PETALS ON THE WIND

Virginia Andrews, who lived in Norfolk, Virginia, studied art at college and during the sixties worked as a fashion illustrator, commercial artist, and later a portrait painter.

Flowers in the Attic was based on a true story and became an immediate bestseller on publication in 1979, receiving tremendous acclaim on both sides of the Atlantic and being adapted for the big screen. It was followed by more books about the Dollanganger family, *Petals on the Wind*, *If There be Thorns*, *Seeds of Yesterday*, and a prequel to *Flowers in the Attic*, *Garden of Shadows*. In addition to these novels, she is also the author of *My Sweet Audrina* and the Casteel family saga: *Heaven*, *Dark Angel*, *Fallen Hearts*, *Gates of Paradise* and *Web of Dreams*, all set in Virginia Andrews' home country, West Virginia, and in Boston.

Virginia Andrews died in 1986, and left a considerable amount of unpublished material.

For automatic updates on your favourite authors visit HarperCollins.co.uk and register for AuthorTracker.

By the same author

FLOWERS IN THE ATTIC
IF THERE BE THORNS
MY SWEET AUDRINA
SEEDS OF YESTERDAY
HEAVEN
DARK ANGEL
GARDEN OF SHADOWS
FALLEN HEARTS
GATES OF PARADISE
WEB OF DREAMS

VIRGINIA ANDREWS

Petals on the Wind

HarperCollins*Publishers*

This novel is entirely a work of fiction.
The names, characters and incidents portrayed in it are
the work of the author's imagination. Any resemblance to
actual persons, living or dead, events or localities is
entirely coincidental.

HarperCollins*Publishers*
77–85 Fulham Palace Road,
Hammersmith, London W6 8JB

www.harpercollins.co.uk

This production 2012

3

First published in the USA by
Pocket Books 1980

First published in Great Britain by
Fontana 1980

ISBN 978 0 00 787376 0

Set in Ehrhardt by Palimpsest Book Production Limited,
Polmont, Stirlingshire

Printed and bound in Great Britain by
Clays Limited, St Ives plc

For Bill and Gene
Who remembered when . . .

PART ONE

FREE, AT LAST!

How young we were the day we escaped. How exuberantly alive we should have felt to be freed, at last, from such a grim, lonely and stifling place. How pitifully delighted we should have been to be riding on a bus that rumbled slowly southward. But if we felt joy, we didn't show it. We sat, all three, pale, silent, staring out the windows, very frightened by all we saw.

The hours passed with the miles. Our nerves grew frazzled because the bus stopped often to pick up and let off passengers. It stopped for rest breaks, for breakfast, then to pick up a single huge black lady who stood alone where a dirt road met the concrete interstate. It took her forever to pull herself on to the bus, then lug inside the many bundles she carried with her. Just as she was finally seated, we passed over the state line between Virginia and North Carolina.

The relief to be gone from that state of our imprisonment! For the first time in years, I began to relax – a little.

We three were the youngest on the bus. Chris was seventeen years old and strikingly handsome with long, waving blond hair that just touched his shoulders, then curled upward. His darkly fringed blue eyes rivalled the colour of a summer sky, and he was in personality like a warm sunny day – he put on a brave face despite the bleakness of our situation. His straight and finely shaped nose had just taken on the strength and maturity that promised to make him all that our father had been – the type of man to make every woman's heart flutter when he looked her way, or even when he didn't. His expression was confident; he almost looked happy. If he hadn't looked at Carrie he might even have been happy. But when he saw her sickly, pale face, he frowned and worry darkened his eyes. He began to pluck on the strings of the guitar strapped to his shoulder. Chris played 'Oh Susannah', singing softly in a sweet melancholy voice that touched my heart. We looked at each other and felt sad with the memories the tune brought back. Like one we were, he and I. I couldn't bear to look at him for too long, for fear I would cry.

Curled up on my lap was my younger sister. She didn't look older than three, but she was eight years old and small, so pitifully small, and weak. In her large, shadowed blue eyes lingered more dark secrets and sufferings than a child her age should know. Carrie's eyes were old, very, very old. She expected nothing: no happiness, no love, nothing – for all that had been wonderful in her life had been taken from her. Weakened by apathy, she seemed willing to pass from life into death. It hurt to see her so alone, so terribly alone now that Cory was gone.

I was fifteen. The year was 1960, and it was November. I wanted everything, needed everything, and I was so terribly afraid I'd never in all my life find enough to make up for what I had already lost. I sat tense, ready to scream if one more bad thing happened. Like a coiled fuse attached to a time bomb, I knew that sooner or later I would explode and bring down all those who lived in Foxworth Hall.

Chris laid his hand on mine, as if he could read my mind and knew I was already thinking about how I would bring hell to those who had tried to destroy us. He said in a low voice, 'Don't look like that, Cathy. It's going to be all right. We'll get by.'

He was still the eternal cockeyed optimist, believing, despite everything, that whatever happened was for the best! God, how could he think so when Cory was dead? How could that possibly be for the best?

'Cathy,' he whispered, 'we have to make the most of what we have left, and that is each other. We have to accept what's happened and go on from there. We have to believe in ourselves, our talents, and if we do, we will get what we want. It works that way, Cathy, really it does. It has to!'

He wanted to be a dull, staid doctor who spent his days in small examination rooms, surrounded by human miseries. I wanted something far more fanciful – and a mountain of it! I wanted all my star-filled dreams of love and romance to be ful-filled – on the stage, where I'd be the world's most famous prima

8

ballerina; nothing less would do! *That would show my mother!*

Damn you, Momma! I hope Foxworth Hall burns to the ground! I hope you never sleep a comfortable night in that grand swan bed, never again! I hope your young husband finds a mistress younger and more beautiful than you! I hope he gives you the hell you deserve!

Carrie turned to whisper: 'Cathy, I don't feel so good. My stomach, it feels funny ...' I was seized by fear. Her small face seemed unnaturally pale; her hair, once so bright and shining, hung in dull, lank strings. Her voice was merely a weak whisper.

'Darling, darling.' I comforted and then kissed her. 'Hang on. We're taking you to a doctor soon. It won't be so long before we reach Florida and there we'll never be locked up.'

Carrie slumped in my arms as I miserably stared out at the dangling Spanish moss that indicated we were now in South Carolina. We still had to pass through Georgia. It would be a long time before we arrived in Sarasota. Violently Carrie jerked upright and began to choke and retch.

I'd judiciously stuffed my pockets with paper napkins during our last rest break, so I was able to clean up Carrie. I handed her over to Chris so I could kneel on the floor to clean up the rest. Chris slid over to the window and tried to force it open to throw out the sodden paper napkins. The window refused to budge no matter how hard he pushed and shoved. Carrie began to cry.

'Put the napkins in the crevice between the seat and the side of the bus,' whispered Chris, but that keen-eyed bus driver must have been watching through his rear-view mirror, for he bellowed out, 'You kids back there – get rid of that stinking mess some other way!' What other way but to take everything from the outside pocket of Chris's camera case, which I was using as a bag, and stuff the smelly napkins in there.

'I'm sorry,' sobbed Carrie as she clung desperately to Chris. 'I didn't mean to do it. Will they put us in jail now?'

'No, of course not,' said Chris in his fatherly way. 'In less than two hours we'll be in Florida. Just try to hang on until then. If we get off now we'll lose the money we've paid for our tickets, and we don't have much money to waste.'

Carrie began to whimper and tremble. I felt her forehead and it was clammy, and now her face wasn't just pale, but white! Like Cory's before he had died.

I prayed that just once God would have some mercy on us. Hadn't we endured enough? Did it have to go on and on? While I hesitated with the squeamish desire to vomit myself, Carrie let go again. I couldn't believe she had anything left. I sagged against Chris while Carrie went limp in his arms and looked heartbreakingly near unconsciousness. 'I think she's going into shock,' whispered Chris, his face almost as pale as Carrie's.

This was when a mean, heartless passenger really began to complain, and loudly, so the compassionate ones looked embarrassed and undecided as to what to do to help us. Chris's eyes met mine. He asked a mute question – what were we to do next?

I was beginning to panic. Then, down the aisle, swaying from side to side as she advanced towards us, came that huge black woman smiling at us reassuringly. She had paper bags with her which she held for me to drop the smelly napkins in. With gestures but no words she patted my shoulder, chucked Carrie under the chin and then handed me a handful of rags taken from one of her bundles. 'Thank you,' I whispered, and smiled weakly as I did a better job of cleaning myself, Carrie and Chris. She took the rags and stuffed them in the bag, then stood back as if to protect us.

Full of gratitude, I smiled at the very, very fat woman who filled the aisle with her brilliantly gowned body. She winked, then smiled back.

'Cathy,' said Chris, his expression more worried than before, 'we've got to get Carrie to a doctor, and soon!'

'But we've paid our way to Sarasota!'

'I know, but this is an emergency.'

Our benefactor smiled reassuringly, then she leaned over to peer into Carrie's face. She put her large black hand to Carrie's clammy brow, then put her fingers to her pulse. She made some gestures with her hands which puzzled me, but Chris said, 'She must not be able to talk, Cathy. Those are the signs deaf people make.' I shrugged to tell her we didn't understand her signs. She frowned, then whipped from a dress pocket beneath a heavy red sweater she wore a pad of multicoloured sheets of notepaper and very swiftly she wrote a note which she handed to me.

My name Henrietta Beech, she'd written, *Can hear, but no talk. Little girl is very, very sick and need good doctor.* I read this, then looked at her hoping she'd have more information. 'Do you know of a good doctor?' I asked. She nodded vigorously, then quickly dashed off another green note. *Your good fortune I be on your bus, and can take you to my own doctor-son, who is very best doctor.*

'Good golly,' murmured Chris when I handed him the note, 'we sure must be under a lucky star to have someone to direct us to such a doctor.'

'Look here, driver,' yelled the meanest man on the bus. 'Get that sick kid to a hospital! Damned if I paid my good money to ride on a stinking bus!'

The other passengers looked at him with disapproval, and I could see in the rear-view mirror that the driver's face flushed with anger, or perhaps it was humiliation. In the mirror our eyes met. He lamely called to me. 'I'm sorry but I've got a wife and five kids and if I don't keep my schedules, then my wife and kids won't eat, because I'll be out of a job.' Mutely I pleaded with my eyes, making him mumble to himself, 'Damn Sundays. Let the weekdays go by just fine, then comes Sunday, damn Sundays.'

This was when Henrietta Beech seemed to have heard enough. Again she picked up her pencil and notepad and wrote. This note she showed to me.

Okay, man in driver's seat who hates Sundays. Keep on ignoring little sick girl, and her parents will sue big shot bus owners for two million!

No sooner had Chris had the chance to skim this note than she was waddling up the aisle and she pushed the note into the driver's face. Impatiently he shoved it away, but she thrust it forward again, and this time he made an attempt to read it while keeping one eye on the traffic.

'Oh, God,' sighed the driver whose face I could clearly see in the mirror. 'The nearest hospital is twenty miles off my route.'

Both Chris and I watched, fascinated, as the mammoth black lady made gestures and signals that left the driver as frustrated as we had been. Once again she had to write a note, and whatever she wrote in that one soon had him turning the bus off the wide highway on to a side road that led into a city named Clairmont. Henrietta Beech stayed with the driver, obviously giving him instructions, but she took the time to look back at us and shine on us a brilliant smile, assuring us that everything would be just fine.

Soon we were rolling along quiet, wide streets with trees that arched gracefully overhead. The houses I stared at were large, aristocratic, with verandas and towering cupolas. Though in the mountains of Virginia it had already snowed once or twice, autumn had not yet laid a frosty hand here. The maples, beeches, oaks and magnolias still held most of their summer leaves, and a few flowers still bloomed.

The bus driver didn't think Henrietta Beech was directing him right, and to be honest I didn't think she was either. Really, they didn't put medical buildings on this kind of residential street. But just as I was beginning to get worried, the bus jerked to a sudden halt in front of a big white house perched on a low, gentle hill and surrounded by spacious lawns and flower beds.

'You kids!' the bus driver bellowed back to us, 'pack your gear, turn in your tickets for a refund, or use them before the time limit expires!' Then quickly he was out of the bus and opening up the locked underbelly, and from there he pulled out forty or so suitcases before he came to our two. I slung Cory's guitar and banjo over my shoulders, as Chris very gently, and with a great deal of tenderness, lifted Carrie in his arms.

Like a fat mother hen, Henrietta Beech hustled us up the long brick walk to the front veranda and there I hesitated, staring at the house, the double black doors. To the right a small sign read FOR PATIENTS ONLY. This was obviously a doctor who had offices in his own home. Our two suitcases were left back in the shade near the concrete sidewalk while I scanned the veranda to spy a man sleeping in a white wicker chair. Our good Samaritan approached him with a wide smile before she gently touched him on the arm, and when he still slept on she gestured for us to advance and speak for ourselves. Next she pointed to the house, and made signals to indicate she had to get inside and prepare a meal for us to eat.

I wished she'd stayed to introduce us, to explain why we were on his porch on Sunday. Even as Chris and I stole on cautious feet towards him, even as I filled with fear, I was sniffing the air filled with the scent of roses and feeling that I'd been here before and knew this place. This fresh air perfumed with roses was not the kind of air I'd grown to expect as the kind deemed worthy for such as me. 'It's Sunday, damn Sunday,' I whispered to Chris, 'and that doctor may not appreciate our being here.'

'He's a doctor,' said Chris, 'and he's used to having his spare time robbed ... but *you* can wake him up.'

Slowly I approached. He was a large man wearing a pale grey suit with a white carnation in his buttonhole. His long legs were stretched out and lifted to the top of the balustrade. He looked rather elegant, even sprawled out as he was with his hands dangling over the arms of the chair. He appeared so comfortable it seemed a terrible pity to awaken him and put him back on duty.

'Are you Dr Paul Sheffield?' asked Chris who had read the sign with the doctor's name. Carrie lay in his arms with her neck arched backwards, her eyes closed and her long golden hair waving in the soft, warm breezes. Reluctantly the doctor came awake. He stared at us long moments, as if disbelieving his eyes. I knew we looked strange in our many layers of clothing. He shook his head as if trying to focus his eyes, and such beautiful hazel eyes they were, bejewelled with flecks of blue, green and gold on soft brown. Those remarkable eyes drank me in, then swallowed me down. He appeared dazzled, slightly drunk, and much too sleepy to put on his customary professional mask that would keep him from darting his eyes from my face to my breasts, then to my legs before he scanned slowly upward. And again he was hypnotized by my face, my hair. It was hair that was far too long, I knew that, and it was clumsily cut on top, and too pale and fragile on the ends.

'You are the doctor, aren't you?' demanded Chris.

'Yes, of course. I'm Dr Sheffield,' he finally said, now turning his attention to Chris and Carrie. Surprisingly graceful and quick, he lifted his legs from the railing, rose to his feet to tower above us, ran long fingers through the mop of his dark hair, and then stepped closer to peer down into Carrie's small, white face. He parted her closed lids with forefinger and thumb and looked for a moment at whatever was revealed in that blue eye. 'How long has this child been unconscious?'

'A few minutes,' said Chris. He was almost a doctor himself, he'd studied so much while we were locked away upstairs. 'Carrie threw up on the bus three times, then began to tremble and feel clammy. There was a lady on the bus named Henrietta Beech, and she brought us here to you.'

The doctor nodded, then explained that Mrs Beech was his housekeeper. He then led us to the door for patients only, and into a section of the house with two small examination rooms and an office, all the while apologizing for not having his usual nurse available. 'Take off all Carrie's clothes but her underpants,' he ordered me. While I set about doing this, Chris dashed back to the sidewalk to fetch our suitcases.

Full of a thousand anxieties, Chris and I backed up against a wall and watched as the doctor checked Carrie's blood pressure, her pulse, her temperature and listened to her heart, front and back. By this time Carrie had come round so he could request her to cough. All I could do was wonder why everything bad had happened to us. Why was fate so persistently against us? Were we as evil as the grandmother had said? Did Carrie have to die too?

'Carrie,' said Dr Sheffield pleasantly after I had dressed her again, 'we're going to leave you in this room for a while so you can rest.' He covered her with a thin blanket. 'Now don't be afraid. We'll be right down the hall in my office. I know that table isn't too soft, but do try and sleep while I talk to your brother and sister.'

She gazed at him with wide, dull eyes, not really caring if the table was hard or soft.

A few minutes later Dr Sheffield was seated behind his big impressive desk with his elbows on the blotter pad, and that's when he began to speak earnestly and with some concern. 'The two of you look embarrassed and ill-at-ease. Don't be afraid you're depriving me of Sunday fun and games, for I don't do much of that. I'm a widower, and Sunday for me is no different than any other day . . .'

Ah, yes. He could say that, but he looked tired, as if he worked too many long hours. I perched uneasily on the soft brown leather sofa, close by Chris. The sunlight filtering through the windows fell directly on our faces while the doctor was in the shadows. My clothes felt damp and miserable, and suddenly I remembered why. Quickly I stood to unzip and remove my filthy outer skirt. I felt quite pleased to see the doctor start in surprise. Since he'd left the room when I undressed Carrie, he didn't realize that I had two dresses on underneath. When I sat again next to Chris, I wore only one dress of blue, princess styled, and it was flattering and unsoiled.

'Do you always wear more than one outfit on Sundays?' he asked.

'Only on the Sundays I run away,' I said. 'And we have only two suitcases and need to save room for the valuables we can hock later on when we have to.' Chris nudged me sharply, mutely signalling I was revealing too much. But I knew about doctors, from him mostly. That doctor behind the desk could be trusted – it was in his eyes. We could tell him anything, everything.

'Sooo,' he drawled, 'you three are running away. And just what are you running from? Parents who offended you by denying you some privileges?'

Oh, if he only knew! 'It's a long story, Doctor,' said Chris, 'and right now all we want to hear about is Carrie.'

'Yes,' he agreed, 'you're right. So we'll talk about Carrie.' All professional now, he continued, 'I don't know who you are, or where you're from, or why you feel you have to run. But that little girl is very, very ill. If this weren't Sunday, I'd admit her to a hospital today for further tests I can't make here. I suggest you contact your parents immediately.'

Just the words to make me panic!

'We're orphans,' said Chris. 'But don't worry about not being paid. We can pay our own way.'

'It's good you have money,' said the doctor. 'You're going to need it.' He swept long, observant looks over both of us, sizing us up. 'Two weeks in a hospital should be sufficient to discover the factor in your sister's illness I can't quite put my finger on.' And while we gasped, stunned that Carrie was *that* sick, he made an approximate guess as to the amount of money it would cost. Again we were stunned. Dear God! Our stolen cache of money wouldn't even pay for one week, much less two.

My eyes clashed with the appalled look in Chris's blue eyes. What would we do now? We couldn't pay that much.

The doctor easily read our situation. 'Are you still orphans?' he asked softly.

'Yes, we're *still* orphans,' stated Chris defiantly, then glanced hard at me to let me know I was to keep my trap shut. 'Once you're an orphan you stay that way. Now, tell us what you suspect is wrong with our sister, and what you can do to make her well again.'

'Hold up there, young man. First you have to answer a few questions.' His was a soft voice, but firm enough to let us know he was in command here. 'First, what is your last name?'

'I am Christopher Dollanganger, and this is my sister, Catherine Leigh Dollanganger, and Carrie is eight years old, whether or not you believe it!'

'Why shouldn't I believe it?' the doctor asked mildly, when just a few minutes ago in the cubelike examination room, he'd shown shock to hear her age.

'We realize Carrie is very small for her age,' said Chris defensively.

'Indeed she is small.' He flicked his eyes to me when he said this, then to my brother, and leaned forward on his crossed arms in a friendly, confidential manner that made me tense in preparation. 'Now look. Let's stop being suspicious of one another. I'm a doctor, and anything you confide to me will remain in my confidence.

'If you really want to help your sister, you can't sit there and make up lies. You have to give me the truth, or else you're wasting my time and risking Carrie's life.'

We both sat silent, holding hands, our shoulders pressed against one another. I felt Chris shudder, so I shuddered too. We were so scared, so damned scared to speak the full truth – for who would believe? We'd trusted those who were supposedly honourable before so how could we trust again? And yet, that man behind the desk ... he looked so familiar, like I'd seen him before. 'All right,' he said, 'if it's that difficult, let me ask more questions. Tell me what all three of you ate last.'

Chris sighed, relieved. 'Our last meal was breakfast very early this morning. We all ate the same thing, hot dogs with every-thing, french fries, and then chocolate milkshakes. Carrie ate only a little of her meal. She's very picky about food under the best of circumstances. I'd say she's never really had a healthy appetite.'

Frowning, the doctor noted this down. 'And all three of you ate exactly the very same things for breakfast? And only Carrie was sick?'

'Right. Only Carrie.'

'Is Carrie often sick?'

'Occasionally, not often.'

'How occasionally?'

'Well ...' said Chris slowly, 'Carrie threw up twice last week, and about five times last month. It's worried me a lot; her attacks seem to be growing more violent as they come more often.'

Oh, the evasive way Chris was telling about Carrie made me really furious! He would protect our mother even now, after all she'd done. Maybe it was my expression that betrayed Chris and made the doctor lean my way, as if he knew he'd hear a more complete story from me. 'Look, you came to me for help, and I'm willing to do what I can, but you aren't giving me a fair chance if you don't give me all the facts. If Carrie hurts inside, I can't look inside to see where it is – she has to tell me, or you have to tell me. I need information to work with – full information. Already I know Carrie is malnourished, under-exercised and underdeveloped for her age. I see that all three of you have enlarged pupils. I see you are all pale, thin and weak looking. Nor can I understand why you hesitate about money when you wear watches that look quite expensive, and someone has chosen your clothes with taste and considerable cost – though why they fit so poorly is beyond my speculation. You sit there with gold and diamond watches, wearing rich clothes and shoddy sneakers, and tell me half-truths. So now I'm going to tell you a few *full truths*!' His voice grew stronger, more forceful. 'I suspect your small sister is dangerously anaemic. And because she is anaemic she is susceptible to myriad infections. Her blood pressure is dangerously low. And there is some elusive factor I can't put my finger on. So, tomorrow Carrie will be admitted to a hospital, whether or not you call your parents, and you can hock those wristwatches to pay for her life. Now . . . if we admit her to the hospital this evening, the tests can begin early tomorrow morning.'

'Do what you feel necessary,' said Chris dully.

'Wait a minute!' I cried, jumping to my feet and moving swiftly to the doctor's desk. 'My brother isn't telling you everything!' I threw Chris a hard glance over my shoulder, while he shot his fierce look to forbid me to reveal the whole truth. I thought bitterly, *Don't worry, I'll protect our precious mother as much as I can*!

I think Chris understood, for tears came to his eyes. Oh, how much that woman had done to hurt him, hurt all of us, and he could still cry for her sake. His tears put tears in my heart too, not for her, but for him, who'd loved her so well, and for me who loved him so well, and tears for all we'd shared and suffered . . .

He nodded, as if saying go ahead, and then I began to tell what must have seemed to the doctor an incredible tale. At first I could tell he thought I was lying, or at least exaggerating. Why was that when every day the newspapers told terrible tales of what loving, caring parents did to their children?

'. . . And so, after Daddy was in that fatal accident, Momma came and told us she was deeply in debt, and she had no way to earn a living for the five of us. She began writing letters to her parents in Virginia. At first they didn't reply, but then one day a letter came. She told us her parents lived in a fine, rich house in Virginia and were fabulously wealthy, but because she had married her half-uncle she'd been disinherited. Now we were going to lose everything we owned. We had to leave our bicycles in the garage, and she didn't even give us time to say goodbye to our friends, and that very evening we set off on a train headed for the Blue Ridge Mountains.

'We felt happy to be going to a fine, rich house, but not so happy about meeting a grandfather who sounded cruel. Our mother told us we'd have to hide away until she could win back his affections. Momma said *one* night only, or maybe two or three, then we could go downstairs and meet her father. He was dying of heart disease and never climbed the stairs so we were safe enough up there as long as we didn't make much noise. The grandmother gave us the attic to play in. It was huge – and dirty, and full of spiders, mice and insects. And that's where we played and tried to make the best of it until Momma won back her father's good will and we could go down and begin to enjoy living like rich children. But soon enough we found out that our grandfather was never going to forgive our mother for marrying his half-brother and we were going to remain "Devil's issue". We'd have to live up there until he was dead!'

I went on, despite the look of pained incredulity in the doctor's eyes. 'And as if that weren't bad enough, being locked up in one room with our playground in the attic, we soon found out our grandmother hated us too! She gave us a long list of what we could do and what we couldn't do. We were never to look out of the front windows, or even open the heavy draperies to let in some light.

'At first the meals the grandmother brought up each morning in a picnic hamper were rather good, but gradually they worsened to only sandwiches, potato salad and fried chicken. Never any desserts, for they would rot our teeth and we couldn't go to a dentist. Of course, when our birthdays came around, Momma would sneak us up ice cream and a bakery cake, and plenty of presents. Oh, you bet she bought us everything to make up for what she was doing to us – as if books and games and toys could ever make up for all we were losing – our health, our belief in ourselves. And, worst of all, we began to lose faith in *her*!

'Another year came, and that summer Momma didn't even visit us at all! Then, in October she showed up again to tell us she'd married a second time and had spent the summer touring Europe on her honeymoon! I could have killed her! She could have told us, but she'd gone away and not said a word to explain! She brought us expensive gifts, clothes that didn't fit, and thought that made up for everything, when it didn't make up for anything! Finally I was able to convince Chris we should find a way to escape that house and forget about inheriting a fortune. He didn't want to go, because he thought that any day the grandfather might die, and he wanted to go to college, then medical school and become a doctor – like you.'

'A doctor like me ...' said Dr Sheffield with a strange sigh. His eyes were soft with sympathy, and something darker too. 'It's a strange story, Cathy, and hard to believe.'

'Wait a minute!' I cried. 'I haven't finished. I haven't told you the worst part! The grandfather did die, and he did write our mother into his will so she'd inherit his tremendous fortune – but he added a codicil that said she could never have children. If it were ever proven she'd given birth to children by her first husband, she'd have to forfeit everything she'd inherited and everything she'd bought with the money!'

I paused. I glanced at Chris who sat pale and weak looking, staring at me with hurt and pleading eyes. But he needn't have worried; I wasn't going to speak of Cory. I turned again to the doctor. 'Now that mysterious, elusive factor you can't put your finger on – the thing wrong with Carrie that makes her throw up, and us too sometimes. It's really very simple. You see, once our mother knew she could never claim us and keep the fortune, she decided to get rid of us. The grandmother began to add sugared doughnuts to the basket. We ate them eagerly enough, not knowing that they were coated with arsenic.'

And so I'd said it.

Poisoned doughnuts to sweeten our imprisoned days as we stole from our room by using the wooden key Chris had fashioned. Day by day dying for nine months while we sneaked into our mother's grand bedroom suite and took all the dollar bills we could find. Almost a year we'd traversed those long, dim corridors, stealing into her room to take what money we could.

'In that one room, Doctor, we lived three years and four months and sixteen days.'

When I'd concluded my long tale the doctor sat very quietly staring at me with compassion, shock, and concern. 'So you see, Doctor,' I said to finish, 'you can't force us to go to the police and tell our story! They might throw the grandmother and our mother in jail, but we'd suffer too! Not only from the publicity, but also from being separated. They'd put us in foster homes, or make us wards of the court, and we've sworn to stay together, always!'

Chris was staring at the floor. He spoke without looking up. 'Take care of our sister. Do whatever is needed to make her well again, and both Cathy and I will find a way to meet our obligations.'

'Hold on, Chris,' said the doctor in his slow, patient way. 'You and Cathy have been fed arsenic too and will need to undergo many of the same tests I order for Carrie. Look at the two of you. You're thin, pale, weak. You need good food, rest and plenty of fresh air and sunshine. Maybe there is something I can do to help.'

'You're a stranger to us, sir,' Chris said respectfully, 'and we don't expect or need anyone's charity or pity. Cathy and I are not that weak or sick. Carrie's the one most affected.'

Full of indignation, I spun about to glare at Chris. We'd be fools to reject help from this kind man just so we could salvage some of our pride that had already gone down in defeat so many times before. What difference did one more time make?

'. . . Yes,' continued the doctor, as if both Chris and I had already agreed to his generous offer to help, 'expenses are not as high for an "out" patient as for an "in" patient – no room and no board to pay. Now listen, this is only a suggestion which you're free to refuse, and travel on to wherever you have in mind – by the way, where are you going?'

'To Sarasota, Florida,' Chris said weakly. 'Cathy and I used to swing from the ropes we tied to the attic rafters, so she thought we could become aerialists, with some practice.' It sounded silly when I heard him say it. I expected the doctor to laugh, but he didn't. He just looked sadder.

'Honestly, Chris, I would hate to see you and Cathy risk your lives like that, and as a doctor I feel I can't allow you to go as you are. Everything in my personal ethics and professional ones too refuses to let you go on without medical treatment. Common sense tells me I should keep my distance and not give a damn about what happens to three kids on their own. For all I know that horrendous story may just be a pack of lies to gain my sympathy.' He smiled kindly to take the sting from his words. 'Yet, my intuition tells me to believe your story. Your expensive clothes, your watches and the sneakers on your feet, your pale skin and the haunted look in your eyes all testify to the truth.'

Such a voice he had, hypnotizing, soft and melodious, with just a bit of Southern accent. 'Come,' he said, charming me, if not Chris, 'forget about pride and charity. Come live in my home of twelve lonely rooms. God must have put Henrietta Beech on that bus to lead you to me. Henny is a terrific worker and keeps my house spotless, but she constantly complains that twelve rooms and four baths are just too much for one woman to care for. Out in the back I have four acres of garden. I hire two gardeners to help, for I just can't devote as much time to the garden as I need to. At this point he riveted his brilliant eyes directly on Chris. 'You can help earn your keep by mowing the lawns, clipping the hedges and preparing the gardens for winter. Cathy can help out in the house.' He shot me a questioning, teasing look with his eyes twinkling. 'Can you cook?'

Cook? Was he kidding? We'd been locked upstairs for more than three years, and we'd never even had a toaster to brown our bread in the mornings, and no butter, or even margarine!

'No!' I snapped. 'I can't cook. I'm a dancer. When I'm a famous prima ballerina I'll hire a woman to do the cooking, like you do. I don't want to be stuck away in some man's kitchen, washing his dishes and fixing his meals and having his babies! That's not for me.'

'I see,' he said, his expression blank.

'I don't mean to sound ungrateful,' I explained. 'I will do what I can to help out Mrs Beech. I'll even learn how to cook for her – and you.'

'Good,' he said. His eyes were laughing, full of sparkling lights as he templed his fingers beneath his chin and smiled. 'You are going to be a prima ballerina, and Chris is going to be a famous doctor, and you are going to achieve all of this by running away to Florida to perform in the circus? Of course I'm of another stodgy generation and I can't fathom your reasoning.

Does it really make good sense to you?'

Now that we were out of the locked room and the attic and in the full light of reality, no, it didn't make good sense. It sounded like foolish, childish and unrealistic folly.

'Do you realize what you'd be up against as professional aerialists?' the doctor asked. 'You would have to compete against people who've trained from early childhood, people descended from long lines of circus performers. It wouldn't be easy. Still, I'll admit there's something in those blue eyes that tells me you two are very determined young people, and no doubt you'll get what you go after if you really want it badly enough. But what about school? What about Carrie? What's she going to do while the two of you swing from trapezes? Now don't bother to answer,' he said quickly when my lips parted. 'I'm sure you can come up with something to convince me, but I must dissuade you. First you have to tend to your health and Carrie's. Any day the two of you could come down as swiftly as Carrie and be just as sick. After all, didn't all three of you exist under the same miserable conditions?'

Four of us, not three, was the whisper in my ears, but I didn't speak of Cory.

'If you meant it about taking us in until Carrie is well,' said Chris with his eyes shining suspiciously, 'we're extremely grateful. We'll work hard, and when we can we'll leave and repay you every cent you spent on us.'

'I meant it. And you don't have to repay me, except by helping out in the house and the yard. So, you see, it isn't pity, or charity, only a business arrangement to benefit all of us.'

A NEW HOME

That's the way it started. We moved quietly into the doctor's home and into his life. We took him over, I know that now. We made ourselves important to him, as if he hadn't had a life before we came. I know that now too. He made it seem we were doing him a favour by relieving him of a dreary, lonely life by adding our youthful presence. He made us feel that *we* were being generous to share *his* life, and oh, we did want to believe in someone.

He gave Carrie and me a grand bedroom to share, with twin beds and four tall windows facing south, and two windows facing east. Chris and I looked at each other with a terrible shared hurt. We were to sleep in different rooms for the first time in ever so long. I didn't want to part from him and face the night with only Carrie, who could never protect me as he had. I think our doctor may have sensed something that told him to fade into the background, for he excused himself and drifted towards the end of the hall. Only then did Chris speak. 'We've got to be careful, Cathy. We wouldn't want him to suspect . . .'

'There is nothing to suspect. It's over,' I answered, but I didn't meet his eyes, guessing, even then, that it would never be over. *Oh, Momma, look what you started by putting the four of us in one locked room, and leaving us there to grow up, knowing how it would be! You of all people should have known!*

'Don't,' Chris whispered. 'Kiss me good night, and there won't be any bedbugs here.'

He kissed me, I kissed him, we said good night, and that was all. With tears in my eyes I watched my brother back down the hall, still holding his eyes on me.

In our room Carrie let out a loud howl. 'I can't sleep in a little bed all by myself!' she wailed. 'I'll fall off! Cathy, why is that bed so little?'

It ended up with Chris and the doctor coming back so they

24

could take away the nightstand that separated the twin beds. Then they shoved the narrow beds so close they appeared one wide bed. This pleased Carrie enormously, but, as the nights passed, somehow the crack between our beds grew ever wider until I, the restless sleeper, finally woke up with one leg and one arm in the crack and Carrie being pulled along with me to the floor.

I loved that room Paul gave us. It was so beautiful with its pale blue wallpaper, and matching curtains. The rug was blue; each of us had a chair with lemon-yellow cushions and all the furniture was antique white. It was the kind of room a girl should have. No gloom. No pictures of Hell on the wall. All the Hell I had was in my mind, put there by thinking back much too often. Momma could have found another solution if she'd really wanted to! She didn't have to lock us up! It was greed, avarice, that damned fortune . . . and Cory was in the ground because of her weakness!

'Forget it, Cathy,' said Chris when we were again saying good night.

I was terribly afraid to tell him what I suspected. My head bowed low against his chest. 'Chris, it was a sinful thing we did, wasn't it?'

'It won't happen again,' he said stiffly, then broke away and almost ran down the hall as if I were chasing. I wanted to lead a good life and hurt no one, especially Chris. But I had to leave my bed around midnight and go to Chris. While he slept I crawled in the bed beside him. He wakened when he heard the bedsprings squeak. 'Cathy, what the hell are you doing here?'

'It's raining outside,' I whispered. 'Just let me lie beside you for a moment or so, and then I'll go away.' Neither of us moved, or even breathed. Then without even knowing how it came about, we were in each other's arms and he was kissing me. Kissing with such ardent fervour it made me respond when I didn't want to. It was evil and wrong! Yet I didn't really want him to stop. That sleeping woman inside of me woke up and took over, wanting what he felt he had to have, and I, the thinking, calculating part, pushed him away. 'What are you doing? I thought you said this would never happen again.'

'You came ...' he said hoarsely.

'Not for this!'

'What do you think I'm made of? Cathy, don't do this again.'

I left him and cried in my own bed, for he was down the hall and not there to waken me if I had a nightmare. No one to comfort me. No one to lend me strength. Then my mother's words came to haunt me with a horrible thought – was I so much like her? Was I going to be the kind of weak, clinging-vine female who always needed a man for protection? No! I was sufficient unto myself!

I believe it was the next day that Dr Paul brought me four pictures to hang. Ballerinas in four different positions. For Carrie he brought a milk-glass vase filled with delicate plastic violets. Already he'd learned about Carrie's passion for all things purple or red. 'Do what you can to make this room yours,' he told us. 'If you don't like the colour scheme, we'll have it changed in the spring.' I stared at him. We wouldn't be here, come spring.

Carrie sat holding her vase of fake violets while I forced myself to speak up and say what I had to. 'Dr Paul, we won't be here in the spring, so we can't afford to let ourselves become too attached to the rooms you've given us.'

He was in the doorway, ready to depart, but he halted and turned to look back at me. He was tall, six two or more, and his shoulders were so wide they almost filled the doorway.

'I thought you liked it here,' he said in a wistful tone, his dark eyes gone bleak.

'I do like it here!' I quickly answered. 'We all like it here, but we can't take advantage of your good nature forever.' He nodded without replying and left, and I turned to see Carrie staring at me with a great deal of animosity.

Daily the doctor took Carrie to the hospital with him. At first she'd wail and refuse to go unless I went along too. She made up fantastic stories about what they did to her in the hospital, and complained about all the questions they asked her.

'Carrie, we never tell lies; you know that. The three of us always tell the truth to each other – but we don't go around telling *everybody* about our past lives upstairs – understand?'

26

She stared up at me with those big, haunted eyes. 'I don't tell nobody Cory went away to heaven and left me. I don't tell nobody but Dr Paul.'

'You told *him*?'

'I couldn't help it, Cathy.' Carrie buried her head in her pillow and cried.

So now the doctor knew about Cory, and how he was supposed to have died in a hospital from pneumonia. How sad his eyes were that night when he questioned Chris and me, wanting all the details of Cory's illness that ended in his death.

Chris and I were huddled up close on the living room sofa when Paul said, 'I'm very happy to report that arsenic has not done any permanent damage to any of Carrie's organs, as we all feared it might have. Now don't look like that. I haven't let out your secret but I had to tell the lab technicians what to look for. I made up a story about how you'd taken the poison accidentally, and your parents were good friends of mine, and I'm considering making you three my legal wards.'

'Carrie's going to live?' I whispered, drowning in relief.

'Yes, she'll live – *if* she doesn't go swinging on trapezes.' He smiled again. 'I've made appointments for the two of you to be examined tomorrow – by me – unless you have some objections.'

Oh, I had objections! I wasn't keen about taking off my clothes and having him go over me, even if a nurse was there. Chris told me I was silly to think a doctor of forty would get any erotic pleasure from looking at a girl of my age. But when he said it, he was looking the other way, so how could I tell what he was really thinking? Maybe Chris was right, for when I was on that examination table, naked and covered by a paper robe, Dr Paul didn't seem the same man whose eyes followed me around when we were in the 'home' side of his house. He did to me the same things he'd done to Carrie, but asked even more questions. Embarrassing questions.

'You haven't menstruated in more than two months?'

'I've never been regular, really! I started when I was twelve, and twice I skipped from three to six months. I used to worry about it, but Chris read up on the subject in one of the medical books Momma brought him, and he told me too many anxieties and too much stress can make a girl miss. You don't think . . . I mean . . . there isn't anything wrong with me, is there?'

'Not that I can tell. You seem normal enough. Too thin, too pale, and you're slightly anaemic. Chris is too, but because of his sex not as much as you are. I'm going to prescribe special vitamins for all three of you.'

I was glad when it was over and I could put on my clothes and escape from that office.

I raced back to the kitchen. Mrs Beech was preparing dinner. Her smile shone big and wide when I came in, lighting up a moon face with skin as slick as oiled rubber. The teeth she displayed were the whitest, most perfect teeth I'd ever seen. 'Golly, am I happy that's over!' I said, falling into a chair and picking up a knife to peel potatoes. 'I don't like doctors poking me over. I like Dr Paul better when he's just a man. When he puts on that long white jacket, he also puts a shade over his eyes. Then I can't see what he's thinking. And I'm very good at reading eyes, Mrs Beech.'

She grinned at me with teasing devilry, then whipped out a pink notepad from the huge square pocket of her starched white apron. With the apron tied about her middle she resembled nothing more than a rolled-up goosedown comforter, waddling about speechless. By now I knew she had a congenital speech defect. Though she was trying to teach Chris, Carrie and me to understand her sign language, as yet none of us had caught on enough to carry on a quick conversation. I think I enjoyed her notes too much – notes she could write lightning-fast in a very abbreviated style. *Doctor says,* she'd written, *young people need lots of good fresh fruit and vegetables, plenty of lean meat, but go easy on starches and desserts. He wants to put on you muscle not fat.*

Already we'd gained some weight in the two weeks of eating Mrs Beech's delicious cooking, even Carrie who was so finicky. Now she ate with enthusiasm, and for her that was remarkable. So, as I peeled the red potatoes, Mrs Beech wrote another note when her signals failed to communicate. *Fairy-Child, from now on call me only Henny. No Mrs Beech.*

She was the first black person I'd known, and though at first I'd felt ill-at-ease with her and a little afraid of her, two weeks of intimacy had taught me much. She was just another human being of another race and colour, with the same sensitivities, hopes and fears we all had.

I loved Henny, her broad smiles, her loose, flowing gowns with flowers blooming riotously, and most of all I loved the wisdom that came from her small pastel paper sheets. Eventually, I did learn to understand her sign language, though I was never as good at it as her 'doctor-son'.

Paul Scott Sheffield was a strange man. So often he looked sad when there was no apparent reason for him to be sad. Then he'd smile and say, 'Yes, God favoured Henny and me that day he put you three on that bus. I lost one family, and grieved for them, and fate was kind enough to send me another, ready-made family.'

'Chris,' I said that evening when we had to reluctantly part, 'when we lived in the room upstairs, you were the man, the head of the household ... Sometimes it feels funny to have Dr Paul around, watching what we do and listening to what we say.'

He blushed. 'I know. He's taking my place. To be honest,' and here he paused and blushed a deeper red, 'I don't like him replacing me in your life, but I'm very grateful for what he's done for Carrie.'

Somehow all that our doctor did for us made Momma seem a thousandfold worse in comparison. *Ten* thousandfold worse!

The next day was Chris's eighteenth birthday, and though I'd never forget, it surprised me that the doctor had planned a party with many fine gifts that sparkled Chris's eyes, and then saddened them with the guilt both he and I felt. Already we'd accepted so much. Already we had been making plans to leave soon. We just couldn't stay on and take advantage of Dr Paul's good nature, now that Carrie was well enough to travel on.

After the party Chris and I sat on the back veranda, mulling this over. One look at his face and I could tell he didn't want to leave the one and only man who could, and would, help him reach his goal of becoming a doctor. 'I really don't like the way he keeps looking at you, Cathy. His eyes follow you about all the time. Here you are, so available, and men his age find girls your age irresistible.'

They did? How fascinating to know. 'But doctors have plenty of pretty nurses available to them,' I said lamely, knowing I would do anything short of murder to see that Chris reached his goal. 'Remember that day we first came? He spoke of the kind of competition we'd be up against in the circus. Chris, he's right. We can't go work for the circus; that's only a silly dream.'

He stared off into space with knitted brows. 'I know all of that.'

'Chris, he's just lonely. Maybe he only watches me because there isn't anything else as interesting to watch as me.' But how fascinating to know that men of forty were susceptible to girls of fifteen. How wonderful to wield over them the power that my mother had.

'Chris, if Dr Paul says the right thing, I mean, if he really honestly wants us, would you stay on?'

He frowned and studied the hedges he'd so recently clipped. After long consideration he spoke slowly, 'Let's give him a test. If we tell him we're leaving, and he doesn't say anything to prevent us, then that will be his polite way to let us know he doesn't really care.'

'Is it fair to test him like that?'

'Yes. It's a good way to give him the chance to get rid of us and not feel guilty about it. You know, people like him often do nice things because they feel they should, not because they really want to.'

'Oh.'

We were not ones to procrastinate. The next evening after dinner, Paul came to join us on the back veranda. *Paul.* I was calling him that in my thoughts – getting familiar, liking him more and more because always he looked so casually elegant, so clean, so nice, sitting in his favourite white wicker rocker, wearing a red cable-knit sweater with grey slacks and slowly, dreamily puffing on a cigarette. We three wore sweaters too, for the evening was chilly. Chris perched beside me on the balustrade while Carrie crouched on the top step. Paul's gardens were fabulous. Shallow marble steps nine feet across took you down a few feet to other steps which took you to a higher level. There was a small Japanese footbridge lacquered red, arching over a

30

small stream. There were nude statues of men and women, placed at random, which lent to his gardens an atmosphere of seduction, of worldly sensuality. They were classic nudes. Graceful, and elegantly posed, and yet, and yet ... I knew that garden for what it was. For I'd been there before in my dreams.

The doctor was telling us, even as the wind turned colder and started to blow dead leaves hither and yon, that he travelled abroad every other year to search out the beautiful marble statues he'd ship home and add to his collection. He'd been so lucky the last time to come across a full-sized copy of Rodin's *The Kiss*.

I sighed with the wind. I didn't want to go. I liked it here with him, with Henny, with the gardens that held me in thrall and made me feel enchanted, beautiful, desirable.

'So all my roses are old-fashioned roses that haven't had the heady scent bred from them,' said Dr Paul. 'Why have roses at all if they don't reek of perfume?'

In the fading, purplish light of the failing day his glimmering eyes met with mine. My pulse quickened and forced another sigh. I wondered what his wife had been like, and how it felt to be loved by someone like him. Guiltily my eyes fled from his long, searching look, afraid he'd see what I was thinking. 'You look disturbed, Cathy. Why?' His question teased me, as if he already knew my secrets. Chris turned his head to give me a hard look of warning.

'It's your red sweater,' I said foolishly. 'Did Henny knit it for you?'

He chuckled softly, then glanced down at the handsome sweater he wore. 'No, not Henny. My older sister knitted the sweater for my birthday, then mailed it to me parcel post. She lives on the other side of town.'

'Why would your sister mail you a gift and not bring it in person?' I asked. 'And why didn't you tell us you had a birthday? We would have given you gifts too.'

'Well,' he began, settling back comfortably and crossing his legs, 'my birthday came and went shortly before you arrived. I'm forty in case Henny hasn't told you. I've been a widower thirteen years, and my sister, Amanda, has not spoken to me since the day my wife and young son died in an accident.' His voice faded away and he stared off into space, moody, solemn, distant.

Dead leaves scuttled on the lawn, chased over the porch and came to nestle near my feet, like brown, dried-up ducklings. All this took me back to a certain forbidden night when Chris and I had so desperately prayed while we huddled on the cold slate roof under a moon that looked like the scowling eye of God. Would there be a price to pay for just one terrible sin committed? Would there? The grandmother would quickly say, *yes! You deserve the worst punishment! Devil's spawn, I knew it all along!*

And while I sat there floundering Chris spoke up. 'Doctor, Cathy and I have been talking this over, and we feel now that Carrie is well we should be leaving. We deeply appreciate everything you've done, and we intend to repay you every cent, though it may take us a few years ...' His fingers squeezed tight around mine, warning me not to say anything different.

'Hold on there, Chris,' interrupted the doctor, jerking upright in his chair and planting both his feet solidly on the floor. Clearly he meant business. 'Don't think for one minute I haven't seen this coming. I've dreaded each morning, fearful I'd wake up to find you gone.

'I've been looking into the legal ramifications of making the three of you my wards. And I've found out it isn't as complicated as I thought. It seems most children who run away say they're orphans, so you'll have to give me proof your father is really dead. If he's alive, I would need his consent, as well as your mother's.'

My breath caught! My mother's consent? That meant we'd have to see her again! I didn't want to see her, not ever!

He went on, his eyes soft as they saw my distress. 'The court would petition your mother to appear at a hearing. If she lived in this state she'd be forced to comply in three days, but since she's in Virginia, they'll give her three weeks. If she doesn't show up, then instead of having only temporary custody of you, I will be granted permanent custody – but only if you're willing to say I've done a good job as a guardian.'

'You've been wonderful!' I cried out. 'But she won't come! She wants to keep us a secret! If the world finds out about us, she'll lose all that money. Her husband might turn against her too if he knew she'd hidden us away. You can bet your life if you dare to try for permanent custody, you'll get it – and you might be sorry in the end!'

Chris's hand tightened more on mine, and Carrie looked up with huge, scared eyes.

'In a few weeks Christmas will be here. Are you going to leave me to spend another lonely holiday by myself? You've been here for almost three weeks, and I've explained to everyone who asked that you were the children of a relative of mine who died recently. I'm not going into this blindly. Henny and I have given this a great deal of thought. She feels, just as I feel, that the three of you are good for us. We both want you to stay on. Having young people in the house makes it more like a home. I feel healthier than I have in years, and happier too. Since the death of my wife and son, I've missed having a family. In all this time I've never gotten used to being a bachelor again.' His persuasive tone grew wistful. 'I feel fate *wants* me to have custody of you. I feel God *planned* for Henny to be on the bus, just so she could bring you to me. When fate steps in and makes the decisions, who am I to deny it? I accept the fact you three are godsent to help me make up for the mistakes I've made in the past.'

Wow! Godsent! I was more than half-won. I knew people could always find the motivation to justify what they wanted; well enough I knew that. Even so, tears filled my eyes as I looked at Chris questioningly. He met my look and shook his head in bewilderment, confused as to what *I* wanted. His hand gripped mine like iron while he spoke, still looking at me, not at Dr Paul. 'We're sorry for the loss of your wife and son, sir. But we can't replace them, and I don't know if we'd be doing right to burden you with the expense of three kids not your own.' Then he added, looking the doctor squarely in the eyes. 'And you should think about this too. You'll have one hell of a time finding another wife when you assume guardianship of us.'

'I don't intend to marry again,' he replied in a strange way. Then he went on with an abstract air, 'Julia was the name of my

33

wife, and my son was named Scotty. He was only three when he died.'

'Oh,' I breathed, 'how terrible to lose a son so young, and your wife too.' His obvious grief and remorse reached out and touched me; I was very in tune with those who grieved. 'Did they die in an accident, a car accident like our father?'

'An accident,' he said sharply, 'but not in a car.'

'Our father was only thirty-six when he was killed, and we were having a surprise birthday party, with a cake, presents ... and he never came, only two state policemen ...'

'Yes, Cathy,' he said softly, 'you've told me. The adolescent years aren't easy for anyone, and to be young and on your own, without the proper education, with little money, no family, no friends –'

'We've got each other!' said Chris staunchly, so as to test him more. 'So, we will never truly be alone.'

Paul went on. 'If you don't want me, and what I have to give you isn't enough, then go on to Florida with my blessings. Throw away all those long hours you studied, Chris, just when you're almost there. And you, Cathy, can forget your dream of being a ballerina. And don't you think for one moment that's going to be a healthy, happy life for Carrie. I'm not persuading you to stay, for you'll do what you want to and have to. So make up your minds – is it to be me and the chance to fulfil your aspirations, or is it to be the hard, unknown world?'

I sat there on the balustrade as close as possible to Chris, with my hand held in his. I wanted to stay. I wanted what the doctor could give to Chris, to say nothing of Carrie and myself.

The southern breezes kept blowing, caressing my cheek and whispering too convincingly that everything would work out right. I could hear Henny in the kitchen making fresh dough for the hot rolls we'd eat in the morning, made golden by dripping butter. Butter was one of the things denied us before, and the luxury Chris had missed most.

Everything here beguiled me, the air, the soft, warm glow in the doctor's eyes. Even the banging of Henny's pots and pans began to work magic, and my heart, so heavily burdened for so long, began to feel lighter. Maybe perfection did exist outside of fairy tales. Maybe we were good enough to walk upright and proud beneath God's blue sky; maybe we were not contaminated shoots grown from the wrong seed planted in the wrong soil.

And more than anything the doctor had said, or anything his sparkling eyes implied, I think it was the roses that still bloomed, though it was winter, that made me feel dizzy from the overwhelming sweetness of their perfume.

But it wasn't Chris and I who decided. It was Carrie. Suddenly she jumped up from the top step and went flying into the doctor's outstretched arms. She flung herself against him and wrapped her thin arms about his neck. 'I don't want to go! I love you, Dr Paul!' she cried out, almost frantic. 'I don't want no Florida and no circus! I don't want to go anywhere!' Then she was crying, letting out all her grief for Cory, withheld for so long. He picked her up and held her on his lap, and put kisses on her wet cheeks before he used his handkerchief to mop up the tears.

'I love you too, Carrie. I always wanted a little girl with blonde curls and big blue eyes, just like yours.' But he wasn't looking at Carrie. He was looking at me.

'And I want to be here for Christmas,' sobbed Carrie. 'I've never seen Santa Claus, not once.' Of course she had, years ago, when our parents took the twins to a department store and Daddy snapped a picture of the two of them on Santa's lap, but maybe she'd forgotten.

How could a stranger come so easily into our lives and give us love, when our own blood kin had sought to give us death?

Carrie decided. We stayed. Even if she hadn't decided, still we would have stayed. How could we not?

We tried to give Dr Paul what money we had left. He refused. 'You keep that money for yourselves. You worked hard to get it, didn't you? And you might as well know I've seen my attorney so he can fill out the petitions that will bring your mother to Clairmont. I know you believe she won't come, but you can never tell. If I'm so lucky as to win permanent custody, I'll give each of you a weekly allowance. No one can feel free and happy without some money in his pocket.' He planned to buy all our clothes and everything else we needed for school. We could only stare at him, amazed he'd be so generous – again.

A few days before Christmas he drove us to a shopping mall that was carpeted in red; the ceiling was a glass dome; throngs of people swarmed about as pop Christmas music played. It was like fairyland! I glowed; so did Carrie and Chris – and our doctor. His huge hand held Carrie's small one as Chris and I held on to each other. I saw him watching us, enjoying our wide-eyed stares. We were charmed by everything. Awed, impressed, very wanting, fearful too he would see and try to satisfy all our yearnings.

I turned in circles when we reached the department that sold clothes for teenage girls. Dazzled and bewildered by so much, I looked at that, and looked at this, and couldn't decide what I wanted when everything was so pretty and I'd never had the chance to shop for myself before. Chris laughed at my indecision. 'Go on,' he urged, 'now that you have the chance to fit yourself perfectly, try on what you like.' I knew what he was thinking, for it had been my mean way to complain that Momma never brought me anything that fitted right.

With great care I selected parsimoniously the outfits I thought suitable for school that would begin for us in January. And I needed a coat, real shoes, and a raincoat and hat and umbrella. Everything that kind-hearted, generous man allowed me to buy made me feel guilty, as if we were taking advantage of him.

To reward me for my slowness and my reluctance to buy too much, Paul said impatiently, 'For heaven's sake, Cathy, don't think we're going shopping like this every week. I want you to buy enough today to last you through the winter. Chris, while we finish up here, you dash on to the young men's section and begin picking out what you want. While you do that, Cathy and I can outfit Carrie with the clothes she needs.'

I noticed that all the adolescent girls in the store were turning to stare at my brother as he made his way to the young men's department.

At last we were going to be normal kids. Then, when I felt tentatively secure, Carrie let out a howl to shatter crystal palaces in London! Her cries jolted the salespeople, startled the customers, and a lady bumped her pram into a dummy who went crashing down. The baby added his screams to Carrie's!

Chris came on the run to see who was murdering his small sister. She stood, feet wide apart, head thrown back, with tears of frustration streaming her cheeks. 'Good God, what's wrong now?' asked Chris as our doctor looked dumbfounded.

Men – what did they know? Obviously Carrie was outraged by the pretty little pastel dresses brought out for her approval. Baby clothes – that's what. Even so, all were too large, and none were red or purple – absolutely not Carrie's style at all! 'Try the toddler department,' suggested the heartless, haughty blonde with the beehive hair. She smiled graciously at our doctor who appeared embarrassed.

Carrie was *eight*! To even mention toddler clothes was insulting! She screwed her face into a puckered prune. 'I can't wear toddler clothes to school!' she wailed. She pressed her face against my thigh and hugged my legs. 'Cathy, don't make me wear pink and blue *baby* dresses! Everybody will laugh! I know they will! I want purple, red – no baby colours!'

Dr Paul soothed her. 'Darling, I adore blonde girls with blue eyes in pastels, so why not wait until you're older to wear all those brilliant colours?'

37

Bittersweet milksop like this was something someone as stubborn as Carrie couldn't swallow. She glared her eyes, balled her fists, prepared her foot for kicking and readied her vocal chords for screaming when a middle-aged, plump woman who must have had someone like Carrie for a granddaughter suggested calmly that she could have her clothes custom made. Carrie hesitated uncertainly, looking from me to the doctor, then to Chris and back to the saleslady.

'A perfect solution!' said Dr Paul enthusiastically, looking relieved. 'I'll buy a sewing machine and Cathy can make you purple, red, and electric-blue clothes, and you'll be a knock-out.'

'Don't want to be a knock-out – just want bright colours.' Carrie pouted while I was left with my mouth agape. I was a dancer, not a seamstress! (Something that didn't escape Carrie's knowledge.) 'Cathy doesn't know how to make good clothes,' she said. 'Cathy doesn't do nothing but dance.'

That was loyalty. Me, who'd taught her and Cory to read, with a little help from Chris. 'What's the matter with you, Carrie?' snapped Chris. 'You're acting like a baby. Cathy can do anything she sets her mind to – remember that!' The doctor readily agreed. I said nothing as we shopped for an electric sewing machine.

'But in the meanting, let's buy a few pink, yellow and blue dresses, all right, Carrie?' Dr Paul grinned mockingly. 'And Cathy can save me tons of money by sewing her own clothes too.'

Despite the sewing I'd have to learn, heaven was ours that day. We went home loaded, all of us made beautiful in barber shops and beauty salons; each of us had on new shoes with hard soles. I had my first pair of high-heeled shoes – and a dozen pairs of nylons! My first nylons, my first bra – and to top it all off, a shopping bag full of cosmetics. I'd taken forever to select makeup while the doctor stood back and watched me with the queerest expression. Chris had grumbled, saying I didn't need rouge or lipstick, or eyeshadow, liner and mascara. 'You don't know anything at all about being a girl,' I answered with an air of superiority. This was my first shopping binge, and by heaven I was making the most of it! I had to have everything I'd seen on Momma's fabulous dressing table. Even her kind of wrinkle cream, plus a mud pack for firming.

No sooner were we out of the car and unloaded than Chris, Carrie and I dashed upstairs to try on all our new clothes. Funny how once new clothes had come to us so easily and hadn't made us happy like this. Not when no one would see us wear them. Yet, being what I was, when I slipped on the blue velvet dress with tiny buttons down the front, I thought of Momma. How ironic that I should want to cry for a mother we'd lost, whom I was determined to hate forever. I sat on the edge of my twin bed and pondered this. Momma had given us new clothes, toys and games out of guilt for what she was doing, depriving us of a normal childhood. A childhood we'd never have the chance to recover. Lost years, some of the best years, and Cory was in a grave, no new suits for him.

His guitar was in the corner where Carrie could wake up and see it and the banjo. Why was it we who always had to suffer, why not her? Then, suddenly it hit me? Bart Winslow was from South Carolina! I ran down to our doctor's study and purloined his big atlas, then back I raced to the bedroom, and there I found the map of South Carolina. I found Clairmont ... but didn't believe my eyes when I saw it was a twin city to Greenglenna! No, that was too much of a coincidence – or was it? I looked up and stared into space. God had meant for us to come here and live near Momma – if she ever visited her husband's home town. God wanted me to have the chance to inflict a little pain of my own. As soon as I could, I was going to Greenglenna to look up all the information I could about him and his family. And I would order a subscription to the local paper that told of all the social activities of the wealthy people who lived near Foxworth Hall.

Yes, I was gone from Foxworth Hall, but I was going to know every move she made, and when she came this way I'd know that too! Sooner or later, Momma was going to hear from me, and know I would never, never forget or forgive. Somehow, in some way, she was going to hurt ten times more than we had!

With this decided, I could join Chris and Carrie in the living room to model all our new clothes for our doctor and Henny. Henny's smile beamed like a dazzling sun. I watched the bejewelled eyes of our benefactor, only to see them shadow over as he frowned reflectively. I saw no admiration or approval. Suddenly, he got up and left the room, offering a weak excuse of needing to do some paperwork.

Soon Henny became my mentor in all things domestic. She taught me to bake biscuits from scratch, and tried to teach me how to make rolls light and fluffy.

Wham! went Henny's hand into the dough. Henny wiped her hands clean of flour and dashed off a note. *Henny got bad eyes for seeing small things like needle eyes. You have good eyes you sew on doctor son's missing shirt buttons – yes?*

'Sure,' I agreed without enthusiasm, 'I can see holes, and I can also knit, crochet, needlepoint and do crewel work. My mother taught me how to do all those things as a way to keep busy.' Suddenly I couldn't speak. I wanted to cry. I saw my mother's lovely face. I saw Daddy. I saw Chris and me as children hurrying home from school, rushing in with snow on our shoulders to find Momma knitting baby things for the twins. I couldn't help but bow my head into Henny's lap and begin to cry, really bawl. Henny couldn't speak, but her soft hand on my shoulder showed she understood. When I glanced upward, she was crying too. Big, fat tears that slid down to wet her bright red dress. 'Don't cry, Henny. I'll be happy to sew on Dr Paul's missing buttons. He's saved our lives, and there's nothing I wouldn't do for him.' She gave me a strange look, then got up to fetch years of mending and perhaps a dozen shirts with missing buttons.

Chris spent every available moment with Dr Paul who was coaching him so he could enter a special school in midterm. Carrie was our biggest problem. She could read and write but she was so very small. How would she manage in a school where children were not always kind?

'It's a private school I have in mind for Carrie,' explained our doctor. 'A very good school for young girls, run by an excellent staff. Since I'm on the board of trustees, I think Carrie will be given special attention, and not subjected to any kind of stress.' He eyed me meaningfully.

That was my worst fear, that Carrie would be ridiculed and

made to feel ashamed because of her overlarge head and undersized body. Once Carrie had been so beautifully proportioned, so very perfect. It was all those lost years when the sun was denied us that made her so small. It was, I knew it was!

I was scared to death Momma would show up on that day she was supposed to appear at the court hearing. But I was certain, almost, that she wouldn't come. How could she? She had too much to lose and nothing to gain. What were we but burdens to bear? And there was jail too, a murder charge...

We sat very quietly with Paul, dressed in our best to appear in the judge's chamber, and waited, and waited, and waited. I was a tight wire inside, stretched so taut I thought I might break and cry. She didn't want us. Again she told us, by not showing up, how little she cared! The judge looked at us with too much pity, making me feel so sorry for all of us – and so angry with her! Oh, damn her to hell! She gave us birth, she claimed to have loved our father! How could she do this to his children – her own children? What kind of mother was she? I didn't want that judge's pity, or Paul's. I held my head high and bit down on my tongue to keep from screaming. I dared to glance at Chris and saw him sitting blank-eyed, though I knew his heart was being shredded, as mine was. Carrie crouched in a tight ball on the doctor's lap, as his hands soothed her, and he whispered something in her ear. I think he said, 'Never mind, it's all right. You have me for a father and Henny for a mother. You'll never want for anything as long as I live.'

I cried that night. I wet my pillow with tears shed for a mother I'd loved so much it hurt to think back to the days when Daddy was alive and our home life was perfect. I cried for all the good things she had done for us back then, and, most of all, for all the love she'd so generously given us – then. I cried more for Cory who was like my own child. And that's when I stopped crying and turned to bitter, hard thoughts of revenge. When you set out to defeat someone, the best way was to think as they did. What would hurt her most? She wouldn't want to think of us. She'd try to forget we ever existed. Well, she wouldn't forget. I'd see to it that she didn't. This very Christmas I would send her a card, and sign it with this, 'From the four Dresden dolls you didn't want,' and I had to change that to 'The three alive Dresden dolls you didn't want, plus the dead one you carried away and never brought back.' I could see her staring at that card.

We had let down our shields and allowed ourselves to be vulnerable again. We allowed faith, hope and trust to come and dance like sugarplums in our heads.

Fairy tales could come true.

They were happening to us. The wicked queen was out of our lives, and Snow White would reign one day. She wouldn't be the one to eat the poisoned red apple. But every fairy tale had a dragon to slay, a witch to overcome or some obstacle to make things difficult. I tried to look ahead and figure out who would be the dragon, and what would be the obstacles. All along I knew who was the witch. And that was the saddest part of being me.

I got up and went out on the upper veranda to stare up at the moon. I saw Chris standing near the railing, gazing up at the moon too. From the slump of his shoulders, usually held so proud, I knew he was bleeding inside, just as I was. I tiptoed over to surprise him. But he turned as I neared and held out his arms. Without thought I went straight into them and put my arms up around his neck. He wore the warm robe Momma had given him last Christmas, though it was much too small. He'd have another from me when he looked under the tree on Christmas morning, with his monogram – CFS – for he wanted never to be called Foxworth, but Sheffield.

His blue eyes gazed down into mine. Eyes so much alike. I loved him as I loved the better side of myself, the brighter, happier side.

'Cathy,' he whispered, stroking my back, his eyes bright, 'if you feel like crying, go ahead, I'll understand. Cry enough for me too. I was hoping, praying that Momma would come and somehow give us a reasonable explanation for doing what she did.'

'A reasonable excuse for murder?' I asked bitterly. 'How

could she dream up one clever enough? She's not that smart.' He looked so miserable I tightened my arms about his neck. One hand stole into his hair and twined there. My other hand lowered to stroke his cheek. Love, it was such an encompassing word, different from sex and ten times more compelling. I felt full of love for him when he lowered his face into my hair and sobbed. He murmured my name over and over again, as if I were the only person in the world who would ever be real and solid, and dependable.

Somehow his lips found mine and we were kissing, kissing with so much passion he was aroused and tried to draw me into his room. 'I just want to hold you, that's all. Nothing else. When I go away to school, I need to have something more to hold to – give me just a little more, Cathy, please.' Before I could answer he had me in his arms again, kissing me with such burning lips I became terrified – and excited too.

'Stop! Don't!' I cried, but he went on, touching my breasts and pushing my gown aside so he could kiss them. 'Chris!' I hissed, angry then. 'Don't love me, Chris. When you're gone, what you feel for me will fade away like it never happened. We'll force ourselves to love others so we can feel clean. We can't be our parents in duplicate. We can't make the same mistake.'

He held me tighter and didn't say a word, yet I knew what he was thinking. There wouldn't be any others. He wouldn't let it come about. One woman had hurt him too deeply, betrayed him too monstrously when he was young and very, very vulnerable. There was only me he could trust.

He stepped back, two tears shining in the corners of his eyes. It was up to me to slice the bond, now, here. And for his own good. Everybody always did everything for someone's good.

I couldn't go to sleep. I kept hearing him calling me, wanting me. I got up and drifted down the hall and again got in his bed, where he lay waiting. 'You'll never be free of me, Cathy, never. As long as you live, it will be me and you.'

'No!'

'Yes!'

'No!' But I kissed him, then jumped from his bed and raced

back to my room, slamming and locking the door behind me. What was the matter with me? I should never have gone to his room and gotten into his bed. Was I as evil as the grandmother said?

No, I wasn't.

I couldn't be!

PART TWO

VISIONS OF SUGARPLUMS

It was Christmas. The tree touched the twelve-foot ceiling, and spread under it were gifts enough for ten children! Not that Chris and I were children any more. Carrie was thrilled by everything Santa had brought for her. Chris and I had used the last of our stolen hoard of money to buy Paul a luscious red lounging robe, and a brilliant gown of ruby-red velvet for Henny. Dazzled and pleased, she held it before her. Then she wrote a thank-you note, *Make good church dress. Make all friends jealous.*

Paul tried on his lavish new lounging robe. He looked divine in that colour and it fitted him beautifully.

Next came the biggest surprise of all. Paul strode over to me and hunkered down on his heels. From his wallet he pulled five large yellow tickets. If he had sat down for a year and thought about nothing but a way to please me most, he couldn't have been more successful. There, fanned in his large, finely shaped hand, were tickets to *The Nutcracker*, performed by the Rosencoff School of Ballet.

'It's a very professional company, I hear,' explained Paul. 'I don't know much about ballet myself, but I've asked around, and they say it is one of the best. They also teach beginner, intermediate and advanced lessons. Which level are you?'

'Advanced!' proclaimed Chris while I could only stare at Paul, too happy to speak. 'Cathy was a beginner when she went upstairs to live. But something wonderful happened to her in the attic – the ghost of Anna Pavlova came and took over her body. And Cathy taught herself how to go on *pointe*.'

That night all of us, including Henny, sat enthralled in the third row, centre section. Those dancers on stage weren't just good – they were superb! Especially the handsome man named Julian Marquet who danced the lead. As in a dream I followed

Paul backstage during intermission, for I was going to meet the dancers!

He led us towards a couple standing in the wings. 'Madame, Georges,' he said to a tiny woman sleek as a seal and a not much larger man by her side, 'this is my ward, Catherine Doll, whom I was telling you about. This is her brother, Christopher, and this younger beauty is Carrie, and you have met Henrietta Beech before . . .'

'Yah, of course,' said the lady who looked like a dancer, talked like a dancer, and wore her black hair just like a dancer would, drawn back from her face and pinned up in a huge chignon. Over black leotards she wore a floating chiffon dress of black, and over that a bolero of leopard skins. Her husband, Georges, was a quiet man, sinewy, pale-faced, with startlingly black hair, and lips so red they seemed made of congealed blood. They were a pair, all right, for her lips were scarlet slashed too, and her eyes were charcoaled smudges in pale pastry dough. Two pairs of black eyes scanned me and then Chris. 'You too are a dancer?' they asked of my brother. My, did they always speak simultaneously?

'No! I don't dance,' said Chris, appearing embarrassed.

'Ah, the pity of that,' sighed the Madame regretfully. 'What a glorious pair the two of you would make on stage. People would flock to stare at beauty such as you and your sister possess.' She glanced down at small Carrie, clinging fearfully to my hand, and casually disregarded her.

'Chris plans to be a doctor,' explained Dr Paul.

'Ha!' Madame Rosencoff scoffed, as if Chris must have taken leave of his senses. Both she and her husband turned their ebony eyes on me, concentrating with such intensity I began to feel hot, sweaty, self-conscious.

'You have studied the daunce?' (Always she said 'daunce', as if it had a 'u'.)

'Yes,' I said in a small voice.

'Your age when you started?'

'I was four years old.'

'And you are now . . . ?'

'In April I will be sixteen.'

'Good. Very, very good.' She rubbed the palms of her long,

46

bony hands together. 'Eleven years and more of professional training. At what age did you go on *pointe*?'

'Twelve.'

'Wonderful!' she cried. 'I never put girls on full *pointe* until they are thirteen, unless they are excellent.' Then she frowned suspiciously. 'Are you excellent, or only mediocre?'

'I don't know.'

'You mean no one has ever told you?'

'No.'

'Then you must be only mediocre.' She half-sneered, turned towards her husband and waved her hand arrogantly to dismiss us.

'Now you wait a minute!' flared Chris, looking red and very angry. 'There's not a dancer on that stage tonight who is as good as Cathy! Not one! That girl out there, playing the lead role of Clara – sometimes she is out of time with the music – Cathy is *never* out of time. *Her* timing is perfect; her *ear* is perfect. Even when Cathy dances to the same melody, each time she varies it just a little, so she never duplicates, always improvises to make it better, and more beautiful, and more touching. You'd be lucky to get a dancer like Cathy in your company!'

Those slanted, jet eyes turned on him, savouring the intensity of his report. '*You* are an authority on the subject of ballet?' she asked with some scorn. '*You* know how to separate the gifted dancers from the horde?'

Chris stood as if in a dream, and spoke as if his feet were firmly rooted there, and even his voice had a huskiness to betray his feelings. 'I only know what I see, and what emotions Cathy makes me feel when she dances. I know when the music turns on, and she begins to move with it, my heart stands still, and when her dance is over, I know I am left aching because such beauty has gone. She doesn't just dance a role, she *is* that character; she makes you believe – because *she* believes – and there's not a girl in your company who reaches out and grabs my heart and squeezes it until it throbs. So go on and turn her away, and let some other dance company benefit from your stupidity.'

The Madame's jet eyes fixed on Chris long and penetratingly, as did our doctor's eyes. Then slowly Madame Rosencoff turned to me, and from head to toe I was assessed, weighed, measured. 'Tomorrow, one o'clock sharp. At my studio you will audition for me.' It was not a request, but a command – not to be disobeyed – and for some reason when I should have been happy, I was angry.

'Tomorrow is too soon,' I said. 'I have no costumes, no leotards, no *pointes*.' All of those things had been left behind in the attic of Foxworth Hall.

'Trifles,' she dismissed, with an arrogant wave of her shapely hand. 'We will supply what you need – just be there – and don't be late, for we demand that our dancers be disciplined in *all* things, including punctuality!' With a queenly gesture we were dismissed, and gracefully she drifted off with her husband in tow, leaving me stunned. Mouth agape, speechless, I caught the strong study of the dancer, Julian Marquet, who must have overheard every word. His dark eyes shone with a glow of interest and admiration. 'Feel flattered, Catherine,' he said to me. 'Customarily she and Georges won't take anyone unless they've waited months, or sometimes years, for an audition.'

I cried that night in Chris's embrace. 'I'm out of practice,' I sobbed. 'I know I'm going to make a fool of myself tomorrow. It isn't fair that she won't let me have more time to prepare! I need to limber up. I'm going to be stiff, clumsy, and they won't want me, I know they won't!'

'Aw, come off it, Cathy,' he said, tightening his arms about me. 'I've seen you in here holding on to the bedpost, and doing your *pliés* and *tendus*. You are *not* out of practice, or stiff, or clumsy – you're just scared. You've got a great big case of stage fright, that's all. And you don't need to worry, you're terrific, *I* know it, *you* know it.'

He brushed a light good-night kiss on my lips, dropped his arms and backed towards the door. 'Tomorrow I'll go down on my knees and pray for you. I'll ask God to let you wow them tomorrow. And I'll be there to gloat when I see their stunned expressions – for no one is gonna believe the dancing wonder of you.'

With that he was gone. And I was left aching and wanting. I

crawled under my covers to lie wide awake and full of trepidation.

Tomorrow was my big day, my chance to prove what I was and if I had that special something you had to have if you were to reach the top. I had to be *the* best, nothing else would do. I had to show Momma, the grandmother, Paul, Chris, everybody! I wasn't evil, or corrupt, or the Devil's issue. I was only me – the best ballerina in the world!

I tossed, turned, fretted in and out of nightmares while Carrie slept on peacefully. In my dreams I did everything wrong at the audition, and, what was worse, I did everything wrong throughout my whole lifetime! I ended up a withered old lady begging on the streets of some huge city. In the dark I passed by my mother and begged for alms. She was still young and beautiful, richly gowned, bejewelled and furred, and escorted by forever-young and faithful Bart Winslow.

I awoke. It was still night. What a long night. I stole down the stairs to find the Christmas tree lights burning, and on the floor, Chris was lying and staring up into the tree branches. It was what the two of us used to do when we were children. Though I should have known better, I was irresistibly drawn towards him, and I lay down beside him. I gazed up into the sparkling other-worldliness of the Christmas tree.

'I thought you'd forgotten,' Chris murmured without looking my way. 'Remember when we were in Foxworth Hall, the tree was so small and it was on a table and we couldn't lie under it like this – and look what happened. Let's never forget again. Even if our future trees are only one foot high, we will hang it up high, so we can lie underneath.'

It worried me the way he said that. Slowly I turned my head to stare at his profile. He was so beautiful, lying there with his fair hair changing colour. Each strand seemed to catch a different rainbowed hue, and when he turned his head to meet my eyes his eyes were glowing too. 'You look . . . so divine,' I said in a tight voice. 'I see candy in your eyes and the crown jewels of England too.'

'No – that's what I am seeing in your eyes, Cathy. You're so very beautiful in that white nightgown. I love you in white nightgowns with blue satin ribbons. I love the way your hair spreads like a fan, and you turn your cheek so it rests on a satin pillow.' He moved closer, so his head was on my hair too. Even closer he inclined his head until our foreheads met. His warm breath was on my face. I moved so my head tilted backward and my neck ached. I didn't feel quite real when his warm lips kissed the hollow of my throat and stayed there. My breath caught. For long, long moments I waited for him to move away. I wanted to pull back myself, but somehow I couldn't. A sweet peace stole over me, quivering my flesh with a tingling sensation. 'Don't kiss me again,' I whispered, clinging harder to him and pressing his head to my throat.

'I love you,' he choked. 'There will never be anyone for me but you. When I'm an old, old man, I'll look back to this night with you under the Christmas tree, and remember how sweet it was of you to let me hold you like this.'

'Chris, do you have to go away and be a doctor? Couldn't you stay on here and decide on something else?'

He lifted his head to stare down into my eyes. 'Cathy – do you have to ask? All my life it's been the only thing I've wanted, but you . . .'

Again I sobbed. I didn't want him to go! I tickled his face with a tress of my hair, until he cried out and kissed my lips. Such a soft kiss, wanting to grow bolder, and afraid I'd turn away if he did. He began to say wild and crazy things when our kiss was over, about how much I looked like an angel. 'Cathy – look at me! Don't turn your head and pretend you don't know what I'm doing, what I'm saying! Look and see the torment you've put me in! How can I find anyone else, when you've been bred into my bones – and are part of my flesh? Your blood runs fast when mine does! Your eyes burn when mine do – don't deny it!' His trembling hands began to fumble with the tiny, lace-covered buttons that opened my nightgown to the waist. I closed my eyes and was again in the attic, when he'd accidentally stabbed me in the side with the scissors, so now I was hurting, bleeding, and I needed his lips to kiss and take away the pain.

'How beautiful your breasts are,' he said with a low sigh, leaning to nuzzle them. 'I remember when you were flat, and then when you began to grow. You were so shy about them, always wanting to wear loose sweaters so I couldn't see. Why were you ashamed?'

Somewhere above I hovered, watching him tenderly kiss my breasts, and somewhere deep inside me I shivered. Why was I letting him do this? My arms drew his body tighter against me, and when my lips again met his, maybe it was my fingers that had unbuttoned his pyjama jacket so his bare chest was against mine. We melded in a hot blend of unsatisfied desire – before I suddenly cried out, 'No – it would be sinful!'

'Then let us sin!'

'Then don't ever leave me! Forget about being a doctor! Stay with me! Don't go and leave me! I'm afraid of myself without you! Sometimes I do crazy things. Chris, please don't leave me alone. I've never been alone, please stay!'

'I *have* to be a doctor,' he said, then groaned. 'Ask me to give up anything else, and I'd say yes. But don't ask me to give up the only thing that's held me together. You wouldn't give up dancing – would you?'

I didn't know, as I responded to his demanding kisses, the fire between us growing larger, overwhelming us both and taking us to the brink of hell. 'I love you so much sometimes I don't know how to handle it,' he cried. 'If only I could have you just once, and there would be no pain for you, only joy.'

The unexpected parting of his hot lips, his tongue that forced my lips open, shot through me with a jolt of electricity! 'I love you, oh, how I love you! I dream of you, think of you all day.' And on and on he went, while his breath came faster, until he was panting and I was overcome by my body ready and willing to be satisfied. While my thoughts wanted to deny him, I wanted him! I gasped with the shame of it!

Before I knew what was happening he had me in his arms and was racing up the back stairs and into my room where he fell with me on my bed. I didn't want this. I didn't want it ever to happen again! 'Stop!' I cried, then rolled away from under him. I fell to the floor. In a flash he was on the floor with me, wrestling. Over and over we turned, two bodies that suddenly collided with something hard.

That was what stopped him. He stared at the box with Oreo cookies, a loaf of bread, apples, oranges, a pound of cheddar cheese, a stick of butter, several cans of tuna fish, beans and tomato juice. Out spilled a can opener, dishes, glasses and silverware. 'Cathy! Why are you stealing Paul's food and hiding it under your bed?'

I shook my head, fuzzy about why I had taken the food and hidden it away. 'Get out! Leave me alone! I don't love you except as a brother, Christopher!'

He came to put his arms about me, and bowed his head on my shoulder. 'I'm sorry. Oh, darling, I know why you took the food. You feel you have to keep food handy – you're afraid someday we will be punished again. Don't you know I'm the only one who *will* understand? Cathy, let me just once give you the pleasure I didn't before, just once to last us both all our lives through.'

I slapped his face! 'No!' I spat. 'Never again! You promised, and I thought you would keep that promise! If you have to be a doctor, and go away and leave me – then it will always be no!' I stopped short. I didn't mean that. 'Chris . . . don't look at me like that, please!'

He flashed me a hurt look. 'There is no life for me if I'm not a doctor, Cathy.'

I put both hands over my mouth to keep from screaming. What was wrong with me? I couldn't demand him to abandon his dream. I wasn't like my mother, making everyone else suffer so she could have her way. I sobbed in his arms. In my brother I had already found my everlasting, forever-green, springtime love that could never, never blossom. Later, as I lay alone on my bed with my eyes open, I realized from the hopeless, flat way I felt that even in a valley without mountains the wind could still blow.

THE AUDITION

It was the day after Christmas. At one o'clock I had to be in Greenglenna, the home of Bart Winslow and the Rosencoff School of Ballet.

We all crowded into Dr Paul's car and we arrived with five minutes to spare.

Madame Rosencoff told me to call her Madame Marisha, if I was accepted. If I failed, I need never address her again, by any name. She wore only black leotards, which showed up every hill and valley of her superb body, kept trim and slim though she must be nearing fifty. Her husband, Georges, was also wearing black to show off his sinewy body which was just beginning to show age with the small protrusion of his belly. Twenty girls and three boys were to audition.

'What music do you choose?' she asked. (It seemed her husband was never going to speak, though he kept his bright bird eyes on me constantly.)

'*Sleeping Beauty*,' I said meekly, believing the role of Princess Aurora the greatest of all testing pieces in the classical repertory – so why choose a less demanding part? 'I can dance *The Rose Adagio* all alone,' I boasted.

'Wonderful,' she said sarcastically. Then added with additional scorn, 'I guessed, just by your looks, you would want *The Sleeping Beauty*.'

That made me wish I'd chosen something lesser.

'What colour leotards do you want?'

'Pink.'

'I thought so.'

She tossed me a pair of faded pink leotards and then, just as casually, picked at random from a triple row of many dozens of *pointe* shoes. She threw me a pair that fitted perfectly, unbelievable as it sounds. When I'd undressed and donned my leotards and slippers, I sat before a long dressing table with a mirror to equal its length and began to bind up my hair. I didn't have to be told Madame would want to see my neck cords, and any *épaulement* I'd perform was sure to displease her. I knew that already.

Hardly had I finished dressing and doing my hair, with a gaggle of giggling girls surrounding me, when Madame Marisha put her head through a partially opened door to see if I was ready. Critically her jet black eyes scanned me. 'Not bad. Follow me,' she ordered, and off she strode, her strong legs heavily muscled. How had she let that come about? I was never going to be on *pointe* so much my legs would look lumpy like hers – never!

She led me out into a big arena with a polished floor that really wasn't as slick as it appeared. Seats for onlookers were lined against the walls, and I saw Chris, Carrie, Henny and Dr Paul. Now I wished I hadn't asked them to come. If I failed, they'd witness my humiliation. Eight or ten other people were there too, though I didn't pay much attention to them. The girls and boys of the company gathered in the wings to watch. I was more afraid than I'd thought I'd be. Sure, I'd practised some since I escaped Foxworth Hall, but not with the same dedication as in the attic. I should have stayed up all night and exercised, and arrived at dawn to warm up more – then maybe I wouldn't feel nervous enough to be sick.

It was my desire to be last, to watch all the others and see the mistakes they made and learn from them, or to see their accomplishments and benefit from those. In this way I could size up what *I* should do.

Georges himself sat down to play the piano. I swallowed over the lump in my throat; my mouth felt dry, and butterflies panicked in my chest as my eyes raked over the spectators to find the lodestone I needed in the blue of Chris's eyes. And as always, he was there to smile, and telegraph his pride and confidence and undying admiration. My dear, beloved Christopher Doll, always there when I needed him, always giving to me and making me better than I would have been without him. God, I prayed, let me be good. Let me live up to his expectations!

I couldn't look at Paul. He wanted to be my father, not my

touchstone. If I failed and embarrassed him, certainly he'd see me differently. I'd lose what charm I had for him. I'd be nobody special.

A touch on my arm made me jump. Whirling about I confronted Julian Marquet. 'Break a leg,' he whispered, then smiled to show his very white and perfect teeth. His dark eyes sparkled wickedly. He was taller than most male dancers, almost six feet, and soon I'd learn he was nineteen. His skin was as fair as mine, though in contrast to his dark hair it made him look too pale. His strong chin sported a devil's cleft and another dimple in his right cheek teased in and out at his will. I thanked him for his wish of good luck, very much taken by his astonishing good looks. 'Wow!' he said when I smiled, his voice husky. 'You're a beautiful girl. Too bad you're only a kid.'

'I'm not a kid!'

'What are you then, some old lady of eighteen?'

I smiled, very pleased to think I looked *that* old. 'Maybe so, maybe not.'

He grinned as if he had all the answers. From the way he bragged of being one of the hottest dancers in a New York company, maybe he *did* have all the answers. 'I'm only here for the holidays – to do Madame a favour. Soon I'll go back to New York where I belong.' He looked around, as if the provinces bored him beyond belief, while my heart did a flip-flop. I was hoping he was one of the dancers I'd work with.

We exchanged a few more words and then my musical cue sounded. Suddenly I was alone in the attic, with coloured paper flowers dangling on long strings; nobody but me and that secret lover who danced always just ahead, never letting me get near enough to see his face. I danced out, fearful at first, and did all the right things, the *entrachets*, the arm flutters, the *pirouettes*. I was sure to keep my eyes open and my face always towards the viewers I didn't see. Then the magic came and took me. I didn't have to plan and count, the music told me what to do, and how to do it, for I was its voice and could do no wrong. And as always that man appeared to dance with me – only this time I saw his face! His beautiful pale, pale face, with the dark and flashing eyes, and the blue-black hair and the ruby lips. Julian!

55

I saw him as in a dream, stretching out his strong arms as he went down on one knee, and the other leg pointed backward gracefully. With his eyes he signalled I was to run, then leap into his receiving arms. Enchanted to see him there, a professional, I was halfway to him when a terrible pain seized my abdomen! I doubled over and cried out! At my feet was a huge pool of blood! Blood streamed down my legs; it stained my pink shoes, my leotards. I slipped and fell to the floor, and grew so weak I could only lie there and hear the screams. Not my screams, but Carrie's. I closed my eyes not caring who it was who came to pick me up. From a far distance I heard Paul's voice and Chris's. Chris's concerned face hovered above me, with his love for me too clearly revealed; it both comforted me and frightened me, for I didn't want Paul to see. Chris said something about not being afraid as blackness came and took me to a far, far place where nobody wanted me.

And my dancing career, not yet begun, was over, over.

Out of a dream of witches I emerged to find Chris sitting on the hospital bed, holding my limp hand ... and those blue eyes, oh, God, those eyes ... 'Hi,' he said softly, squeezing my fingers. 'I've been waiting for you to come around.'

'Hi yourself.'

He smiled and leaned to kiss my cheek. 'I'll tell you this, Catherine Doll, you sure know how to end a dance dramatically.'

'Yeah, that's talent. Real talent. I guess I'd better go into acting.'

He shrugged indifferently. 'You could, I guess, though I doubt you will.'

'Oh, Chris,' I stormed weakly, 'you know I've ruined what chance I had! Why did I bleed like that?' I knew my eyes were full of fear. Fear that he saw and knew the cause. He leaned to draw me up into his embrace and held me fast against his chest.

'Life offers more than one chance, Cathy, you know that. You needed a D & C. You'll be fine and on your feet by tomorrow.'

'What's a D & C?'

He smiled and stroked my cheek tenderly, always forgetting I wasn't as medically sophisticated as he was. 'It's short for a

56

procedure in which a woman is dilated, and an instrument called a curette is used to scrape waste material from the lining of the uterus. Those missed periods of yours must have clotted and then broke free.'

Our eyes met. 'That's all it was, Cathy ... *all*, nothing else.'

'Who did the scraping?' I whispered, scared it was Paul.

'A gynaecologist named Dr Jarvis, a friend of our doctor. Paul says he's the best around.'

I lay back on the pillows, not knowing what to think. Of all times for something like that to happen – in front of everyone I was trying to impress. My God, why was life so cruel to me?

'Open your eyes, my lady Catherine,' said Chris. 'You're making too much out of this, when it doesn't matter. Take a look at that dresser over there and see all the pretty flowers, real flowers, not paper ones. I hope you don't mind if I took a peek at the cards.' Of course I didn't mind what *he* did, and soon he was back from the dresser and putting a small white envelope in my flaccid hand. I stared at the huge floral bouquet, thinking it was from Paul, and only then did my eyes flick to the card in my hand. My fingers shook as I extracted from the envelope the small note that read:

Hope you recover soon. I expect to see you next Monday, three o'clock sharp.

Madame Marisha.

Marisha! I was accepted! 'Chris, the Rosencoffs want me!'

'Of course they do,' he said mildly. 'They'd be just plain dumb if they didn't, but that woman scares the hell out of me! I wouldn't want her controlling my life, even if she is little. But, I guess you can handle her fine; you can always bleed on her feet.'

I sat up and threw my arms about him. 'Is it going to work out for us, Chris? Do you really think it will? Can we be that lucky?'

He nodded, smiled and then pointed to another bouquet, one from Julian Marquet with another short note. *I'll be seeing you*

*when I fly down from New York again, Catherine Doll, so don't
forget me.*

And over Chris's shoulder, while his arms held me tight, Paul
came into the room and hesitated near the doorway, frowning as
he stared at the two of us, and then he put on a smile and came
forward. Quickly Chris and I drew apart.

SCHOOL DAYS RENEWED

There came a day in January when we had to part. We'd taken exams to grade our abilities, and, much to Chris's surprise, and mine, we'd all done extremely well. I qualified for the tenth grade, Carrie for the third, and Chris for a junior college. But there was no happiness on Carrie's face when she screamed out, 'No! No!' Her foot was ready for kicking, her fists balled to do battle with anyone who tried to force her. 'Don't want no private school for funny lookin' girls! I won't go! You can't make me go! I'm going to tell Dr Paul, Cathy!' Her face was red with fury and her weeping voice was a siren's wail.

I wasn't overjoyed by the idea of putting Carrie in a private school ten miles outside the city. The day after she left, Chris would be leaving too. I'd be left alone to attend high school – and we'd sworn a solemn vow never, never to part. (I'd forced myself to put back the hidden cache of food – and no one knew about that but Chris.) I lifted Carrie on to my lap to explain to her how Dr Paul had selected this very special school and had already paid an enormous tuition. She squinched her eyes shut and tried not to hear. 'And it is *not* a school for funny little girls, Carrie,' I said soothingly and then kissed her forehead. 'It's a school for *rich* girls with parents who can afford the best. You should feel proud and very lucky to have Dr Paul as our legal guardian.' Did I convince her? Had I ever convinced her of anything?

'I still don't want to go,' she wailed stubbornly. 'Why can't I go to *your* school, Cathy? Why do I have to go off all alone with nobody?'

'Nobody?' I laughed to hide what I was feeling, a reflection of her own fears. 'You won't be alone, darling. You'll be with hundreds of other girls near your own age. Your school is an elementary one; I have to go on to high school.' I rocked her to and fro in my arms, and stroked her long, shining cascade of hair, then tilted her piquant dollface to mine. Oh, she was a pretty little thing. Such a beauty she'd be if only her body would grow in proportion to her large head. 'Carrie you have four people who love you very much. Dr Paul, Henny, Chris and me. We all want what's best for you, and even though a few miles separate us, you'll be in our hearts, in our thoughts, and you can come home every weekend. And, believe it or not, school is not such a dreary place, it's fun, really. You'll share a lovely room with a girl your own age. You'll have expert teachers and, best of all, you'll be with girls who will think you're the prettiest thing they've ever seen. And you must want to be with other children. I know that being with a great many girls is loads of fun. You play games, and have secret societies and parties, and whisper and giggle all through the night. You'll love it.' Yeah. Sure. She'd love it.

Carrie acquiesced only after she'd shed a waterfall of tears, her pleading eyes telling me she was going only to please me and her big benefactor whom she loved well. She'd sleep on nails to please him. And to her that school for girls was a bed of nails to endure. Just in time to hear, 'Am I going to stay there a long, long time?' Paul and Chris entered the living room. The two of them had been sequestered in Paul's study for hours, with Paul coaching Chris on some of the chemistry he'd neglected studying while locked away. Paul gave Carrie just one glance, saw her misery, then headed for the hall closet. Shortly, he was back with a big box wrapped in purple paper and tied with red satin ribbon three inches wide. 'This is for my favourite blonde,' he said kindly.

Carrie's big, haunted eyes stared up at him before she smiled thinly. 'Oh!' she cried in delight to open her gift and see the bright red leather luggage, complete with a cosmetic case outfitted with a gold comb, brush, mirror and little plastic jars and bottles, and a leather stationery case for writing letters home to us. 'It's bea-u-ti-ful!' she exclaimed, won over at once by everything red and so fine. 'I never knew they made red suitcases and put gold mirrors and things in them.'

I had to look at Paul, who certainly didn't think a little girl needed makeup.

As if he read my thoughts, he said, 'I know it's rather adult, but I wanted to give her something she can use for many, many years. When she sees it years from now, she'll think of me.'

'That's the prettiest luggage I ever saw,' I said cheerily. 'You can put your toothbrushes, your toothpaste, your bath powder and your toilet water in your makeup case.'

'I'm not going to put any nasty toilet water in my suitcases!'

That made all of us laugh. Then I was up and running towards the stairs, hurrying to my room to fetch a small box that I rushed back to Carrie. Gingerly I held that box in my hands, wondering if I should give it to her and awaken old memories. 'Inside this box are some old friends of yours, Carrie. When you're in Miss Emily Dean Calhoun's School for Properly Bred Young Ladies and feel a little lonely, just open this box and see what's inside. Don't show the contents to everybody, just to very special friends.'

Her eyes grew large when she saw the tiny porcelain people and the baby she'd loved so much, all stolen by me from that huge, fabulous doll's house that she'd spent so many hours playing with in the attic. I'd even taken the crib.

'Mr and Mrs Parkins,' breathed Carrie, tears of happiness shining in her big, blue eyes, 'and little baby Clara! Where did they come from, Cathy?'

'You know where they came from.'

She looked at me, holding the box full of cotton to cushion the fragile dolls and hand-made wooden crib, all priceless heirlooms. 'Cathy, where is Momma?'

Oh, God! Just what I didn't want her to ask. 'Carrie, you know we are supposed to tell everybody both our parents are dead.'

'*Is* Momma dead?'

'No ... but we have to pretend she is.'

'Why?'

Once again I had to explain to Carrie why we could never tell anyone who we really were, and that our mother still lived, or else we'd end up back in that dreary northern room. She sat on the floor near her shiny new red luggage, with the box of dolls in her lap, and stared at me with haunted eyes and no comprehension at all.

'I mean this, Carrie! You are *never* to mention any family but Chris and me, and Dr Paul and Henny. Do you understand?'

She nodded, but she didn't understand. It was in her lips that quivered and in her wishful expression – she still wanted Momma!

Then came the terrible day when we drove Carrie ten miles outside the city limits of Clairmont to enter her in that fancy private school for the daughters of the affluent. The building was large, painted white, with a portico in front and the customary white columns. A brass plaque near the front door read, ESTABLISHED IN 1824.

We were received in a warm and cosy-looking office by a descendant of the school founder, Miss Emily Dean Dewhurst. A stately, handsome woman with startling, white hair and not a wrinkle to betray her age. 'She's a lovely child, Dr Sheffield. Of course we'll do what we can to make her happy and comfortable while she learns.'

I leaned to embrace Carrie who trembled and I whispered, 'Cheer up, make an effort to enjoy yourself. Don't feel abandoned. Every weekend we'll come to take you home with us. Now is that so bad?'

She brightened and forced a smile. 'Yes, I can do it,' she murmured weakly.

It wasn't easy to drive away and leave Carrie in that beautiful white plantation house.

The very next day was Chris's time to depart for his school, and oh, how I hurt to see him pack up his things. I watched but couldn't speak. Chris and I couldn't even bear to look at one another.

His school was even farther away. Paul drove thirty miles before we reached the campus with buildings of rose-coloured bricks and, again, the obligatory white columns. Sensing we needed to be alone, Paul made some flimsy excuse of wanting to inspect the gardens. Chris and I weren't really alone, but in an alcove with big bay windows. Young men were constantly passing by to glance in and stare at us. I wanted to be in his arms, with my cheek against his. I wanted this to be a farewell to love, so complete we'd know it was forever gone, at least forever gone from being wrong. 'Chris,' I stammered, near tears, 'whatever am I going to do without you?'

His blue eyes kept changing colour, jumbling his kaleidoscope emotions. 'Cathy, nothing will change,' he whispered hoarsely, clinging to my hands. 'When next we see each other, we'll still feel the same. I love you. I always will – right or wrong, I can't help it. I'll study so diligently I won't have time to think about you, and miss you, and wonder what's going on in your life.'

'And you'll end up the youngest graduate from medical school in the history of mankind,' I chided, though my voice was as hoarse as his. 'Save a little love for me, and store it away in the deepest part of your heart, the same as I'm going to store my love for you. We can't make the same mistake our parents did.'

He sighed heavily and hung his head, studying the floor at his feet, or maybe he was studying my feet in the high heels that made my legs look so much prettier. 'You'll take care of yourself.'

'Of course. You take care of yourself. Don't study too much. Have some fun, and write me at least once a day; I don't think we should run up phone bills.

'Cathy, you're awfully pretty. Maybe too pretty. I look at you and see our mother all over again, the way you move your hands, and the way you tilt your head to the side. Don't enchant our doctor too much. I mean, after all, he's a man. He has no wife – and you'll be living in the same house with him.' He looked up, his eyes suddenly sharp. 'Don't rush into anything trying to escape what you feel for me. I mean it, Cathy.'

'I promise to behave myself.' It was such a weak promise when *he'd* awakened that primitive urge in me that should have been held back until I was old enough to handle it. Now all I wanted was to be fulfilled and loved by someone I could feel good about.

'Paul,' Chris said tentatively, 'he's a great guy. I love him. Carrie loves him. What do you feel for him?'

'Love, the same as you and Carrie. Gratitude. That's not wrong.'

'He hasn't done anything out of the way?'

63

'No. He's honourable, decent.'

'I see him looking at you, Cathy. You're so young, so beautiful, and so ... needing.' He paused and flushed, looking away guiltily before he went on. 'I feel ugly asking you, when he's done so much to help us, but still, sometimes I think he took us in only because, well, only because of you. Because he wants you!'

'Chris, he's twenty-five years older than me. How can you think like that?'

Chris looked relieved. 'You're right,' he said. 'You are his ward, and much too young. There must be plenty of beauties in those hospitals who'd be happy to be with him. I guess you're safe enough.'

Smiling now, he pulled me gently into his embrace and lowered his lips to mine. Just a soft, tender kiss of goodbye-for-a-while. 'I'm sorry about Christmas night,' he said when our kiss was over.

My heart was an aching ruin as I backed off to leave him. How was I going to live without him nearby? Another thing *she'd* done to us. Made us care too much, when we should never have cared in the way we did. Her fault, always her fault! Everything gone wrong in our lives could be laid at her door!

'Don't overwork yourself, Chris, or soon you will be needing to wear glasses.' He grinned, promised, made a reluctant gesture of farewell. Neither of us could manage to speak the word 'goodbye'. I spun about to run out, with tears in my eyes as I raced down the long halls, and then out into the bright sunshine. In Paul's white car I crouched down low and really sobbed, like Carrie when she bawled.

Suddenly Paul showed up from nowhere and silently took his place behind the wheel. He switched on the ignition, backed the car out and turned to head for the highway again. He didn't mention my reddened eyes or the sodden handkerchief I clutched in my hand to dab at the tears that kept coming. He didn't ask why I sat so silently when usually I teased, and gibed, and rattled on nonsensically just to keep from hearing silence. *Quiet, silence. Hear the feathers fall, listen to the house squeal. That was the attic gloom.*

Paul's strong, well-cared-for hands guided the car with an easy, casual skill, while he sat back relaxed. I studied his hands, for, next to a man's eyes, I noticed his hands. Then I moved my glance to his legs. Strong, well-shaped thighs which his tight, blue knit trousers showed up well, perhaps too well, for all of a sudden I wasn't sad, or gloomy, but felt an onrush of sensuality.

Giant trees lined the wide, black road, trees gnarled and dark, thick and ancient. 'Bull Bay magnolias,' said Paul. 'It's a pity they aren't in bloom now, but it won't be too long. Our winters are short. One thing you must remember: never breathe on a magnolia blossom, or touch one; if you do it will wither and die.' He threw me a teasing look so I couldn't tell whether or not he was speaking the truth.

'I used to dread turning on to my street, before you came with your brother and sister. I was always so alone. Now I drive home happily. It's good to feel happy again. Thank you, Cathy, for running south instead of north or west.'

As soon as we got home Paul headed for his office and I headed upstairs to try to work off my loneliness by exercising at the barre. Paul didn't come home for dinner, and that made it even worse. He didn't show up after dinner either, so I went to bed early. All alone. I was all alone. Carrie was gone. My steadfast Christopher Doll, gone too. For the first time we were to sleep under separate roofs. I missed Carrie. I felt awful, afraid. I needed someone. The silence of the house and the deep dark of the night were screaming all about me. *Alone, alone, you are alone, and nobody cares, nobody cares.* I thought about food. I'd worried that I hadn't kept a big supply at hand. Then I remembered I needed some warm milk. Warm milk was supposed to help you fall asleep – and sleep was what I needed.

ENCHANTRESS ... ME?

Soft firelight glowed in the living room. The grey logs had gutted into ashes in the hearth, and Paul, wrapped in his warm red robe, sat in a wing-backed chair and slowly drew on a pipe.

I gazed at his smoke-haloed head and saw someone warm, needing, wistful and yearning, as I yearned, and I wished. And being the fool I often was, I drifted towards him on bare feet that didn't make a sound. How nice he'd wear our gift so soon. I wore a gift from him – a soft, turquoise peignoir of airy fabric that floated over a gown of the same colour.

He started to see me there, so near his chair, in the middle of the night, though he didn't speak to break the spell that was somehow binding us together in a mutual need.

There was a lot I didn't know about myself, nor did I understand what impulse lifted my hand to caress his cheek. His skin felt raspy, as if he needed a shave. He put his head back against the chair and tilted his face to mine.

'Why are you touching me, Catherine?'

His question was asked in a tight, cold voice, and I could have felt rebuked and hurt, but his eyes were soft, limpid pools of desire, and I had seen desire before, only not in the kind of eyes he had. 'Don't you like to be touched?'

'Not by a seductive young girl wearing flimsy clothes who is twenty-five years my junior.'

'Twenty-four and seven months your junior,' I corrected, 'and my maternal grandmother married a man of fifty-five, when she was only sixteen.'

'She was a fool and so was he.'

'My mother said she made him a good wife,' I added lamely.

'Why aren't you up in your bed asleep?' he snapped.

'I can't sleep. I guess I'm too excited about school tomorrow.'

'Then you'd better go to bed so you'll be at your best.'

I started to go, really I did, for the thought of warm milk was still in my head, but I had other thoughts, too, more seductive. 'Dr Paul...'

'I hate it when you call me that!' he interrupted. 'Use my first name or don't speak to me at all.'

'I feel I should show you the respect you deserve.'

'A fig for respect! I'm not any different than other men. A doctor isn't infallible, Catherine.'

'Why are you calling me Catherine?'

'Why shouldn't I call you Catherine? It's your name, and it sounds more grown up than Cathy.'

'A moment or so ago, when I touched your cheek, you flared your eyes at me, as if you didn't want me to be grown up.'

'You're a witch. In a second you change from a naïve girl into a seductive, provocative woman – a woman who seems to know exactly what she's doing when she lays her hand on my face.'

My eyes fled before the onslaught of his. I felt hot, uneasy, and wished now I'd gone directly to the kitchen. I stared at the fine books on the shelves and the miniature *objets d'art* he seemed to crave. Everywhere I looked was something to remind me that what he needed most was beauty.

'Catherine, I'm going to ask you something now that is none of my business, but I must ask. Just what is there between you and your brother?'

My knees began to click together nervously. *Oh, dear God. Did it show on our faces?* Why did he have to ask? It wasn't any of his business. He had no right to ask such a question. Common sense and good judgement should have glued my tongue to the roof of my mouth and kept me from saying what I did in a shamed, lame way. 'Would you be shocked to hear that when we were locked up in one room, always together, four of us, and each day was an eternity, that sometimes Chris and I didn't always think of ourselves as brother and sister? He attached a barre in the attic for me, so I could keep my muscles supple, so I could keep on believing some day I'd be a ballerina. And while I danced on that soft, rotten wood, he'd study in the attic schoolroom, poring for hours over old encyclopedias. He'd hear my dance music and come and stand in the shadows to watch...'

'Go on,' he urged when I paused. I stood with my head

67

bowed, thinking backward, forgetting him. Then he suddenly leaned forward and seized hold of me. 'Tell me the rest.'

I didn't want to tell him, yet his eyes were hot, demanding, making him seem a different person.

Swallowing first, I continued with reluctance, 'Music has always done something special for me, even when I was small. It takes me over and lifts me up and makes me dance. And when I'm up there's no way to come down except by feeling love for someone. If you come down and feel your feet on the floor, and there's no one there to love, then you feel empty and lost. And I don't like to feel lost or empty.'

'And so you danced in the attic, and dwelled in your fanciful imagination, and came back to the floor and found the only one there to love was your brother?' he said with icy heat, burning his eyes into mine. 'Right? You had another kind of love you reserved for your little twins, didn't you? You were mother to them. I know that. I see that every time you look at Carrie and speak Cory's name. But what kind of love do you have for Christopher? Is it *motherly*? Sisterly? Or is it –' He paused, flushed, and shook me. 'What did you do with your brother when you were locked up there, when you were alone?'

Seized by panic, I shook my head, and pushed his hands from my shoulders. 'Chris and I were decent! We did the best we could!'

'"The best you could"?' he fired, looking hard and belligerent, as if the kindly, gentle man I knew had been only a disguise. 'What the hell does that tell me?'

'All you need to know!' I flared back and flashed my eyes with temper as hot and red as his. 'You accuse me of seducing you. That's what you're doing; you sit and you watch every move I make! You undress me with your eyes. You talk about ballet classes, and sending my brother to college and medical school, and all the while you imply that sooner or later you are going to demand your payment, and I know what kind of payment you want!' I took my hands and ripped open the peignoir so the skimpy bodice of the nightgown was revealed. 'Look at the kind of gift you gave me. Is this the kind of nightgown a girl of fifteen wears? No! It's the kind of gown a bride wears on her wedding night! And you gave it to me, and you saw Chris frown, and you didn't even have the decency to blush!'

His laughter mocked me. I smelled the strong red wine he liked to drink before retiring. His breath was hot on my face, his face very close to mine so I could see each strong dark hair that poked from his skin. It was the wine that made him act as he did, I thought. Only the wine. Any woman would serve – *any woman*! He stared at me and then, suddenly shocked to find his hand cupping my left breast, he yanked it away as if my flesh burned him. He pulled the fabric of my frail peignoir together and hid what his hungry eyes had devoured before. He stared at my lips that were slightly parted and waiting to be kissed. I think he planned to kiss me just before he gained control. At that moment thunder crashed overhead, and a lightning bolt sizzled jaggedly to crackle with fire as it struck a telephone wire outside. I jumped! Cried out!

As suddenly as he had withdrawn his hand, he snapped out of his fog and into what he was customarily – a detached, lonely man who was determined to keep himself aloof. How wise I was in my innocence to know this even before he snapped, 'What the hell are you doing sitting on my lap half naked? Why did you let me do what I did?'

I didn't say anything. He was ashamed; I could see that now in the glow of the dying fire, and in the intermittent flashes of lightning. He was thinking of all sorts of self-condemning thoughts, chastising, berating, whipping himself – I knew it was my fault; as always it was my fault.

'I'm sorry, Catherine. I don't know what possessed me to do what I did.'

'I forgive you.'

'Why do you forgive me?'

'Because I love you.'

Again he jerked his head into profile, and I couldn't see his eyes well enough to read them. 'You don't love me,' he said calmly, 'you're only grateful for what I've done.'

'I love you – and I'm yours, when, or if, you want me. And you can say you don't love me, but you'll be lying, for I see it in your eyes each time you look at me.' I pressed closer against him and turned his face to mine. 'When I was put away by Momma, I swore that when I was free, if love came and demanded of me I'd open my door and let it in. The first day I came I found love in your eyes. You don't have to marry me, just love me, when you need me.'

He held me and we watched the storm. Winter fought with spring and finally conquered. Now it only hailed, and the thunder and lightning were gone, and I felt so ... so right. We were much alike, he and I. 'Why aren't you afraid of me?' he softly asked, as his big, gentle hands stroked my back, my hair. 'You know you shouldn't be here, letting me hold you, touch you.'

'Paul ...' I began tentatively, 'I'm not bad; neither is Chris. When we were locked away, we did do the best we could, honest. But we were locked in one room and growing up. The grandmother had a list of rules that forbade us to even look at each other and now I think I know why. Our eyes used to meet so often and without a word spoken he could comfort me, and he said my eyes did that for him too. That wasn't bad, was it?'

'I shouldn't have asked, and of course you had to look at each other. That's why we have eyes.'

'Living like we did for so long, I don't know a lot about other girls my age, but ever since I was only table high, any kind of beauty has made me light up. Just to see the sun falling on the petals of a rose, or the way light shines through tree leaves and shows the veins, and the way rain on the road turns the oil iridescent, all that makes me feel beautiful. More than anything, when music is playing, especially my kind, ballet music, I don't need the sun or flowers or fresh air. I light up inside and wherever I am magically turns into marble palaces, or I am wild and free in the woods. I used to do that in the attic, and always just ahead a dark-haired man danced with me. We never touched, though we tried to. I never saw his face, though I wanted to. I said his name once, but when I woke up I couldn't remember what it was. So, I guess I'm really in love with *him*, whoever he is. Every time I see a man with dark hair who moves gracefully I suspect he's the one.'

He chuckled and twined his long fingers into my unbound

hair. 'My, what a romantic you are.'

'You're making fun of me. You think I'm only a child. You think if you kissed me it wouldn't be exciting.'

He grinned, accepted the challenge and slowly, slowly his head inclined until his lips met mine. Oh! So this was what it was like, a kiss from a stranger. Electric tingles sizzled madly up and down my arms, and all those nerves that a child my age wasn't supposed to have burned with fire! I drew away sharply, afraid. I was wicked, unholy, still the Devil's spawn!

And Chris would be shocked!

'What the hell are we doing?' he barked, coming out of the spell I'd cast. 'What kind of little devil are you to let me handle you and kiss you? You are very beautiful, Catherine, but you are only a child.' Some realization darkened his eyes as he guessed at my motives. 'Now get this straight in your pretty head – you don't owe me, not anything! What I do for you, for your brother and sister, I do willingly, gladly, without expecting any repayment – of any kind – do you understand?'

'But ... but...' I sputtered. 'I've always hated it when the rain beats hard and the wind blows at night. This is the first time I've felt warm and protected, here, with you, before the fire.'

'Safe?' he teased lightly. 'You think you're safe with me as you kiss me like that? What do you think I'm made of?'

'The same as other men, only better.'

'Catherine,' Paul said, his voice softer and kinder now, 'I've made so many mistakes in my life, and you three give me an opportunity to redeem myself. If I so much as lay a hand on you again, I want you to scream for help. If no one is here, then run to your room, or pick up something and bash me over the head.'

'Ooh,' I whispered, 'and I thought you loved me!' Tears trickled down my cheeks. I felt like a child again, chastised for presuming too much. How foolish to have believed love was already knocking on my door. I sulked as he lifted me away from him. Then he gently lifted me to my feet, but kept his hands on my waist as he looked up into my face.

'My God, but you are beautiful and desirable,' he said with a sigh. 'Don't tempt me too much, Catherine – for your own good.'

'You don't have to love me.' My head bowed to hide my face and my hair was something to hide behind as I shamelessly said, 'Just use me when you need me, and that will be enough.'

He leaned back in the chair and took his hands from my waist. 'Catherine, don't ever let me hear you offer such a thing again. You live in fairyland, not reality. Little girls get hurt when they play grown-up games. You save yourself for the man you marry – but for God's sake, wait to grow up first. Don't rush into having sex with the first man who desires you.'

I backed off, scared of him now, while he stood to come within arm's reach. 'Beautiful child, the eyes of Clairmont are fixed upon you and me, wondering, speculating. I don't have a gilt-edged reputation. So, for the health of my medical practice and the good of my soul and conscience, stay away from me. I'm only a man, not a saint.'

Again I backed off, scared. I flew up the stairs as if pursued. For he wasn't, after all, the kind of man I wanted. Not him, a doctor, perhaps a womanizer – the last kind of man who could fulfil my dreams of faithful, devoted and forever-green-springtime-romantic love!

The school Paul sent me to was big and modern with an indoor swimming pool. My schoolmates thought I looked good and talked funny, like a Yankee. They laughed at the way I spoke. I didn't like being laughed at. I didn't like being different. I wanted to be like the others, and though I tried I found out I was different. How could it be otherwise? *She* had made me different. I knew Chris was feeling lonely in his school because he too was an alien in a world that had gone on without us. I was fearful for Carrie in her school, all alone, made different too. Damn Momma for doing so much to set us apart, so we couldn't blend into the crowd and talk as they did and believe as they did. I was an outsider, and in every way they could all my schoolmates made me feel it.

Only one place made me feel I belonged. Straight from my school classes I'd catch a bus and ride to ballet class, toting my bag with leotards, *pointes* and a small handbag tucked inside. In the dressing room the girls shared all their secrets. They told ridiculous jokes, sexy stories, some of them even lewd. Sex was in the air, all around us, breathing hotly and demandingly down our necks. Girlishly, foolishly, they discussed whether they should save their bodies for their husbands. Should they pet with clothes on or off – or go 'all the way' – and how did they stop a guy after they had turned him on?

Because I felt so much wiser than the others I didn't contribute anything. If I dared to speak of my past, of those years when I was living 'nowhere' and the love that had sprung up from barren soil, I could imagine how their eyes would pop! I couldn't blame them. No, I didn't blame anyone but the one who'd made it all happen! Momma!

One day I ran home from the bus stop and dashed off a long, venomous letter to my mother – and then I didn't know where to send it. I put it aside until I found out the address in Greenglenna. One thing for sure, I didn't want her to know where we lived. Though she had received the petition, it didn't have Paul's name on it, or our address, only the address of the judge. Sooner or later though, she'd hear from me and be sorry she did.

Each day we began bundled up in heavy, woollen, knitted leg-warmers, and at the barre we exercised until our blood flowed fast and hot and we could discard the woollens as we began to sweat. Our hair, screwed up tight as old ladies' who scrubbed floors, soon became wet too, so we showered two or three times a day – when we worked out eight or ten hours on Saturdays. The barre was not meant for holding on to tightly, but was meant only for balance, to help us develop control, grace. We did the *pliés*, the *tendus*, and *glissés*, the *fondus* the *ronds de jambe à terre* – and none of it was easy. Sometimes the pain of rotating the hips in the turnouts could make me scream. Then came the *frappes* on three-quarter pointe, the *ronde de jambe en l'air*, the *petite* and *grande battlements*, the *développes* and all the warm-up exercises to make our muscles long, strong and supple. Then we left the barre and used the centre arena to repeat all of that without the aid of the barre.

And that was the easy part – from there on the work became

increasingly difficult, demanding technical skills awesomely painful to do.

To hear I was good, even excellent, lifted me sky-high ... so there had been some benefits gained from dancing in the attic, dancing even when I was dying, so I thought as I *pliéd un, deux*, and on and on as Georges pounded on the old upright piano. And then there was Julian.

Something kept drawing him back to Clairmont. I thought his visits were only ego trips so we could sit in a circle on the floor and watch him perform in the centre, showing off his superior virtuosity, his spinning turns that were blurrily fast. His incredible, leaping elevations defied gravity, and from these *grand jetés* he'd land goose-down soft. He cornered me to tell me it was his kind of dancing that added so much excitement to the performance.

'Really, Cathy, you haven't seen ballet until you see it done in New York.' He yawned as if bored and turned his bold, jet eyes on Norma Belle in her skimpy see-through, white leotards. Quickly I asked why, if New York was the best place to be, he kept coming back to Clairmont so often.

'To visit with my mother and father,' he said with a certain indifference. 'Madame is my mother, you know.'

'Oh, I didn't know that.'

'Of course not. I don't like to boast about it.' He smiled then, devastatingly wicked. 'Are you still a virgin?' I told him it was none of his business and that made him laugh again. 'You're too good for this hick place, Cathy. You're different. I can't put my finger on it, but you make the other girls look clumsy, dull. What's your secret?'

'What's yours?'

He grinned and put his hand flat on my breast. 'I'm great, that's all. The best there is. Soon all the world will know it.' Angry, I slapped his hand away. I stomped down on his foot and backed away. 'Stop it!'

Suddenly, as quickly as he'd cornered me, he lost all interest and walked away to leave me staring.

Most days I'd go straight home from class and spend the evening with Paul. He was so much fun to be with when he wasn't tired. He told me about his patients without naming them, and told tales of his childhood, and how he'd always wanted to be a doctor, just like Chris. Soon after dinner he'd have to leave to make his rounds at three local hospitals, including one in Greenglenna. I'd try and help Henny after dinner while I waited for Paul to come back. Sometimes we watched TV, and sometimes he took me to a film. 'Before you came, I never went out.'

'Never?' I asked.

'Well, almost never,' he said. 'I did have a few dates before you came, but since you've been here my time just seems to disappear. I don't know what uses it all up.'

'Talking to me,' I told him, teasing with my finger that I trailed along his closely shaven cheek. 'I think I know more about you than I know about anyone else in the world, except Chris and Carrie.'

'No,' he said in a tight voice, 'I don't tell you everything.'

'Why not?'

'You don't need to know all my dark secrets.'

'I've told you all my dark secrets, and you haven't turned away from me.'

'Go to bed, Catherine!'

I jumped up and ran over to him and kissed his cheek, which was very red. Then I dashed for the stairs. When I was at the top, I turned to see him at the newel post, staring upward, as if the sight of my legs under the short, rose, baby-doll nightie fascinated him.

'And don't run around the house in such things!' he called to me. 'You should wear a robe.'

'Doctor, you brought this outfit to me. I didn't think you'd want me to cover myself. I thought you wanted to see me with it on.'

'You think too much.'

In the mornings I was up early, before six, so I could eat breakfast with him. He liked me to be there, though he didn't say so. Nevertheless, I could tell. I had him bewitched, charmed. I was learning more and more how to be like Momma.

I think he tried to avoid me, but I didn't let him. He was the

75

one to teach me what I needed to know.

His room was down the hall from mine, but I never dared to go to him at night as I had to Chris. I longed for Chris and for Carrie. When I woke up, I ached not to see them in the room beside me; I ached more not to see them at the breakfast table, and if Paul hadn't been there, I think I might have started off each and every day with tears instead of forced smiles.

'Smile for me, my Catherine,' Paul said one morning when I sat staring down at my plate of scrambled eggs and bacon. I looked up, caught by something I heard in his voice, something wistful, as if he needed me.

'Don't ever say my name like that again,' I said hoarsely. 'Chris used to call me his lady Cath-er-ine, and I don't like to hear anyone else call me his Catherine.'

He didn't say anything more, just laid aside the newspaper, got up and went out to the garage. From there he'd drive to the hospitals, then back to his home offices, and I wouldn't see him again until dinner time. I didn't see enough of him, never enough of anyone I cared about.

Only on weekends, when Chris and Carrie were home, did he seem really at ease with me. And yet, when Chris and Carrie were back in their schools, something would come between us, some subtle spark that revealed that he was just as attracted to me as I was to him. I wondered if the real reason was the same as my own. Was he trying to escape memories of his Julia by letting me into his heart? Just as I was trying to escape Chris?

But my shame was worse than his, or so I thought then. I thought I was the only one with a dark, ugly past. I never dreamed anyone as fine and noble as Paul could have ugliness in his life too.

Only two weeks passed and Julian flew down from New York again. This time he made it very obvious he'd come just to see me. I felt flattered and a little awkward, for he'd already gained success, while I was still only hoping. He had an old ricky-tin car he said had cost him nothing but his time, for all the pieces had come from the junkyard. 'Next to dancing, I love to tinker with cars,' he explained as he drove me home from dance class.

'Some day, when I'm rich, I'm going to have luxury cars, three or four, or maybe seven, one for each day of the week.'

I laughed; it sounded so outrageous and ostentatious. 'Does dancing pay that much?'

'It will when I hit the big-time money,' he answered confidentially. I had to turn my head and stare at his handsome profile. If you took his features apart one by one, you could find fault with them, for his nose could have been better, and his skin needed more colour, and perhaps his lips were too full and red, and too sensual. But when he was put all together, he was sensational looking. 'Cathy,' he began, throwing me a long look as his tinny car chugged and choked along, 'you'd love New York. There's so much to do, so much to see and experience. That doctor you live with isn't your real father, you shouldn't stick around just to please him. Think about moving to New York as soon as possible.' He put his arm about my shoulders to draw me closer to his side. 'What a team we'd make, you and I,' he said softly, cajolingly, and painted for me bright pictures of what our life would be like in New York. Clearly he made me understand I'd be under his wing, and in his bed.

'I don't know you,' I answered, pulling away to sit as far from him as possible. 'I don't know your past, and you don't know mine. We're nothing at all alike, and though you flatter me with your attention you also scare me.'

'Why? I won't rape you.'

I hated him for saying that. It wasn't rape I was afraid of. In fact I didn't know what made me afraid of him, unless I was more afraid of myself when I was with him. 'Tell me who you are, Julian Marquet. Tell me about your childhood, your parents. Tell me why you think you are God's gift to the dance world and to every woman you meet.'

Casually he lit up a cigarette, which he wasn't supposed to do. 'Let me take you out tonight and I'll give you all the answers you want.'

We'd reached the big house on Bellefair Drive. He parked in front, while I stared towards the windows softly lit in the rosy twilight glow. I could barely discern the dark shadow of Henny who peered out to see who was parking in front of her home. I thought of Paul, but more than anyone else I thought of Chris, my better half. Would Chris approve of Julian? I didn't think he would, and still I said yes, I'd date him that night. And what a night it turned out to be.

MY FIRST DATE

I was hesitant about bringing up the subject of Julian to Paul. It was Saturday night; Chris and Carrie were home, and, truthfully, I'd just as soon have gone out with them and Paul. It was with great reluctance that I brought up the fact I had a date with Julian Marquet. 'Tonight, Paul, you don't mind, do you?'

He flashed me a tired look and a weak smile. 'I think it's about time you started dating. He's not too much older, is he?'

'No,' I whispered, feeling a little disappointed that he didn't object.

Julian showed up promptly at eight. He was slicked up in a new suit, with his shoes shined, his unruly hair tamed, his manners so perfect he didn't seem himself. He shook hands with Paul, leaned to kiss Carrie's cheek. Chris glared at him. The two had been bicycling when I'd told Paul about my first date, and even as Julian held my new spring coat I felt Chris's disapproval.

He drove to a very elegant restaurant where coloured lights flickered and rock music played. With surprising confidence Julian read the wine list, then tasted what the waiter brought and nodded, saying it was fine. This was all so new to me I felt on edge, afraid of making a mistake. Julian handed me a menu. My hands trembled so much I turned it over to him and asked him to select. I couldn't read French, and it seemed he could from the speedy way he chose our meal. When the salad and main course came it was just as good as he'd promised.

I was wearing a new dress, cut low in front and much too old for a girl of my age. I wanted to appear sophisticated, even though I wasn't.

'You're beautiful,' he said, while I was thinking the same thing about him. My heart felt funny, as if I were betraying someone. 'Much too beautiful to be stuck here in Hicktown for years on end while my mother exploits your talents. I'm not a male lead like I told you before, Cathy; I'm second string in the *corps*. I wanted to impress you, but I know if I had you with me, as my partner, both of us could make it big. There's a certain magic between us I've never had with another dancer. Of course you'd have to begin in the *corps*. But soon enough Madame Zolta would see your talent far surpasses your age and experience. She's an old crow, but no dummy. Cathy, I've danced my head off to get where I am – but I could make it easier for you. With me to back you up you'll make it quicker than I did. Together we'd made a sensational team. Your fairness complements my darkness; it's the perfect foil.' And on and on he talked, half-convincing me I was great already, when a certain part of me knew deep down I wasn't that sensational, and not nearly good enough for New York. And there was Chris whom I couldn't see if I went to New York, and Carrie who needed me on the weekends. And Paul, he fitted in my life somewhere, I knew he fitted somewhere. The problem was – where?

Julian wined and dined me, then danced me out on to the floor. Soon we were dancing to rock like no one else in the place could. Everyone drew back just to watch, then applaud. I was giddy with the nearness of him and the amount of wine I'd consumed. On the way home Julian drove on to a secluded lane where lovers parked to make out. I'd never made out and wasn't ready for someone as overwhelming as Julian.

'Cathy, Cathy, Cathy,' he murmured, kissing my neck, behind my ears, while his hand sought to stroke my upper thigh.

'Stop!' I cried. 'Don't! I don't know you well enough! You go too fast!'

'You're acting so childish,' he said with annoyance. 'I fly all the way from New York just to be with you, and you can't even let me kiss you.'

'Julian!' I stormed, 'take me home!'

'A kid,' he muttered angrily and turned on the ignition. 'Just a damned beautiful kid who tantalizes but won't come through. Wise up, Cathy. I'm not going to hang around forever.'

He was in my world, my dancing, glamorous world, and suddenly I was afraid of losing him. 'Why do you call yourself Marquet when your father's name is Rosencoff?' I asked, reaching to turn off the ignition.

He smiled and leaned back, then turned to me. 'Okay, if you want to talk. I think you and I are a lot alike, even if you won't admit it. Madame and Georges are my mother and father, but they have never seen me as a son, especially my father. My father sees me as an extension of himself. If I become a great dancer, it won't be to my credit; it will be just because I am *his* son and bear *his* name. So I put an end to that idea by changing my name. I made it up, just like any performer does when he wants to change his name.

'You know how many baseball games I've played? None! They wouldn't let me. Football was out of the question. Besides, they kept me so busy practising ballet positions, I was too tired for anything else. Georges never let me call him Father when I was little. After a while I wouldn't call him Father if he got down on his knees and begged. I tried my damnedest to please him, and I never could. He'd always find some flaw, some minute mistake I'd made to keep any performance from being perfect. So, when I make it, I'm making it on my own steam, and nobody is going to know he is my father! Or that Marisha is my mother. So don't go shooting off your mouth to the rest of the class. They don't know. Isn't it funny? I throw a tantrum if he even dares to mention he has a son, and I refuse to dance. That kills him, so he let me go on to New York, thinking I wouldn't make it without his name. But I have made it, and without his help. I think that kills him. Now tell me about you. Why are you living with that doctor and not your own parents?'

'My parents are dead,' I said, annoyed he'd asked. 'Dr Paul was a friend of my father, so he took us in. He felt sorry for us and didn't want us to go into an orphanage.'

'Lucky you,' he said with a certain sourness. '*I'd* never be so lucky.' Then he leaned over until his forehead was pressed against mine and our lips were only inches apart. I could feel his breath hot on my face. 'Cathy, I don't want to say and do anything wrong with you. I want to make you the best thing that's ever happened to me. I am thirteenth in a long line of male dancers who have married ballerinas, most of them. How do you think that makes me feel? Not lucky, you can bet. I've been in

New York since I was eighteen, and last February I turned twenty. That's two years, and still I'm not a star. With you I could be. I've got to prove to Georges I'm the best, and better than he ever was. I've never told anyone this before, but I hurt my back when I was a kid, trying to lift an engine that was too heavy. It bothers me all the time, but still I dance on. And it's not just because you're small and don't weigh much. I know other dancers who are smaller and lighter, but something about your proportions seems to balance just right when I lift. Or maybe it's what you do to your body that adjusts to my hands . . . Whatever it is you do, you fit me to a tee. Cathy, come with me to New York, please.'

'You wouldn't take advantage of me if I did?'

'I'd be your guardian angel.'

'New York is so big . . .'

'I know it like the palm of my hand. Soon you'll know it just as well.'

'There's my sister and my brother. I don't want to leave them yet.'

'Eventually you'll have to. The longer you stay the harder it will be to make the break. Grow up, Cathy, be your own person. You never are when you stay home and let others dominate you.' He looked away, his scowl bitter. I felt sorry for him, and touched too.

'Maybe. Let me think about it more.'

Chris was on the upper veranda outside my bedroom when I went in to undress. When I saw him out there in his pyjamas, his slouched shoulders drew me to him.

'How'd it go?' he asked without looking at me.

Nervously my hands fluttered around. 'Okay, I guess. We had wine with dinner. Julian got a little drunk, I think. Maybe I did too.'

He turned to stare in my eyes. 'I don't like him, Cathy! I wish he'd stay in New York and leave you alone! From what I hear from all the girls or boys in your dance company, Julian has claimed you so now no other dancer will ask you out. Cathy, he's from New York. Those guys up there move fast, and you're only fifteen!' He moved to cradle me in his arms.

'Who are you dating?' I asked with a sob in my throat. 'Don't tell me you're not seeing any girls.'

His cheek was against mine when he answered slowly, 'There's no girl I've met who can compare to you.'

'How are your studies going?' I asked, hoping to take his mind off me.

'Great. When I'm not thinking of all I have to do in the first year of medical school – gross anatomy, microanatomy and neuroanatomy – I get around to preparing for college.'

'What do you do in your spare time?'

'What spare time? There's none left when I finish worrying about what's happening to you! I like school, Cathy. I'd really enjoy it if you weren't constantly on my mind. I wait for the weekends when I can see you and Carrie again.'

'Oh, Chris ... you've got to try to forget me and find someone else.'

But just one long look into his tortured eyes revealed that what had been started so long ago wasn't going to be easy to stop.

I had to try to find someone else and then he'd know it was over, forever over. My thoughts took wing to Julian who was striving so to prove himself a better dancer than his father. How like me, who had to be better in all ways than my mother.

I was ready the next time Julian flew down. When he asked me for a date, this time I didn't hedge. It might as well be him; we did have the same goals. Then, after the film and a soft drink in a club for me, and beer for him, he again drove to the lovers' lane every city seemed to have. I allowed him this time to do a bit more than just kiss me, but too soon he was breathing hot and fast, and touching me with so much expertise that soon I was responding even when I didn't want to. He pushed me back on the seat. Suddenly I realized what he was about to do – and I grabbed up my handbag and began to beat him on his face. 'Stop! I told you before, go slower!'

'You asked for it!' he raged. 'You can't lead me on, then turn me off. I despise a tease.'

I thought of Chris and began to cry. 'Julian, please. I like you, honest I do. But you don't give me a chance to fall in love with you. Please stop coming at me so fast.'

He seized my arm and ruthlessly twisted it behind my back until I cried out from the pain. I thought he meant to break it. But he released it just when I was about to scream.

'Look, Cathy. I'm half in love with you already. But no girl strings me along like I'm some country bumpkin. There are plenty of girls willing to give out – so I don't need you as much as I thought – not for anything!'

Of course he didn't need me. Nobody really needed me but Chris and Carrie, though Chris needed me in the wrong way. Momma had twisted and warped him, and turned him towards me, and now he couldn't turn away. I couldn't forgive her for that. She had to pay for everything wrong she'd caused. If he and I had sinned, *she had made us.*

I thought and thought that night of how I could make Momma pay, and I came up with the exact price that would hurt most. It wouldn't be money, she had too much of that. It would have to be something she prized more than money. Two things – her honourable reputation which was a bit tarnished from marrying her half-uncle, and her young husband. Both would be gone when I was through with her.

Then I was crying. Crying for Chris, for Carrie who didn't grow and for Cory who was by now, probably, only bones in his grave.

I turned over to grope for Carrie, reaching to draw her into my arms. But Carrie was in a private school for girls, ten miles outside the city limits. Chris was thirty miles away.

It began to rain hard. The staccato beats on the roof overhead were military drums to take me into dreams and back to exactly where I didn't want to go. I was dumped down in a locked room cluttered with toys and games and massive, dark furniture, and pictures of Hell on the walls. I sat in an old wooden rocker, half coming apart, and on my lap I held a ghostly small brother who called me Momma, and on and on we rocked, and the floorboards creaked, and the wind blew, and the rain pelted down, and below us, around us, above us, the enormous house of countless rooms was waiting to eat us up.

I hated the rain so close above my head, like it used to be when we were upstairs. How much worse our lives had been when it rained, and the room was damp and chill, and in the attic there was nothing but miserable gloom and dead faces that lined the wall. Bands like the grandmother's grey iron came to tighten about my head, smothering my thoughts, making me confused and terrified.

Unable to sleep, I left the bed and slipped on a filmy negligee. For some curious reason I stole to Paul's bedroom and cautiously eased open his closed door. The alarm clock on his nightstand read two o'clock – and still he wasn't home! Nobody in the house but Henny who was so far, far away – away at the other end of the house in her room adjacent to the kitchen.

I shook my head and stared again at Paul's smoothly made bed. Oh, Chris was crazy to want to be a doctor! He'd never have a full night's rest. And it was raining. Accidents happened so often on rainy nights. What if Paul should be killed? What would we do then! *Paul, Paul*, I screamed to myself as I raced towards the stairs and flew down them, then sped on to where I could peer out the French windows in the living room. I hoped to see a white car parked in the drive, or turning into the drive. God, I prayed, don't let him have an accident! Please, please – don't take him like you took Daddy!

'Cathy, why aren't you in bed?'

I whirled about. There was Paul sitting comfortably in his favourite chair, puffing on a cigarette in the dark. There was just enough light to see he wore the red robe we'd given him for Christmas. I was so overwhelmed with relief to see him safe and not spread out dead on a morgue slab. Morbid thoughts. *Daddy, I can barely remember how you looked, or how your voice sounded, and the special smell of you has faded away.*

'Is something wrong, Catherine?'

Wrong? Why did he call me Catherine at night when we were alone, and only Cathy during the day? *Everything* was wrong! The Greenglenna newspapers and the Virginia one I'd subscribed to and had delivered to my ballet school both told stories of how Mrs Bartholomew Winslow would make her second 'winter' home in Greenglenna. Extensive renovation was being done so her husband's home would be as it was when it was new.

Only the best for my mother! For some reason I couldn't fathom I lit into Paul like a shrew. 'How long have you been home?' I demanded sharply. 'I've been upstairs worrying about you so much I can't sleep! And here you were, all the time! You missed your dinner; you missed last night's dinner; you were supposed to take me out last night and you forgot all about it! I finished my homework early, dressed in my best clothes and sat around waiting for you to show up, and you forgot it! Why do you let your patients make so many demands on your time so you don't have a life of your own?'

For a long time he didn't answer. Then when my lips parted to speak again, he said in a mild tone, 'You really do sound upset. I guess the only excuse I can offer is to say I'm a doctor, and a doctor's time is never his own. I apologize for not calling and telling you there was an emergency and I couldn't leave.'

'Forget – how could you forget?'

'I'm sorry again. Sometimes I have things on my mind.'

'Are you being sarcastic?'

'I am trying to control my temper. It would be nice if you could control yours.'

'I'm not mad!' I shouted. He was so like Momma, so much in control, so poised, when I never was! He didn't care. That's why he could sit there and look at me like that! He didn't really care if he made promises and broke them – like her! I ran forward as if to strike him, but he caught my fists and stared up at me in utter surprise. 'Would you hit me, Catherine? Does missing a film mean so much to you that you can't understand how I could forget? Now say you're sorry for screaming at me, as I said I was sorry for disappointing you.'

What tortured me was more than mere disappointment! Nowhere was there anyone I could depend on – only Chris who was forbidden to me. Only Chris who would never forget anything I needed or wanted.

I shuddered. Oh, what kind of person was I? Was I so like Momma I had to have what I wanted, when I wanted, no matter what the cost to others? Was I going to make Paul pay for what she'd done? None of it was his fault. 'Paul, I am sorry I yelled at you. I do understand.'

'You must be very tired. Perhaps you take your ballet classes too seriously. Maybe you should let up a little.'

How could I tell him I couldn't let up? I had to be the best, and to be the best at anything meant hours and hours of work. I fully intended to give up all the pastimes other girls my age enjoyed. I didn't want a boy-friend who wasn't a dancer. I didn't want any girl-friends who didn't dance. I didn't want anything to come between me and my goal, and yet, and yet ... sitting there, looking up at me, was a man who said he needed me, and who was hurt by the hateful way I'd acted.

'I read about my mother today,' I said lamely, 'and a house she's having remodelled and redecorated. She always gets what she wants. I never get anything. So I act ugly to you and forget all that you've done.' I backed off a few feet, aching with the shame I felt. 'How long have you been home?'

'Since eleven-thirty,' he answered. 'I ate the salad and the steak Henny left for me in the warming oven. But I don't sleep well when I'm exceptionally tired. And I don't like the sound of the rain on the roof.'

'Because the rain shuts you off and makes you feel lonely?'

He half-smiled. 'Yeah, something like that. How did you know?'

How he felt was all over his face as dim as it was in that big room. He was thinking of her, his Julia, his dead wife. He always looked sad when Julia was on his mind. I approached his chair and impulsively reached out to touch his cheek. 'Why do you have to smoke? How can you tell your patients to quit the habit and keep on smoking yourself?'

'How do you know what I tell my patients?' he asked in that soft voice, in a way that tingled my spine. Nervously I laughed, telling him he didn't always close his office door tight, and if I happened to be in the back hall, sometimes, despite my will, I couldn't help overhearing a few things. He told me to go to bed and stop hanging around in the back hall where I didn't belong – and he'd smoke if he wanted to smoke.

'Sometimes you act like a wife, asking such questions, getting angry at me for forgetting to come home to you.'

Now he had me feeling a fool, and again I was angry. 'From

now on, I'll be prepared to be disappointed when you don't come home and that way I *won't* be disappointed. I might as well get used to expecting the worst from everyone.'

'Catherine! You can hate me if that's what you want, make me pay for everything you have suffered, and then, perhaps, you can go to sleep at night and not toss and turn and cry out in your sleep, and call for your mother like a child of three.'

Stunned, I stared at him. 'I call out for *her*?'

'Yes,' he said, 'many, many times I've heard you call for your mother.' I saw the pity in his eyes. 'Don't be ashamed of being human, Catherine. We all expect only the best from our mothers.'

I didn't want to talk about her, so I stepped nearer. 'Julian is back in town. I went out with him tonight since you stood me up last night. Julian thinks I'm ready for New York. He thinks his dance instructor, Madame Zolta, would develop me quicker than his mother. He thinks together we'd make a brilliant team.'

'And what do *you* think?'

'I think I'm not ready for New York yet,' I whispered, 'but he comes on so strong, sometimes he makes me believe, because he seems so convinced.'

'Go slowly, Catherine. Julian is a handsome young man, with arrogance enough for ten men. Use your own good common sense and don't be influenced by someone who might only want to use you.'

'I dream every night of being in New York, on stage. I see my mother in the audience staring up at me with disbelieving eyes. She wanted to kill me. I want her to see me dance and realize I have more to give the world than she does.'

He winced. 'Why do you need revenge so much? I thought if I took you three in and did the best I could for you, you'd find peace and forgiveness. Can't you forgive and forget? If there's one chance we poor humans have of reaching godliness, it's in learning to forgive and forget.'

'*You* and Chris,' I said bitterly. 'It's easy for you to talk about forgiving and forgetting – because you haven't been a victim, and I have. I've lost my younger brother who was like my own son. I loved Cory, and she stole away his life. *I hate her for that!* I hate her for ten million reasons – so don't talk to me about forgiving and forgetting – when she's got to pay for what she did! She lied to us, betrayed us in the worst possible way! She said nothing to let us know our grandfather had died, and kept right on letting us stay locked up – for nine long, long months – and in those long months we were eating poisoned doughnuts! So don't you dare talk to me of forgiving and forgetting! I don't know how to forgive and forget! All I know how to do is hate! And you don't know what it's like to hate as I do!'

'Don't I?' he asked in a flat voice.

'No, you don't know!'

He drew me down on his lap when I sobbed and tears streamed down my face. He comforted me as a father would, with little kisses and kind, stroking hands. 'Catherine, I've got a story of my own to tell. Maybe in some ways it equals the horror or yours. Maybe if I tell you you'll be able to use some of what I've learned.'

I stared up into his face. His arms held me tightly as I leaned back. 'Are you going to tell me about Julia and Scotty?'

'Yes.' A hard edge toned his voice. His eyes fixed on the rain-washed windows, and his hand that found mine squeezed tight. 'You think only your mother commits crimes against those she loves – well, you're wrong. It's done every day. Sometimes it's done to gain money, but there are other reasons.' He paused, sighed, then went on. 'I hope when you've heard my story, you can go to bed tonight and forget about vengeance. If you don't, you'll hurt yourself more than anyone else.'

I didn't believe that because I didn't want to believe that. But I was eager enough to hear the tale of how Julia and Scotty both died on the same day.

When Paul began to speak of Julia, I feared the ending. I squeezed my eyelids closed, wishing now my ears didn't have to hear, for I didn't need more to add to the anguish I already felt for one little dead boy. But he did it for my sake, to save me, as if anything could.

'Julia and I were childhood sweethearts. She never had another boy-friend; I never had another girl-friend. Julia belonged to me, and I let every other boy know it. I never gave myself, or her, the chance to experience what others were like – and that was a terrible mistake. We were foolish enough to believe our love would last forever.

'The older Julia grew, the more beautiful she became. I thought I was the luckiest guy in the world, and she thought I was perfect. We both had each other up on pedestals. She was going to be the perfect doctor's wife, and I was going to be the perfect husband, and we'd have three children. Julia was an only child, and her parents doted on her. She adored her father; she used to say I was like him.' His voice deepened here, as if what he had to say was very painful.

'I put an engagement ring on Julia's finger the day she was eighteen. I was nineteen at the time. When I was in college, I'd think of her back here and wonder what man had his eye on her. I was afraid I'd lose her to someone else if we didn't marry. So at age nineteen she married me. I was twenty.'

His voice turned bitter while his eyes went blank, and his arms tightened about me. 'Julia and I had kissed many times, and we always held hands, but she would never let me do anything truly intimate – that had to wait until she had a wedding band on her finger. I'd had a few sexual encounters, not many. She was a virgin and thought I was. I didn't take my marriage vows lightly, and I meant to be exactly the kind of husband who'd make her happy. I loved her very much. So, on our wedding night, she took two hours to undress in the bathroom. She came out of the bathroom wearing a long white gown, and her face was as white as that gown. I could tell she was terrified. I convinced myself I would be so tender, so loving, she would enjoy being my wife.

'She didn't enjoy sex, Cathy. I did the best I could to arouse her, while she cringed back with her eyes wide and full of shock, and then she screamed when I tried to take off her nightgown. I stopped and thought I'd try again the next night, after she pleaded for me to give her more time. The next night it was the same thing all over again, only worse. "Why, why can't you just lie here and hold me?" she asked tearfully. "Why does it have to be so ugly?"

'I was just a kid myself, and didn't know how to handle a

situation like that. I loved her, and I wanted her, and in the end I raped her – or so she said time and again. Still I loved her. I'd loved her most of my life and I couldn't believe I'd made the wrong choice. So I began to read every book on lovemaking I could find, and I tried all the techniques to arouse her and make her want me – and she was only repulsed. I took to drinking after I graduated from medical school, and when I felt like it I found some other woman who was glad to have me in her bed. The years passed while she held herself aloof, cleaned my house, washed my clothes, ironed my shirts and sewed on my missing buttons. She was so lovely, so desirable and so near that sometimes I'd force her, even if she cried afterwards. Then, she found out she was pregnant. I was delighted, and I think she was too. Never was a child more loved and pampered than my son, and, fortunately, he was the kind of child who couldn't be spoiled by too much love.'

His voice took on an even deeper register while I huddled closer in his arms, fearing what was to come, for I knew it would be terrible.

'After Scotty's birth Julia told me flatly she'd done her duty and given me a son, and that from now on I was to leave her alone. I left her alone, but I was deeply wounded. I talked to her mother about our problem, and her mother hinted at some dark secret in Julia's past, a cousin of hers who'd done something to Julia when she was only four. I never learned just what he'd done, but whatever it was, it spoiled sex forever for my wife. I suggested to Julia we should both visit a marriage counsellor or a psychologist but she'd have none of that – it would be too embarrassing – why couldn't I leave her alone?

'I did leave her alone after that,' he went on. 'There are always women around willing to accommodate a man, and in my office I had a lovely receptionist who let me know she was more than available, any time, any place. We had an affair that lasted several years. I thought we were both very discreet, and no one knew. Then one day she came and told me she was pregnant with my child. I couldn't believe her, for she'd told me she was on the pill. I couldn't even believe the child was mine since I knew she had other lovers. So I said no, I couldn't divorce my wife and risk losing Scotty to father a child who might not be mine. She blew up.

'I went home that evening to confront a wife I'd never known before. Julia lashed out at me for being unfaithful, when she'd done the best she could and given me the son I wanted. And now I'd betrayed her, broken my vow and made her the laughing stock of the town! She threatened to kill herself. I pitied her as she screamed out *she'd make me hurt*! She'd threatened suicide before but she'd never done anything.

'I thought this blow-up would clear the air between us. Julia never spoke to me again about my affair. In fact she stopped speaking to me at all except when Scotty was around, for she wanted him to have a normal home with ostensibly happy parents. I had given her a son she loved beyond reason.

'Then came June and Scotty's third birthday. She planned a party for him and invited six small guests, who naturally had to bring along their mothers as well. It was on a Saturday. I was home, and to help calm Scotty, who was very excited about his party, I gave him a sailboat to go with the sailor suit he was going to wear. Julia came down the stairs with him, dressed in blue voile. Her lovely dark hair was bound back with a blue satin ribbon. Scotty clung to his mother's hand, and in his free hand he carried the sailboat. Julia told me she was afraid she hadn't bought enough sweets for the party, and it was such a beautiful day that she and Scotty would walk to the nearest shop and buy some more. I offered to drive her there. She refused. I offered to walk along with them. She said she didn't want me to. She wanted me to wait and be there in case any of the guests arrived early. I sat down on the front veranda and waited. Inside, the dining table was all set for the party, with balloons suspended from the chandelier, and crackers, hats and other presents, and Henny had made a huge cake.

'The guests began to arrive around two. And still Julia and Scotty didn't return. I began to worry so I got in my car and drove to the shop, expecting to see them on the way home. I didn't see them. I asked the assistants if they'd been there; no one had seen them. That's when I began to feel really frightened. I cruised the streets looking for them, and stopped to ask passers-by if they'd seen a lady dressed in blue with a little boy in a sailor suit. I guess I'd questioned four or five before a boy on a bicycle told me yes, he'd seen such a lady in blue, with a little boy carrying a sailboat, and he pointed out the direction they'd taken.

'They were headed for the river! I drove as far as I could then jumped out of the car and ran down the dirt path, fearing every moment I'd get there too late. I couldn't bring myself to believe she'd really do it. I kept calming myself by thinking Scotty only wanted to float his boat on the water, like I used to do. I ran so fast my heart hurt, and then I reached the grassy river bank. And there they were, the two of them, both in the water floating face upward. Julia had her arms locked around Scotty who'd clearly tried to free himself from her hold, and his little boat was sailing with the tide. The blue ribbon had come unbound from her hair, and it floated too, and all about her hair streamed like dark ribbons to twine in the weeds. The water was only knee-high.'

I made some small sound that choked my throat, feeling his terrible anguish, but he didn't hear. He went on, 'In no time at all I had them both in my arms and I carried them to shore. Julia was barely alive, but Scotty seemed dead, so it was him I worked over first in a futile effort to bring him around. I did everything possible to pump the water from his lungs, but he was dead. I then turned to Julia and did the same for her. She coughed and choked out the water. She didn't open her eyes but at least she was breathing. I put both of them in my car and drove them to the nearest hospital where they slaved to bring Julia back, but they couldn't. No more than I could bring Scotty back to life.'

Paul paused and stared deep into my eyes. 'That is my story for a girl who thinks she's the only one who has suffered, and the only one who has lost, and the only one who grieves. Oh, I grieve just as much as you do but I also bear the guilt. I should have known how unstable Julia was. We had watched *Medea* on TV only a few nights before Scotty's birthday and she showed unusual interest in it, and she didn't care for television. I was stupid not to know what she was thinking and planning. Yet, even now, I cannot understand how she could kill our son when she loved him so much. She could have divorced me and kept him. I wouldn't have taken him from her. But that wasn't enough revenge for Julia. She had to kill the thing I loved best, my son.'

I couldn't speak. What kind of woman had Julia been? Like my own mother? My mother killed to gain a fortune. Julia killed for revenge. Was I going to do the same thing? No, no, of course not. My way would be better, much better, for she'd live to suffer on, and on, and on.

'I'm sorry,' I said brokenly, so sorry I had to kiss his cheek. 'But you can have other children. You can marry again.' I put my arms about him when he shook his head.

'Forget Julia!' I cried, throwing my arms about his neck and snuggling closer in his arms. 'Don't you tell me all the time to forgive and forget? Forgive yourself, and forget what happened to Julia. I remember my mother and father; they were always loving and kissing. I've known since I was a little girl that men need to be loved and touched. I used to watch my mother to see how she tamed Daddy down when he was angry. She did it with kisses, with soft looks and small touches.' I tilted my head back and smiled at him as I'd seen my mother smile at my father. 'Tell me how a wife should be on her wedding night. I wouldn't want to disappoint my bridegroom.'

'I will tell you no such thing!'

'Then I'll just pretend you're my bridegroom, and I have just come from the bathroom after getting undressed. What do you think?'

He cleared his throat and tried to shove me away, but I clung like a burr. 'I think you ought to go to bed and forget games of pretending.'

I stayed where I was. Over and over again I kissed him and soon he was responding. I felt his flesh grow warmer but then his lips beneath mine tightened into a firm line as his hands went under my knees and shoulders. He stood with me in his arms and headed towards the stairs. I thought he was going to take me to his room and make love to me and I was frightened, ashamed – and excited and eager too. But he headed straight for my room and there by my narrow bed he hesitated. He held me close against his heart for an excruciatingly long time as the rain pelted

94

down and beat on the window glass. Paul seemed to forget who I was as his raspy cheek rubbed against mine, caressing with his cheek, not his hands this time. And again, as always, I had to speak and spoil it all.

'Paul.' My timid voice drew him out of some deep reverie that might, if I'd stayed silent, have led me sooner towards that forever-withheld ecstasy my body yearned for. 'When we were locked away upstairs our grandmother always called us Devil's spawn. She told us we were evil seed planted in the wrong soil, that nothing good would ever come of us. She made us all unsure of what we were, or whether we had the right to be alive. Was it so terrible what our mother did, to marry her half-uncle when he was only three years older than she? No woman with a heart could have resisted him. I know I couldn't have. He was like you. Our grandparents believed our parents had committed an unholy sin so they despised us, even the twins who were so little and adorable. They called us unwholesome. Were they right? Were they right to try to kill us?'

I'd said exactly the right words to snap him back into focus. Quickly he dropped me. He turned his head sideways so I couldn't read his eyes. I hated for people to hide their eyes from me so I couldn't see the truth.

'I think your parents were very much in love and very young,' he said in a strange, tight voice, 'so much in love they didn't pause to consider the future and the consequences.'

'Oh!' I cried, outraged. 'You think the grandparents were right – and we are evil!'

He spun about to face me, his full, sensual lips open, his expression furious. 'Don't take what I say and twist it about to suit your need for revenge. There's no reason, ever, to justify murder, unless it's a case of self-defence. You're not evil. Your grandparents were bigoted fools who should have learned to accept what was and make the best of it. And they had much to be proud of in the four grandchildren your parents gave them. And if your parents took a calculated gamble when they decided to have children, I say they won. God and the odds were on your side and gave you too much beauty and appreciation of it, and perhaps too many talents. Most certainly there is one very young girl who smoulders with adult emotions too large for her size and age.'

'Paul . . . ?'

'Don't look at me like that, Catherine.'

'I don't know how I'm looking.'

'Go to sleep, Catherine Sheffield, this instant!'

'What did you call me?' I asked as he backed off towards the door.

He smiled at me. 'It wasn't a Freudian slip, if that's what you're thinking. Dollanganger is too long a name. Sheffield would be a much better choice. Legally we can arrange to have your surname changed.'

'Oh.' He made me feel sick with disappointment.

'Look here, Catherine,' he said from the doorway. He was so large he blocked out the light from the hall. 'You're playing a dangerous game. You're trying to seduce me and you're very lovely and very hard to resist. But your place in my life is as my daughter – nothing else.'

'Was it raining that day in June when you put Julia and Scotty in the ground?'

'What difference does that make? *Any day* you put someone you love underground it's raining!' And he was gone from my door, striding quickly down the hall to his room where he slammed the door hard.

So, I'd tried twice and he'd rejected me twice. Now I was free to go on my merry, destructive way to dance and dance until I reached the top. And that would show Momma, who could do nothing but embroider and knit, just who had the most talent and brains. She would see who could make a fortune on her own without selling her body, and without stooping to murder to inherit it!

The whole world was going to know about me! They'd compare me to Anna Pavlova and say I was better. She'd come to a party they threw in my honour, and with her would be her husband. She'd look old, jaded, tired, while I'd be fresh and young, and her darling Bart would come straight to me, his eyes dazzled as he kissed my hand. 'You are the most beautiful woman I've ever seen,' he'd say, 'and the most talented.' And with his eyes alone I'd know he loved me, loved me ten times more than he had ever loved her. And then when I had him and she was alone, I'd tell him who I was, and he'd not believe at first. Then he would. And he'd hate her! He'd take all her money from her. Where would it go? I paused, stumped. Where would the money go if it were taken from Momma? Would it go back to the grandmother? It wouldn't come to us, not Chris, Carrie or me, for we just didn't exist as Foxworths. Then I smiled to myself, thinking of the four birth certificates I'd found sewn under the lining of one of our old suitcases. I began to laugh. Oh, Momma, what stupid things you do! Imagine, hiding the birth certificates. With those I could prove Cory existed, and without them it would be her word against mine, unless the police went back to Gladstone and found the doctor who had delivered the twins. And then there was our old babysitter, Mrs Simpson – and Jim Johnston. Oh, I hoped none had moved away and that they could still remember the four Dresden dolls.

I knew I was evil, just like the grandmother said from the beginning, born to be bad. I'd been punished before I'd even done anything evil, so why not let the punishment fit the crime that was to be? There was no reason why I should be haunted and ruined just because once upon a miserable time, I had turned for refuge into the arms of my brother. I'd go to the man who needed me most. If that was evil, to give what his words denied and his eyes pleaded for, then let me be evil!

I began, as I grew sleepy, to plan how it would be. He wouldn't turn away and put me off, for I'd make it impossible. He wouldn't want to hurt me. He'd take me and then he'd think to himself he had to, and then he wouldn't feel guilty at all.

The guilt would all be mine. And Chris would hate me and turn, as he had to, to someone else.

SWEETER THAN ALL THE ROSES

I was sixteen in April of 1961. There I was, at the blossoming, ripe age when all men, young and old, and most of all those past forty, turned to stare at me on the streets. When I waited on the corner for a bus, cars slowed because male drivers couldn't keep from gaping at me.

And if they were enraptured, I was even more so. I preened before the many mirrors in Paul's home and saw, sometimes by surprise, a lovely, even breathtakingly beautiful girl – and then that glorious revelation – that was *me*! I was dazzling and I knew it. Julian flew down often to turn his desiring eyes upon me, telling me he knew what *he* wanted even if I didn't. I saw Chris only on the weekends and I knew he still wanted me, still loved me more than he'd ever love anyone again.

Chris and Carrie came home for my birthday weekend and we laughed and hugged and talked so fast, as if we'd never have the time to say enough, especially Chris and I. I wanted to tell Chris that Momma would be living in Greenglenna soon but I was afraid he'd try to stop me from doing what I had planned so I never mentioned it. After a while Carrie drew away to sit with big, sad eyes and stare at our kind benefactor. That big, handsome man who ordered me to dress up in my very best. 'Why not wear that dress you've been saving for a special occasion? For your birthday I'm treating all of you to a gourmet feast at my favourite restaurant, The Plantation House.'

Right away I had to rush upstairs and begin dressing. I was going to make the most of my birthday. My face didn't really need makeup, yet I put it on, the whole works, including mascara black as ink, and then I used tongs to curl my lashes. My nails gleamed like lustrous pearls and the gown I wore was Paris pink. Oh, did I feel pretty as I preened and primped before a cheval glass bought for my vanity.

'My lady Catherine,' said Chris from the open doorway. 'You

do look gorgeous but it is in appallingly bad taste to admire yourself so much you have to kiss your own reflection. Really, Cathy, wait for compliments from others – don't give them to yourself.'

'I'm afraid no one will tell me,' I said defensively, 'so I tell it to myself to give myself more confidence. Do I look beautiful and not just pretty?'

'Yeah,' he said in a funny, tight voice, 'I doubt I'll ever see another girl as beautiful as you look right now.'

'Would you say I'm improving with age?'

'I'm not going to compliment you any more! It's no wonder the grandmother broke all the mirrors. I've got a good mind to do that myself. Such conceit!'

I frowned, not liking to be reminded of that old woman. '*You* look fantastic, Chris,' I said, giving him a big, warm smile. 'I'm not ashamed or embarrassed to hand out compliments when they're deserved. You're as handsome as Daddy.'

Every time he came home from his school he looked more mature and more handsome. Though, when I peered closer, wisdom was putting something strange in his eyes, something that made him seem much, much older than I was. He also appeared sadder, more vulnerable, and the combination was extremely appealing. 'Why aren't you happy, Chris?' I asked. 'Is life disappointing you? Is it less than you thought it would be when we were locked away and we had so many dreams for the future? Are you sorry now that you decided on being a doctor? Are you wishing instead to be a dancer like me?'

I had neared to watch his oh, so revealing eyes, but he lowered them to hide away and his hands tried to span my waist, but my waist wasn't that small or his hands weren't that large. Or was he just doing something to touch me? Making a game out of what was serious. Was that it? I ducked to peer into his face and I saw the love I was looking for and then wished I didn't know.

'Chris, you haven't answered.'

'What did you ask?'

'Life, medical training, is it living up to your expectations?'

'What does?'

'That sounds cynical. My style, not yours.'

He raised his head and smiled brightly. *Oh, God!* 'Yes,' he said, 'life on the outside is what I thought it would be. I was realistic, unlike you. I like school and the friends I've made. But I still miss you; it's hard being separated from you, always wondering what you're up to.' His eyes shifted again and became shadowed as he yearned for the impossible. 'Happy birthday, my lady Cath-er-ine,' he softly said, and then brushed my lips with his. Just a feathery little kiss that didn't dare much. 'Let's go,' he said resolutely, taking hold of my hand. 'Everyone is ready but fussy, prissy you.'

We descended the stairs hand in hand. Paul and Carrie were all dressed and waiting, with Henny too. The house felt strange, so hushed and expectant – so weirdly dark, with all the lights off but in the hall. How funny.

Then, suddenly, out of the dark came, *'Sur-prise! Sur-prise!'* Screamed by a chorus of voices as the lights all came on, and members of my ballet class, thronging about Chris and me.

Henny carried in a birthday cake of three layers, each smaller than the one underneath and proudly said she'd made it and decorated it herself. *Let me always succeed at what I set out to do,* I wished with my eyes closed when I blew out all the candles. *I'm gaining on you, Momma – getting older and wiser each day, so when the time comes, I'll be ready – your match.*

I blew so well the melted pink wax smeared the sugary pink roses nestled sweetly on pale green leaves. Across from me was Julian. His ebony eyes riveted as mutely he asked the same question over and over.

Whenever I tried to meet eyes with Chris he had his turned another way or lowered to stare at the floor. Carrie crowded close beside Paul, who sat some distance away from the boisterous revelry and tried not to look stern. As soon as I had all the presents opened Paul got up, picked Carrie up in his arms, and both disappeared up the stairs.

'Good night, Cathy,' called Carrie, her small face happy and flushed with sleepiness, 'this is the best birthday party I've ever been to.'

I could have cried from the pain of that, for she was almost nine years old and the birthday parties she could remember, except Chris's last November, had been pitiful attempts to make much out of little.

'Why are you looking sad?' asked Julian who came up and swung me into his embrace. 'Rejoice – for now you have me at your feet, ready to set your heart on fire along with your body.'

Truly I hated him when he acted like that. He tried to demonstrate in every way possible that I belonged to him and him alone. His gift had been a leather tote to carry my leotards, shoes and other ballet things. I danced away from him, not wanting to be claimed tonight. All the girls who weren't already infatuated with Julian immediately fell for Chris, and this in no way enhanced Julian's liking for my brother. I don't know what happened to put the match to the grass but suddenly Chris and Julian were in a corner arguing and about to exchange blows. 'I don't give a damn what you think!' stormed Chris. 'My sister is too young for a lover and not ready for New York!'

'You! You –' fired Julian back. 'What do *you* know about the dance? You know nothing! You can't even manage to move your feet without stepping on yourself!'

'That may be true,' said Chris in an icy voice, 'but I have other skills. And we're talking about my sister and the fact that she is still under age. I won't have you persuading her to accompany you to New York when she hasn't even finished high school yet!'

My head swivelled from one to the other and between the two it was hard to say which was the better looking. I felt sick that they would show everyone their hostility, and sick because I wanted so much for them to like each other. I trembled on the brink of crying out, *stop, don't do this!* But I said nothing.

'Cathy,' called Chris, not moving his eyes for one second from Julian who appeared ready to throw a blow or deliver a kick, 'do you honestly believe you are ready to make your début in New York?'

'No ...' I said in a near whisper.

Julian's eyes raged my way, for he was at me, demanding of me every second we were together, wanting me to accompany him to New York and be his mistress and dance partner. I knew why he wanted me – my weight, my height, my balance suited his abilities perfectly. It was of utmost importance to find the perfect partner when you wanted to impress in a *pas de deux*.

'May all your birthdays be hell on earth!' Julian said as he headed for the front door, and he slammed it hard behind him. That's how my party ended, with everyone going home looking embarrassed. Chris stalked up to his room without wishing me good night. With tears in my eyes I began to pick up the trash from the living-room carpet. I found a hole burned in the plushy green from a carelessly held cigarette. Someone had broken one of Paul's prized pieces of hand-blown glass – a transparent rose of shimmering crystal. I held it, thinking about buying glue that would put it back together again, even as I planned a way, for there had to be a way, to cover up the holes in the carpet and take the white rings from the tables.

'Don't worry about the rose,' Paul's voice came from behind me, 'it's just a cheap knickknack. I can always buy another.'

I turned to look at him. He was standing so casually in the archway of the foyer, meeting my teary look with his soft, kind eyes. 'It was a beautiful rose,' I choked, 'and I know it was expensive. I'll buy you another if I can find a duplicate, and if I can't I'll buy you something better when I can ...'

'Forget it.'

'Thank you again for the beautiful music box.' Nervously my hands fluttered to my daring décolletage and sought to hide the cleavage. 'My father gave me a silver music box with a ballerina inside once but I had to leave it ...' My voice trailed off and I could speak no more, for thoughts of my father always left me in childish ruins of bleakness without hope.

'Chris told me about the music box your father gave you and I tried to find one just like it. Did I succeed?'

'Yes,' I said, though it wasn't the same.

'Good. Now go to bed. Forget the mess – Henny will clean up. You look sleepy.'

I was soon up the stairs and into my room, where to my surprise Chris was waiting for me.

'What is going on between you and Julian?' he shot out fiercely.

'Nothing is going on!'

'Don't lie to me, Cathy! He doesn't fly down here so often for *nothing*!'

'Mind your own damned business, Christopher!' I said viciously. 'I don't try to tell you what to do and I demand the same from you! You are not a saint and I am not an angel! The trouble is you're just another man who thinks you can do anything *you* want while I have to sit prim and prissy on the sidelines and wait for someone to come along and marry me! Well, I'm not that kind of woman! Nobody is going to push me around and make me do what I don't want to – never again! Not Paul! Not Madame! Not Julian – and not you either!' His face paled as he listened and restrained himself from interrupting. 'I want you to stay out of my life, Christopher. I'll do what I have to, anything I have to, to get to the top!'

He glared at me with his heavenly blue eyes shooting devilish electric sparks. 'I take it you'll sleep with just any man if that's necessary.'

'I'll do what I have to!' I raged back, though I hadn't given that any thought.

He seemed on the verge of slapping me, and the control it took to keep his hands at his sides made him clench them into fists. A white line etched about his tightened lips. 'Cathy,' he began in a hurt voice, 'what's come over you? I didn't think you'd ever become another opportunist.'

Bitterly I met his eyes. What did *he* think he was doing? We'd stumbled fortunately upon an unhappy, lonely man and we were using him, and sooner or later there'd be a price to pay. Our grandmother had always told us nobody did anything for nothing. But somehow I couldn't hurt him more, and I couldn't speak a word against Paul who'd taken us in and was doing everything he could. Truthfully, I had reason enough for knowing he didn't expect any reward.

'Cathy,' he pleaded, 'I hate every word you just said. How can you talk to me like that when you know how much I love and respect you? There isn't a day that passes that I don't long for you. I live for the weekends when I can see you and Carrie. Don't turn from me, Cathy, I need you. I'll always need you. It scares the hell out of me to think I'm not nearly that necessary in *your* life.' He had hold of my arms and would have pulled me against his chest, but I yanked away and turned my back. How could I tell what was wrong and what was right when nobody seemed to care any more?

'Chris,' I began brokenly, 'I'm sorry I spoke like that. It matters to me very much what you think. But I'm all torn up inside. I think I have to have everything immediately to help make up for all I've lost and suffered. Julian wants me to go with him to New York. I don't think I'm ready yet and I don't have the discipline I need – Madame tells me that all the time and she's right. Julian says he loves me and will take care of me. But I'm not sure what love is, or if he loves me at all or only wants me to help him reach his goal. But his goal is my goal. So tell me how I can tell if he loves me or if he only wants to use me?'

'Have you let him make love to you?' he asked flatly, his eyes dead looking.

'*No!* Of course not!'

His arms encircled me and held me fast. 'Wait at least one more year, Cathy. Trust Madame Marisha, not Julian. She knows more than he does.' He paused and forced me to lift my bowed head. I studied his handsome face and wondered why he hesitated and didn't go on.

I was an instrument of yearning, filled with a ravenous desire for romantic fulfilment. I was scared too of what was inside me. So scared I was like Momma. When I looked in the mirrors I saw my mother's face beginning to emerge more definitely. I was exalted that I looked like her, and paradoxically I hated myself for being her reflection. No, no, I wasn't like her inside, only on the outside. My beauty was not only skin deep.

I kept telling myself this as I made a special trip to Greenglenna downtown. In the city hall there I made some flimsy excuse about looking up my mother's birth certificate just so I could look up the birth certificate of Bart Winslow. I found out he was eight years younger than my mother and I also discovered exactly where he lived. I walked fifteen blocks until I came to a quiet, elm-lined street where old mansions were in a state of decaying disrepair. All but the home of Bart Winslow! His home had scaffolding all around. Dozens of workmen were putting up storm windows on a freshly painted brick home with white trim around the windows and a white portico.

Another day found me in the Greenglenna library where I read up on the Winslow family. Much to my delight, when I searched back through the old newspapers I found a society editor who seemed to devote most of her column to Bart Winslow and his fabulously wealthy and very beautiful wife with her aristocratic background. 'The heiress to one of the country's greatest fortunes.'

That column I snipped out furtively and sneaked home to Chris. I didn't want him to know Momma would live in Greenglenna. He showed some distress as he scanned the column. 'Cathy, where did you find this article?'

I shrugged. 'Oh, it was in some Virginia paper they sell in a newsstand.'

'She's in Europe again,' he said in a queer way. 'I wonder why she keeps going to Europe.' He turned his blue eyes my way and a dreamy expression softened his features. 'Remember the summer she went on her honeymoon?'

Remember? As if I could ever forget. As if I would ever let myself forget. Some day, some day when I was rich and famous too, Momma was going to hear from me and when she did, she'd better be well prepared, for bit by bit I was forming my strategy.

Julian didn't come to Greenglenna as much as he had before my sixteenth birthday party. I figured Chris had scared him off. I didn't know if that made me happy or not. When he did visit his parents he ignored me. He began to pay attention to Lorraine DuVal, my best friend. For some reason I felt hurt and resentment, not only against him but also against Lorraine. In the wings I half-hid myself and watched them dance a passionate *pas de deux*. That was when I determined I'd study twice as hard as I had before, for I was going to show Julian too! I was going to show everyone just what *I* was made of!

Steel, covered over with frilly, silly tulle tutus!

OWL ON THE ROOF

Now I'm going to recount an event in Carrie's life, for this is her story and Chris's as well as mine. When I look back now and reflect on how life turned out for Carrie, I truthfully believe what happened to Carrie in Miss Emily Dean Calhoun's School for Properly Bred Young Ladies had a great deal to do with how she thought of herself in the future.

Ah, dig me a well to cry in before I begin, for I loved her so, and what pain she had to bear I bear, even now.

From the jigsaw pieces that I've gathered from Carrie herself and from Miss Dewhurst, and from several other students at that school, this was Carrie's nightmare to endure, and I will report it as honestly as possible.

Carrie spent her weekends with us but she had retreated into that quiet, little apathetic creature who'd grieved so when her twin died. Everything about Carrie worried me. When I asked her questions she insisted everything was all right and refused to say anything against the school or the girls or the teachers. She said one thing, and one thing only, to express her feelings – and what a clue it was. 'I like the carpet – it's coloured like grass.' That was it. She left me wondering, worried, trying to guess what was troubling her. Something was wrong, I knew it, and she wouldn't tell me what it was.

Each Friday about four Paul would drive to fetch Carrie and Chris and bring them back home. He did his best to make all our weekends memorable. Though Carrie appeared happy enough with us, she seldom laughed. Try as we would, all we could pull from her was a weak smile.

'What's wrong with Carrie?' whispered Chris. I could only shrug. Somewhere along the way I'd lost Carrie's confidence. Her big blue eyes fastened on Paul. They mutely pleaded with him. But he was looking at me, not Carrie.

As the time approached for her to be driven back to school

Carrie would grow very quiet; her eyes would become blank and resigned. We'd kiss her goodbye and tell her to be good, make friends, 'and if you need us, you know how to call.'

'Yes,' she said weakly, her eyes downcast. I pressed her against me telling her again how much I loved her, and if she was unhappy she had to speak up and say so. 'I'm not unhappy,' she answered with her eyes fixed sadly on Paul.

It was truly a beautiful school. I'd have loved to attend such a school. Each girl was allowed to decorate her side of a double room as she saw fit. Miss Dewhurst had only one restriction, and that was each girl had to choose 'proper, ladylike' appointments. Soft, passive femininity was greatly stressed in the South. Soft, whispering clothes, drifting chiffon, dulcet voices, shy, downcast eyes, weak, fluttery hands to express helplessness, and absolutely no opinions that would conflict with male ones – and never, never let a man know you had a brain that might be better than his. And I'm afraid, after reconsidering, it wouldn't be the proper school for me after all.

Carrie's bed was twin size, covered by a bright purple spread. On it she had decorator pillows of rose, red, purple, violet and green. Beside her bed was a nightstand with the milk-glass vase filled with plastic violets given to her by Paul. Whenever he could he brought her real flowers. Strangely, she adored that little pot of violets more than the real flowers that soon withered and died.

Since Carrie was the smallest girl in the school of one hundred students, she was given as a room mate the next smallest girl, named Sissy Towers. Sissy had brick-red hair, emerald eyes that were long and narrow, thin, paper-white skin, and a spiteful, mean temper which she never displayed to any adult, but saved for the girls she knew how to intimidate. Worst of all, though she was the second smallest, she towered over Carrie by six inches!

Carrie had celebrated her ninth birthday with a party the week before her ordeal began. It was May, and it began on a Thursday.

The school days ended at three. The girls had two hours to play outside before dinner at five-thirty. They all wore uniforms of colours determined by what grade they were in. Carrie was in the third grade; her uniform was of yellow broadcloth with a dainty white organdie pinafore to top it off. Carrie had a strong dislike for the colour yellow. Yellow represented to her, as it did to Chris and me, the colour of all the best things we couldn't have when we'd been locked away and made to feel unwholesome, unwanted and unloved. Yellow was also the colour of the sun that was denied us. The sun was what Cory had wanted most to see, and now that all yellow things were so easily accessible, and Cory wasn't, yellow was a hateful thing.

Sissy Towers adored yellow. She envied Carrie's long, golden locks and despised her own head of crinkly rust. Perhaps too she envied the beauty of Carrie's doll-like face, and those big blue eyes with the long, dark, curling lashes, and her lips ripe as strawberries. Oh, yes, our Carrie was a doll with an exquisite face, sensational Goldilocks hair and, the pity of it all, this beauty hovered above a body much too thin, too small, and a neck too delicate to support a head that belonged on someone bigger and taller.

Yellow dominated Sissy's side of the room; yellow spread, yellow slip-covered chairs; her dolls were blondes wearing yellow, her books wore yellow jackets, homemade. Sissy even wore yellow sweaters and skirts when she went home. The fact that Sissy looked unbecomingly sallow in yellow did not lessen her determination to annoy Carrie with the colour – come what may. And on this day, for some trifling reason that was never explained, she began to taunt Carrie in a mean, spiteful way.

'Carrie is a dwarf . . . a dwarf . . . a dwarf,' sang Sissy in a sing-song chant.

'Carrie should be in a circus . . . a circus . . . a circus,' Sissy chanted on and on. Then she jumped up on the top of her desk and in the loud, brassy manner of a barker touting a freak show at a carnival Sissy really began to shout, *'Come one! Come all! Come pay your quarter to see the living sister of Tom Thumb! Come see the world's smallest woman! Come, pay your money and see the little one with the huge, huge eyes – like an owl's! Come view the huge, huge head on the little, scrawny neck! Come pay your quarter to see our little freak naked!'*

Dozens of little girls crowded into the room to stare at Carrie who crouched in a corner on the floor, with her head hanging low and her long hair hiding her shamed, terrified face.

Sissy opened up her small purse to receive the quarters the affluent little girls dropped in willingly. 'Now take off your clothes, little freak,' ordered Sissy. 'Give the customers their money's worth!'

Quivering and beginning to cry, Carrie crouched into a tighter ball and pulled up her knees and prayed that God would somehow open up the floor. But floors never graciously open up and swallow you when they should. It remained hard and unyielding beneath her as the taunting voice of Sissy went on and on.

'Look at her tremble ... look at her shake ... she's gonna make ... an earthquake!'

All the girls giggled, except one average-sized girl of ten who looked on Carrie with pity and sympathy. 'I think she's cute,' said Lacy St John. 'Leave her alone, Sissy. It's not nice what you're doing.'

'Of course it's not nice!' Sissy said with a laugh. 'But it's such fun! She's such a timid little mouse! You know, she *never* says anything. I don't think she *can* talk!' Down from the chair Sissy jumped to run to where Carrie was, and there she prodded Carrie with her foot. 'Have you got a tongue, little freak? Come, little big-eyes, tell us how you got to be so funny-looking. Did the cat steal your tongue? Do you have a tongue? Stick it out!'

Carrie hung her head even lower.

'See, she doesn't have a tongue!' proclaimed Sissy, jumping up and down. Sissy whirled around and spread her arms wide. 'Look at what they gave me for a room-mate – an owl without a tongue! What can we do to make her talk?'

Lacy moved protectively closer to Carrie. 'Come on, Sissy, enough is enough, leave her alone.'

Pivoting, Sissy stomped down hard on Lacy's foot. '*Shut up!* This is my room! When you're in my room, you do as I say! And I'm just as big as you are, Lacy St John, and my daddy's got more money too!'

'I think you are a mean, nasty, ugly girl to torment Carrie!' said Lacy.

Sissy raised her fist in the manner of a professional boxer, dancing around to take quick jabs at Lacy. 'You wanna fight? C'mon, put up your dukes! Just see if you can get me before I blacken your eyes!' And before Lacy could raise her hands for protection, Sissy shot out a right that caught Lacy squarely on the left eye. Then Sissy's left hook smashed Lacy's fine straight nose! Blood spurted everywhere!

This was when Carrie lifted her head, saw the only girl who'd shown her the least bit of kindness being beaten to a pulp, and that was cause enough for Carrie to use her most formidable weapon – her voice. She began to scream. Full blast, using every bit of vocal power she had, Carrie threw back her head and let go!

Down in her study on the first floor, Miss Emily Dean Dewhurst bolted upright and smeared the ink in her ledger. She ran to sound an alarm in the hall to bring each and every teacher on the run.

It was eight o'clock in the evening. Most of the teachers had retired to their rooms. Clad in bathrobes, negligees, and one in a scarlet evening gown, apparently ready to slip out on the sly, the teachers raced towards the clamour. They burst into the room Carrie shared with Sissy and found a frightful scene. Twelve girls all doing battle, while others stood back and watched. One girl, like Carrie, only screamed, but the others were yelling, kicking, wrestling on the floor, pulling hair, biting and tearing off clothes – and above all the racket of the fray resounded the blaring trumpet of one small human in terror.

'Where is the man – the man?' cried out Miss Longhurst, the one in the scarlet evening gown with her bosom about to fall out of the low-cut bodice.

'Miss Longhurst, control yourself!' ordered Miss Dewhurst, who promptly assessed the situation and planned her strategy. 'There is no man here. *Girls*!' she boomed, '*Stop this fracas this very second, or every one of you will be denied liberty this weekend!*' Then she said in a low voice to the sexy Longhurst, '*You* report to my office when this is under control.'

Every girl in that room about to have her hair pulled or her face scratched jerked abruptly still and quiet. With horrified eyes they looked around and saw the room full of teachers – and worst of all Miss Dewhurst, who was not known for showing mercy once bedlam broke loose, as it often did. All hushed. All but Carrie who kept right on screaming, her eyes squeezed shut, her small, pale hands in tight fists.

'Why is that child screaming?' asked Miss Dewhurst as a guilty-looking Miss Longhurst sneaked away to take off her incriminating evidence – that somewhere a man *was* hiding and waiting.

Naturally, it was Sissy Towers who recovered first. 'She's the one who started it all, Miss Dewhurst. It's *all* Carrie's fault. She's like a baby. You've just got to give me a new room-mate or I'll die living so close to a baby.'

'Repeat what you just said, Miss Towers. Tell me again what I *must* do.'

Intimidated, Sissy smiled uneasily. 'I mean, I would like to have a new room-mate; I don't feel good living so close to someone so unnaturally small.'

Coldly Miss Dewhurst eyed Sissy. 'Miss Towers, *you* are unnaturally cruel. From now on you will room on the first floor in the room next to mine where I can keep an eye on you.' She flashed her sharp gaze around the room. 'As for the rest of you, I'm going to notify your parents that your weekend leaves are cancelled! Now, each of you report to Miss Littleton so she may mark your records with demerits.' The girls groaned and one by one drifted out to have their names recorded with minus marks. Only then did Miss Dewhurst advance to where Carrie was on her hands and knees; her voice faded to a whimper, but her head kept moving from side to side in a hysterical way. 'Miss Dollanganger, are you calm enough now to tell me what happened?'

Carrie was beyond speech. Terror and the sight of blood had taken her back to the locked room, to a hungry day when she had been forced to drink blood or starve to death. Miss Dewhurst was touched and bewildered. Forty years she'd seen girls come and go, and she knew girls could be just as devastatingly ugly and cruel as boys. 'Miss Dollanganger, unless you respond to me, you will not visit your family this weekend. I know you've had a hard time of it and I want to be kind to you. Can't you please explain what happened?'

Fallen flat on the floor now, Carrie looked up. She saw the older woman towering above her, and the blue skirt she wore was almost grey. Grey was the colour the grandmother always wore. And the grandmother did terrible things; somehow the grandmother had caused Cory to die – and now she had come to get Carrie too!

'I hate you! I hate you!' screamed Carrie over and over, until finally Miss Dewhurst was driven from the room and the school nurse was sent in to give Carrie a sedative.

That Friday, I answered the telephone when Miss Dewhurst called to say twelve of her girls had broken her rules and disobeyed her orders, and Carrie was one of them. 'I'm sorry, really I am. But I can't give your sister privileges and still punish the others. She was in the room and she refused to quiet when I ordered her to.'

I waited until evening at the dinner table to discuss it with Paul. 'It's a terrible mistake to leave Carrie over the weekend, Paul. You know we promised her she could come home *every* weekend. She's too little to be the cause of anything, so it's not fair she should be punished too!'

'Really, Cathy,' he said, putting down his fork, 'Miss Dewhurst called me right after she talked to you. She does have rules, and if Carrie misbehaved then she has to suffer along with the rest of the girls. And I respect Miss Dewhurst even if you don't.'

Chris, home for the weekend, spoke up and agreed with Paul. 'Sure, Cathy, you know as well as I do that Carrie can cut up when she wants to. If she did nothing but scream she could drive you batty – and deaf.'

That weekend was a flop without Carrie. I couldn't get her off my mind. I stewed, fretted, worried over Carrie. I seemed to hear her calling to me. I closed my eyes and I saw her small, white face with her eyes huge and haunted by fear. She *was* all right! She had to be, didn't she? What could happen to a little girl in an expensive school controlled by such a responsible, respectable woman as Miss Emily Dean Dewhurst?

When Carrie was hurting and at odds with herself and all the world, and there was no one near who loved her, she retreated to yesterdays and the safe comfort of the tiny porcelain dolls she'd carefully hidden away beneath all of her clothes. Now she was the only girl in the school with a room all to herself. She'd never been alone before. Not once in all her nine years had Carrie spent a night in a room alone. She was alone now and she knew it. Every girl in the school had turned against her, even Lacy St John.

From her very secret place Carrie would take her dolls, Mr and Mrs Parkins and dear little baby Clara, and she'd talk to them as she used to do when she was locked away in the attic. 'And Cathy,' she told me later, 'I thought maybe Momma was up in God's heaven, in the garden with Cory and Daddy, and I felt so mean at you and Chris because you let Dr Paul put me in that place, and you know how much I liked to be with all of you. And I hated you, Cathy! I hated everybody! I hated God for making me so small so people laugh at my big head and little body!'

In the short halls and long corridors of green carpeting Carrie heard the girls whispering. Furtively they shifted their eyes when she looked their way. 'I told myself I didn't care,' whispered Carrie hoarsely to me, 'but I did care. I told myself I could be brave like you and Chris and Dr Paul wanted. I kept on making myself feel brave but I wasn't really brave. I don't like the dark. And I told myself God was going to hear my prayers and make me grow taller, 'cause everybody grows taller when they grow older, and so would I.

'It was so dark, Cathy, and the room felt so big and scary. You know I don't like night and darkness with no lamp burning, with nobody there but me. I even wanted Sissy back, she seemed better than nobody. Something in the shadows moved and I was terrified, and though we're not supposed to I turned on a lamp. I wanted to take all my little dolls to bed with me so I'd have company. I was going to be so careful not to toss and turn and break off their heads.

'I always put Mr and Mrs Parkins left and right with baby Clara in the middle in the bottom drawer of my dresser. I picked up the cotton wadding that was in the middle first and felt something hard. But when I looked, Cathy, when I looked there was no baby, only a little stick! I unwrapped Mr and Mrs Parkins, and they were only sticks too – bigger ones! It hurt so bad not to find them I began to cry. All my little dolls gone, all turned to wood, so I knew God was never going to let me grow tall when he would make my pretty dolls into only sticks.

'Something funny happened to me then, like I turned into wood too. I felt stiff and couldn't see too well. I went and crouched in a corner and waited for something bad to happen. The grandmother said something terrible would happen if I broke a doll, didn't she?' Not another word would she say, but I learned from others what happened after that.

In the dark, long after midnight, the twelve little rich girls Miss Dewhurst had denied liberty all stole furtively into Carrie's room. It was Lacy St John who had the integrity to tell me, but only when Miss Dewhurst was out of hearing.

Twelve girls, all wearing long white cotton nightgowns, the official sleeping garments of the school, filed into Carrie's room, each bearing a single candle held so her face was lit up under her chin. Such lighting made their eyes appear sunken, dark hollows and lent their youthful faces an eerie, ghoulish appearance – enough to terrify a little girl still crouched in the corner, already in a trance of haunted fear.

They came to form a semicircle around Carrie, to stare down at her as each put over her head a pillowcase with holes for eyes. Then came the ritual of weaving the candles intricately in formalized patterns as they chanted in the way of real witches. They sought to drive the smallness out of Carrie. They sought to set her free and themselves free from whatever evil they were driven to do for self-protection from someone so unnaturally small and strange.

One voice shrilled above all the others and Carrie knew it was Sissy Towers. To Carrie, all those shrouded girls in their long nightgowns with white hoods over their heads and the black holes for eyes were devils straight from Hell! She began to whimper, to tremble, and oh, she was so scared, as if once more the grandmother were in the room, only this time she had multiplied until there were twelve of her!

'Don't you cry, don't you fear,' soothed the nightmarish voice from a mouthless hood. 'If you live through this night, through this initiation, you, Carrie Dollanganger, will become a member of our most private and very exclusive society. If you succeed from this night forward, you will share in our secret rituals, our secret parties, our secret hoards of goodies.'

'Ohhh,' moaned Carrie, 'go away, leave me alone, go away, leave me alone.'

'*Quiet!*' ordered the shrill voice of the hidden speaker, 'you have no chance to become one of us unless you sacrifice your most beloved and precious possessions. It is either that or suffer our trial.'

Crouched in the corner, Carrie could only stare at the moving shadows behind the white witches who threatened her. The glows from the candles grew larger, larger, turning her world into one of yellow and scarlet fire.

'Give to us what you dearly cherish or you must suffer, suffer, suffer.'

'I have nothing,' whispered Carrie honestly.

'The dolls, the pretty little china dolls, give us those,' intoned the austere voice of the speaker. 'Your little clothes won't fit us; we don't want those; give us your dolls, your pretty man, woman and child dolls.'

'They're gone,' cried Carrie, fearful they would set fire to her. 'They turned to wooden sticks.'

'Ho-ho! A likely story! You lie! So now you must suffer, little owl, to become one of us – or die. Take your choice.'

It was an easy decision. Carrie nodded and tried not to sniffle.

'All right, from this night forward you, Carrie Dollanganger, funny name, funny face, will be one of us.'

It hurts to write of how they took Carrie and blindfolded her, then tied her small hands behind her back, then pushed her out into the hall, then up a flight of steep stairs, and suddenly they were outside. Carrie felt the cool night air, the slant of the support beneath her bare feet, and guessed correctly the girls had taken her on to the roof! There was only one thing she feared more than the grandmother and that was the roof – any roof! Anticipating her screams the girls had gagged Carrie. 'Now lie or sit still as a proper owl should,' said the same harsh voice. 'Perch here on the roof, near the chimney under the moon, and in the morning you will be one of us.'

Struggling and frantic now, Carrie tried to resist the strength of so many who forced her to sit. Then, even worse, they suddenly took away their hands and left her there in the darkness on the roof – all alone. Far away she heard the whispering titters of their retreat and the slight click of a door latching down.

Cathy, Cathy, she screamed to herself, *Chris, come save me! Dr Paul, why did you put me here? Doesn't anybody want me?* Sobbing, making small mewing sounds while blindfolded, gagged and bound, Carrie braved the steep incline of the huge, strange roof and began to move towards where the latching sound had come from. Inch by inch, sitting up and sliding along on her bottom, Carrie moved forward, praying every time she moved an inch not to fall. It seemed that she heard, above and from behind the oncoming spring thunderstorm, the sweet and distant voice of Cory singing as he strummed his melancholy song of finding his home and the sun again. In the faltering report she gave me later, she said,

'Oh, Cathy, it was so strange way up there high, and the wind started to blow, and the rain began to fall, and the thunder rumbled and the lightning struck so I could see the brightness through the blindfold – and all the time Cory was singing and leading me to the trapdoor that opened when I used my feet to force it upwards, and somehow I wiggled through. Then I fell down the stairs! I fell into blackness and I heard a bone break. And the pain, it came like teeth and bit me so I couldn't see or feel anything or even hear the rain any more. And Cory, he went away.'

Sunday morning came and Paul, Chris and I were at the breakfast table eating brunch.

Chris had a hot, homemade buttery roll in his hand, his lips parted wide to put at least half inside with one bite, when the telephone in the hall rang. Paul groaned as he put down his fork. I groaned too, for I had made my first cheese soufflé and it had to be eaten right away. 'Would you mind getting that, Cathy?' he asked. 'I really want to dig into your soufflé. It looks delicious and it smells heavenly.'

'You sit right there and eat,' I said, jumping up and hurrying to answer, 'and I'll do what I can to protect you from the pesky Mrs Williamson ...'

He softly laughed and flashed me an amused look as he picked his fork up again. 'It may not be my lonely widow lady with another of her minor afflictions.' Chris went on eating.

I picked up the phone and in my most adult and gracious way I said, 'Dr Paul Sheffield's residence.'

'This is Emily Dean Dewhurst calling,' said the stern voice on the other end. 'Please put Dr Sheffield on the phone immediately!'

'Miss Dewhurst!' I said, already alarmed. 'This is Cathy, Carrie's sister. Is Carrie all right?'

'You and Dr Sheffield are needed here immediately!'

'Miss Dewhurst –'

But she didn't let me finish. 'It seems that your younger sister has disappeared rather mysteriously. On Sundays those girls who are being punished by weekend liberty denial are required to attend chapel services. I myself called the roll and Carrie did not respond to her name.' My heart beat faster, apprehensive of what I was to hear next, but my finger moved to push a button that would put Miss Dewhurst's message on to the attached microphone so Chris and Paul would hear even as they ate.

'Where was she?' I asked in a small voice, already terrified.

She spoke calmly. 'A strange hush came in the air this morning when your sister's name was called and when I asked where she was. I sent a teacher to check your sister's room and she wasn't there. I then ordered a thorough search of the grounds and the entire school building from basement to attic, and still your sister wasn't found. I would, if your sister was of a different character, presume she'd run off and was on her way home. But something in the atmosphere warns that at least twelve of the girls here know what has happened to Carrie and they refuse to talk and incriminate themselves.'

My eyes widened. 'You mean you still don't know where Carrie is?'

Paul and Chris had stopped eating. Now both stared at me with mounting concern. 'I'm sorry to say I don't. Carrie hasn't been seen since nine o'clock last night. Even if she walked all the way home she should have reached there by now. It's almost noon. If she is not there and she is not here, then she is either injured, lost or some other accident has befallen her ...'

I could have screamed. How could she speak so dispassionately! Why, why every time something terrible came into our lives was it a flat, uncaring voice that told us the bad news?

Paul's white car sped down Overland Highway towards Carrie's school. I was sandwiched in the front seat between Paul and Chris. My brother had his bag so he could catch a bus and go on to his school after he found out what had happened to Carrie. He had my hand squeezed tight in his to reassure me that *this* child of ours was going to live! 'Stop looking so worried, Cathy,' said Chris as he put an arm about my shoulder and drew my head to his shoulder. 'You know how Carrie is. She's probably hiding and just won't answer. Remember how she was in the attic? She wouldn't stay even when Cory wanted to. Carrie'd take off to do her own thing. She hasn't run away. She'd be too afraid of the dark. She's hiding somewhere. Somebody did something to hurt her feelings and she's punishing them by letting them worry. She couldn't face the world in the dead of night.'

Dead of night! Oh, God! I wished Chris hadn't mentioned the attic where Cory had almost died in a trunk before he went on to meet Daddy in heaven. Chris kissed my cheek and wiped away my tears. 'Come now, don't cry. I said all of that wrong. She'll be all right.'

'What do you mean you don't know where my ward is?' fired Paul in a hard voice as he coldly eyed Miss Dewhurst. 'It was my understanding the girls in this school were properly supervised twenty-four hours a day!'

We were in the posh office of Miss Emily Dean Dewhurst. She was not seated behind her impressive, large desk, but restlessly pacing the floor. 'Really, Dr Sheffield, nothing like this has ever happened before. Never have we lost a girl. We make a room check every night to see the girls are tucked in bed with lights out, and Carrie was in her bed. I myself looked in on her, wanting to comfort her if she'd let me, but she refused to look at me or to speak. Of course it all began with that fight in your ward's room and the demerits that resulted in their loss of their weekend liberty. Every member of the faculty has helped me search and we've questioned our girls who profess to know nothing about it – which I imagine they do – but if they won't talk, I don't know what to do next.'

'Why didn't you notify me when you first found her missing?' Paul asked. I spoke up then and asked to be taken to Carrie's room. Miss Dewhurst turned eagerly to me, anxious to escape the doctor's wrath. As we three followed her up the stairs she spilled forth lengthy excuses so we'd understand how difficult it was to handle so many mischievous girls. When we finally entered Carrie's room several students trailed behind us, whispering back and forth about how much Chris and I looked like Carrie, only we weren't 'so freakishly small'.

Chris turned to scowl at them. 'No wonder she hates it here if you can say things like that!'

'We'll find her,' assured Chris. 'If we have to stay all week and torture each little witch here we'll make them tell us where she is.'

'Young man,' shot out Miss Dewhurst, 'nobody tortures my girls but me!'

I knew Carrie better than anyone and around the grooves of her brain I ambled. Now, if I were Carrie's age, would I try to escape a school that had unjustly kept me from going home? Yes! *I* would do exactly that. But I was not Carrie; I would not run away in only a nightgown. All her little uniforms were there, custom-sewn by Henny, and her small sweaters, skirts and blouses, and pretty dresses, all there. Everything she'd brought to this school was in its proper place. Only the porcelain dolls were missing.

Still on my knees before Carrie's dresser, I sat back on my heels and looked up at Paul and showed him the box that contained nothing but cotton wadding and sticks of wood. 'Her dolls aren't here,' I said dully, not comprehending the sticks at all, 'and as far as I can tell the only article of her clothing that's missing is one of her nightgowns. Carrie wouldn't go outside wearing only her nightgown. She's got to be here – somewhere no one has looked.'

'We have looked *everywhere*!' Miss Dewhurst spoke impatiently, as if I had no voice in this matter, only the guardian, the doctor, whose favour she sought even while Paul turned on her another of his stern, hard looks.

For some reason I can't explain I swivelled my head about and caught a cat-who's-eaten-the-canary look on the pale and sickly face of a frizzled, rust-haired, skinny girl whom I detested merely from hearing the little Carrie had told me about her room-mate. Maybe it was just her eyes, or the way she kept fingering the big square pocket of her organdie pinafore that narrowed my own eyes as I tried to pierce the depths of hers. She blanched and shifted her green eyes towards the windows, shuffled her feet about uneasily and quickly yanked her hand from her pocket. It was a lined pocket and it bulged suspiciously.

'You,' I said, 'you're Carrie's room-mate, aren't you?'

'I was,' she murmured.

'What is that you have in your pocket?'

Her head jerked towards me. Her eyes sparked green fire as the muscles near her lips twitched. 'None of your business!'

'Miss Towers!' whiplashed Miss Dewhurst. 'Answer Miss Dollanganger's question!'

'It's my purse,' said Sissy Towers, glaring at me defiantly.

'It's a very lumpy purse,' I said, and suddenly I lunged forward and seized Sissy Towers about the knees. With my free hand, as she struggled and howled, I pulled from her pocket a blue scarf. From that scarf tumbled Mr and Mrs Parkins and baby Clara. I held the three porcelain dolls in my hand and demanded, 'What are you doing with my sister's dolls?'

'They're my dolls!' said the girl, her gimlet eyes narrowing to slits. The girls gathered around began to snicker and made whispering remarks to one another.

'Your dolls? These dolls belong to my sister.'

'You lie! You are stealing from me and my father can have you thrown in jail! Miss Dewhurst,' ordered the small demon, her hand reaching for the dolls, 'you make this person leave me alone! I don't like her, any more than her *dwarf* sister!'

I got to my feet and towered threateningly above her. Protectively I put the dolls behind my back. She'd have to kill me to get to them!

'Miss Dewhurst!' shrieked the imp as she attacked me. '*My mommy and daddy gave me those dolls for my Christmas!*'

'You lying little devil!' I said, itching to slap her defiant face. 'You stole those dolls and the crib from my sister. And because you did Carrie is at this very moment in extreme danger!' I knew it. I felt it. Carrie needed help and fast. 'Where is my sister?' I raged.

I stared hard at that red-haired girl named Sissy, knowing she had the answer to where Carrie was but knowing she'd never tell me. It was in her eyes, her mean, spiteful eyes. It was then that Lacy St John spoke up and told us what they'd done to Carrie the night before.

Oh, God! There was no place in the world more terrifying to Carrie than a roof – any roof! I went reeling back into the past, when Chris and I had tried to take the twins out on the roof of Foxworth Hall so we could hold them in the sunlight and keep them in the fresh air so they'd grow. And like children out of their minds from fright they'd screamed and kicked.

I squeezed my eyelids very tight, concentrating fully on Carrie, where, where, where? And behind my eyes I saw her crouched in a dark corner in what seemed a canyon rising tall on either side of her.

'I want to look in the attic myself,' I said to Miss Dewhurst, and she quickly said they'd already thoroughly searched the attic and called and called Carrie's name. But they didn't know Carrie like I did. They didn't know my small sister could go off to a Never-Never land where speech didn't exist, not when she was in shock.

Up the attic stairs all the teachers, Chris, Paul and I climbed. It was so much like it used to be, a huge, dim and dusty place. But not full of old furniture covered with dusty grey sheets or remnants of the past. Up here were only stacks upon stacks of heavy wooden crates.

Carrie was here. I could sense it. I felt her presence as if she reached out and touched me, though when I looked around I saw nothing but the crates. 'Carrie!' I called as loudly as possible. 'It's me, Cathy. Don't hide and keep quiet because you're afraid! I've got your dolls and Dr Paul is with me and so is Chris. We've come to take you home, and never again are we going to send you away to school!' I nudged Paul, 'Now you tell her that too.'

He abandoned his soft voice and boomed, 'Carrie, if you can hear me, it's just as your sister says. We want you to come home with us to stay. I'm sorry, Carrie. I thought you'd like it here. Now I know you couldn't possibly have been happy. Carrie, please come out, we need you.'

Then I thought I heard a soft whimper. I raced in that direction with Chris close at my heels. I knew about attics, how to search, how to find.

Abruptly I drew to a halt and Chris collided with me. Just ahead, in the dim shadows created by the towers of heavy wooden crates, still in her nightgown, all torn, dirty and bloody, gagged and still blindfolded, I spied Carrie. Her spill of blonde hair gleamed in the faint light. Beneath her a leg was twisted in a grotesque way. 'Oh, God,' whispered Chris and Paul at the same time, 'her leg looks broken.'

'Wait a minute,' Paul cautioned in a low voice, clamping both his hands down on my shoulders when I would heedlessly run forward and rescue Carrie. 'Look at those crates, Cathy. Just one careless move on your part and they will all come crashing down on both you and Carrie.'

Somewhere behind me a teacher moaned and began to pray. How Carrie had managed to drag herself down that close passageway while blind and bound was unbelievable. A fully adult person couldn't have done it – but I could do it – I was still small enough.

Even as I spoke I planned the way. 'Carrie, do exactly as I say. Don't lean to the right or to the left. Lie flat on your stomach, aim for my voice. I'm going to crawl in to you and take hold of you under your arms. Raise your head high so your face won't be scraped. Dr Paul will grab hold of my ankles and pull us both out.'

'Tell her it's going to hurt her leg.'

'Did you hear Dr Paul, Carrie? It's going to hurt your leg so please don't thrash about if you feel pain; everything will be over in a second or two and Dr Paul will make your leg well again.'

It seemed to take hours for me to inch down that tunnel while the crates teetered and rocked, and when I had her by the shoulders I heard Dr Paul cry out, 'Okay, Cathy!' Then he pulled, fast and hard! Down thundered the wooden crates! Dust flew everywhere. In the confusion I was at Carrie's side, removing the gag and blindfold while the doctor untied her bonds.

Then Carrie was clinging to me, blinking because the light hurt, crying from the pain, terrified to see the teachers and her leg so crooked.

In the ambulance that came to take Carrie to the hospital Chris and I rode and shared the same stool, each of us holding one of Carrie's hands. Paul followed in his white car so he'd be there to supervise the orthopaedist who would set Carrie's broken leg. Lying face upward on the pillow near her head with fixed smiles and rigid bodies were Carrie's three dolls. That's when I remembered. Now the crib was missing too, just as the cradle had disappeared years ago.

Carrie's broken leg spoiled the long summer vacation trip our doctor had planned for all of us. Again I raged inwardly at Momma. Her fault; always we were punished for what she'd caused! It wasn't fair that Carrie had to be laid up and we couldn't journey north – while out mother gallivanted from here to there, going to parties, hobnobbing with the jet set and the movie stars as if we didn't exist at all! On the French Riviera now. I cut that item from Greenglenna's society column and pasted it into my huge scrapbook of revenge. That was one article I showed to Chris before I put it into the book. I didn't show him all of them. I didn't want him to know I had subscribed to the Virginia newspaper that reported on everything the Foxworths did.

'Where did you get this?' he demanded, looking up from the clipping he handed back to me.

'The Greenglenna newspaper – it's more concerned with high society than Clairmont's *Daily News*. Our mother is a hot item, didn't you know?'

'I try to forget, unlike you!' he said sharply. 'We don't have it so bad now, do we? We're lucky to be with Paul, and Carrie's leg will mend and be as good as ever. And other summers will come when we can go to New England.'

How did he know that? Nothing was ever offered twice. Maybe in other summers to come we'd be too busy or Paul would. 'You realize, being almost a doctor, don't you, that her leg might not grow while she's in that cast?'

He looked strangely ill-at-ease. 'If she grew like average kids I guess there might be that risk. But, Cathy, she doesn't grow very much, so there's little chance one leg will be shorter than the other.'

'Oh, go bury your nose in *Gray's Anatomy*!' I flared, angry because he'd always make light of anything I said that made Momma the fault of anything. He knew why Carrie didn't grow as well as I did. Deprived of love, of sunshine and freedom, it was a marvel she'd lived to survive! Arsenic too! Damn Momma to hell!

Busily, day by day, I added to my collection of news clippings and blurry photographs cut from many newspapers. That's where most of my 'pin money' went. Though I stared at all the pictures of Momma with hate and loathing, I looked at her husband with admiration. How very handsome, how powerfully built her young husband was with his long, lean, darkly bronzed skin. I stared at the photograph that showed him lifting a champagne glass high as he toasted his wife on their second wedding anniversary.

I decided that night to send Momma a short note. Sent first class, it would be forwarded.

Dear Mrs Winslow,

How well I remember the summer of your honeymoon. It was a wonderful summer, so refreshingly pleasant in the mountains in a locked room with windows that were never opened.

Congratulations and my very best wishes, Mrs Winslow, and I do hope all your future summers, winters, springs and falls will be haunted by the memory of the kind of summers, winters, springs and falls your Dresden dolls used to have.

> Not yours any more,
> The doctor doll,
> The ballerina doll,
> The small doll,
> And the dead doll.

I ran to post the letter and no sooner had I dropped it in the postbox on the corner than I was wishing I had it back. Chris would hate me for doing this.

It rained that night and I got up to watch the storm. Tears streaked my face as much as the rain streaked the window glass. Because it was Saturday Chris was home. He was out there on the veranda, allowing the wind-driven rain to wet his pyjamas and glue them to his skin.

He saw me just about the time I saw him, and he stepped into my room without saying a word. We clung together, me crying and him trying hard not to. I wanted him to go, even as I held hard to him and cried on his shoulder. 'Why, Cathy, why all the tears?' he asked as I sobbed on and on.

'Chris,' I asked when I could, 'you don't still love *her*, do you?'

He hesitated before he answered. That made anger simmer my blood into a rolling boil. '*You do!*' I cried. 'How can you after what she did to Cory and to Carrie? Chris, what's wrong with you that you can go on loving when you should hate as I do?'

Still he didn't say anything. And his very silence gave me the answer. He went on loving her because he had to if he were to go on loving me. Every time he looked in my face he saw her and what she'd been like in her early youth. Chris was just like Daddy, who had been just as vulnerable to the kind of beauty I had. But it was only a surface resemblance. I wasn't weak! I wasn't without abilities! I could have thought of one thousand ways to earn a living, rather than lock my four children in a miserable room and leave them in care of an evil old woman who wanted to see them suffer for sins that weren't even theirs!

While I thought my vengeful thoughts and made my plans to ruin her life when I could, Chris was tenderly kissing me. I hadn't even noticed. 'Stop!' I cried when I felt his lips pressing down on mine. 'Leave me alone! You don't love me like I want to be loved, for what I am. You love me because my face is like hers! Sometimes I hate my face!'

He looked terribly wounded as he backed towards the door. 'I was only trying to comfort you,' he said in a broken voice. 'Don't turn it into something ugly.'

My fear that Carrie's leg would come out of the cast shorter than the other proved groundless. In no time at all after her leg was cut free from the plaster she was walking around as well as ever.

As fall neared, Chris, Paul and I conferred and decided that a public school where Carrie could come home every afternoon would be best for her after all. All she'd have to do was board a bus three blocks from home; the same bus would bring her home at three in the afternoon. In Paul's big homey kitchen she'd stay with Henny while I attended ballet class.

Soon September was upon us again, then November had gone by, and still Carrie hadn't made a single friend. She wanted most desperately to belong, but always she was an outsider. She wanted someone as dear as a sister but she found only suspicion, hostility and ridicule. It seemed Carrie would walk the long halls of that elementary school forever before she found a friend.

'Cathy,' Carrie would tell me, 'nobody likes me.'

'They will. Sooner or later they will know how sweet and wonderful you are. And you have all of us who love and admire you so don't let others worry you. Don't care what they think!' She sniffed, for she did care, she did!

Carrie slept on her twin bed pushed close beside mine, and every night I saw her kneel beside her bed, temple her small hands under her chin, and with lowered head she prayed, 'And please, God, let me find my mother again. My real mother. And most of all, Lord God, let me grow just a little bit taller. You don't have to make me as tall as Momma, but almost as tall as Cathy, please God, please, please.'

Lying on my bed and hearing this, I stared bleakly up at the ceiling and I hated Momma, really despised and loathed her! How could Carrie still want a mother who'd been so cruel? Had Chris and I done right in sparing her the grim truth of how our own mother had tried to kill us? How she'd caused Carrie to be as small as she was?

Carrie placed all her unhappiness and loneliness upon her smallness. She knew she had a pretty face and sensational hair, but what did they matter when the face and the hair were on a head much too large for the thin little body? Carrie's beauty did nothing at all to win her friends and admiration, just the opposite. 'Doll face, Angel Hair. Hey you, midget, or are you a dwarf? Are you going to join a circus and be their littlest freak?' And home she'd run, all three blocks from the bus stop, scared and crying, tormented again by children without sensitivity.

'I'm no good, Cathy!' she wailed with her face buried in my lap. 'Nobody likes me. They don't like my body 'cause it's too little, and they don't like my head 'cause it's too big, and they don't even like what is pretty 'cause they think it's wasted on somebody too little like me!'

I said what I could to comfort her but I felt so inadequate. I knew she watched my every movement and compared my proportions to hers. She realized I was very much in proportion and how much she was constructed grotesquely.

If I could have given her a part of my height, gladly I would have done so. Instead, I gave her my prayers. Night after night, I too went down on my knees and prayed to God, 'Please let Carrie grow! Please, God, she's so young, and it hurts her so much, and she's been through so much. Be kind. Look down, God! See us! Hear us!'

One afternoon Carrie went to the only one who could deliver almost everything – so why not size?

Paul was sitting on his back veranda, sipping wine, nibbling cheese and crackers. I was at ballet class, so I heard only Paul's version of what happened.

'She came to me, Cathy, and asked if I didn't have a stretching machine to pull her out longer.'

I sighed when he told me.

' "If I had such a machine," I told her' – and I knew he'd done it with love, kindness and understanding, not with mockery – ' "it would be a very painful process. Have patience, darling, you're taller than you were when you came. Time will make you grow. Why, I've seen the shortest young people suddenly just shoot up overnight after they reach puberty." She stared at me with those big blue haunted eyes and I saw her disappointment. I had failed her. I could tell from the way she ambled off with her shoulders drooping and her head hung so low. Her hopes must have ridden high when those cruel kids at her school chided her about finding a "stretching machine".'

'Isn't there one thing modern medicine can do to help her grow?' I asked Paul.

'I'm looking into it,' he said in a tight voice. 'I'd give my soul to see Carrie reach the height she wants. I'd give her inches of my height, if only I could.'

MOMMA'S SHADOW

We had been with our doctor for one year and a half, and what exhilarating and baffling days they were. I was like a mole coming out of darkness only to find the brilliant days weren't at all like I had supposed they would be.

I'd thought once we were free of Foxworth Hall and I was almost an adult life would lead me down a clear and straight path to fame, fortune and happiness. I had the talent; I saw that in the admiring eyes of Madame and Georges. Madame especially harped on every little flaw of technique, of control. Every criticism told me I was worth all her efforts to make me not only an excellent dancer but a sensational one.

During summer vacation Chris obtained a job as a waiter in a café from seven in the mornings to seven in the evenings. In August he would leave again for Duke University where he would begin his second year in college. Carrie fiddled away her time playing on the swing, playing with her little-girl toys, though she was ten now and should be outgrowing dolls. I spent five days a week in ballet class, and half of Saturday. My small sister was like a shadow tagging after me when I was at home. When I wasn't she was Henny's shadow. She needed a playmate of her own age but she couldn't find one. She had only the porcelain dolls to confide in now that she felt too old to act the baby with Chris and me, and suddenly she stopped complaining about her size. But her eyes, those sad, sad yearning eyes, told how she longed to be as tall as the girls we saw walking in the shopping malls.

Carrie's loneliness hurt so much that again I thought of Momma and damned her to everlasting hell! I hoped she was hung over the eternal fires by her heels and prodded by imps with spears.

More and more often I was writing Momma short notes to torment her sunny life wherever she was. She never settled down in one place long enough to receive my letters, or if she did she didn't respond. I waited for the letters to come back stamped ADDRESS UNKNOWN but none ever did.

I read the Greenglenna newspaper carefully every evening, trying to find out just what my mother was up to and where she was. Sometimes there was news.

Mrs Bartholomew Winslow left Paris and flew on to Rome. I cut out that clipping and added it to my scrapbook. Oh, what I would do when I met up with her! Sooner or later she'd have to come to Greenglenna and live in that home of Bart Winslow's which was newly repaired, redecorated and refurbished. I cut out that news article too and stared long and hard at a photograph which was not flattering. This was unusual. Customarily she could put on a brilliant smile to show the world how happy and contented she was with her life.

Chris left for college in August, two weeks before I went back to high school. In late January I would graduate. I couldn't wait to be finished with high school so I studied like mad.

The autumn days flew swiftly by, so much in contrast to other autumns when time had crept monotonously while we grew older and youth was stolen from us. Just keeping track of my mother's activities kept me busy, and then when I really put my nose on the trail of Bart's family history I used up more of my precious time.

In Greenglenna I pored for hours over old books written about the founding families of Greenglenna. His ancestors had arrived just about the same time mine had, back in the eighteenth century, and they too had been from England, settling down in Virginia in the part that was now North Carolina. I looked up and stared into space. After the Revolution the Winslows had moved to South Carolina. How odd. Now the Foxworths too were in South Carolina.

Not a day passed as I shopped and travelled on the busy streets of Greenglenna that I didn't expect to see my mother. I stared after every blonde I saw. I went into expensive shops looking for her. Snobbish salesladies would come up silently behind me and enquire if they could help. Of course they couldn't help. I was looking for my mother, and she wasn't hanging from a clothes rack. But she was in town! The society column had given me this information. Any day I would see her!

One sunny Saturday I was rushing to do an errand for Madame Marisha when I suddenly spotted on the sidewalk ahead of me a man and a woman so familiar my heart almost stopped beating! It was them! Just to see her strolling so casually at his side, enjoying herself, put me in a state of panic! Sour gall rose in my throat. I dared to draw nearer, so I was very close behind them. If she turned she'd be sure to see me – and what would I do then? Spit in her face? Yes, I would like to do that. I could trip her and make her fall and watch how she lost her dignity. That would be nice. But I didn't do anything but tremble and feel ill as I listened to them talk.

Her voice was so soft and sweet, so cultivated and genteel. I marvelled at how svelte she still was, how lovely her pale, gleaming hair that waved softly back from her face. When she turned her head to speak again to the man at her side I saw her profile. I sighed. Oh, God, my mother in that expensive, rose-coloured suit. The beautiful mother I had loved so well. My murdering mother who could still take my heart and wring it dry, for once I had loved her so very much and trusted her ... and deep inside of me was that little girl, like Carrie, who still wanted a mother to love. Why, Momma? Why did you have to love money more than you loved your children?

I stifled the sob that she might have heard. My emotions raged out of control. I wanted to run up and scream accusations before her husband, and shock him and terrify her! I also wanted to run up and throw my arms about her, cry out her name and plead that she love me again. But all the tempestuous emotions I felt were submerged in the tidal wave of spite and vengeance I felt. I didn't accost her, for I wasn't ready to face her yet. I wasn't rich or famous. I wasn't anybody special and she was still a great beauty. She was one of the wealthiest women in the area and also one of the luckiest.

I dared much that day but they didn't turn to see me. My mother was not the type to look behind her or stare at passers-by. She was accustomed to being the one who drew all the admiring glances. Like a queen among peasants she strolled as if no one was on the street but her and her young husband.

When I had my fill of viewing her, I looked at her husband and drank up the special kind of virile handsomeness that was his. He no longer sported a huge thick moustache. His dark hair was waved smoothly back and was styled modishly. He reminded me a bit of Julian.

I followed where they led, daring fate to let them see me. They were here, living in the home of Bart Winslow. As I tagged along, full of vengeful schemes, despising her, admiring him, I planned which way to hurt her most. And what did I do – I chickened out! I did nothing, absolutely nothing! Furious with myself I went home and raged in front of the mirror, hating my image because it was her all over! Damn her to hell! I picked up a heavy paperweight from the special little French provincial desk Paul had bought me and I hurled it straight at the mirror! *There, Momma! You're broken in pieces now! Gone, gone, gone!* Then I was crying, and later a workman came and replaced the glass in the mirror frame. Fool, that's what I was. Now I'd wasted some of the money I was planning to use for a wonderful gift for Paul's forty-second birthday.

Some day I'd get even, and in a way in which I wouldn't be hurt. It would be more than just a broken mirror. Much, much more.

A BIRTHDAY GIFT

Medical conventions ruined many a plan of mine, as did patients. On this unique day I skipped ballet class to rush straight home from high school. I found Henny in the kitchen slaving over a gourmet menu I had planned – all Paul's favourite dishes. A Creole jambalaya with shrimp, crabmeat, rice, green bellpeppers, onions, garlic, mushrooms and so many other things I thought I'd never finish measuring out half teaspoons of this and that. Then all the mushrooms and other vegetables had to be sautéed. It was a troublesome dish I wasn't likely to make again.

No sooner was this in the oven than I began another cake from scratch. The first was sunk in the middle and was soggy. I covered up the hollow with thick frosting and gave it to the neighbourhood kids. Henny bustled and bumbled around, shaking her head and throwing me critical glances.

I had the last rose squeezed from the pastry tube when Chris dashed in the back door bearing his gift. 'Am I late?' he asked breathlessly. 'I can't stay longer than nine o'clock; I have to be back at Duke before roll call.'

'You're just in time,' I said, all flustered and in a flurry to get upstairs and bathe and dress. 'You set the table while Henny finishes up with the salad.' It was beneath his dignity, of course, to set a table, but for once he obliged without complaint.

I shampooed my hair and set it on large rollers, and polished my nails a glowing, silvery pink, my toenails too. I painted my face with an expertise born of hours of practice and long consultations with Madame Marisha and the beauty assistants in the department stores. When I was done no one would have guessed I was only seventeen. Down the stairs I drifted, borne aloft by the admiration that shone from my brother's eyes and by the envy from Carrie's and a big grin that split Henny's face from ear to ear.

Fussily I arranged the table again, changing around the noise-makers, the crackers and the colourful, ridiculous paper clown hats. Chris blew up a few balloons and suspended them from the chandelier. And then we all sat down to wait for Paul to come and enjoy his surprise party.

When he didn't show up and the hours passed, I got up to pace the floor as Momma had done at Daddy's thirty-sixth birthday party when he never came home, not ever.

Finally Chris had to leave. Then Carrie began to yawn and complain. We fed her and let her go to bed. She slept in her own room now, especially decorated in purple and red. Next it was only Henny and me watching TV as the Creole casserole kept warming and drying out, and our salad was wilting, and then Henny yawned and left for bed. Now I was left alone to pace and worry, my party ruined.

At ten I heard Paul's car turn into the drive and through the back door he strode, bearing with him the two suitcases he'd taken to Chicago. He tossed me a casual greeting before he noticed my fancy attire. 'Hey . . .' he said, throwing a suspicious glance into the dining room and seeing the party decorations, 'have I somehow managed to spoil something you planned?'

He was so damned casual about being three hours late I could have killed him if I hadn't loved him so much. Like those who always try to hide the truth, I lit into him. 'Why did you have to go to that medical convention in the first place? You might have guessed we'd have special plans for your birthday! And then you go and call us up and tell us what time to expect you home, and then you're three hours late –'

'My flight was delayed –' he started to explain.

'I've been slaving to make you a cake that tastes as good as your mother's,' I interrupted, *'and then you don't show up!'* I brushed past him and pulled out the casserole in the oven.

'I'm ravenous,' said Paul humbly, apologetically. 'If you haven't eaten, we might as well make the most of what looks like it could have been a very festive and happy occasion. Have mercy on me, Cathy. I don't control the weather.'

I nodded stiffly to indicate I was at least a little understanding.

He smiled and lightly brushed the back of his hand over my cheek, 'You look absolutely exquisite,' he breathed softly, 'so take the frown off your face and get things ready, and I'll be down in ten minutes.'

In ten minutes he had showered and shaved and changed into fresh clothes. By the light of four candles the two of us sat down at the long dining table with me to his left. I had arranged this meal so I wouldn't have to hop up and down to serve him. Everything that was needed was put upon a serving cart. The dishes that had to be served hot were on electrical heating units, and the champagne was cooling in a bucket. 'The champagne is from Chris,' I explained. 'He's developed a liking for it.'

He lifted the champagne bottle from the ice and glanced at the label. 'It's a good year and must have been expensive; your brother has developed gourmet tastes.'

We ate slowly and it seemed whenever I lifted my eyes they met with his. He'd come home looking tired, mussy; now he looked completely refreshed. He'd been gone two long, long weeks. Dead weeks that made me miss his presence in the open doorway of my bedroom as I practised at the barre, doing my warm-up exercises before breakfast to beautiful music that sent my soul soaring.

When our meal was over I dashed into the kitchen, then glided back bearing a gorgeous coconut cake with miniature green candles fitted into red roses made of icing. Across the top I'd written as skilfully as I could with that pastry tube, *Happy Birthday to Paul*.

'What do you think?' Paul asked after he blew out the candles.

'Think about what?' I questioned back, carefully setting down the cake with twenty-six candles, for that was the age he appeared to me, and the age I wanted him to be. I felt very much an adolescent, floundering in the world of adult quicksand. My short, formal gown was flame-coloured chiffon, with shoestring straps and lots of cleavage showing. But if my attempts to look sophisticated had succeeded, inside I was in a daze as I tried to play the role of seductress.

'My moustache – surely you've noticed. You've been staring at it for half an hour.'

'It's nice,' I stammered, blushing as red as my gown. 'It becomes you.'

'Now ever since you came you've been hinting how much more handsome and appealing I'd be with a moustache. And now that I've taken the trouble to grow one you say it's *nice*. Nice is such a weak word, Catherine.'

'It's because ... because you do look so handsome,' I stumbled, 'that I can find only weak words. I fear that Thelma Murkel has already found all the strong words to flatter you.'

'How the hell do you know about her?' He fired this at me as he narrowed his beautiful eyes.

Gosh, he should know – gossip – and so I told him this: 'I went to that hospital where Thelma Murkel is the head nurse on the third floor. And I sat just beyond the nurses' station and watched her for a couple of hours. In my opinion she's not quite beautiful, but handsome, and she seemed to me terribly bossy. And she flirts with all the doctors, in case you don't know that.'

I left him laughing with his eyes lit up. Thelma Murkel was a head nurse in the Clairmont Memorial Hospital and everyone there seemed to know she had her mind set on becoming the second Mrs Paul Scott Sheffield. But she was only a nurse in a sterile white uniform, miles and miles away, and I was under his nose, with my intoxicating new perfume tickling his senses (as the advertisement had said, a bewitching, beguiling, seductive scent no man could resist). What chance did Thelma Murkel, age twenty-nine, have against the likes of me?

I was giddy from three glasses of Chris's imported champagne and hardly alert at all when Paul began to open the gifts Carrie, Chris and I had saved up to buy for him. I'd embroidered for him a crewel painting of his gingerbread white house with trees showing above the roof and a part of the brick wall to the sides with a little of the flowers showing. Chris had sketched it for me and I'd slaved many hours to make it perfect.

'It's a stunningly beautiful work of art!' he said with impressed awe. I couldn't help but think of the grandmother, and how she'd cruelly rejected our tedious and hopeful gesture to win her friendship. 'Thank you very much, Catherine, for thinking so much of me. I'm going to hang it in my office where all my patients can see it.'

Tears flooded my eyes, smeared my mascara as I furtively tried to blot them away before he realized it wasn't just the candlelight making me this beautiful, but three hours of preparation. He didn't notice the tears or my handkerchief that came from the cleavage of my low-cut gown. He was still admiring the small stitches I'd so carefully made. He put the gift aside, caught my glance with his own shining eyes and stood to help me up. 'It's too beautiful a night to go to bed,' he said as he glanced at his watch. 'I've got a yearning to walk in the garden by moonlight. Do you ever have yearnings like that?'

Yearnings? I was made of yearnings, half of them adolescent and too fanciful to ever come true. Yet as I strolled by his side through the magic of his Japanese garden and over the little red-lacquered footbridge, and as we ascended marble steps and walked on hand in hand, I felt we'd both entered a magical Never-Never-land. It was the marble statues, of course, life-size marble statues standing in their cold and perfect nudity.

The breezes were blowing the Spanish moss, and Paul had to duck to escape it, while I could stand straight and smile because having height did cause a few problems I could escape. 'You're laughing at me, Cath-er-ine,' he said, just as Chris used to tease, and separate my name into slow and distinct syllables. *My lady Cath-er-ine.*

I ran on ahead and down the marble steps. Everything seemed silvery-bluish and unreal, and the moon was big and bright, full and smiling, with long dark clouds streaking its face and making it seem sinister one moment and gay the next. I sighed, for it was like that strange night that put Chris and me up on the roof of Foxworth Hall, both of us fearful we'd roast over the eternal fires of Hell.

'It's a pity you are here with me and not with that beautiful boy you dance with,' said Paul, yanking me back from thoughts of yesterday.

'Julian?' I asked in surprise. 'He's in New York this week – but I suspect he'll be back again next week.'

'Oh,' he said. 'Then next week will belong to him, and not me.'

'That all depends ...'

'On what?'

'Sometimes I want him and sometimes I don't. Sometimes he seems just a boy and I want a man. Then again, sometimes he's very sophisticated and that impresses me. And when I dance with him I fall madly in love with the prince he's supposed to be. He looks so splendid in those costumes.'

'Yeah,' he said, 'I've noticed that myself.'

'His hair is jet black, while yours is sort of brownish smoky black.'

'I suppose jet black is more romantic than brownish smoky black?' he teased.

'That all depends.'

'Catherine, you are female through and through – stop giving me enigmatic answers.'

'I'm not enigmatic, I'm just telling you love isn't enough, nor romance. I want skills to see me through life so I'll never have to lock away my children to inherit a fortune I didn't earn. I want to know how to earn a buck and see us through, even if we don't have a man to lean on and support us.'

'Catherine, Catherine,' he said softly, taking both my hands in his and holding them tight. 'How hurt you've been by your mother. You sound so adult, so hard. Don't let bitter memories deprive you of one of your greatest assets – your soft, loving ways. A man likes to take care of the woman he loves and his children. A man likes to be leaned on, looked up to, respected. An aggressive, domineering woman is one of God's most fearsome creatures.'

I yanked free of him and ran on to the swing and threw myself down on the seat. I pushed myself high, higher, fast, faster, flying so high it took me back to the attic and the swings there when the nights were long and stuffy. Now here I was, free, on the outside and swinging crazily to put myself *back* into the attic! It was seeing Momma and her husband again that was making me desperate, making me want what should be put off until I was older.

I flew so high, so wildly, with such abandon that my skirts fanned up into my face and made me blind. Dizzy, I suddenly fell to the ground! Paul came running to my side, falling down on his knees to lift me up in his arms. 'Are you hurt?' he asked, and kissed me before I could answer. No, not hurt. I was a dancer who knew how to fall. He started murmuring the love words I needed to hear between his kisses that came slower and lasted longer, and the look in his eyes made me fill with a drunkenness far headier and far more sparkling than any imported French champagne.

My lips parted beneath his prolonged kiss. I gasped because his tongue touched mine. His kisses came hot, soft, moist on my eyelids, my cheeks, my chin, neck, shoulders, cleavage as his hands endlessly roamed and sought all my most intimate places.

'Catherine,' he gasped, pulling away and gazing down at me with his eyes on fire, 'you're only a child. We can't let this happen. I swore I'd never let this happen, not with you.' Useless words that I snuffed out by encircling his neck with my arms. My fingers sank into the thickness of his dark hair as I murmured huskily, 'I wanted to give you a shiny silver Cadillac for your birthday, but I didn't have enough money. So I thought I'd give you second best – me.'

He moaned softly. 'I can't let you do this – *you don't owe me.*' I laughed and kissed him, shamelessly kissed him long and deep.

'Paul, it's *you* who owes me! You've given me too many long, desiring looks to tell me you don't want me now. If you say that you're lying. You think of me as a child. But I grew up a long time ago. Don't love me, I don't care. For I love you and that's enough. I know you'll love me the way I want to be loved, because even though you won't admit it, you do love me and want me.'

The moon lit up his eyes and made them shine. Even as he said, 'No, you're a fool to think it will work,' his eyes were speaking differently.

To my way of thinking, his very restraint proved exactly how very much he *did* love me. If he had loved me less he would have eagerly taken long ago what I wouldn't have denied. So when he made a move to rise, to leave me and have done with temptation, I took his hand and put it where it would pleasure me most. He groaned. And groaned even louder when I put *my* hand where it would pleasure *him* most. Shameless what I did, I knew it. I shut off my thoughts of what Chris would think, of how the grandmother would consider me a scarlet harlot. Oh, was it fortunate or just the opposite that that book in Momma's nightstand drawer had shown me well what to do to pleasure a man and how to respond?

I thought he would take me there on the grass under the stars, but he picked me up and carried me back into the house. Up the back stairs he stole quietly. Neither of us spoke though my lips travelled over his neck and face. Far off, in the room to the rear of the kitchen, I could hear Henny's TV as she listened to a late-night talkshow.

On his bed he laid me down and with his eyes alone he began his lovemaking, and in his eyes I drowned, and things grew blurry as my emotions swelled higher like a tidal wave engulfing both of us. Skin to skin we pressed, just holding close at first and thrilling in the exaltation of sharing what the other had to give. With each touch of his lips, of his hands I was shot through with electrifying sensations, until at last I was wild to have him enter me, no longer tender, but fervent with his own fierce, demanding need to reach the same heights I was seeking.

'Catherine! Hurry, hurry, *come!*'

What was he talking about? I was there beneath him, doing what I could. Come where? He was slippery and wet with sweat. My legs were raised and clutched about his waist and I could feel the terrible effort of his restraint as he kept telling me to come, come, come! Then he groaned and gave up.

Hot juices spurted forth to warm up my insides pleasantly five or six times, and then it was over, all over, and he was pulling out. And I hadn't reached any mountain high, or heard bells ringing, or felt myself exploding – not as he had. It was all over his face, relaxed and at peace now, vaguely smeared with joy. How easy for men, I thought, while I still wanted more. There I was on the verge of everything and it was all over. All over but for his sleepy hands that roamed over my body, exploring all hills and crevices before he fell asleep. Now his heavy leg was thrown over mine. I was left staring up at the ceiling with tears in my eyes. *Goodbye, Christopher Doll – now you are set free.*

Sunlight through the window wakened me early. Paul was propped up on an elbow gazing dreamily down at me. 'You are so beautiful, so young, so desirable. You aren't sorry, are you? I hope you don't wish now you had done it differently?'

I snuggled closer against his bare skin. 'Explain one thing, please. Why did you keep asking me to come?' He roared with laughter.

'Catherine, my love,' he finally managed. 'I nearly killed myself trying to hold back until you could climax. And now you lie there with those big innocent blue eyes and ask what I meant! I thought those dancing playmates of yours had explained everything to you. Don't tell me there is one subject you haven't read about in a book!'

'Well, there was a book I found in Momma's table drawer . . . But I just looked at the photographs. I never read the text, though Chris did, but then he stole more often to her bedroom suite than I did.'

He cleared his throat. 'I could tell you what I meant by what I said, but demonstrating would be more fun. Really, you don't have the least idea?'

'Yes,' I said defensively, 'of course I do. I'm supposed to feel stunned by lightning bolts so I stiffen out and go unconscious and then I'm split wide apart into atoms that float around in space and then gather together and sizzle me with tingles so I can float back to reality with dream-stars in my eyes – like you had.'

'Catherine, don't make me love you too much.' He sounded serious, as if I'd hurt him if he did.

'I'll try to love you the way you want.'

'I'll shave first,' he said, throwing back the covers and making ready to get up.

I reached to pull him back. 'I like the way you look now, so dark and dangerous.'

Eagerly I surrendered to all Paul's desires. We developed delicate ways of keeping our trysts secret from Henny. On Henny's day off I washed the bed linens that were duplicates of the ones soiled that I hid away until they could be washed. Carrie could have been in another world she was so unobservant. But when Chris was home we had to be more discreet and not even look at each other, lest we betray ourselves. I felt strange with Chris now, like I'd betrayed him.

I didn't know how long the rapture between Paul and me would last. I longed for passion undying, for ecstasy everlasting. Yet my suspicious self guessed nothing as glorious as what Paul and I had could go on indefinitely. He would soon tire of me, a child whose mental capacities couldn't compete with his, and he'd go back to his old ways – maybe with Thelma Murkel. Maybe Thelma Murkel had gone with him to that medical convention, though I was wise enough not to question him ever about what he did when I wasn't with him. I wanted to give him everything Julia had denied, and give gladly with no recriminations when we parted.

But in the moment of our flaming obsession with each other I felt so large, so generous, and I gloated in our selfless abandonment. And I think the grandmother with her talk of evil and sin had made it ten times more exciting because it was so very, very wicked.

And then again I'd flounder, not wanting Chris to think I was wicked. Oh, it mattered so much to me what Chris would think. *Please, God, let Chris know why I'm doing this. And I do love Paul, I do!*

After Thanksgiving Chris still had a few days of vacation, and while we were at the dinner table with Henny hovering nearby, Paul asked all of us what we wanted for Christmas. This would be our third Christmas with Paul. In late January I'd be graduating from high school. I didn't have much time to go, for my next step, I hoped, would be New York.

I spoke up and told Paul what I wanted for Christmas. I wanted to go to Foxworth Hall. Chris's eyes widened and Carrie began to cry. 'No!' said Chris firmly. 'We will not open healed wounds!'

'*My wounds are not healed!*' I stated just as firmly. '*They will never be healed until justice is done!*'

FOXWORTH HALL, FROM THE OUTSIDE

The minute the words left my mouth he shouted, '*No!* Why can't you let bygones be bygones?'

'*Because I am not like you, Christopher!* You like to pretend that Cory didn't die of arsenic poisoning, but of pneumonia, because you feel more comfortable with that! Yet you were the one who convinced me *she* was the one who did it! So why can't we go up there and see for ourselves if any hospital has a record of Cory's death?'

'Cory could have died of pneumonia. He had all the symptoms.' How lamely he said that, knowing full well he was protecting her.

'Now wait a minute,' said Paul who had kept quiet, and spoke only when he saw the fire blazing from my eyes. 'If Cathy feels she must do this thing, why not, Chris? Though if your mother admitted Cory to a hospital under a false name it won't be easy to check up.'

'She had a fake name put on his tombstone too,' said Chris, giving me a long, hateful look. Paul gave that some thought, wondering aloud how we could find a grave when we didn't know the name. I believed I had all the answers. If she registered Cory in a hospital for treatment under a certain name, then naturally she'd use the same name when he was buried. 'And Paul, since you're a doctor you can gain entry to all the hospital records, right?'

'You really want to do this?' he asked. 'It's sure to bring back a lot of unhappy memories and, like Chris just said, open up healed wounds.'

'My wounds are *not* healed, and will never be healed! I want to put flowers on Cory's grave. I think it will comfort Carrie to know where he's buried, then we can visit him from time to time. Chris, you don't have to go if you are so dead set against it!'

What I wanted Paul tried to deliver, despite Chris's oppo-sition. Chris did travel with us to Charlottesville, riding in the back seat with Carrie. Paul went inside several hospitals and charmed the nurses into giving him the records he wanted. He looked and I looked while Carrie and Chris stayed outside. Not one eight-year-old boy had died of pneumonia two years ago in late October! Not only that, the cemeteries didn't have a record of a child his age being buried! Still stubbornly determined, I had to trek through all the cemeteries, feeling Momma might have lied and put Dollanganger on his headstone after all. Carrie cried, for Cory was supposed to be in heaven, not in the ground lightly frosted with a recent snowfall.

Fruitless, time-consuming, unrewarding waste! As far as the world was concerned, no male child of eight years had died in the months of October and November 1960! Chris insisted we go back to Paul's. He tried to persuade me that I didn't really want to see Foxworth Hall.

I whirled to glare at Chris. '*I do want to go there! We do have time!* Why come this far and turn back without seeing that house? At least once in the daylight, on the outside – why not?'

It was Paul who reasoned with Chris by telling him I needed to see the house. 'And to be honest, Chris, I'd like to see it myself.'

Brooding sullenly in the back seat beside Carrie, Chris relented. Carrie cried as Paul headed his car towards the climbing mountain roads that Momma and her husband must have traversed thousands of times. Paul stopped at a gas station to ask directions to Foxworth Hall. We could have easily guided Paul to The Hall, if we knew where the train tracks were and could find the mail depot that was a stop-off point.

'Beautiful country,' said Paul as he drove. Eventually we did came upon that grand house that sat all alone on a mountain-side. 'That's the one!' I cried, terribly excited. It was huge as a hotel, with double wings that jutted out front and back from the long main stem constructed of pink brick with black shutters at all the windows. The black slate roof was so sharply pitched it looked scary – how had we ever dared to walk up there? I counted the eight chimneys, the four sets of dormer windows in the attic.

'Look over there, Paul,' I directed, pointing out the two windows on the northern wing where we had been held prisoners for so long, waiting endlessly for our grandfather to die.

While Paul stared at those two windows, I looked up at the dormer windows of the attic and saw that the fallen slat from one of the black shutters had been replaced. There wasn't a scorch mark anywhere or signs of a fire. The house hadn't burned! God hadn't sent an errant breeze to blow the candle flame until it caught a dangling paper flower on fire. God wasn't going to punish our mother or the grandmother, not for anything!

All of a sudden Carrie let out a loud howl. 'I want Momma!' she screamed. 'Cathy, Chris, that's where we used to live with Cory! Let's go inside! I want Momma, please let me see my real momma!'

It was frightful the way she cried and pleaded. How could she remember the house? It had been dark the night we arrived, with the twins so sleepy they couldn't have seen anything. The morning we stole away it was before dawn and we'd left by the back door. What was it that told Carrie this was our prison of yesteryear? Then I knew. It was the houses lower down the street. We were at the end of the cul-de-sac and up much higher. We'd often peeked out the windows of our locked room and gazed down on all the fine houses. Forbidden to look out of the windows – and yet we dared, on occasion.

What had been accomplished by our long journey? Nothing, nothing at all except more proof that our mother was a liar beyond belief. I mulled it over, day after day.

'Paul,' I asked, my eyes downcast, 'it's not sinful what we're doing, is it? I keep thinking of the grandmother and all her talk of evil. Tell me that love makes this all right.'

'Open your eyes, Cathy,' he said softly. 'Look at what you see.' When I'd looked, he tilted my face upwards and then lifted me so he could hold me close. Holding me in his tight embrace, he began to talk, and every word he said told me our love was beautiful and right.

I couldn't speak. Silently I cried inside, for so easily I could have ended up the prude the grandmother wanted to make of me.

Like a young child I allowed him to comfort me, and do what he would with his kisses and caresses, until the embers always ready between us caught fire and he picked me up and carried me to his bed.

When our passion was sated, I lay in the circle of his arms and thought of all I could do. Things that would have shocked me as a child. Things that once I would have considered terribly gross, ugly, for I had thought then only of the acts and not of the feelings of giving. How strange that people were born so sensual and had to be stifled for so many years. I recalled the first time his tongue had touched me *there* and the electrifying jolt I'd felt.

Oh, I could kiss Paul everywhere and feel no shame, for loving him was better than smelling roses on a sunny summer day, better than dancing to beautiful music with the best of all partners.

That was what loving Paul was like for me when I was seventeen and he was forty-two.

He had restored me and made me whole, and deeper down I shoved the remorse I felt for Cory.

There was hope for Chris, he was alive.

There was hope for Carrie, that she could grow and find love too.

And maybe, if things turned out right – there was hope for me too.

TOWARDS THE TOP

Julian didn't fly down as often as he used to, and his mother and father complained about this. When he did come, he danced better than ever, but not once did I see him glance my way. I had the suspicion, though, he did plenty of looking when he knew I couldn't see him. I was getting better, more disciplined, more controlled . . . and I worked. Oh, how I worked!

From the very first I'd been included in the professional group of the Rosencoff Ballet Company, but only as a member of the *corps de ballet*. This Christmas we were to alternate performances of *The Nutcracker* and *Cinderella*.

Long after the others had gone home I had the dance studio all to myself on a Friday afternoon, and I was lost in the world of the Sugarplum Fairy, intent upon giving this role something different, when suddenly Julian was dancing with me. He was like my shadow, doing what I did, even pirouetting, making a mockery of what I did.

He frowned, then grabbed up a towel to dry his face and hair. I wiggled my toes and started towards the dressing room. I was going out to dinner with Paul that evening.

'Cathy, hold up!' he called. 'I know you don't like me –'

'I don't.'

He grinned wickedly, leaning forward to stare into my eyes. His lips brushed my cheek as I cringed away, then he had me pinioned in his arms, with his palms flat against the wall to prevent my running away. 'You know what, I think you should be the one to dance Clara, or Cinderella.' He tickled under my chin, then kissed near my ear. 'If you're nice to me I could see to it that you dance both lead roles.'

I ducked and ran. 'Come off it, Julian!' I flared. 'Your favours would demand a price . . . and you don't interest me.'

Ten minutes later I had showered and dressed and was ready to leave the building when Julian showed up in his street clothes.

'Cathy, seriously, I think you're ready for New York now. Marisha thinks so too.' His smile was wry, as if his mother's opinion wasn't as worthy as his own. 'No strings attached. Not unless some day you decide you want strings.'

Now I didn't know what to say, so I said nothing. I did get chosen for both the roles for the Rosencoff performances. I thought the other girls would be jealous and resentful, but instead they applauded when it was announced. We all worked well together, making it one merry, hectic time. Then came my début as Cinderella!

Julian didn't even knock before he entered the girls' dressing room to survey me in my costume of rags and tatters. 'Stop being so damned nervous. They're only people out there. You don't think I'd come back here to dance with a girl who wasn't sensational, do you?'

As we stood in the wings his arm stayed about my shoulders, lending me confidence as we both counted towards my cue to go on. His parts didn't come until much later. I couldn't see Paul, Chris, Carrie or Henny out in the darkened audience. I trembled more as the footlights dimmed and the overture was played, and then the curtain rose. My mounting anxiety disappeared and took all my insecurity along with it, as some astonishing kinaesthetic memory took over and I allowed the music to control and direct me. I wasn't Cathy, or Catherine, or anybody but Cinderella! I swept ashes from the hearth and enviously watched two hateful stepsisters prepare for the ball, feeling love and romance would never come into my life.

If I made mistakes, if my technique wasn't perfect, I didn't know it. I was in love with the dance, with performing before a large audience, with being young and pretty, and most of all I was in love with life and all it had to offer outside of Foxworth Hall.

Red, yellow and pink roses came to fill my arms. I thrilled when the audience rose to give us a standing ovation. Three times I handed Julian a rose of a different colour; each time our eyes met and clung. See, his were saying to me mutely, we *do* create magic together! We *are* the perfect dancing partners!

He cornered me again during the buffet party. 'Now you've

had a taste of what it's like,' he said softly and persuasively, his dark eyes pleading. 'Can you give up the applause? Can you keep on staying here, in a hick town, when New York is waiting for you? Cathy, as a team we'll be sensational! We look so right together. I dance with you better than I dance with any other ballerina. Oh, Cathy, you and I could reach the top so much sooner together. I swear to take good care of you. I'll look out for you and never let you feel lonely.'

'I don't know,' I said miserably, though I was lit up inside. 'I have to finish school first – but do you really think I'm good enough? Up there they expect the best.'

'You *are* the best! Trust me, believe in me. Madame Zolta's company isn't the largest, or top rank, but she's got what it takes to make our company rate as high as the larger and older ones – once she has a couple of fantastic dancers like us!'

I asked what Madame Zolta was like. Somehow that made him confident I'd already agreed and, laughing first, he managed to plant a kiss on my lips. 'You're going to adore Madame Zolta! She's Russian and the sweetest, kindest, most gentle little old lady you ever met. She'll be like your mother. [Good God!] She knows everything there is about dance. Life in New York is like living on Mars compared to here, another world, a better world. In no time at all you'll love it. I'll take you to famous restaurants where you'll eat food such as you've never tasted before. I'll introduce you to movie stars, TV celebrities, actors, actresses, authors.'

I tried to resist him by fastening my eyes on Chris, Carrie and Paul, but Julian moved so he blocked out my view. All I could see was him. 'It's the kind of life you were born for, Cathy,' and this time he sounded sincere and deeply earnest. 'Why have you studied and put yourself through so much torture, if not for success? Can you achieve the kind of fame you want here?'

No. I couldn't.

But Paul was here. Chris and Carrie were here. How could I leave them?

'Cathy, come with me to where you belong, behind the footlights, on stage, with roses in your arms. Come with me, Cathy, and make my dreams come true too.'

Oh, he was winning that night, and I was heady with my first success, and even when I wanted to say no, I nodded and said, 'Yes . . . I'll go, but only if you come down here and fly with me. I've never been on a plane, and I wouldn't know where to go once I landed.'

He took me in his arms then, tenderly, and held me as his lips brushed my hair. Over his shoulder, I could see both Chris and Paul staring our way, both of them looking astonished and more than a little hurt.

In January of 1963 I graduated from school. I wasn't particularly brilliant, like Chris, but I'd made it through.

Chris was so clever it was more than likely he'd finish college in three years rather than four. Already he'd won several scholarships to help take the financial burden of his education from Paul's shoulders, though he never mentioned a word about any of us paying him back – for anything. It was understood, though, that Chris would become an associate with Paul when he had his MD. I marvelled that Paul could keep spending on us and never complain, and when I asked, he explained. 'I enjoy knowing I'm helping to contribute to the world the wonderful doctor Chris will make – and the super ballerina you will be one day.' He looked so sad when he said that, so terribly sad. 'As for Carrie, I hope she decides to stay home with me and marry a local boy, so I can see her often.'

'When I'm gone it will be Thelma Murkel for you again, won't it?' I asked with some bitterness, for I wanted him to stay faithful, no matter how many miles I put between us.

'Maybe,' he said.

'You won't love anyone else as much as you love me, say you won't.'

He smiled. 'No. How could I love anyone as much as I love you? No other could dance into my heart the way you did, could she?'

'Paul, don't mock me. Say the word and I won't go. I'll stay.'

'How can I say the words to make you stay when you have to fulfil your destiny? You were born to dance, not to be the wife of a stodgy, small-town doctor.'

Marriage! He'd said wife! He'd never mentioned marriage before.

It was more than awful to tell Carrie I was leaving. Her screams were deafening and pitiful. '*You cannot go!*' she bellowed, tears streaming. '*You promised we would all stay together, and now you and Chris both go away and leave me! Take me too! Take me!*' She beat at me with small fists, kicked at my legs, determined to inflict some pain for what Chris and I were giving her – and already I felt pain enough for the world in leaving her. 'Please try and understand, Carrie, I will be coming back, and Chris will too – you won't be forgotten.'

'I hate you!' she screamed. 'I hate both you and Chris! I hope you die in New York! I hope you both fall down and die!' It was Paul who came to save me.

'You've still got me every day, and Henny,' he said, hefting Carrie's slight weight up in his arms. 'We're not going anywhere. And you'll be the only daughter we have when Cathy is gone. Come, dry your tears, put a smile on your face and be happy for your sister. Remember this is what she'd been striving for all those long years when you were locked up.'

I ached inside as I wondered if I really wanted a dance career as much as I had always thought. Chris threw me a long, sad look then bent to pick up my new blue suitcases. He hurried out the front door trying not to let me see the tears in his eyes. When we all went out, he stood near Paul's white car, his shoulders squared off, his face set, determined not to show any emotion.

Henny had to pile in with the rest of us; she didn't want to be left home to cry alone. Her eloquent brown eyes spoke to me, wishing me good luck as her hands were kept busy wiping the tears from Carrie's face.

At the airport Julian paced back and forth, constantly glancing at his watch. He was afraid I'd back out and wouldn't show up. He looked very handsome in his new suit as his eyes lit up when he saw me approach. 'Thank God, I was thinking I flew down here for nothing – and I wouldn't do this twice.'

The evening before, I'd already said a private goodbye to Paul. His words rang in my ears to haunt me even as I boarded the plane. 'We both knew it couldn't last, Catherine. From the beginning I warned you, April just can't marry with September.'

Chris and Paul followed us up the ramp to help with the many pieces of hand luggage I wouldn't trust to the baggage compartment, and once more I had to hug Paul close. 'Thank you, Catherine,' he whispered so neither Chris nor Julian could overhear, 'for everything. Don't look back with any regrets. Forget about me. Forget all the past. Concentrate on your dancing and wait before you fall in love with anyone – and let it be someone near your own age.'

Choking, I asked, 'And what about you?'

He forced a smile and then a chuckle. 'Don't worry about me. I've got my memories of a beautiful ballerina and that's enough.'

I burst into tears! Memories! What were they? Just something to torture yourself with, that's all! Blindly I turned to find myself locked in Chris's arms. My Christopher Doll who was six feet tall now, my knight, gallant, chivalrous and sensitive. Finally I, could pull away and then he took my hands, both of them, as our gazes met and locked. We too had shared a great deal, even more than Paul and I. *Goodbye my walking, talking, cheerful, chiding, and living set of encyclopedias, my fellow prisoner of hope ... You don't need to cry for me ... Cry for yourself ... or don't cry at all. It's over. Accept it, Chris, like I have, like you have to. You're only my brother. I'm only a sister, and the world is full of beautiful women who'd love you better than I can, or could.*

Every word I didn't speak I knew he heard, and still he kept on looking at me with his heart in his eyes, making me hurt all over.

'Cathy,' he said hoarsely, loud enough for Julian to hear, 'it's not that I'm afraid you won't make it, I'm sure you will if you don't get so damned impulsive! Please don't do anything reckless that you'll regret later on. Promise to think of all the ramifications first before you jump in with both feet. Go easy on sex and love. Wait until you're old enough to know what you want in a man before you choose one.'

I'm sure my smile was crooked, for already I'd chosen Paul. I flicked my eyes from Paul who looked serious, to Julian who was frowning and glaring at Chris, then at Paul. 'You go easy on sex and love too,' I said jokingly to Chris, making sure my tone was light. I hugged him tight once more, hurting to let him go. 'And write to me often, and come to New York with Paul, Carrie and Henny whenever you can – or come alone, but come – promise?'

Solemnly he promised. Our lips met briefly, and then I turned to take my seat near the window. Since this was my first plane trip, Julian graciously gave up that privilege. I waved like mad to my family whom I couldn't even see from the plane window.

Julian, so adroit and adept on stage, was at a loss when it came to handling a girl who sobbed on his shoulder, trembling, already homesick, wishing she wasn't going even before the plane was five thousand feet up. 'You've got me,' he said smoothly. 'Didn't I swear to take care of you? And I will, honest to God. I'll do everything possible to make you happy.' He grinned at me and kissed me lightly. 'And, my love, I'm afraid I exaggerated the charms of Madame Zolta just a wee, wee bit, as you'll soon find out.'

I stared at him. 'What do you mean?'

He cleared his throat and without the slightest embarrassment he told me about his first meeting with the once-famous Russian dancer. 'I don't want to spoil the surprise in store when you meet up with this great beauty, so I'll save that and let you see for yourself. But I'll warn you about this, Madame Z is a toucher. She likes to feel you, your muscles, how hard and firm they are. Would you believe she put her hand directly on my fly to find out the size of what was underneath?'

'No! I don't believe that!'

He laughed merrily and threw his arm about me. 'Oh, Cathy, what a life we're going to live, you and I! What heaven will be ours when you find out you've got sole property rights to the handsomest and most gifted and graceful *danseur* ever born.' He drew me even closer and whispered in my ear, 'And I haven't said a word about the talented lover I am.'

I laughed too – and shoved him away. 'If you aren't the most conceited, arrogant person I've ever met! And I suspect you can be quite ruthless too when it comes to getting what you want.'

'Right on!' he said with a following laugh. 'I'm all of that and more too, as you'll soon find out. After all, wasn't I ruthlessly determined to get you where I want you?'

NEW YORK, NEW YORK

It was snowing when our plane landed in New York. The cold in my nostrils stunned me. I'd forgotten bitter winters like this. The wind howling down those narrow canyons seemed to want to rip the skin from my face. Ice seemed to enter my lungs and shrivel them with constricting pain. I gasped, laughed, turned to glance at Julian who was paying the cab driver, and then I pulled from my coat pocket a red knitted scarf Henny had made for me. Julian took it and helped me swathe it about my head and neck so it half-covered my face. Then I shocked him by pulling from the other pocket a red scarf I had knitted for him.

'Gosh, thanks. I never thought you cared.' He seemed very pleased as he wrapped his neck and ears.

On this day of days the cold had made his cheeks as red as his lips, and with that blue-black hair that curled just above his coat collar and those sparkling dark eyes the sheer beauty of him was enough to steal anyone's breath. 'Okay,' he said, 'pull yourself together, and prepare to meet ballet personified – my sweet, delicate, delicious dance instructor whom you will positively adore.'

Just to be here had me on edge, so I clung as close as possible to Julian, staring at all the people who dared to brave such ferocious weather.

The luggage we'd brought was left in a waiting room of the huge building, and in the flurry of scurrying after Julian I didn't notice much of anything until we were in the office of our ballet mistress Madame Zolta Korovenskov. Her stance, her arrogance immediately reminded me of Madame Marisha. But this woman was much older, if all those wrinkles could be counted as tree-rings to indicate her age.

Queenly stiff she rose from behind a desk that was impressively wide. Coolly, all business, she stalked over to us and looked us over with bead-black eyes as small as those of a mouse.

What hair she had was skinned back from her dry brittle face like fine white floss. She wasn't five feet tall, but radiated six feet of authority. Her half-moon glasses perched precariously on the end of an astonishingly long thin nose. Above those half-discs she peered at us, squinting, so her minute eyes almost disappeared in the crows' feet. Julian was so unlucky as to gain her scrutiny first.

Her puckered little prune mouth drew up like a drawstring purse. I watched and waited for a smile to come and break her parchment skin. I expected her voice to crackle, cackle, witchlike.

'So!' she spat at Julian. 'You take off *when* you want, and come back *when* you want and you expect me to say I'm glad to see you! Bah! Do that one more time and out you go! Who is this girl with you?'

Julian gave the old hag a charming smile, and quickly put his arm about her. 'Madame Zolta Korovenskov, may I introduce you to Miss Catherine Doll, the wonderful dancer I've been telling you about for months and months – and she is the reason why I left without your permission.'

She looked me over with very interested gimlet eyes. 'You come from some nowhere too?' she whiplashed. 'You've got the look of another place, like my black devil here does. He's a very good dancer, but not as good as he thinks. Can I believe him about you?'

'I guess, Madame, you'll just have to watch me dance and judge for yourself.'

'Can you dance?'

'As I said before, Madame, wait and judge for yourself.'

'See, Madame,' Julian said eagerly, 'Cathy's got spirit, fire! You must see her dance. She's so fast she's a blur!'

'Ha!' she snorted, then came to encircle me and next she gave my face such a close scrutiny I was blushing. She felt my arms, my chest, even my breasts, then put her bony hands on my neck and felt the cords. Those audacious hands roamed down the length of my body while I wanted to scream out I wasn't a slave to be sold in the marketplace. I was grateful she didn't put her hand on my crotch as she'd done to Julian. I stood still and endured the inspection and felt all the while a deep, hot blush. She looked up to see it and smiled sarcastically.

When she'd done and I'd been physically appraised and evaluated, she delved the depths of my eyes to drink up my essence. I felt she was trying to absorb my youth with her eyes and drain it from me. Then she was touching my hair. 'When do you plan to marry?' she shot out.

'Sometime when I'm near thirty, maybe, or maybe never,' I answered uneasily. 'But most certainly I'm going to wait until after I'm rich and famous, and the world's best ballerina.'

'Hah! You have many illusions about yourself. Beautiful faces don't usually go with great dancers. Beauty thinks it needs no talent and can feed on itself, so it soon dies. Look at me. Once I was young and a great beauty. What do you see now?'

She was hideous! And she couldn't have ever been beautiful, or there'd be some evidence.

As if sensing my doubt to her claim, she gestured arrogantly to all the photographs on the walls, on her desk, on the tables, bookshelves. All showed the same lovely young ballerina. 'Me,' she proudly informed. I couldn't believe it. They were old photos, brownish in colour, the costumes outdated, and yet she had been lovely. She gave me a wide, amused smile, patted my shoulder and said, 'Good. Age comes to everyone and makes everyone equal. 'Who did you study with before Marisha Rosencoff?'

'Miss Denise Danielle.' I hesitated, fearful of telling her about all the years I'd danced alone and been my own instructor.

'Ah,' she sighed, looking very sad, 'I saw Denise Danielle dance many times, such a brilliant performer, but she made the old mistake and fell in love. End of promising career. Now, all she do is teach.' Her voice rose and fell, quivering, gaining strength, then losing it. 'Big-head Julian says you are a great dancer, but I have to see you dance before I believe, and then I will decide if beauty is its own excuse for being.' Once more she sighed. 'You drink?'

'No.'

'Why is your skin so pale? Do you never go in sun?'

'Too much sun burns me.'

'Ah ... you and your lover boy – afraid of the sun.'

'Julian is *not* my lover!' I said between clenched teeth, shooting him a fierce look, for he must have told her we were.

Not an element of our expressions missed the keen observation of those ebony-bead eyes. 'Julian, did you or did you not tell me you were in love with this girl?'

He flushed and lowered his eyes, and had the decency to look embarrassed for once. 'Madame, the love is all on my side, I'm ashamed to admit. Cathy feels nothing for me ... but she will, sooner or later.'

'Fine,' the old witch said with a birdlike nod. 'You have a big passion for her, she has none for you – that makes for sizzling, sensational dancing on your part. Our box office will overflow. *I see it coming!*'

That was, of course, the reason she took me on, knowing Julian had his unsatisfied lust and knowing I had a smouldering desire to find someone else offstage. Onstage, he was everything beautiful, romantic and sensual – my dream lover. If we could have danced through all our days and nights, we could have set the world on fire. As it was, when he was only himself, with his glib and often smutty tongue, I ran from him. I went to bed each night thinking of Paul prowling his lonely gardens, and refused to let myself dream of Chris.

I was soon ensconced in a small apartment twelve blocks from the dance studio. Two other dancers shared the three small rooms and one tiny bath with me. Two floors above, Julian shared an apartment with two male dancers in rooms no bigger than those we three girls had. His room-mates were Alexis Tarrell and Michael Michelle, both in their early twenties, and both just as determined as Julian to become the best male *danseur* of their generation. I was astonished to find out Madame Zolta considered Alexis the best, and Michael next, and Julian third. I soon found out why she held him back – he had no respect for her authority. He wanted to do everything in his own way, and because of this she punished him.

My room-mates were as different as night and day. Yolanda Lange was half British, half Arab, and the strange combination made for one of the most exotic, dark-haired, sloe-eyed beauties I'd ever seen. She was tall for a dancer, five eight, the same height as my mother. Her breasts, when I saw them, were small hard lumps, all large dark nipples, but she wasn't ashamed of their size. She delighted in walking about naked, showing off, and soon I found out her breasts mirrored her personality – small, hard and mean. Yolanda wanted what she wanted when she wanted it and she'd do anything to get it. She asked me a thousand questions in less than an hour, and in that same hour told me her life story. Her father was a British diplomat who'd married a belly-dancer. She'd lived everywhere, done everything. I immediately disliked Yolanda Lange.

April Summers was from Kansas City, Missouri. She had soft brown hair, blue-green eyes; we were both the same height, five feet four and a half inches. She was shy and seldom did she raise her voice above a whisper. When loud, raucous Yolanda was around, April seemed to have no voice at all. Yolanda liked noise; at all times the record player or the television had to be turned on. April spoke of her family with love, respect and pride, while Yolanda professed hatred for parents who'd pushed her into boarding schools and left her alone on holidays.

April and I became fast friends before our first day together was over. She was eighteen and pretty enough to please any man, but for some strange reason the boys of the academy didn't pay April one whit of attention. It was Yolanda who made them hot and panting, and soon enough I learned why – she was the one who gave out.

As for me, the boys saw me, they asked for dates, but Julian made it clear I wasn't available – I was *his*. He told everyone we were lovers. Though I persistently denied this, he would tell them in private I was old-fashioned and ashamed to admit we were 'living in sin'. He chidingly explained in my very presence, 'It's that old Southern-belle tradition. Gals down South like guys to think they're sweet, shy, demure, but underneath that cool magnolia exterior – sexpots – every one!' Of course they believed him and not me. Why should they believe the truth when a lie was so much more exciting?

I was happy enough though. I adapted to New York as one

native born, rushing about as every New Yorker had to – get there fast, don't waste a second, there was so much to prove before someone else with a pretty face and more talent showed up to knock you off the board. But while I was ahead in the game, it was wild and heady stuff, exhausting and demanding. How grateful I was that Paul kept sending me a weekly cheque, for what I earned at the dance company wouldn't have paid for my cosmetics.

The three of us who shared rooms 416 required at least ten hours of sleep. We got up at dawn to limber up at our home barre before breakfast. Breakfast had to be very light, as was lunch. Only during the last meal of the day, after a performance, could we really satisfy our ravenous appetites. It seemed I was always hungry, that I never had enough to eat. In just one performance in the *corps de ballet* I lost five or six pounds.

Julian was with me constantly, shadowing me too closely, keeping me from dating anyone else. Depending on my mood or state of exhaustion, I was resentful of this, and other times happy to have someone around who wasn't a stranger.

Madame Zolta said one day in June, 'Your name is silly! Change it! Catherine Doll – what kind of name for dancer? An inane, unexciting name – it doesn't suit you at all!'

'Now you wait a minute, Madame!' I snapped back, abandoning my attitude position. 'I chose that name when I was seven and my father liked it. *He* thought it suited me fine, so I'm going to use it, stupid or not!' I longed to tell her Madame Naverena Zolta Korovenskov wasn't exactly what I'd call a lyrical name either.

'Don't argue with me, girl, change it!' She used her ivory walking cane to pound on the floor. But, if I changed my name, how would my mother know when I reached the top? She had to know! Still that wretched little witch in her outdated, silly costume could narrow her fierce dark eyes and lift that cane and brandish it so I was forced to yield, or else! Julian slouched nearby and grinned.

I agreed I would change the spelling of my last name from Doll to Dahl. 'That is better,' she said sourly, 'somewhat.'

Madame Z rode my back. She nagged. She criticized. She

complained if I was innovative and complained when I wasn't. She didn't like the way I wore my hair and said I had too much. 'Cut it off!' she ordered but I refused to snip off even an inch, for I believed my long hair a great asset for the role of Sleeping Beauty. She snorted when I said this. (Snorting was one of her favourite means of expression.) If she hadn't been a wonderfully gifted instructor we'd have all hated her. Her very dour nature forced the best from us, for we so wanted to see her smile. She was also a choreographer, but we had another too who came and went and supervised when he wasn't in Hollywood, in Europe, or off in some remote spot dreaming up new dancing scores.

One afternoon after class, when we dancers were playing about foolishly, I jumped up to dance wildly to a popular song. Madame came in and caught me, then exploded, 'We dance *classical* here! No modern dance here!' Her dry, wrinkled face screwed into a dried, headhunter's belt ornament. 'You, Dahl, explain the difference between classical and modern.'

Julian winked at me, then fell backward to rest on his elbows and cross an elegant ankle over a knee, as he delighted in my discomfort. 'Succinctly, Madame,' I began with my mother's poise, 'the modern form of ballet consists mostly of grovelling about on the floor and posturing, while classical stands up on its toes, whirls, spins, and is never too seductive or awkward. And it tells a story.'

'How right you are,' she said icily. 'Now get you home to bed and posture and grovel there if you feel the need to express yourself in such a manner. Never let me catch you doing such before my eyes again!'

Modern and classical could be blended and made beautiful. The tightness of that small shrew enraged me. 'Find yourself another dancer. *I'm going home!*' I flounced off towards the dressing room, leaving all the dancers standing in shock staring after me.

I ripped off my practice clothes and yanked on underwear. Into the dressing room stalked the grim-faced witch, her eyes mean, her lips pressed tightly together. 'If you go home you never come back!'

'I don't want to come back!'

'You will wither away and die!'

'You're a fool if you think that!' I snapped without regard to her age or respect for her talent. 'I can live my life without dancing, and happily too – so go to hell, Madame Zolta!'

As if a spell had been broken that old hag smiled at me, and sweetly too. 'Ah ... you have spirit. I was wondering if you did. Tell me to go to hell, it is nice to hear. Hell is better than heaven anyway. Now, seriously, Catherine,' she said in a kind tone, kinder than I'd ever heard from her, 'you are a wonderfully gifted dancer, the best I have, but you are so impulsive you abandon the classical and toss in whatever comes to your mind. I only try to teach you. Invent all you want, but keep it classical, elegant, beautiful.' Tears glistened her eyes. 'You are my delight, did you know? I think you are the daughter I never had; you take me back to when I was young and thought all life was one big romantic adventure. I'm so afraid life will steal your look of enchantment, your childish wonderment. If you can hang on to that expression, you'll soon have the world at your feet.'

It was my attic face she was speaking of. That enchanted expression that used to so enthrall Chris. 'I'm sorry, Madame,' I said humbly. 'I was rude. I was wrong to scream, but you pick on me all the time, and I'm tired, homesick too.'

'I know, I know,' she crooned as she came to embrace me, then rocked with me back and forth. 'To be young and in a strange city is hard on the nerves and confidence. But remember, I only needed to know what you are made of. A dancer without fire is no dancer at all.'

I'd been living in New York seven months, working even on the weekends until I fell into bed dead tired, before Madame Zolta thought I should be given a chance to dance a lead role with Julian to partner me. It was Madame's rule to alternate lead roles, so that there would be no stars in her company, and though she'd hinted many times she wanted me for Clara in *The Nutcracker*, I thought she just used that to dangle before me, like a rich plum I'd never be allowed to eat. Then it became a reality. Our company was in competition with much larger and better-known companies, so it was an absolute stroke of genius that she was able to sell a television producer on the notion that people who couldn't afford to buy ballet tickets could be reached by television.

I called Paul long distance to tell him my great news. 'Paul, I'm going to appear on TV in *The Nutcracker*. I'll be Clara!' He laughed and congratulated me. 'I guess that means you won't be coming home this summer,' he said rather sadly. 'Carrie misses you an awful lot, Cathy. You've only paid us one short visit since you went away.'

'I'm sorry, I want to come but I need this chance to star, Paul. Please explain to Carrie so her feelings won't be hurt. Is she there?'

'No, she's finally made a friend and is "sleeping-over". But call again tomorrow night and reverse the charges, and tell her yourself.'

'And Chris, how is he?' I asked.

'Fine, fine. He gets nothing but A's, and if he can manage to keep that up, he'll be accepted for an accelerated programme and can finish out his fourth year of college while starting his first year in medical school.'

'Simultaneously?' I asked, marvelling that anyone, even Chris, could be that smart and accomplish so much.

'Sure, it can be done.'

'Paul, what about you? Are you well? Are you working too much, too many long hours?'

'I'm healthy and yes, I do work long hours, as every doctor does. And since you can't come to visit us, I think it would be nice for Carrie if we came to visit you.'

Oh, that was the best idea I'd heard in months and months. 'And bring Chris,' I said. 'He'll love to meet all the pretty ballerinas I can introduce him to. But you, Paul, you'd better not look at anyone but me.'

He made a strange sound in his throat before he chuckled. 'Don't worry, Catherine, there's not a day that passes that I don't see your face before me.'

In early August the television production of *The Nutcracker* was taped for Christmastime release. Julian and I sat close together and watched the rushes, and when it was over he turned to take me in his arms, and for the first time he told me with the kind of sincerity I could believe, 'I love you, Cathy. Please stop taking me so lightly!'

Hardly had we rested up from *The Nutcracker* when Yolly fell and sprained her ankle, and April was visiting her parents, so I had the chance to be Sleeping Beauty! Since Julian had played two roles in the TV production, both Alexis and Michael thought it should be their turn to partner me. Madame Zolta frowned and looked at Julian, then at me. 'Alexis, Michael, I promise you the very next lead roles, but let Julian dance with Catherine. They have a rare magic between them that is spellbinding. I want to see how they do in a really lavish production like *The Sleeping Beauty*.'

Oh, the thoughts I had on stage as I lay so still on the purple velvet couch, waiting for my lover to come and put on my lips an arousing, come-alive kiss. The glorious music made me feel more real on that couch than when I was just me with no royal blood at all. I felt enchanted, surrounded by an aura of beauty as I quietly, gracefully lay with my arms folded on my breasts and my heart pulsated in rhythm with the glorious music. Out in the dark audience, Paul, Chris and Carrie and Henny were watching for the first time a New York performance. Truly, I felt in my bones I was that mystical medieval princess.

I saw him dreamily from beneath almost closed eyes, my prince. He danced about me, then down one knee he knelt to tenderly gaze upon my face before he dared to put a hesitant kiss upon my closed lips. I awakened, shy, disoriented, fluttering my eyelids. I feigned love on sight, but was so frightened, so maidenly virtuous, he had to woo me with more dancing and coax me to dance too, and in the most passionate *pas de deux* I soon succumbed to his charms and in conquest he lifted me high and up on the flat of his palm that knew well the exact spot to balance my weight just right, and I was carried offstage.

The last act ended; the applause thundered and resounded as time and again the curtain rose and came down. Julian and I took eight curtain calls of our very own! Red roses were thrust again and again into my arms, and flowers were tossed on to the stage. I looked down to see one single yellow buttercup weighted down by a folded slip of paper. I bent to pick it up and knew it was from Chris even before I had the chance to read his note. Daddy's four yellow buttercups – and here was one put in a freezer to keep it fresh until it could be thrown to me as a tribute to what we used to be.

Blindly I stared out into an audience of blurred faces, searching to see those I loved. All I could see was the attic, the gloomy, awesomely huge attic with its paper flowers, and over there, near the stairwell, was Chris standing in the shadows, near the shrouded sofa and the big trunk and his yearning desire was on his face as he watched me dance on and on.

I was crying, and the audience loved it. They gave me a standing ovation. I turned to hand a red rose to Julian, and again they thundered their applause. And he kissed me! Right in front of thousands – he dared to kiss me – and it wasn't respectful, it was possessive. 'Damn you for doing that!' I hissed, feeling humiliated.

'Damn you for not wanting me!' he hissed back.

'I'm not yours!'

'You will be!'

My family came backstage to lavish me with praise. Chris had grown taller but Carrie was very much the same – maybe a bit taller, not much. I kissed Henny's firm, round cheek. Only then could I look at Paul. Our eyes locked and held. Did he still love me, want me, need me? He hadn't answered my last letter. Easily hurt, I'd written only to Carrie to tell her of the upcoming performances, and only then did Paul call to say he was bringing my family to New York.

After the performance came the buffet party given for us by the rich patrons Madame Z cultivated. 'Wear the costumes you have on,' she instructed. 'The aficionados get a big thrill seeing dancers up close in costumes – but take off the stage makeup, use what you wear every day to look stunning. Never for one second give the public the idea you are less than glamorous!'

Music was playing and Chris took me in his arms for a waltz, the dance I had taught him so many years ago. 'This is still the way you dance?' I chided.

He grinned in a self-effacing way. 'Can't help it if you got all the dancing talent and I got all the brains.'

'Remarks like that could easily make me think you have no brains.'

He laughed again and I was drawn closer. 'Besides, I don't have to dance and posture to win over the girls. Just take a look at your friend Yolanda. She's quite a beauty, and she's been giving me the eye all evening.'

'She gives every good-looking guy the eye, so don't feel so flattered. She'll sleep with you tonight if you want that, and tomorrow night with someone else.'

'Are you like her too?' he shot back, narrowing his eyes.

I smiled at him wickedly, thinking, no, I was like Momma, sweet and cool and able to handle men – at least, I was learning. To prove this I winked at Paul, seeing if he'd come over and cut in. Swiftly Paul was on his feet, moving gracefully across the dance floor to take me from Chris. My brother's lips tightened, then he strolled straight from me to Yolanda. In a minute or two they disappeared.

'I guess you think I'm all hands and clumsy feet, after dancing with Julian,' said Paul, who could dance better than Chris. Even when the music changed to a faster rhythm with a jungle beat he followed along, surprising me that he could let go of his dignity and jiggle around almost as abandoned as a college kid. 'Paul, you're wonderful!' He laughed and said I made him feel young again. It was so much fun to see him like this, relaxed, that I went a bit wild with my dancing.

Carrie and Henny looked tired and ill-at-ease. 'I'm sleepy,' complained Carrie, rubbing her eyes. 'Can't we go to bed now?' It was twelve o'clock when we dropped Henny and Carrie off at their hotel, then Paul and I sat in a quiet Italian café and looked at one another. He still wore the moustache – not a neat, dandy one, but a thick brush above his sensual lips. He'd gained a few pounds, but it didn't detract from his looks or his appeal. He reached across the table to gather both my hands in his, then lifted them to his face so he could rub his cheek against them. And all the while he did this, his eyes asked a burning question, forcing a question from me. 'Paul, have you found someone else?'

'Have you?'

'I asked first.'

'I'm not looking for anyone else.'

It was an answer to make my heartbeats quicken, for it had been so long and I loved him too much. I watched him pay the bill, pick up my coat and hold it, and then his own for me to hold. Our eyes met – and then we almost ran from the restaurant to the nearest hotel where he registered us as Mr and Mrs Paul Sheffield. In a room painted dark red, he took off my clothes with such seductive slowness I was ready even before he went down on his knees to kiss me everywhere. Then he held me close, caressed and cherished me, kissed and pleasured until we were again made one.

After we were spent, he traced his finger along my lips, looking at me so tenderly. 'Catherine, what I wrote on that hotel register I meant,' he said, kissing me softly.

I stared at him, disbelieving. 'Paul, don't tease me.'

'I'm not teasing, Catherine. I've missed you so much since you've been away. I realized what a fool I've been to deny you and myself the chance to find happiness. Life is too short to have so many doubts. Now you're finding success in New York; I want to share it with you. I don't want us to have to sneak around behind Chris's back, I don't want to have to worry about the small-town gossips. I want to be with you, I want you forever, I want you to be my wife.'

'Oh Paul,' I cried, throwing my arms about his neck, 'I'll love you forever, I promise!' My eyes filled with tears, I was so relieved he'd asked me to marry him at last. 'I'll make you the best wife any man has ever known.' I meant it too.

We didn't sleep that night. We stayed awake, planning how it would be when we were married. I would stay with the company, somehow we'd work it out. The only shadow that darkened our joy was Chris. How would we tell Chris? We decided to wait until Christmas, when I would be in Clairmont. Until then I had to keep my happiness a secret, hide it from the world, so no one would guess I was about to become Mrs Paul Scott Sheffield.

A FIGHTING CHANCE

That was the autumn of my happiness, of my burgeoning success, of my love for Paul. I thought I had fate fully under my control; I dared it to stop me, for I was free and running true on my course. Almost on top now. I had nothing to fear now, nothing at all. I couldn't wait to tell the world about my engagement to Paul. But stealthily I protected my secret. I told no one, not Julian, nor Madame Zolta, for there was much at stake, and I had to bide my time, to make sure everything would continue to go my way. Right now I still needed Julian to partner me, just as much as he needed me. And I needed Madame Zolta to have complete confidence in me. If she knew I was going to be married, something she did not highly approve of, she might not give me all the lead roles, she might think I was a lost cause and not worth her time. And I still had to be famous. I still had to show Momma how much better I was than she.

Now that Julian and I were achieving a little recognition, Madame Zolta began to pay us more money. Julian came running to me one Saturday morning, terribly excited as he grabbed me up and swung me off my feet in a circle. 'Guess what? The old witch said I could buy her Cadillac on a part payment plan! It's only two and a half years old, Cathy.' He looked wistful. 'Of course, I always hoped my first Cadillac would be a brand new one, but when a certain ballet mistress is scared to death a certain sensational *danseur* might join another ballet company and take along with him her best ballerina – how can that certain someone refuse to almost give away her Cadillac?'

'Blackmail!' I cried. He laughed and grabbed my hand, and we dashed to look at his new car parked outside our apartment building. My breath pulled in, it looked so new! 'Oh, Julian, I love it! You couldn't blackmail her if she didn't want you to have one of her pets – she knows you will pamper it – and don't ever, ever sell it.'

'Oh, Cathy,' his eyes shone brilliantly with unused tears. 'Can't you see why I love you so? We're alike – why can't you love me, just a little?' Proudly he swung open the door to give me the rare privilege of being the first girl to ride in his first Cadillac.

We had a wild and crazy kind of day from there on. We drove through Central Park and all the way up through Harlem, to the George Washington Bridge and back. It was raining but I didn't mind. It was warm and cosy in the car.

Then Julian started in again. 'Cathy ... you're never going to love me, are you?' It was a question he put to me at least once or twice a day, in one form or another. I longed to tell him of my engagement to Paul, to put an end to his questions once and for all. But I steadfastly kept my secret.

'It's because you're still a virgin, isn't it? I'll be so gentle, so tender, Cathy ... give me a chance, please.'

'Good God, Julian, is that all you ever have on your mind?'

'Yeah!' he snarled. 'You're damned right it is! And I'm sick and tired of the game you play with me!' He guided the car out into a heavy stream of traffic. 'You're a cockteaser. You lead me on while we dance, then kick me in the groin when we're not!'

'Take me home, Julian! I find that kind of talk disgusting!'

'Right! You bet I'll take you home!' he spat at me as I crouched near the passenger door he had locked. He shot me a fierce, distraught look then bore down hard on the gas pedal! We sped down all those rain-slick streets, and every so often he'd glance my way to see how I was enjoying the terrifying ride! He laughed, wild and crazy, then braked so fast I was flung forward so my forehead struck the windshield! Blood trickled from the cut. Next he snatched the handbag from my lap, leaned to unlock my door, then he shoved me out into the pouring rain!

'To hell with you, Catherine Dahl!' he shouted as I stood there in the rain, refusing to beg. My coat pockets were empty. No money. 'You've had your first and your last ride in my car. I hope you know your way around!' He saluted me with an evil smile. 'Get home the best way you can, puritan saint,' he spat out, 'if you can!'

He drove off leaving me on the street corner in the downpour, in Brooklyn where I'd never been before. I didn't have even a nickel. I couldn't make a phone call, or use a subway, and the rain came down strong. My lightweight coat was soaked through. I knew I was in an unsavoury district where anything could happen ... and he'd left me here, when he'd sworn to take care of me!

I began to walk, not knowing north from south, east from west, and then I saw a cab cruising by and hailed it. Nervously I leaned forward to watch the metre click away the miles – and the dollars. *Damn you again, Julian, for taking me so far!* Finally we reached my apartment building – at the cost of fifteen dollars!

'What do you mean you ain't got it on yuh?' the cab driver flared. 'I'll drive ya straight to the police precinct!'

We bickered back and forth, with me trying to explain he couldn't be paid unless he let me out to go for money, and all the while the meter was running. Finally he agreed. 'But you'd better be back, chicky, in five minutes – or else!'

An English fox chased by a hundred hounds couldn't have run faster than I did. The elevator crawled upward, creaking all the way. Never did I step in that thing when I wasn't afraid it would stop between floors and I'd be trapped. Finally, the door opened, and I raced down the hall to bang on the door, praying April or Yolanda would be there to let me in. Crazy Julian had my handbag and my key!

'Take it easy!' bellowed Yolanda. 'I'm comin'. Who is it anyway?'

'Cathy! Let me in quick! I've got a taxi driver waiting with his meter running!'

'If you think you're going to put the bite on me, forget it!' she said, swinging open the door. She wore only nylon briefs, and her freshly shampooed head was wrapped with a red towel. 'You look like something the sea coughed up,' she said invitingly. I wasn't one to pay much attention to Yolanda. I shoved her aside, ran to where I hid my secret cache of emergency money – then I went slack. The small key to my locked treasure chest was in the bag Julian had – if he hadn't thrown it away. 'Please, Yolly, loan me fifteen and a buck for a tip.'

Shrewdly she looked me over while she removed the towel and began to comb her long dark hair. 'What yah got to trade for small favours like that?'

'I'll give you anything you want. Just give me the money.'

'Okay – you just keep your promise to repay.' Slowly she took a twenty from her fat billfold. 'Give the driver a fiver; that will cool him down – and anything I want – right?' I agreed and raced off.

No sooner did the driver grab the twenty, than he was smiling, friendly as he tipped his cap. 'See you around, chicky.' I hoped he'd drop dead!

I was so chilled the first thing I did was to run a tub of hot water, but only after I'd scrubbed off the dirty ring Yolly had left.

My hair was still wet as I pulled on clothes, planning to go to Julian and demand my purse back, when Yolly blocked my way. 'Come on, Cathy . . . I want you to keep your bargain – anything I want, right?'

'Right,' I said, disgusted. 'What do you want?'

She smiled and leaned provocatively against a wall. 'Your brother . . . I want you to invite him up next weekend.'

'Don't be ridiculous! Chris is in college. He can't come up here any time he wants.'

'You get him up here any way you have to. Say you're sick, say you desperately need him, but get him up here! And then you can keep the twenty.'

I turned to stare at her with hostility. 'No! I've got the money to pay you back . . . I'm not going to let Chris get involved with the likes of you!'

Still wearing only the briefs, she smeared on scarlet lipstick without looking in a mirror. 'Cathy, love, your dear, precious brother is already involved with the likes of me.'

'I don't believe you! You're not his type!'

'Nooo,' she purred, her eyes narrowing as she watched me finish dressing, 'let me tell you something, dollface, there isn't a guy alive who doesn't go for *my* type. Including your dear brother and your lover-boy Julian!'

'You lie!' I cried. 'Chris wouldn't touch you with a ten-foot pole – and as for Julian, I don't give a damn if he sleeps with ten whores like you!'

Suddenly her face flamed red, she stiffened and came at me with her hands raised and her fingers curled into claws with long red fingernails! 'Bitch!' she snarled. 'Don't you dare call me a whore! I don't take pay for what I want to give out – and your brother likes what I give out – go and ask him how many times he's –'

'Shut up!' I yelled, not letting her finish. 'I don't believe anything you say! He's too smart to do anything but use you for physical needs ... Beyond that, you couldn't mean more than dirt to him!'

She grabbed me and I belted her back, hard. Hard enough so she fell to the floor. 'You're nothing but a shallow, mean tramp, Yolanda Lange!' I screamed with fury. 'Not nearly good enough for my brother to wipe his feet on! You've slept with every dancer in the company. I don't care what you do ... just leave *me*, and leave *my brother* alone!'

Her nose was bleeding ... Oh, I didn't know I'd hit that hard, and her nose was also beginning to swell. Quickly she jumped to her feet, but for some reason she backed off from me. 'Nobody talks to me like that and gets away with it ... You're gonna regret this day, Catherine Dahl! I'll get your brother. And what's more, I'll take Julian from you too! And when he's mine, you'll find out that without him you're nothing! Nothing but a hick dancer Madame Z would throw out if Julian didn't insist on keeping you on because he's got the hots for a virgin.'

What she screamed out could be so true. Maybe she was right, that without Julian I wouldn't be anything special. I felt sick and I hated her – hated her for soiling Chris and my image of him. I began to throw my clothes in my suitcases, determined I'd go back to Clairmont before I'd live another hour near Yolanda!

'Go on!' she hissed between her clenched teeth. 'Run away, little prude – what a fool you are. I'm not a whore! It's just I'm not the tease you are – and between the two, I choose my kind!'

Heedless of what she said, I finished packing, then strapped the handles of my three bags together so I could drag them out into the hall, and under my arm I carried a soft leather satchel stuffed full. I turned at the door to look back at Yolanda who had sprawled on the bed like a sleek cat. 'You really do terrify me, Yolanda. I'm so scared I could laugh. I've faced up to bigger and better than you, and still I'm alive ... so don't you come near me again, or it will be *you* who lives to regret this day!'

Shortly after I slammed the door I was on Julian's floor. Dragging along my tied-together luggage, I banged on the door to Julian's apartment with both fists! 'Julian!' I cried, 'if you're in there, open this door and give me back my bag. Open this door or you'll never have me for a dance partner again!'

He opened the door quickly enough, wearing nothing but a bath towel wrapped about his narrow hips. Before I knew what was happening he dragged me into the room and threw me down on the bed. I looked around frantically, hoping to see Alexis or Michael, but it was my bad luck he had the apartment to himself. 'Sure,' he barked, 'you can have your damned bag back – after you answer a few questions!'

I jumped up from the bed – and he shoved me down again, then knelt so he straddled my body, and in no way could I escape! 'You let me go, you beast!' I yelled. 'I walked six blocks in the rain and was freezing cold – now let me up and give me my bag!'

'Why can't you love me?' he shot out, holding me down with both hands as I struggled to free myself. 'Is it because you're in love with someone else? Who is it? It's that big doctor who took you in, isn't it?'

I shook my head, terribly afraid of him. I couldn't tell him the truth. He looked almost insane with jealousy. His hair was so wet from his recent shower he dripped water on me. 'Cathy, I've had about all I can take from you! It's been about three years since we met, and I'm not getting anywhere. It can't be me that's wrong – so it must be you! Who is it?'

'Nobody!' I lied. 'And you are all wrong for me! The only thing I like about you, Julian Marquet, is the way you dance!'

Blood flooded his face. 'You think I'm blind and stupid, don't you?' he asked, so furious he could likely explode. 'But I'm not blind, I'm not stupid and I've seen the way you look at that doctor – and so help me God if I haven't seen you look at your own brother in the same way! So don't go getting up on your high horse of morals, Catherine Dahl, for I've never seen a brother and sister so fascinated with each other before!'

I slapped him then! He slapped back, twice as hard! I tried to fight him off, but he was like an eel as he wrestled me down to the floor where I feared he'd soon rip off my clothes and rape me – but he didn't do that. He only held me beneath him and breathed heavily until he had some control of his raging emotions, and only then did he speak. 'You're mine, Cathy, whether you know it or not . . . you belong to me. And if any man comes between us, I'll kill him – and you too. So remember that before you turn your eyes on anyone but me.'

He gave me my bag then, and told me to count my money to see if he'd stolen any. I had forty-two dollars and sixty-two cents, it was all there.

Shakily I gained my feet, when he allowed me to, and I trembled as I backed to the door, opened it, and stepped out into the hall clutching my bag tight. Only then did I dare to speak what I thought.

'There are institutions for madmen like you, Julian. You can't tell me whom to love, and you can't force me to love you. If you had deliberately set out to make yourself repugnant to me, you couldn't have done a better job of it. Now I can't even like you – and as for dancing together again, forget it!' I slammed the door in his face, then hurried away.

But as I reached the elevator, he had the door open again, and he cursed something so terrible I can't repeat it, except it ended with, 'Damn you to hell, Cathy . . . I've said it before, and I'll say it again . . . and you'll wish to God you were in hell before I'm done with you!'

After that terrible sceme with Yolanda, then Julian, I sought out Madame Zolta and told her I just couldn't live any longer in an apartment with a girl determined to ruin my career.

'She afraid of you, Catherine, that's all. Yolanda was the superstar in my small company until you came along. Now she feels threatened. Make up with her . . . Be a good girl, and go and say you're sorry for whatever it was.'

'No, Madame. I don't like her, and I refuse to live in the same apartment with her. So if you don't give me more money, I'll have to go to another company and see if they will, and if they won't then I'll go back to Clairmont.'

She groaned, bowed her skeleton head into her bony hands and moaned some more. Oh, how grand Russians were at expressing emotions! 'Okay . . . you blackmail me, and I give in. I'll give you a small raise, and tell you where to find cheap apartment – but it won't be so nice as one you left.'

Hah! That had been nice? But she was right. The only apartment I could find would fit in Paul's smallest bedroom, all two rooms of it. But it was my own . . . the very first place I'd had all to myself, and for a few days I exulted in fixing it up as best I could. Then I really began to sleep restlessly, waking up every few minutes to listen to all the squeaks and squeals the old building made. I longed for Paul. I longed for Chris. I heard the wind blow, and there was no one in another bed three feet from mine to comfort me with soft words and sparkling blue eyes.

Chris's eyes were in front of me as I got up and sat at my kitchen table to write a note to 'Mrs Winslow'. I sent her my first rave review, one with a sensational photo of Julian and me in *The Sleeping Beauty*. And I wrote at the bottom of my letter,

It won't be long now, Mrs Winslow. Think about that every night before you fall asleep. Remember somewhere I'm still alive, and I'm thinking of you, and planning.

I even mailed off that letter in the middle of the night before I had the chance to reconsider and tear it up. I raced home, threw myself on my bed and sobbed. Oh God, I was never going to be set free! Never! And despite all my tears I woke up again, thinking of how I could hurt her so she'd never be the same. *Be happy now, Momma, for it won't be long!*

I bought six copies of all papers that had anything to say about me. Unfortunately, most often my name was coupled with Julian's. Paul and Chris were also favoured with my reviews; the others I kept for myself – or Momma. I pictured how she'd look when she opened the envelope, though it was my fear she'd just pitch it in the trashcan after she'd torn up the envelope with its contents unread. Not once did I call her Mother or Momma, but kept my salutations always formal and cold. There would come a day when she would see me face to face and I would call her Mother and I would watch her pale, then shudder.

One morning I was awakened by someone banging on my door. 'Cathy, let me in! I have terrific news!' It was Julian's voice.

'Go away!' I said sleepily, getting up and pulling on a robe before I stumbled over to make him stop pounding on the door. 'Stop that!' I yelled. 'I haven't forgiven you – I never will – so stay out of my life!'

'Let me in or I'll kick the door down!' he bellowed. I unlocked the deadbolts, and swung the door open a crack. Julian barged in to sweep me up in his arms and plant on my lips a long, hot kiss while I was half yawning. 'Madame Zolta ... yesterday after you left, she broke the news! We're going on tour in London! Two weeks there! I've never been to London, Cathy, and Madame is so delighted they've taken official notice of us over there!'

'Really?' I asked, catching his excitement. Then I staggered off towards my minute kitchen ... Coffee, had to have coffee before I could think straight.

'God, are you always so disoriented in the morning?' he asked, following me into the kitchen where he straddled a chair backwards and leaned on his elbows to watch my every move. 'Wake up, Cathy! Forgive me, kiss me, be my friend again. Hate me all you want tomorrow, but love me this day – for I was born for this day, you too – Cathy, we're going to make it! I know we are! Madame Zolta's company was never noticed before we became a team! It isn't her success – it's ours!'

His modesty deserved a medal. 'You've eaten breakfast?' I asked, and hoped. I had only two slices of bacon and wanted both for myself.

'Sure I have; I grabbed a bite before I came over, but I can eat again.'

Naturally he could eat again! He could always eat ... and that's when it hit me ... London! Our company going to

175

London! I spun around, crying, 'Julian, what you said, you're not kidding? We're going over there – all of us?'

He jumped up. 'Yes, all of us! It's a big break, our chance to make it big! We'll make the world sit up and take notice! And you and I, we'll be the stars! Because together we're the best, and you know it as well as I do.'

I shared my meal and listened to him rhapsodize on the long and fantastic career we had just ahead. We'd be rich, and when we grew older, we'd settle down and have a couple of kids, and then teach ballet, I'd like that, wouldn't I? I hated to spoil his plans, but I had to say it. 'Julian, I don't love you, so we can never be married. We'll go to London and dance together, and I'll do my best – but I plan to marry someone else. I'm already engaged. I have been for a long time now.'

His long, glaring look of disbelief and pure hatred delivered and redelivered a series of visual slaps on my face. 'You're lying!' he screamed. I shook my head to deny it. 'God damn you to hell for leading me on!' he raged, then hurled himself out of my apartment. I'd never led him on, except when we were dancing, and that was my role to play ... That was all, all there was between us.

WINTER DREAMS

I was going home for Christmas. The unpleasantness with Julian was forgotten in my happy anticipation of seeing Paul, and bringing with me such good news. Thank God I had Paul to escape to. And I wasn't going to let Julian take the joy from this Christmas. For this was the time Paul and I had agreed to announce our engagement, and the only person who could ruin my happiness now was Chris.

At two o'clock in the morning Chris and Paul met me at the airport. It was bitterly cold even in South Carolina. It was Chris who reached me first to catch me up in his strong arms, and he tried to put a kiss on my lips but I turned my face so his kiss landed on my cheek. 'Hail to the conquering ballerina!' he cried, hugging me tight and looking at me with so much pride. 'Oh, Cathy, you are so beautiful! Each time I see you, you make my heart hurt.'

He made my heart hurt too, to see him more handsome than even Daddy had been. Quickly I looked in another direction. I tore away from my brother's embrace and ran towards Paul who stood and watched. He stretched out his hands to take mine in them. *Careful, careful*, warned his long look, *mustn't let our news escape too soon.*

That was our best Christmas ever, from beginning to end – or almost to the end. Carrie had grown half an inch, and I see her sitting on the floor on Christmas morning with her big blue eyes happy and glowing as she exclaimed over the red velvet dress I'd bought her, found after hours and hours of searching almost every shop in New York. She looked like a radiant, small princess when she tried the dress on. I tried to picture Cory seated cross-legged on the floor looking at his gifts too. It was impossible for me to leave the memory of him out of any happy occasion. Oh, many a time I'd glimpsed a small boy with blond curls and blue eyes on the streets of New York, and I'd run to chase after, hoping by some miracle it would be him – and it never was, never was.

Chris put a small box into my hands. Inside was a tiny gold heart-locket and in the centre of the lid was a genuine diamond, a small one, but a diamond nevertheless. 'Paid for by my own hard-earned cash,' he said as he fastened the chain about my neck. 'Waiting on tables pays well when you give good service with a smile.' Then, furtively, he slipped a folded note in my hand. An hour later, when I had the chance, I read a note that made me cry:

To my lady Catherine,
I give you gold with a diamond you can barely see,
But the gem would be castle-sized if it expressed all I feel for thee.
I give you gold because it endures, and love like the eternal sea.
Only your brother, Christopher.

I hadn't read that note when Paul gave me his gift wrapped in gold foil and topped by a huge red satin bow. My hands trembled as I fumbled with the many layers of tissue, all while he watched expectantly. A *grey fox* coat! 'The kind of coat you really need for New York winters,' he said, his eyes shining with all the warmth and love he felt.

'It's too much,' I choked, 'but I love it, absolutely love it!'

He smiled, made happy so easily. 'Every time you wear it, it's essential you think of me, and it should keep you warm on those cold, foggy days in London too.'

I told him it was the most beautiful coat I'd ever seen, though I felt uneasy. It brought back thoughts of Momma and her closet full of many furs, gained only because she had the heartless cruelty to lock us away, and thus gain a fortune, and furs, and jewellery, and everything else money could buy.

Chris jerked his head around to catch something on my face that must have betrayed my love for Paul. His brows drew together in a scowl before he shot a glance at Paul. Then he got up and left the room. Somewhere upstairs a door slammed violently. Paul pretended not to notice. 'Look over in the corner, Catherine – that's a gift for all of us to enjoy.'

I stared at the huge cabinet TV set that Carrie jumped up and ran to turn on. 'He bought it just so we could watch you dance in *The Nutcracker* in *colour*, Cathy. Now he won't let me touch it.'

'It's only because it is the devil to tune in correctly,' Paul apologized.

Throughout the rest of Christmas Day I saw very little of Chris, except at mealtimes. He wore the bright blue sweater I'd knitted for him – and it did fit – and under it the shirt and tie I'd given him as well. But none of my gifts to him could equal that gold and diamond locket with the small poem that left my heart bleeding. I hated it that he kept caring so much, and yet – when I thought about it later – I would hate it more if he didn't.

That evening we all settled down comfortably before the new colour TV. I curled up on the floor near Paul's leg as he sat in a chair, with Carrie close at my side. Chris sat far away, deep in a mood that took him even farther away than the actual feet that separated us. So I didn't feel as happy as I should have as I watched the credits roll by on the colourful screen. A tape which had been made in August and only now was to be seen in hundreds of cities across the country. How beautiful the sets looked in colour; they hadn't appeared nearly so ethereal in reality. I gazed at myself as Clara – did I really look like that? I forgot myself and leaned unconsciously against Paul's thigh, and I felt his fingers twine into my hair – and then I didn't know where I was, except on stage, with Julian now transformed by magic from the ugly nutcracker into the handsome prince.

When it was over I came back to myself and the first thing I thought of was my mother. *God, let her be home this night, and let her have seen me. Let her know what she tried to kill! Let her hurt, cry, grieve … please, please!*

'What can I say, Cathy,' said Paul in an awed way. 'No dancer could have performed that role better than you did. And Julian was superb too.'

'Yeah,' said Chris coldly, getting to his feet and coming to lift Carrie up in his arms. 'You both were sensational – but it sure wasn't the kiddy performance I remember seeing when *I* was a child. The two of you made it seem a romance. Really, Cathy, turn that guy off, and quickly!' With those words he strode from the room and up the stairs to tuck Carrie into bed.

'I think your brother is suspicious,' said Paul mildly, 'not only of Julian, but also of me. All day he has treated me as a rival. He's not going to be happy when he hears our news.'

Because like others I wanted to put off what was unpleasant, I suggested we not tell him until the next day. Then, when I was curled up on Paul's lap and we had our arms wrapped about each other, we exchanged the kind of passionate kisses held back until now. I was aching for him. After we'd turned off all the lights we stole up the back stairs and with the zeal born of starvation made love on his bed. Later on we slept, then woke up to make love again. At dawn I kissed him once more, then slipped on a robe to sneak down the hall to my own room. To my utter dismay, just as I stepped from Paul's room into the hall, Chris opened his door and came out! Abruptly he jerked to a stop and stared at me with astonished, hurt eyes. I cringed backward, so ashamed I could cry! Neither of us said a word. His eyes were the first to break from the frozen stare that also stilled our limbs. He ran for the stairs, but halfway there he turned to throw me a look of outraged disgust. I wanted to die! I went in to look at Carrie who was sound asleep with her red velvet dress clutched in her arms. And on my bed I lay trying to think of what to say to Chris to make it right between us again. Why did I feel in my heart that I was betraying him?

The day after Christmas was for returning the gifts you hated, didn't want, or those that didn't fit. I forced myself to approach Chris who was in the garden, fiercely snipping at the rose bushes with hedge clippers. 'Chris, I need to talk to you and explain a few things.'

He exploded. 'Paul had no right to give you a fur coat! A gift like that makes you seem a kept woman! Cathy, give him back that coat! And, most of all, stop what you are doing with him!'

First I took the clippers from his hands before he ruined Paul's beloved roses. 'Chris, it isn't as bad as you believe. You see ... Paul and I ... well, we are planning to marry in the spring. We love each other, so it isn't wrong what we do together. It's not an affair to be forgotten tomorrow; he needs me and I need him.' I stepped closer when he turned his back to hide his expression. 'It's better this way for me and for you too,' I said softly. I circled his waist and twisted about to stare up into his face. He seemed stunned, like a healthy man who learns suddenly he has a terminal illness – and all hope had fled from him.

'He's too old for you!'

'I love him.'

'So, you love him. What about your career? Are you throwing away all those years of dreaming, of working? Are you going to break your word? You know we swore to each other to go after our goals and not let those lost years make a difference.'

'Paul and I have discussed that. He understands. He thinks we can work it out...'

'*He* thinks? What does a doctor know about the dancer's life? You'll never be with him. He'll be here; you'll be God knows where, with men your own age. You don't owe him anything, Cathy, you don't! We'll pay him back every cent he's spent on us. We'll give him the respect he deserves, and the love – but you don't owe him your life.'

'Don't I?' I asked in a whisper, aching inside for Chris. 'I think I do owe him my life. You know how I felt when I came here. I thought no one could be trusted or depended on. I expected the worst to happen to us, and it would have too without him. And I don't love him just for what he's done. I love him because of who and what he is. Chris, you don't see him as I do.'

He whirled about, seizing the shears from my hands. 'And what about Julian? You are going to be married to Paul and dance with Julian? You know Julian is mad for you. It's all over him, the way he looks at you, the way he touches you.'

I backed off, stricken. Chris wasn't talking *just* of Julian. 'I'm sorry if this has ruined your holiday,' I said, 'but you'll find someone too. You love Paul, I know you do. And when you've thought about this, you'll know we are right for each other, despite our age difference, despite everything.' I went off, leaving Chris in the garden with the hedge clippers.

Paul drove me to Greenglenna while Carrie stayed home to enjoy the new colour TV set and all her new clothes and games. Paul chatted happily of the party he planned for all of us tonight at his favourite restaurant. 'I wish I could be selfish and leave Chris and Carrie at home. But I want them there when I put the ring on your finger.' I fixed my eyes on the winter landscape rolling by, the trees bare, the grass brown, the pretty houses with decorations and outdoor lights turned on after dark. Now I was part of the show, no longer just a spectator locked away – and yet I felt so torn, so miserable.

'Cathy, you are seated beside the happiest man in the world!'

And back in his garden, I'd left a man just as miserable as I felt.

In my bag I had a ring I'd bought for Carrie in New York. A tiny ruby for a very small finger, and even so, it was too large for anything but her thumb. As I stood there, in the better jewellery department of the best store in town, discussing just how the ring could be reduced in size without ruining the setting, I suddenly heard a very familiar voice! A sweet, husky, dulcet-toned voice. As in slow motion, I cautiously turned my head.

Momma! Standing right next to me! If she'd been alone, perhaps she would have seen me, but she was absorbed in chatting to her female companion who was dressed just as elegantly as she was. I'd changed considerably since she saw me last – still, if she looked, she would have to know who I was. The two of them were discussing the party they had attended last night. 'Really, Corrine, Elsie does carry the festive theme through to an outrageous extreme – all that red!'

Parties! Was that all she did, go to parties! My heart went pounding in fox-trot time. My spirits went limp, sagged out by disappointment. A party – I should have known! She never stayed at home and watched TV! She hadn't seen me! Oh, but I was angry! I turned to *make* her see me! A small standing mirror on the glass jewellery showcase reflected her profile, and showed me how lovely she was still. A bit older looking, but striking nonetheless. Her flaxen hair was drawn back to emphasize the perfection of her small gem of a nose, her pouting red lips, her long and naturally dark lashes that were made thicker by mascara. Her ears glittered with gold and diamonds, the real things – and she was speaking.

'Can't you show me something just right for a lovely young girl?' she asked the saleslady. 'Something in good taste, not gaudy, or too large, but something a young girl can keep all her life and be proud of.'

Who? What girl did she have to give gifts to? I felt jealous and watched her select a lovely gold locket very much like the one Chris had given me! Three hundred dollars! Now our dear mother was spending money on a girl not her own, forgetting about us. Didn't she think of us, wonder how we were faring? How could she sleep at night when the world could be so cold, ugly and cruel to children on their own?

As far as I could tell, she was completely without guilt or regrets. Maybe that was what millions could do – nail a satisfied smirk to one's face – despite what it covered. I wanted to speak and see her poise collapse! I wanted her smiles to peel off like bark from a tree and she'd be revealed before her friend for what she was – a monster without a heart! A killer! A fraud! But I said nothing.

'Cathy,' said Paul, coming up behind me and putting his hands on my shoulders, 'I've returned everything – how about you? Ready to go now?'

I wanted desperately for my mother to see me with Paul, a man every bit as handsome as her darling 'Bart'. I wanted to shout it out. *See, I too can attract intelligent, kind, educated and handsome men!* So quickly I glanced to see if Momma had heard Paul speak my name, hoping to delight in her stunned surprise, her guilt, her shame. But she'd moved on farther down the counter, and if she heard the name, Cathy, it didn't cause her to turn her head.

For some reason I didn't understand, I sobbed.

'Are you all right, darling?' asked Paul. He saw something on my face that puzzled him and put concern in his eyes. 'You're not having second thoughts about us, are you?'

'No, of course not!' I denied. But I was having second thoughts about *me*. Why hadn't I done something? Why hadn't I put out my foot this time and tripped her? Then I could have seen her sprawled on the floor, her poise vanished – maybe. It would be like her to fall gracefully and have all the men in the store hurry to assist her up – even Paul.

I was dressing for the big affair at The Plantation House when Chris came into my bedroom and sent Carrie away. 'Go watch TV,' he said with more sharpness than I'd ever heard him use with her. 'I want to speak to your sister.' Carrie threw him, then me, an odd look before she skipped out of the room.

No sooner had Carrie closed the door behind her, than Chris was at my side and seizing my shoulders. He shook me violently. 'Are you going through with this farce? You don't love him! You still love me! I know you do! Cathy, please, don't do this to me! I know you're trying to set me free by marrying Paul, but that's not a good reason for marrying a man.' He hung his head, released my shoulders, and looked terribly ashamed. His voice came so low I had to keen my ears to hear his words. 'I know it's wrong what I feel for you. I know I should try and find someone else, like you try to do . . . but I can't stop loving you and wanting you. I think about you all during my days, every day. I dream about you at night. I want to wake up and see you in the room with me. I want to go to bed and know you're there, very close, where I can see you, touch you.' A sob tore from his throat before he could go on. 'I can't bear to think of you with another man! Damn it, Cathy, I want you! You don't plan to have children anyway, so *why can't it be me?*'

I'd drawn away when he released my shoulders. When his words stopped I ran to fling my arms about him, as he clutched at me, as if I were the one and only woman who could save him from drowning. And we'd both drown if I did as he wanted. 'Oh, Chris, what can I say? Momma and Daddy made their mistake in marrying each other – and we were the ones to pay the price. We can't risk repeating their mistake!'

'Yes we can!' he fervently cried. 'We don't have to have a sexual relationship! We can just live together, be together, just brother and sister, with Carrie too. Please, please, *I beg you not to marry Paul!'*

'*Shut up!'* I screamed. '*Leave me alone!'* I struck at him then, wanting to hurt him, as every word he said hurt me. 'You make me feel so guilty, so ashamed! Chris, I did the best I could for you when we were prisoners. Maybe we did turn to each other, but only because we had no others! If there had been, you would never have wanted me, and I would never have given you a second glance! You are only a *brother* to me, Chris, and I want to keep you where you should be ... which isn't in my bed!'

Then he had me in his arms, and I couldn't help but cling to him with my cheek pressed against his thudding heart. He was having a hard time controlling his tears. I wanted him to forget ... but every second he held me hard against him raised his hopes, and he was aroused! And he was the one who thought we could live platonically together! 'Let me go, Chris. If you love me for the rest of your life, keep it to yourself; I never want to hear about it again! I love Paul, and nothing you say will keep me from marrying him!'

'You're lying to yourself,' he choked, holding me tighter. 'I see you watching me before you turn your eyes his way. You want me, and you want him. You want everyone, and everything! Don't ruin Paul's life when already he's suffered enough! He's too old for you – and age *does* count! He'll be old and dried up sexually when you're at your peak! Why, even Julian would be better!'

'You are one big fool if you believe that!'

'Then I'm a fool! I've always been a fool, haven't I? When I put my love and trust in you that was the biggest mistake of my life, wasn't it? You are just as heartless, in your own way, as our mother! You want every man who appeals to you, regardless of the consequences ... but I would let you have whomever you wanted, as long as you always came back to me.'

'Christopher, you're jealous because I found someone to love before you did! And don't stand there and glare your icy blue eyes at me – for you've had plenty of affairs! I know you've slept with Yolanda Lange, and God knows how many others. And what did you tell them? You told them you loved them too! Well,

I don't love you now! I love Paul, and there's not one thing you can do to stop us from marrying each other!'

He stood there, pale faced and quivering all over, and then he said in a hoarse whisper, 'Yes, there is. I could tell him about us ... he wouldn't want you then.'

'You wouldn't tell him that. You're much too honourable, and besides, he already knows.'

For long, long moments we glared at each other ... and then he ran from the room, slamming the door so hard behind him it put a long crack in the ceiling plaster.

Only Carrie accompanied Paul and me to The Plantation House. 'It's too bad Chris doesn't feel well. I hope he doesn't have the flu ... Everyone else does.'

I didn't say anything, just sat and listened to Carrie chatter on and on about how much she loved Christmas and the way it made everything ordinary look so pretty.

Paul slipped a two-carat diamond ring on my finger while a huge fire crackled the Yule log, and soft music played. I did my best to make it a joyous occasion, laughing, smiling, exchanging long, romantic looks while we sipped champagne and toasted each other and our long and happy future together. I danced with him under the giant crystal chandeliers and kept my eyes closed, picturing Chris home alone, sulking in his room and hating me.

'We're going to be so happy, Paul,' I whispered, standing on the toes of my high-heeled silver slippers. Yes, this was the way our life together would be. Easy. Sweet. Effortless. Just like the lilting, old-fashioned waltz we danced to. Because when you truly loved there were no problems that love couldn't overcome.

Me ... and my ideas.

Drive. Dedication. Desire. Determination. The four D's of the ballet world we had to live by. If Madame Z had been tough on us before Christmas, now she clamped down on us such a heavy schedule of practice all we did was work. She lectured on how perfect the Royal Ballet was, strictly classical – but we were to do everything in our own unique American way, classical . . . but more beautiful and innovative.

Julian was absolutely ruthless, even demonic. I began to really despise him! We were both wet with sweat and our hair hung in strings. My leotard was glued to my skin. Julian wore only a loin cloth. He yelled as if I were deaf, 'Do it right this time, damn it! I don't want to be here all night!'

'Stop yelling at me, Julian! I can hear perfectly well!'

'Then *do it right*! First take three steps and then you kick, then jump for me to catch, and for God's sake this time lay back immediately! Don't stay upright and stiff, the moment I catch you fall backwards and go limp – if you can manage to do anything right or graceful today.'

That was my trouble. I didn't trust him now. I was afraid he was going to try to hurt me. 'Julian, you yell at me as if I'm deliberately doing everything wrong!'

'It seems to me you are! If you really wanted to do it right you could. All you have to do is take three steps, kick, then jump, and I lift and let you fall back. Now see if you can get it right at least one time out of fifty tries!'

'Do you think I like this? Look at my armpits,' I said as I lifted my arms to show him. 'See how raw they are, how you've rubbed the skin off? And tomorrow I'll be black and blue all over from the bruises you make with your hard grasps!'

'Then *do it right*!' He raged not only with his voice, but with his jet eyes, and I was terribly afraid he was just waiting for the opportunity to let me fall – on purpose – for revenge. But I got up, and we did it again. And again I failed to fall back and fully trust him. This time he threw me to the floor where I lay panting, gasping, and wondering why the hell I kept this up.

'You're gasping for breath?' he asked sarcastically, towering above me, his bare feet wide apart and straddling my legs. His bare chest glistened with perspiration that dripped down to fall on me. 'I do all the hard work, and you lie there sprawled out and exhausted looking. What happened to you down there? Did you use all your energy making it with your doctor?'

'Shut up! I'm tired from twelve hours of continuous practice, that's all!'

'If you're tired, I'm ten times more so – so get up, and let's do it again – and get it right this time, goddamn you!'

'Don't you swear at me! Get yourself another partner! You tripped me up and made me fall so my knee hurt for three days afterwards – so how can I run and jump into your arms – you're mean enough to cripple me permanently!'

'Even if I hated you, I wouldn't let you fall. And, Cathy, I don't hate you. *Not yet.*'

After practising over and over again to the piano music, counting, timing, repeating the same series of steps, at last I got it right, and even Julian could smile and congratulate me. Then came the final dress rehearsal and the performance of *Romeo and Juliet*.

It was the stunning sets and dazzling costumes that brought out the best in all of us when combined with a full orchestra. Now I could give to the role of Juliet all the little nuances that would make her real, and not some wooden stick that Yolanda appeared tonight, as she did her *pliés* while her eyes seemed glassy, unfocused. Madame Z came up to peer closely into her face, and then she sniffed Yolly's breath. 'By God ... you been smoking grass! No dancer of mine goes spaced out on to the stage and cheats my audience – get home and to bed. Catherine, get ready to play Juliet!'

Yolanda staggered past me, then tried to give me a savage kick as she hissed, 'Why did you have to come back? Why didn't you stay down there where you belong?'

I didn't think of Yolanda and her threats as I stood on the

flimsy balcony and gazed dreamily down into Julian's pale face that tilted upward to mine. He appeared so beautiful under the bluish lights, wearing white tights, with his dark hair gleaming, his jet eyes glittering along with the fake jewels on his medieval costume. He seemed to be my attic lover who would ever bound away from me, and never let me near enough to see the features of his face.

The applause thundered as the curtain lowered. And behind it, out of breath, Julian sprang up to hug me close. 'You were sensational tonight! How do you manage to frustrate me right up until the moment of performance?' The curtain rose for our bows – then he kissed me full on the lips. 'Bravo,' they cried, for this was the sort of drama and passion all balletomanes craved.

It was our night, the best yet, and drunk with success I dashed past photographers and autograph hounds towards my dressing room, for there was a big party afterwards, a celebration before our company took off for London. Quickly I lathered on cold cream to take off the makeup, then I changed from my last-act costume into a short formal of periwinkle blue. Madame Zolta rapped on my door and called out, 'Catherine, a lady here says she has flown all the way from your home town to watch you dance. Come, open your door and we will hold up the party until you arrive.'

A tall attractive woman entered. Dark-haired, dark-eyed, her clothes were expensive and flattering to her figure. For some strange reason, it seemed I'd met her before, or she reminded me of someone. She looked me over from head to toe, and only then did she turn to stare around the small dressing room filled with plastic bags jammed with all the costumes I was taking with me to England, each labelled with my name and the name of the ballet the costumes were designed for. I waited impatiently for her to have her say, then go, so I could get on to putting on my coat.

'I don't think I know you,' I said to hurry her up.

She smiled crookedly, then sat down uninvited to cross her nicely shaped legs. Rhythmically she swung one foot in a high-heeled black pump back and forth.

'Of course you don't know me, my dear child ... but I know a great deal about you.'

There was something in her sweet and too-smooth tongue to warn me, and I stiffened, prepared for whatever she'd come to deliver – and it would be bad. I could tell from the mean look that hid beneath the false sweet one.

'You're very pretty, maybe even beautiful.'

'Thank you.'

'You dance exceptionally well – that surprised me. Though of course you would have to dance well to be with this company which I've heard is fast becoming an important one.'

'Thank you again,' I said, thinking she'd never come to the point.

She took a long time before she spoke again, keeping me in suspense, on edge. I picked up my coat, trying to signal to her that I was trying to leave.

'Nice fur coat,' she commented. 'I suppose my brother gave you that. I've heard he's throwing away his money like a drunken sailor. Giving all he's saved to three nobodies who came on a bus and took over his life.' She laughed low and sarcastically, the way women of culture know how to laugh. 'Now I know why, seeing you; though I've heard from others you were pretty enough to make any man foolish. Still, I had no idea a child such as you could look so voluptuous, so sensual and skinny all at the same time. You're a peculiar blend, Miss Dahl. All innocence and sophistication too. Such a brew must be heady intoxication for a man of my brother's type.' She chortled. 'There's nothing like the combination of youth, long blonde hair, a beautiful face and full breasts to bring out the beast even in the best of men.' She sighed, as if pitying me. 'Yes, that's the trouble with being too young and beautiful. Men are made their worst selves. Paul's made an ass of himself before, you know. You're not his first little playmate; though he's never given one a fur coat before, and a diamond ring. Just as *if* he could possibly marry you.'

So this was Paul's sister, Amanda – the queer sister who knitted him sweaters and mailed them off, but refused to speak to him on the street.

Amanda got up and prowled around me. A cat on the stalk, ready to spring. Her perfume was Oriental, musky, heavy, as she moved in on what she must think a timid prey. 'Such flawless skin you have,' she said, reaching to stroke my cheek, 'so firm, like porcelain. You won't keep that skin, or all that hair once you're thirty-five or so, and long before then he'll have tired of you. He likes his women young, very young. He likes them pretty, intelligent and talented. I have to acknowledge he has good taste, if not good sense. You see,' she smiled again that hateful smile, 'I really don't give a damn what he does as long as it stays within the limits of decency and doesn't reflect on *my* life.'

'Get out of here,' I managed to say. 'You don't know your brother at all. He's an honourable, generous man and in no way could he harm *your* life.'

Pityingly she smiled.

'My dear child, don't you realize you are ruining his career? Are you fool enough to think this affair has gone unnoticed? In a town the size of Clairmont everybody knows everything. Though Henny can't talk, the neighbours do have eyes and ears. Gossip, that's all I hear, gossip – throwing away his money on juvenile delinquents who take advantage of his good nature, and soon enough he'll be broke, and he won't have a medical practice left!' She was heating up now, and I feared any moment she'd rake my face with her long red nails.

'Get out of here!' I ordered hotly. 'I know all about you, Amanda, for gossip has reached my ears too! Your trouble is you think your brother owes you the rest of his life because you worked to help put him through college and medical school. But I used to keep his books, and he's paid you back, plus ten per cent interest – so he doesn't owe you anything! You're a liar to try and make him seem small in my eyes – for you can't do that! I love him, and he loves me, and nothing you can say can stop our marriage!'

She laughed again, hard and mirthless, then her face turned hard, determined. 'Don't order *me* to do anything! When I'm ready to go, I'll leave – and that's when I've had my say! I flew up here just to see his newest little paramour, his dancing doll . . .

and believe me you won't be his last. Why, Julia used to tell me he –'

I hotly interrupted, 'Get out! Don't you dare say one word more about him! I know about Julia. He's told me. If she drove him to others, I don't blame him; she wasn't a real wife; she was a housekeeper, a cook – not a wife!'

Merrily she laughed – God how she liked to laugh! She was enjoying this, someone competitive enough to fight back, someone she could claw. 'Fool girl! That's the same old line every married man passes on to his newest conquest. Julia was one of the dearest, sweetest, kindest and most wonderful women who ever lived. She did everything she could to please him. Her one fault lay in the fact she couldn't give him all the sex he wanted, or the kind of sex he demanded, so yes, in a way, he did have to turn to others – like you. I'll admit most married men fool around, but they still don't do what he did!'

I hated the spiteful witch now, really detested her. 'What's he done that was so terrible? Julia drowned his three-year-old son – there's nothing on earth that would make *me* take the life of my child! I don't need revenge that much!'

'I agree,' she said, back to the mild tone now. 'That was an insane thing for Julia to do. Scotty was such a handsome, lovely boy – but Paul drove her to do what she did. I understand her reasoning. Scotty was the thing Paul loved most. When you seek to destroy someone emotionally, you kill what he loves best.'

Oh! The horror of her!

'He wears a hair shirt, doesn't he?' she asked in a gloating way, her dark, pretty eyes glowing with satisfaction. 'He tortures himself, blames himself, longs for his son, and then you came along, and he put a baby in you. Don't think the whole town doesn't know about your abortion! We know! We know everything!'

'You lie!' I shrieked. 'It wasn't an abortion! It was because my periods weren't regular!'

'It's on the hospital records,' she said to me smugly. 'You miscarried a two-headed embryo with three legs – twins who didn't separate properly. You poor thing, don't you know you had an abortion?'

Drowning, drowning, I was going under, black swirls of water all around ... two headed? Three legs? Oh, God – the monster baby I so dreaded! But Paul hadn't touched me then, not Paul. 'Don't cry,' she soothed, and I yanked from the touch of her large hand that flashed with diamonds, 'all men are beasts, and I guess he didn't tell you. But don't you see, you can't marry him. I'm doing this for your own good. You're beautiful, young, gifted, and to live in sin with a married man is a pure waste. Save yourself while you can.'

Tears blurred my vision. I rubbed at my eyes as a child would, feeling a child in a crazy adult world as I stared dully at her bland, smooth face. 'Paul's not a married man. Paul's a widower. Julia's dead. She killed herself the day she drowned Scotty.'

Like a mother she patted my shoulder. 'No, child, Julia *is not* dead. Julia lives in an institution where my brother put her after she drowned Scotty. She's still his legal wife, insane or not.'

She thrust into my slack hand several snapshots, pictures of a thin, pitiful-looking woman lying on a hospital bed, her face in profile in both. A woman ravaged by suffering. Her eyes were wide open and staring blankly into space, and her dark hair lay like strings on the pillows. Yet I'd seen too many pictures of Julia not to recognize her, even as changed as she was.

'By the way,' said Paul's sister, leaving me with the snapshots, 'I enjoyed the performance. You're a marvellous dancer. And that young man – he's spectacular. Take *him*. He's obviously in love with you.' She left then. Left me in a daze of broken dreams and floundering in despair. How was I ever going to learn to swim in an ocean of deceit?

Julian took me to the big party which was being thrown in our honour. Hordes of people surrounded us, congratulated us, said so many flattering words. They meant nothing to me. All I could think was Paul had lied to me, lied to me, took me when he knew he was married – *lies*, I hated lies!

Never had Julian been sweeter or more considerate. He held me close in one of those slow, old-fashioned dances, so close I could feel every hard muscle of his lean body, and the maleness of him pressed hard, hard. 'I love you, Cathy,' he whispered. 'I want you so much I can't sleep at night. I want to hold you, make love to you. If you don't let me soon, I'll go mad.' He buried his face in my piled-up hair. 'I've never had anyone brand new, like you. Cathy, please, please love me, love me.'

His face swam before me. He seemed dream-godlike, perfect, and yet, and yet ... 'Julian, what if I told you I wasn't *brand new*?'

'But you are! I know you are!'

'How can you tell?' I giggled drunkenly. 'Is there something written on my face that says I am still a virgin?'

'Yes,' he said firmly. 'Your eyes. Your eyes tell me you don't know what it's like to be loved.'

'Julian, I fear *you* don't know much.'

'You underestimate me, Cathy. You treat me like a little boy one minute, and the next like some hungry wolf who will eat you up. Let me make love to you, then you'll know no man has ever touched you before.'

I laughed. 'All right – but one night only.'

'If you have me for one night, you will never, never want me to go,' he warned, and his eyes glowed and sparkled, black as coal.

'Julian ... I don't love you.'

'But you will – after tonight.'

'Oh, Julian,' I said with a long yawn, 'I'm tired, and partially drunk – go away, leave me alone.'

'Not on your life, kiddo. You said yes, and I'm holding you to it. It's me tonight ... and every night for the rest of your life – or mine.'

On a rainy Saturday morning, with all our luggage already piled into the taxis that would take our company to the airport, Julian and I stood in the city hall with our best friends to support us, and a judge said the words that would bind us together until 'death you do part'. When it came my turn to speak my vows, I hesitated, wanting to run away and fly to Paul. He would be crushed when he found out. Then there was Chris. But Chris would rather see me marry Julian than Paul; that's what he'd told me.

Julian held tight to me, his dark eyes soft and shining with love and pride. I couldn't run. I could only say what I was supposed to, and then I was married to the one man I'd sworn I would never allow to touch me intimately. Not only Julian was happy and proud, but also Madame Zolta who beamed at us and gave us her blessings, kissed our cheeks and shed motherly tears. 'You've done the right thing, Catherine. You will be so happy together, such a beautiful couple . . . but remember not to make any babies!'

'Darling, sweetheart, love,' Julian whispered when we were on the plane flying over the Atlantic, 'don't look so sad. This is our day for rejoicing! I swear you will never be sorry. I'll make you a fantastic husband. I'll never love anyone but you.'

My head bowed down on his shoulder, then I bawled! Crying for everything that should have been mine on my wedding day. Where were my birdsongs, the bells that should chime? Where was the green grass, and the love that was mine? And where was my mother who was the cause of everything gone wrong? *Where?* Did she cry when she thought of us? Or did she, more likely, just take my notes with the newsclippings and tear them up? Yes, that would be like her, never to face up to what she'd done. How easily she tripped away on her second honeymoon and left us in the care of a merciless grandmother, and back she came, all smiling and happy, telling us of what a wonderful time she had. While we, locked up, had been brutalized and starved, and she'd never even looked at Cory and Carrie who didn't grow. Never noticed how shadowed their hollow eyes, how thin their weak legs and arms. Never noticed anything she didn't want to see.

The rain kept coming down, down, forecasting what was ahead. That cold blasting torrent of freezing water put ice on the wings of the plane that was carrying me farther and farther from all those I loved. That ice was in my heart too. And tonight I had to sleep with a man I didn't even like when he wasn't on stage, and dressed in costume, and playing the role of a prince.

But to give Julian his due, he was all he boasted of being in bed. I forgot who he was, and pretended he was someone else as his kisses played over my body, and not one inch went unexplored, unkissed or uncaressed. Before he finished, I wanted him. I was more than willing to have him take me . . . and try to erase the persistent thought that I had just made the worst mistake of my life.

And I had made many mistakes.

LABYRINTH OF LIES

Before our bodies had adjusted to jet lag, we went into rehearsals with the Royal Ballet looking on, comparing our style to theirs. Already Madame Z had told us their way was strictly classical, but we were to do everything in our own way, and were not to be intimidated. 'Stick to your guns, keep it pure, but make each dance your very own. Julian, Catherine, as newlyweds, all eyes will be upon you two – so make every scene as romantic as you can. The two of you together touch my heart and make it cry . . . and if you keep it up, what you're doing, you may make ballet history.'

She smiled, and tears filled the deep furrows about her tiny eyes. 'Let us all prove that America too can produce the very best!' She broke then and turned her back, so we couldn't see her face crumple. 'I love all of you so much,' she sobbed. 'Now go away . . . leave me be . . . and make me proud of you.'

We were determined to do our very damnedest to make Madame Zolta's name famous once more, not as a dancer, but as a teacher. We practised until we fell exhausted into our beds.

The Royal Opera House, Covent Garden shared its space with the ballet company, and when I first saw it I sucked in my breath and held fast to Julian's hand. The red and gold auditorium seated more than two thousand people. Its sparkling swirl of balconies that rose up to a high dome with a sunburst design in the middle stunned me with its old-fashioned splendour. Soon we were to find out that backstage was far less opulent, with no charm in its crowded dressing rooms and a rabbit warren of tiny offices and workrooms; worst of all, no rehearsal studios at all!

And all the time Julian stayed glued to my side. Privacy was something he'd never heard of and had no respect for. Even when I was in the bathroom he had to be there, so I'd race to lock the door and leave him pounding. 'Let me in! I know what you're doing, why all the secrecy?'

Not only that, he wanted to crawl into my mind and know all my past, all my thoughts, everything I'd done. 'And so your mother and father were killed in an auto crash, what happened next?' he asked, holding me in an iron embrace. Why did he have to hear it again? I swallowed. By now I had concocted a believable story about the law wanting to put us in an orphanage, so Chris, Carrie and I had to run away. 'We had a little money saved up, you know, from birthdays, Christmas, and such. We caught a bus that would take us to Florida, but Carrie was sick and threw up, and this huge fat black lady came and took us to her "doctor son". I guess he felt sorry for us; he took us in . . . and that's all there is to it.'

'All there is to it,' he repeated slowly. 'There's a hell of a lot you're not telling me! Though I can guess the rest. He saw a rich plum in a young beautiful girl, and that's why he was so damned generous. Cathy – just how intimate were you with him?'

'I loved him, and I planned to marry him.'

'Then why didn't you?' he shot out. 'Why did you finally say yes to me?'

Tact and subtlety were never among my virtues. I grew angry because he was making me explain, when I didn't want to explain. 'You were at me all the time!' I stormed. 'You made me believe I could learn to love you – but I don't think I can! We've made a mistake, Julian! A horrible mistake!'

'Don't you say anything like that again, you hear!' Julian sobbed as if I'd wounded him terribly, and I was reminded of Chris. I couldn't go through my life damaging everyone I met, so my rage vanished as I allowed him to take me in his arms. His dark head lowered so he could kiss my neck. 'Cathy, I love you so much. More than I ever wanted to love any woman. I've never had anyone love me for myself. Thank you for trying to love me, even though you say you don't.'

It hurt to hear the quiver in his voice. He seemed a small boy who was pleading for the impossible to happen, and perhaps I was doing him an injustice. I turned and wrapped my arms around his neck. 'I do want to love you, Jule. I did marry you, and I am committed, so I'll try and make you the best wife I can. But don't push at me! Don't make demands – just let love come as I learn more about you. You're almost a stranger to me, even though we've known each other for three years.'

He winced, as if I ever really knew him, then love would be, indeed, impossible. He doubted himself so much. Oh, God, what had I done? What kind of person was I, that I could turn from an honest, sincere, honourable man and rush headlong into the arms of someone I suspected was a brute?

Momma had a way of acting impulsively, and being sorry when it was too late. I *wasn't* like her underneath; I couldn't be! I had too many talents to be like someone who had none ... none but for making every man fall in love with her, and that wasn't intelligence. No, I wanted to be like Chris ... and then I floundered again, caught, as always, in the quicksand of *her* making. All of it was her fault, even my marriage to Julian!

'Cathy, you're going to have to learn to overlook a lot of flaws,' said Julian. 'Don't put me up on a pedestal, don't expect perfection. I have feet of clay, as you already know, and if you try to make me into the Prince Charming I think you want ... you are going to fail. You have that doctor of yours on a pedestal too; I think you might be the kind to put all the men you love up so high they are bound to come tumbling down. Just love me and try not to see what doesn't please you.'

I wasn't good at overlooking faults. I'd always seen Momma's when Chris never had. I always flipped over the brightest coin and looked for the tarnish. Funny. Paul's tarnish had seemed all Julia's fault until Amanda came with her horror story. Another reason to hate Momma, making me doubt my instinct!

Long after Julian returned to bed I sat by the windows and contemplated myself, my eyes fixed on the long shiverlets of ice striking the glass. The weather was only telling me what lay ahead. Spring was back there in the garden with Paul ... and I'd done it myself. I didn't have to believe Amanda. God help me if I turned out to be like Momma inside, as well as out!

Our weeks in London were busy, exciting and exhausting – but I dreaded the time when we returned to New York. How long could I keep putting off telling Paul? Not forever. Sooner or later he had to know.

Shortly before the first day of spring, we flew back to Clairmont, and we took a taxi to Paul's house. It was the place of our deliverance, and it seemed nothing there had changed. Only I had, for I was coming to devastate a man who didn't need to be hurt again.

I stared at the boxwoods neatly clipped into cones and spheres, and the wisteria trees that were blooming; azaleas rioted colourfully everywhere, and the big magnolias were ripe and soon to flower, and over everything emerald draped the dangling grey Spanish moss, misting and fogging, to create shreds of living lace. I sighed. If at twilight there was anything more beautiful and somehow romantically, sadly mystical than a live oak dripping with Spanish moss that would in the end kill its host, I'd yet to see it. Love that clung and killed.

I thought I could take Julian inside, then tell Paul our news – but I couldn't. 'Would you mind waiting on the veranda until I tell Paul?' I asked. For some reason he only nodded. I'd expected an argument. Agreeably, for a change, he sat in a white wicker rocker, the same one Paul had been in when first we found him dozing on that Sunday afternoon, after the bus put us off. He'd been forty then. He was now forty-three.

Quivering a little, I went on alone to open the front door with my own key. I could have telephoned or sent a cable. But I had to see his face and watch his eyes, and try to read his thoughts. I needed to know if I'd really injured his heart, or only wounded his pride and ego.

No one heard me open the door. No one heard my footsteps on the hard parquet of the foyer. Paul was sprawled in his favourite chair before the colour television and the fireplace, dozing. His long legs were stretched to rest on the matching ottoman, his ankles crossed and his shoes off. Carrie was sitting cross-legged on the floor near his chair, as always needing to be near someone who loved her. She was deeply engrossed in her play with the small porcelain dolls. She wore a white sweater banded at the neck and wrists with purple, and over this her red corduroy jumper. She looked like a pretty little doll.

My eyes went again to Paul. In his light dozing sleep he had the expression of someone anxiously waiting. Even his feet moved often to cross and uncross, while his fingers flexed into fists, then unflexed. His head was thrown back to rest on the high back of his chair, but that too kept moving from side to side . . . dreaming, I thought, maybe of me. Then his face turned in my direction. Did he sense my presence even in his sleep?

Ever so slowly his eyelids fluttered open. He yawned and lifted a hand to cover his mouth . . . then stared at me fuzzily. As if I were merely an apparition. 'Catherine,' he murmured, 'is that you?'

Carrie heard his question, jumped up and came flying to me, crying out my name as I caught her and swung her high. I lavished on her small face a dozen or so kisses, and hugged her so tight she cried out, 'Ouch, that hurts!' She looked so pretty, so fresh and well fed. 'Oh, Cathy, why did you stay away *so long*? We wait every day for you to come home, and you never do. We make plans for your wedding, but when you don't write, Dr Paul says we should wait. Why did you send only postcards? Didn't you have time to write long letters? Chris said you must be awfully busy.' She had pulled out of my arms and was back on the floor near Paul's chair, and staring at me reproachfully. 'Cathy . . . you forgot all about us, didn't you? All you care about is dancing. You don't need a family when you dance.'

'Yes, I do need a family, Carrie,' I said absently, with my eyes fixed on Paul, trying to read what he was thinking.

Paul got up and came towards me, his eyes locked with mine. We embraced and Carrie sat quietly on the floor and watched, as if studying the way a woman should act with the man she loved. His lips only brushed over mine. Yet his touch shivered me as Julian's never did. 'You look different,' he said to me in his slow, soft way. 'You've lost weight. You look tired too. Why didn't you telephone or telegraph to let me know you were on the way? I would have met you at the airport.'

'You look thinner too,' I said in a hoarse whisper. His weight loss was far more becoming than mine. His moustache seemed darker, thicker. I touched it tentatively, longingly, knowing it wasn't mine to feel now – and he had grown it just to please me.

'It hurt when you stopped writing to me every day. Did you stop when your schedule became too crowded?'

'Something like that. It's tiring to dance every day, and try to see as much as possible at the same time ... I got so busy, I never had enough time.'

'I subscribe to *Variety* now.'

'Oh ...' was all I could say, praying they didn't write about my marriage to Julian. 'I've nominated myself as your clipping service, though Chris is keeping a scrapbook too. Whenever he's home, we compare clippings; if one of us has something the other doesn't, we have it photocopied.' He paused as if puzzled by my expression, my demeanour, something. 'They are all rave reviews, Catherine, why do you look so ... so ... emotionless?'

'Tired, like you said.' I hung my head not knowing what to say, or how to meet his eyes. 'And how've you been?'

'Catherine, is something the matter? You act strange.' Carrie was staring at me ... as if Paul had expressed her thoughts too. I gazed around the big room filled with the beauty of all that Paul had collected. Sunlight through the ivory sheers shone on the miniatures in his tall étagère with the glass shelves, the black, gold-veined mirror behind them, and lit from the top and bottom. How easy to hide away in looking around, pretending everything was all right, when everything was all wrong.

'Catherine, speak to me!' Paul cried. 'There is something wrong!'

I sat down, knees weak, my throat tight. Why couldn't I ever do anything right? How could he have lied to me, deceived me, when he knew I'd had enough of lying and deceit? And how could he look so trustworthy still?

'When will Chris be home?'

'Friday, for Easter vacation.' His long look was reflective, as if he thought it strange when usually Chris and I kept in constant communication. Then there was Henny to greet and hug and kiss ... and I could put it off no longer ... though I found a way. 'Paul, I brought Julian home with me ... He's out on the veranda waiting. Is that all right?'

He gave me the strangest look, and then nodded. 'Of course.

Ask him in.' Then he turned to Henny. 'Set two more places, Henny.'

Julian came in, and, as I'd cautioned him, he didn't say a word to let anyone know we were married. Both of us had taken off our wedding rings and had them in our pockets. It was the strangest of quiet meals, and even when Julian and I handed out the gifts the stiffness grew, and Carrie only glanced at her bracelet of rubies and amethysts, though Henny beamed a broad smile when she put on her solid gold bracelet.

'Thank you for the lovely figurine of yourself, Cathy,' said Paul, putting it carefully aside on the closest table. 'Julian, would you please excuse Cathy and me for a while? I'd like to have a private talk with her.' He said this as a doctor requesting a private interview with the responsible family member of a critically ill patient. Julian nodded and smiled at Carrie. She glared back at him.

'I'm going to bed,' stated Carrie defiantly. 'Good night, Mr Marquet. I don't know why you had to help Cathy buy me that bracelet, but thank you anyway.'

Julian was left in the living room to stare at the TV as Paul and I took off for a stroll in his magnificent gardens. Already his fruit trees were in bloom, and climbing red, pink and white roses made a brilliant display on the white trellises.

'What's wrong, Catherine?' Paul asked. 'You come home to me and bring along another man, so maybe you don't have to explain at all. I can guess.'

Quickly I put out my hand to seize hold of his. 'Stop! Don't say anything!' Falteringly and very slowly I began to tell him about his sister's visit. 'Why did you lead me to believe Julia was dead, Paul? Did you think me such a child I couldn't bear to hear it? I could have understood if you had told me. I loved you, don't you ever doubt that I did! I didn't give to you because I thought I owed you anything. I gave because I wanted to give, because I desperately needed you. I knew better than to expect marriage, and I was happy enough in the relationship we had. I would have been your mistress forever – but you should have told me about Julia! You should have known me well enough to realize I'm impulsive, I act without thought when I'm hurt – and it hurt terribly that night Amanda came and told me your wife was still alive!

'Lies!' I cried. 'Oh, how I hate liars! *You* of all people to lie to me! Besides Chris, there was no one I trusted more than you.'

He'd stopped strolling, as I had. The nude marble statues were all around, mocking us. Laughing at love gone awry. For now we were like them, frozen and cold.

'Amanda,' he said, rolling her name on his tongue as something bitter and fit to be spat out. 'Amanda and her half-truths. You ask why – why didn't you ask *why* before you flew to London? Why didn't you give me the chance to defend myself?'

'How can you defend lies!' I hit back meanly, wanting him to hurt as I'd hurt that night when Amanda slammed out of the theatre.

He walked away to lean against the oldest oak, and from his pocket he drew a pack of cigarettes.

'Paul, I'm sorry. Tell me now what your defence would have been.'

Slowly he puffed on the cigarette, and exhaled smoke. That smoke came my way and weaved around my head, neck, body – and chased off the scent of roses. 'Remember when you came,' he began, taking his time, 'you were so bitter from your loss of Cory, to say nothing of how you felt about your mother. How could I tell you my own sordid story when already you'd known too much pain? How was I to know you and I would become lovers? You seemed to me only a beautiful, haunted child – though you've touched me deeply – always you've touched me. You touch me now, standing there with your accusing eyes. Though you are right. I *should* have told you.' He sighed heavily.

'I told you about the day Scotty was three, and how Julia took him down to the river and held him under the water until he was dead. But what I didn't tell you was that she lived on . . . A whole team of doctors worked on her for hours on end trying to bring her out of the coma, but she never came out.'

'Coma,' I whispered. 'She's alive now, and still in the same coma?'

He smiled so bitterly, and then looked up at the moon that was

204

smiling too, sarcastically, I thought. He turned his head and allowed his eyes to meet mine. 'Yes, Julia lived on, with her heart beating, and before you came along with your brother and sister I drove every day to visit her in a private institution. I'd sit beside her bed, hold her hand, and force myself to look at her gaunt face and skeleton body ... It was the best way I had to torment myself and try to wash away the guilt I felt. I watched her hair become thinner each day – the pillows, covers, everything covered by her hair as she withered away before my very eyes. She was connected to tubes that helped her to breathe, and a tube was in her arm through which she was fed. Her brain waves were flat, but her heart kept on beating. Mentally she was dead, physically she was alive. If she ever came out of the coma, she'd never speak, move, or even be able to think. She'd have been a living dead woman at the age of twenty-six. That's how old she was when she took my son down to the river to hold him under the shallow water. It was hard for me to believe a woman who loved her child so much could drown him and feel his struggles to live ... and yet she did it just to get back at me.' He paused, flicked the ash from his cigarette and turned his shadowed eyes to me. 'Julia reminds me of your mother ... Both could do anything when they felt justified.'

I sighed, he sighed, and the wind and flowers sighed too. I think those marble statues sighed along as well, in their lack of understanding the human condition. 'Paul, when did you see Julia last? Doesn't she have any chance at all for a full recovery?' I began to cry.

He gathered me in his arms and kissed the top of my head. 'Don't cry for her, my beautiful Catherine. It's all over for Julia now; she is finally at peace. The year we became lovers, she died less than a month after we started. Quietly she just slipped away. I remember at the time you looked at me as if you sensed something was wrong. It wasn't that I felt less for you that made me stand back and look at myself. It was a blend of painful guilt and sorrow that someone as sweet and lovely as Julia, my childhood sweetheart, had to leave life without once experiencing all the wonderful, beautiful things it had to give.' He cupped my face between my palms, and tenderly kissed away my tears.

'Now smile and say the words I see in your eyes, say you love me. When you brought Julian home with you, I thought it was over between us, but now I can tell it will never be over. You've given me the best you have within you, and I'll know that even when you're off thousands of miles, dancing with younger and handsomer men ... you'll be faithful to me, as I'll be faithful to you. We'll make it work, because two people who are sincerely in love can always overcome obstacles no matter what they are.'

Oh ... how could I tell him now? 'Julia's dead?' I asked, quivering, deep in shock, hating myself and Amanda! 'Amanda lied to me ... She knew Julia was dead, and yet she flew to New York to tell me a lie? Paul, what kind of woman is she?'

He held me so tight I felt my ribs ache, but I clung just as fast to him, knowing this was the last time I could. I kissed him wildly and passionately, knowing I'd never feel his lips again on mine. He laughed jubilantly, sensing all the love and passion I had for him, and in a happy, lighter voice he said, 'Yes, my sister knew when Julia died; she was at her funeral. Though she didn't speak to me. Now please stop crying. Let me dry your tears.' He used his handkerchief to touch to my cheeks and the corners of my eyes, then held it so I could blow my nose.

I'd acted the child, the impulsive, impatient child Chris had warned me not to be – and I had betrayed Paul who trusted me. 'I still don't understand Amanda,' I said in a mournful wail, still putting off that moment of truth I didn't know if I could face. He held me and stroked my back, my hair, as I clung with my arms about his waist, staring up into his face.

'Sweetheart, Catherine, why do you look and act so strange?' he said in his voice that had gone back to normal. 'Nothing my sister said should rob us of taking what joy we can from life. Amanda wants to drive me out of Clairmont. She wants to take over this house so she can leave it to her son, so she does her best to ruin my reputation. She's very active socially and fills the ears of her friends with lies about me. And if there were women before Julia drowned my son, that was lesson enough for me to change my ways. There was no other woman until *you*! I've even heard it rumoured that Amanda has spread it about that I made you pregnant and you had an abortion. You see what a spiteful woman can do – anything!'

Now it was too late, too late. He asked me again to stop crying. 'Amanda,' I said stiffly, my control about to break. 'She said that I had an abortion. She said you kept the embryo, one with two heads. I've seen that thing in your office in a bottle. Paul, how could you keep it? Why didn't you have it buried? A monster baby! It isn't fair – it isn't – why, why?'

He groaned and wiped his hand over his eyes, to quickly deny everything. 'I could kill her for telling you that! A lie, Catherine, all a lie!'

'Was it a lie? It could have been mine, you know that. For God's sake, Chris doesn't know – he didn't lie to me too, did he?'

He sounded frantic as he denied everything, and sought once more to embrace me, but I jumped backwards, and thrust forth both arms to ward him off. 'There *is* a bottle in your office with a baby like that inside! I saw it! Paul, how could you? You, of all people, to save something like that!'

'No!' he flared immediately. 'That thing was given to me years ago when I was in medical school – a joke, really – students play all sorts of jokes you'd find gruesome, and I'm telling you the truth, Catherine, you didn't abort.' Then he stopped abruptly, just as I did, with my thoughts reeling. I'd betrayed myself!

I began to cry. *Chris, Chris, there was a baby, there was a monster just like we feared.*

'No,' said Paul again and again, 'it's not yours, and even if it were, it wouldn't make any difference to me. I know you and Chris love each other in a special way. I've always known it, and I do understand.'

'Once,' I whispered through my sobs, 'only once on one terrible night.'

'I'm sorry it was terrible.'

I stared up at him then, marvelling that he could look at me with so much softness and so much respect, even knowing the full truth. 'Paul,' I asked tremulously, timidly, 'was it an unforgivable sin?'

'No ... an understandable act of love, I'd call it.'

He held me, he kissed me, he stroked my back and began telling me his plans for our wedding. '... and Chris will give you away, and Carrie will be your bridesmaid. Chris was very hesitant and wouldn't meet my eyes when I discussed this with him. He said he thought you weren't mature enough to handle a complicated marriage like ours will be. I know it's not going to be easy for you, or for me. You'll be touring the world, dancing with young, handsome men. However, I'm looking forward to accompanying you on a few of those tours. To be the husband of a prima ballerina will be inspiring, exciting. Why, I could even be your company doctor. Surely dancers need doctors on occasion?'

I went dead inside. 'Paul,' I began dully, 'I can't marry you.' Then, quite out of context, I went on, 'You know, wasn't it stupid of Momma to hide our birth certificates inside the linings of our two suitcases? She didn't do too good a job and the linings ripped and I found them. Without my birth certificate I couldn't have applied for a passport, and I also needed that certificate to prove I was of age to apply for a marriage licence. You see, several days before our company flew to London Julian and I had blood tests and our marriage ceremony was just a simple one, with Madame Zolta and the company dancers there, and even as I said my marriage vows, and swore fidelity to Julian ... I was thinking of you, and Chris, and hating myself, and knowing I was doing the wrong thing.'

Paul didn't say anything. He reeled backwards, then staggered over to fall upon a marble bench. For moments he just sat, and then his head drooped into his hands and he hid his face.

I stood. He sat. He lost himself somewhere, while I waited for him to come back and rail at me. But his voice when it came was as soft as a whisper, 'Come, sit beside me for a while. Hold my hand. Give me time to realize it's all over between us.' I did as he said and held his hand, while both of us stared up at the sky full of diamonds and dark clouds.

'I'll never hear your kind of music again without thinking of you ...'

'Paul, I'm sorry! I wish to God I'd listened to my instinct that told me Amanda was lying. But the music was playing where I was too and you were far away, and Julian was there, pleading with me, telling me he loved and needed me, and I believed him, and convinced myself you didn't really love me. I can't bear to be without someone who loves me.'

'I'm very happy he loves you,' he said, then got up quickly and started for the house, his strides so long and fast I'd never catch up even if I ran. 'Don't say another word! Leave me alone, Catherine! Don't follow me! You did the right thing – don't doubt that! I was an old fool, playing with a young one, and you don't have to tell me I should have known better – I already know that!'

TOO MANY LOVES TO LOSE

Gone as deaf and stony as one of Paul's marble statues, I sat on the veranda and stared up at the night sky that was turning stormy and black with clouds. Julian came out to sit beside me and in his embrace I began to cry softly. 'Why?' he asked. 'You do love me a little, don't you? Your doctor can't be really hurt; he was very kind to me, and told me to come out and comfort you.'

It was then that Henny came out to signal with her lightning-fast signs that her doctor-son was packing for a trip and I was to stay here. 'What's she saying to you?' asked Julian with annoyance. 'Damn, it's like hearing someone talk in a foreign tongue. I feel so left out.'

'Stay here and wait!' I ordered, then jumped up to race into the house and fly up the back stairs, then on into Paul's room where he was flinging his clothes into an open suitcase on his bed. 'Look,' I cried in distress, 'there's no reason why you have to leave! This is your home. *I'll* go. I'll take Carrie with me, so you need never see my face again!' He turned to give me a long and bitter look as he went on putting shirts in his bag.

'Cathy, you've taken the wife I expected to have, and now you want to take away my daughter. Carrie is like my own flesh and blood, and she wouldn't fit into your kind of life. Let her stay with me and Henny. Let me have something to call my own. I'll be back before you go ... and you should know that Julian's father is very, very ill.'

'Georges is ill?'

'Yes. Perhaps you don't know that he's had kidney disease for several years, and has been on a dialysis machine for months. I don't think he'll live much longer. He's not my patient, but I stop in to visit him as often as I can, more or less to hear about you and Julian. Now will you please get out, Cathy, and not force me to say things I'd regret.'

I cried face down on my bed until Henny came into my room.

Strong, motherly, dark hands patted my back. Henny's misting, liquid brown eyes spoke when her tongue couldn't. She talked to me with her gestures, and then took from her apron pocket a clipping from the local newspaper. An announcement of my marriage to Julian! 'Henny,' I wailed, 'what am I going to do? I'm married to Julian, and I can't demand a divorce; he depends on me, believes in me!'

Henny shrugged her broad shoulders, expressing that people were as complex to her as they were to me. Then quickly she signalled, 'Big sister always been big trouble maker. One man already hurt, no good hurting two. Doctor good man, strong man, will survive disappointment, but young dancing man might not. Wipe away tears, cry no more, put on big smile and go downstairs and take hand of new husband. For everything work out for the best. You see.'

I did as Henny directed, and joined Julian in the living room, and there I told him about his father being in the hospital, and not expected to live. His pale face went even whiter. Nervously he chewed on his lower lip. 'It's really that serious?'

It had been my opinion that Julian didn't care much for his father, so I was surprised to see his reaction. At that moment Paul came into the living room with his suitcase and offered to drive us to the hospital. 'And remember, my house has plenty of rooms, and there is no reason at all why the two of you should even consider a hotel. Stay as long as you like. I'll be back in a few days.'

He backed his car out of the garage so Julian and I could join him on the front seat. Hardly a word was said until he let us out in front of the hospital, and sadly I hesitated before the steps, watching Paul drive away into the night.

They had Georges in a private room, and with him was Madame Marisha. When I saw Georges in the bed, I drew in my breath! Oh! To be like that! He was so thin he seemed already dead. His face had a greyish pallor, and every bone he had jutted forward to make jagged peaks beneath the thin skin. Madame M was crouched at his side, staring down into his gaunt face pleading with her eyes, commanding him to hold on and live! 'My love, my love, my love,' she crooned as to a baby, 'do not go, do not leave me alone. We have so much to do yet, to experience yet . . . Our son has to reach fame before you die . . . Hold on, my love, hold on.'

Only then did Madame Marisha glance up to see us there, and with her same old authority she snapped, 'Well, Julian. You did finally come! And after all the cables I sent you! What did you do, tear them up and dance on, as if nothing matters?'

I blanched, very surprised, and looked from him to Madame. 'My dear mother,' he said coldly, 'we were on tour, you know that. We had engagements and contracts, so my wife and I kept our commitments.'

'You heartless brute!' she snarled, then gestured for him to come closer. 'Now you say something kind and loving to that man on the bed,' she hissed in a whisper, 'or so help me God I'll make you wish you were never born!'

Julian had a great deal of trouble making the effort to approach the bed, so much so I had to give him a shove, while his mother sobbed into a handful of pink tissues. 'Hello, Father,' was all he could manage, along with, 'I'm sorry you are so ill.' Quickly he came back to me, and held me hard against him. I felt his whole body trembling.

'See, my love, my sweetheart, my darling,' crooned Madame Marisha again, once more bending above her husband and smoothing back his damp dark hair. 'Open your dear eyes and see who has flown thousands of miles to be at your side. Your own Julian and his wife. All the way from London they flew the moment they knew you were so sick. Open your eyes, my heart, see him again, see them together, such a beautiful pair of newlyweds – please open your eyes, please look.'

On the bed the pale, thin wraith of a man slitted his dark eyes and they moved slowly, trying to focus on Julian and me. We were at the foot of his bed, but he didn't seem to see us. Madame got up to push us closer, and then held Julian there so he couldn't back off. Georges opened his eyes a bit wider and thinly smiled. 'Ah, Julian,' he sighed. 'Thank you for coming. I have so much to say to you – things I should have said before . . .' He faltered, stammered, 'I should have –' and then he broke off. I waited for him to continue – and I waited. I saw his wide-open eyes glaze and go blank and his head stayed so still. Madame screamed! A doctor and nurse came on the run, and shooed us out as they began to work over Georges.

We formed a pitiful group in the hall outside his room, and in only a short while the grey-haired doctor came out to say he was sorry, all had been done that could be done. It was over. 'It is better so,' he added. 'Death can be a good friend to those in extreme pain. I wondered how he held on so long ...'

I stared and stared at Julian, for we could have come back sooner. But Julian made his eyes blank and refused to speak. 'He was your father!' screamed Madame as tears streaked her cheeks. 'For two weeks he suffered, waiting to see you before he could let himself die and escape the hell of living on!'

Julian whirled, his pale skin flamed with bright red fury, as he lashed out at his mother, 'Madame, just what did my father give me? All I was to him was an extension of himself! All he was to me was a dance instructor! Work, dance, that's all he ever said! He never discussed what I wanted besides the dance; he didn't give a damn what else I wanted, or what else I needed! I wanted him to love me for myself; I wanted him to see me as his son, not just as a dancer. I loved him; I wanted him to see I loved him, and say he loved me in return ... but he never did! And try as I would to dance perfectly, he never gave me a compliment – for I didn't do anything nearly as well as he could have done it when he was my age! So, that is what I was to him, somebody to step into his shoes and carry on his name! But, damn him, and you, I've got my own legal name ... Julian Marquet, not Georges Rosencoff, and his name will not live on and steal from me what fame I achieve!'

I held Julian in my arms that night, understanding him as I hadn't before. When he broke down and cried, I cried along with him, for a father he'd professed to despise, when underneath he loved him. And I thought of Georges, and how sad it was that he tried, too late, to say what he should have years and years ago.

So we'd come from a honeymoon where we had achieved a certain amount of fame and publicity, and given many, many hours of hard work, only to attend the funeral of a father who wouldn't live to know about his son's accomplishments. All the glory of London now seemed shrouded in funereal mists.

Madame Marisha held out her arms to me when the graveside ceremony was over. She held me in her thin arms, as she might have once held Julian, and in a sort of hypnotic trance we rocked back and forth, both of us crying. 'Be good to my son, Catherine,' she sobbed and sniffled. 'Have patience with him when he acts wild. His has not been an easy life, for much of what he says is true. Always he felt himself in competition with his father, and never could he surpass his father's abilities. Now I will tell you something. My Julian has a love for you that is almost holy. He thinks you are the best thing that has ever happened in his life, and to him you are without flaw. If you have flaws, hide them. He won't understand. A hundred times he's been in then out of love, all within the space of a few months. For years you frustrated him. So now that he's your husband, give to him generously all the love that's been denied, for I am not a demonstrative woman. I have always wanted to be, but somehow I could never humble myself to touch first. Touch him often, Catherine. Take his hand when he would pull from you and go off and sulk alone. Understand why he's moody, and love him three times as much. That way you will bring out the best in him, for he does have admirable qualities. He has to, for he is Georges's son.'

She kissed me, and said goodbye for a while, and made me swear to come with Julian often on visits. 'Fit me in the corners of your life,' she said with sadness making her face long and hollow eyed. But when I promised, and turned to look, Julian was glaring hard at the both of us.

Chris came home for his Easter vacation, and less than eagerly he greeted Julian. I noticed Julian glaring at him with narrowed, suspicious eyes.

No sooner were Chris and I alone when he bellowed, 'You married *him*? Why couldn't you wait? How could you be so intuitive when we were locked away and so damned dumb now that we're out! I was wrong not wanting you to marry Paul only because he is so much older. And I admit it, I was jealous, and

didn't want you to marry anyone. I had a dream of you and me
... some day. Well ... you know what I dreamed. But if it had to
be a choice between Paul and Julian, then it should have been
Paul! He's the one who took us in, and fed and clothed us, and
gave us the best of everything. I don't like Julian. He'll destroy
you.'

He hesitated, turning his back so I couldn't see his face. He
was twenty-one and beginning to take on the virile strength of a
man. In him I could see so much of our father – and our mother.
And when I wanted to, I could take things and twist them to suit
my purpose, and so I thought he was more like Momma in some
ways than like Daddy. I started to say this, and then I too
floundered, for I couldn't. He wasn't anything at all like our
mother!

Chris was strong ... she was weak. He was noble, she was
without any honour at all. 'Chris ... don't make it harder for me.
Let's be friends again. Julian is hot-headed and arrogant and a
lot of things that irritate on the surface, but underneath he's a
little boy.'

'But you don't love him,' he said without meeting my eyes.

In a few hours Julian and I would be leaving. I asked Carrie if
she would like to come and live in New York with us, but I had
lost her trust; I had betrayed her too many times already and she
let me know it. 'You go on back to New York, Cathy, where it
snows all the time – but you leave me here! I used to want to be
with you, now I don't care! You went and married that Julian
with the black eyes when you could have been Dr Paul's wife,
and my real mother. I'll marry him! You think he won't want me
'cause I'm too little – but he will. You think he's too old for me,
but I won't be able to get anybody else, so he'll feel sorry and
marry me, and we'll have six children – you just wait and see!'

'Carrie –'

'Shut up! I don't like you now! *Go away! Stay away! Dance
until you die! Chris and me don't want you! Nobody here wants
you!*'

Those screamed words hurt! My Carrie, yelling at me to go
away, when I'd been like a mother to her most of her life. Then I
looked over to where Chris was standing before the pink

215

sweetheart roses, his shoulders sagging, and in his eyes, oh, those blue, blue eyes ... that look would always follow me. Never, never was his love going to set me free to love anyone without reservations as long as he kept loving me.

Just an hour before we had to leave for the airport Paul's car turned into the drive. He smiled at me as he always smiled, as if nothing between us had changed. He had some tale to tell Julian of a medical convention that had kept him away, and he was terribly sad and sorry to hear his father had died. He shook hands with Chris, then slapped him heartily on the back, the way men so commonly showed affection to one another. He greeted Henny, kissed Carrie and gave her a little box of candy, and only then did he look at me.

'Hello, Cathy.'

That told me so much. I was no longer Catherine, a woman he could love as an equal, I had been moved back to only a daughter. 'And, Cathy, you can't take Carrie with you to New York. She belongs with me and Henny so she can see her brother from time to time, and I'd hate for her to change schools too.'

'I wouldn't leave you for nothing,' said Carrie staunchly. Julian went upstairs to finish packing his things, and I dared to follow Paul out into the garden, despite the forbidding look Chris gave me. He was down on his knees, still wearing a good suit, pulling up a few weeds someone had overlooked. He got up quickly when he heard my steps and brushed the grass from his trousers, then he stared off into space as if the last thing he wanted to do was to look at me.

'Paul ... this would have been our wedding day.'

'Would it? I'd forgotten.'

'You haven't forgotten,' I said, drawing closer, ' "The first day of spring, a fresh start" you said. I'm so sorry I spoiled everything. I was a fool to have believed Amanda. I was a double fool not to have waited to talk to you first before I married Julian.'

'Let's not talk about it any more,' he said with a heavy sigh. 'It's all over now, and finished.' Voluntarily he stepped close

216

enough to draw me into his arms. 'Cathy, I went away to be alone. I needed that time to think. When you lost faith in me, you turned impulsively, but truthfully, to the man who has loved you for a number of years. Any fool with eyes could see that. And if you can be honest with yourself, you have been in love with Julian almost as long as he's loved you. I believe you put your love for him on a shelf because you thought you owed me ...'

'Stop saying that! I love you, not him. I'll always love you!'

'You're all mixed up, Cathy ... You want me, you want him, you want security, you want adventure. You think you can have everything, and you can't. I told you a long time ago April wasn't meant for September. We did and said a lot of things to convince ourselves that the years between us didn't matter, but they do matter. And it isn't only the years, it's the space that would separate us. You'd be somewhere dancing and I'd be here, rooted and tied down but for a few weeks a year. I'm a doctor first and a husband second – sooner or later you'd find that out and you'd turn to Julian eventually anyway.' He smiled, and tenderly kissed away the tears I always had to shed, and he told me fate always dealt out the right cards. 'And we'll still see each other – it isn't as if we're forever lost to one another – and I have my memories of how wonderfully sweet and exciting it was between us.'

'You don't love me!' I cried accusingly. 'You never loved me, or you wouldn't be taking this so agreeably!'

Softly he chuckled and cuddled me close again, as a father would. 'Dear Catherine, my hot-blooded, feisty dancer, what man wouldn't love you? How did you learn so much about loving locked away in a cold, dim, northern room?'

'From books,' I said, but the lessons taught were not all from books.

His hands were in my hair and his lips were near mine. 'I'll never forget the best birthday gift I ever had.' His breath was warm on my cheeks. 'Now here's the way it's going to be from now on,' he said firmly. 'You and Julian will go back to New York, and you will make him the best wife you are capable of being. The two of you will do your damnedest to set the world on fire with your dancing, and you've got to determine never to look back with regrets, and forget about me.'

'And you – what about you?'

He lifted his hand and fingered his moustache. 'You'd be surprised what this moustache has done for my sex appeal. I might never shave it off.'

We both laughed, real laughter, not faked. I took then the two-carat diamond ring he'd given me and tried to return it to him. 'No! I want you to keep that ring. Save it to hock, when or if you ever need a bit of extra cash.'

Julian and I flew back to New York and hunted for weeks before we found just the right cosy apartment. He wanted something much more elegant, but between us we didn't earn enough for the penthouse apartment he thought was our due. 'Sooner or later though, I'll see we live in that kind of place, near Central Park, in rooms filled with real flowers.'

'We don't have time to baby along real plants and flowers,' I said, having experienced all the time and trouble it took to keep flowers and plants alive and healthy. 'And when we go to visit Carrie, we can always enjoy Paul's gardens.'

'I don't like that doctor of yours.'

'He's not *my* doctor!' I felt fluttery inside, afraid for no reason at all. 'Why don't you like Paul? Everybody else likes him well enough.'

'Yeah, I know,' he answered shortly, pausing with his fork held midway between his plate and his mouth. He gave me a heavy, solemn look. 'That's the trouble, my darling wife, I think you like him *too* much, even now. And what's more, I'm not crazy about your brother, either. Your sister is okay. You can ask her up for visits once in a while – but don't you ever forget, not for one second, that I come first in your life now. Not Chris, not Carrie, and, most of all, not that doctor you were engaged to. I'm not blind or stupid, Cathy. I've seen him look at you, and though I don't know how far you went with him before you'd better let it be dead now!'

My head bowed with the panic I felt. My brother and sister were like extensions of myself! I needed them in my life, not just on the fringes. What had I done? I had the blinding precognition that he was going to be my loving keeper, my gaoler, and I'd be as imprisoned with him as I'd been in the locked room in Foxworth Hall! Only this time I'd be as free to come and go as far as his invisible chain would allow. 'I love you like crazy,' he said, polishing off the last of his meal. 'You are the best thing that's ever happened to me. I want you at my side all the time, *never* out of sight. I need you to keep me straight. I drink too much sometimes, and then I get mean, real mean, Cathy. I want you to make me over into what you think I am on stage; I don't want to hurt you.'

He touched me then, for I knew he'd been terribly hurt, as I'd been hurt, and he'd been so disappointed in his father, as my mother had disappointed me. And he needed me. Maybe Paul was right. Fate had used Amanda to deal out the right cards so Julian and I would be winners, not losers. Youth did call to its own age, and he was young, handsome, a talented dancer – and charming when he wanted to be. He had a cruel, dark side, I knew that. I'd experienced some of that ... but I could tame him. I wouldn't let him be my ruler and my judge, my superior or my master. We'd make it fifty-fifty, share and be equals, and eventually, one bright and sunny morning, I'd wake up and see his darkly stubbled face and know I loved him. Know I loved him better than anyone I'd loved before – anyone.

PART THREE

DREAMS COME TRUE

While Julian and I worked slavishly to reach the top of the ballet world, Chris whizzed his way through college, and in his fourth year he entered an accelerated programme for medical students, completing his fourth year of college while simultaneously beginning his first year of medical school.

He flew to New York and explained it to me while we strolled hand in hand in Central Park. It was spring and the birds were chirping and merrily collecting the trash they needed to build nests.

'Chris, Julian doesn't know you're here, and I'd rather he didn't find out. He's terribly jealous of you, and Paul too. Would you feel insulted if I didn't ask you over for dinner?'

'Yes,' he said stubbornly. 'I came up to visit my sister, and visit my sister I will. Not furtively either. You can tell him I came to visit Yolanda. Besides, I only intend to stay for the weekend.'

Julian was obsessively possessive of me. He was like an only child who needed constant pampering, and I didn't mind, except when he tried to keep me from my family. 'Okay. He's rehearsing now, and he thinks I'm home doing housework before I join him this afternoon. But stay away from Yolanda, Chris. She's nothing but trouble. Whatever she does with any man is news for the class the next day.'

He gave me a strange look. 'Cathy, I don't give a damn about Yolanda. She was just my excuse to see you; I know your husband hates me.'

'I wouldn't call it hate ... not exactly.'

'All right, call it jealousy, but whatever it is, he's not keeping me from you.' His tone and his look grew serious. 'Cathy, always you and Julian seem just on the verge of making it big, and then something happens, and you never become the stars you should be. What is it?'

I shrugged. I didn't know what it was. I thought Julian and I were as dedicated to the dance as any others, and even more so, and still Chris was right ... we'd put on a spectacular performance and draw rave reviews, and then we'd slide backwards. Perhaps Madame Zolta didn't want us to become superstars, lest we leave her company and join another.

'How is Paul?' I asked as we sat on a bench dappled with sunlight and shade.

Chris had my hand in his and tightly he held it. 'Paul's Paul ... he never changes. Carrie adores him; he adores her. He treats me like a younger brother he's very proud of. And really, Cathy, I don't think I would have made it as well without all the tutoring he gave me.'

'He hasn't found anyone else to love?' I asked in a tight voice. I didn't fully believe Paul's letters that said there weren't any women he cared for.

'Cathy,' said Chris, putting his fingers tenderly under my chin to tilt my face upwards to his, 'how can Paul find anyone to equal you?' I could have cried from the expression in his eyes. Would the past never set me free?

No sooner did Julian see Chris than the two of them were at it. 'I don't want you sleeping under my roof!' stormed Julian. 'I don't like you and I never have and never will – so get the hell out and forget you've got a sister!' Chris left to stay at a hotel, and on the sly we met once or twice before he went back to his school. Dully I went back to attend class with Julian, then the afternoon rehearsal and the evening performance. Sometimes we had the lead roles, sometimes only minor ones, and sometimes, as punishment for some sarcastic remark Julian would make to Madame Zolta, we both had to dance in the *corps*. Chris didn't visit New York again for three years.

When Carrie was fifteen she came to spend her first summer with us in New York. Hesitating and frightened-looking from the long flight she'd made all alone, she ambled slowly through the bustling, noisy crowds at the airport terminal. Julian spotted her first and he cried out, then bounded forward to sweep her up in his arms. 'Hi there, gorgeous sister-in-law!' he greeted, planting a hearty kiss on her cheek. 'My, how much you grow to look like Cathy – first thing you know I won't even know the difference – so watch out! Are you positively sure the dancing life isn't for you?'

She was made happy and secure by his pleasure to see her again, and quickly she responded by throwing her arms about his neck. In the three years Julian and I had been married, she'd learned to love him for what he appeared to be. 'Don't you dare call me Tinkerbell!' she said, laughing. It was our standing joke, for Julian thought Carrie just the right size to play a fairy – and kept telling her it still wasn't too late for her to become a dancer. If someone else had even suggested such a thing, she would have been deeply insulted, but for Julian, someone she deeply admired, she would be a fairy only by flitting around and fluttering her arms. She knew he meant 'fairy' as a compliment, and not a criticism of her small size.

Then it was my turn to have Carrie in my arms. I loved her so much I was overwhelmed by the force that swept over me and made me feel I was holding a child born of my own flesh. Though there was never a time I could look at Carrie and not long for Cory who should be at her side. I wondered too, if he had lived, would he too stand only four feet six inches tall? Carrie and I laughed and cried, exchanged news and then she whispered so Julian wouldn't overhear, 'I don't wear a training bra any more. I've got on a *real* one.'

'I know,' I whispered back. 'The first thing I noticed was your bosom.'

'Really?' She appeared delighted. 'You can see them? I didn't think they showed that much.'

'Well, of course they show,' said Julian, who shouldn't have sneaked so close to eavesdrop on this sisterly confidence. 'That's the first thing my eyes go for once they get past a fabulous face. Carrie, do you realize you have a fabulous face? I just might kick out my wife and marry you.'

It was a remark that didn't sit well with me. Many an argument we'd have because he cared too much for very young girls. However I was determined to let nothing spoil Carrie's vacation in New York, the first time she'd come alone, and Julian and I had mapped out a schedule so we could show her everything. At least there was one member of my family Julian would accept.

The months flew swiftly by, and then the spring we'd waited for so long was upon us.

Julian and I were in Barcelona, enjoying our first real vacation since we'd married. Five years and three months of married life, and still there were times when Julian seemed a stranger. Madame Zolta had suggested the vacation, thinking it a good idea if we visited Spain so we could study the Flamenco style of dancing. In a hired car we drove from one town to another, loving the beautiful countryside. We liked the late evening meals, the sleepy siesta afternoons lying on the rocky shores of the Côte d'Azur – but, most of all, we loved Spanish music and dancing.

Madame Z had mapped our tour throughout Spain, listing all the villas that charged nominal rates. She was thrifty and taught all her dancers her tricks. If visitors occupied one of the small cottages near a hotel, and cooked their own meals, the fee was even less. So this was where Julian and I were on the day Chris's graduation invitation arrived. It had followed us all over Spain, to catch up with us here.

My heart jumped when I spied the thick creamy envelope, knowing it contained the graduation announcement of Chris's achievement – his medical degree – at long last! It was almost as if I myself had completed college, then medical school all within seven years.

Very carefully I used a letter opener so I could put this souvenir in my scrapbook of dreams, some of which were coming true. Inside was not only the formal announcement, but also a note on which Chris had written modestly:

I am embarrassed to tell you this, but I am the top grad in a class of two hundred. Don't you dare find an excuse to keep away. You have to be there to bask in the glow of my excitement, as I bask in the radiance of your admiration. I cannot possibly accept my MD if you aren't there to see. And you can tell Julian this when he tries to prevent your coming.

The bothersome thing about this was Julian and I had signed a contract some time ago to tape a TV production of *Giselle*. It was set for June, but now in May they wanted us both. We were sure the television exposure would make us the stars we'd strived so long to be.

It seemed a perfect time to approach Julian with the news. We had returned to our cottage after touring old castles. As soon as our evening meal was over we sat out on the terrace sipping glasses of a red wine he was nuts about, but that gave me a headache. Only then did I dare to timidly approach going back to the States in time for Chris's May graduation. 'Really, we do have the time to fly there, and be back in plenty of time to go into rehearsals for *Giselle*.'

'Oh, come off it, Cathy!' he said impatiently. 'It's a difficult role for you, and you'll be tired, and you'll need to rest up.'

I objected. Two weeks was plenty of time . . . and a TV taping didn't take too long. 'Please, darling, let's go. I'd be sick not to see my brother become a doctor, just as you'd be if your brother was reaching the goal he'd strived for year after year.'

'Hell, no!' he flared, narrowing his dark eyes and shooting sparks my way. 'I get so damned sick and tired of hearing Chris this, and Chris that, and if it isn't his name you drum in my ears, then it's Paul this and that! *You are not going!*'

I pleaded with him to be reasonable. 'He's my only brother, his graduation day is as important to me as it is to him. You can't understand how much this means not only to him, but to me as well! You think he and I lived lives of luxury compared to yours, but you can rest assured, it was no picnic!'

'Your past is something you don't talk about to me,' he snapped. 'It's exactly as if you were born the day you found your precious Dr Paul! Cathy, you are *my* wife now, and your place is with me. Your Paul has Carrie, and they'll be there, so your brother won't lack applause when he gets that damned MD!'

'You can't tell me what I can do and what I can't do! I'm your wife, not your slave!'

'I don't want to talk about this any more,' he said, standing and seizing hold of my arm. 'C'mon, let's hit the sack. I'm tired.' Without speaking I allowed him to tug me into the bedroom where I began to undress. But he came over to help, and in this way I was informed it was to be a night of love, or rather sex. I shoved his hands away. Scowling, he put them back on my shoulders and leaned to nibble on my neck; he fondled my breasts before he reached to unhook my bra. I slapped his hands away. But he persisted in taking off my bra. Easy as a mask to take off, he threw away his anger and put on his dreamy-eyed romantic look.

There had been a time when Julian had appeared to me the epitome of everything sophisticated, worldly, elegant, but compared to the way he was now, since his father's death, he'd been only a country-bumpkin. There were times I actually detested him. This was such a time. 'I *am* going, Julian. You may come with me, or you may meet me in New York after I fly back from the graduation ceremony. Or you can stay on here and sulk. Whatever – *I am going*. I want you to come with me and share in the family celebration, for you never share in anything – you hold me back, so I don't share either – but this time *you can't stop me*! It's too important!'

Quietly he listened and he smiled in a way that sent chills down my spine. Oh, how wicked he could look. 'Hear this, beloved wife, when you married me, I became your ruler, and by my side you will stay until I kick you out. And I'm not yet ready to do that. You are not leaving me alone in Spain.'

'Don't threaten me, Julian,' I said coolly, though I backed off and felt a terrible pounding of panic. 'Without me you don't have anyone who cares, except your mother, and since you don't care for her, who have you got left?'

Lightly he reached out to slap both my cheeks. I closed my eyes, resigned to accept anything he did, as long as I could go to Chris. I allowed him to undress me and do what he would, even though he clutched my buttocks so hard they hurt. I could, when I chose, withdraw until I was outside of myself, looking on, and what he did to me that was appalling didn't really matter – for I wasn't truthfully there – unless the pain was great – as sometimes it was.

'Don't try and sneak away,' he warned, his words muffled because he was kissing everywhere, teasing me as a cat who plays with a mouse when it's not hungry. 'Swear on your word of honour that you will stay and miss your dearly beloved brother's graduation – stay with the husband who needs you, who adores you, who can't live without you.'

He was mocking me, though his need for me was that of a child needing his mother. That was what I had become – his mother, in everything but sex. I had to choose his suits, his socks and shirts, his costumes, his practice outfits, though he consistently refused to let me handle the household accounts.

'I will not swear to anything so unfair. Chris has come to see you perform and you have gloried in showing off to him. Now let him have his turn. He's worked hard for it.' I pulled free from him then, and strolled to pick up a black lace nightgown he liked me to wear. I hated black nightgowns and underwear; they reminded me of whores and call-girls – and my own mother who'd had a fancy for black lingerie. 'Get up off your knees, Julian. You look ludicrous. You can't do anything to me if I choose to go. A bruise would show, and besides, you've grown so accustomed to my weight and balance you can't even lift another dancer properly.'

He came at me angrily. 'You're mad because we haven't made it to the top, aren't you? You're blaming me because our booking was cancelled. And now Madame Z has given us leave so I can sober up and come back refreshed, made wholesome by playing games with my wife. Cathy, I don't know how to entertain myself except by dancing; I'm not interested in books or museums like you are, and there are ways of hurting and humiliating you that won't leave any bruises – except on your ego – and you should know that by now.'

Foolishly I smiled, when I should have known better than to challenge him when he was feeling less than confident. 'What's the matter, Jule? Didn't your sex break satisfy your lust for perversion? Why don't you go out and find a schoolgirl, for I'm not going to cooperate.'

I'd never before thrown in his face that I knew about his debaucheries with very young girls. It had hurt at first when I found out, but now I knew he used those girls like he used paper napkins, to casually toss away when soiled, and back he'd come to me, to say he loved me, needed me, and I was the *only* one.

Slowly he advanced, using his pantherlike stalk that told me he would be ruthless, but I held my head high, knowing I could escape by shutting off my mind, and he couldn't afford to hit me. He paused one foot away. I heard the clock on the nightstand ticking.

'Cathy, you will do as I say if you know what's good for you.'

He was cruel that night, evil and spiteful; he forced upon me what should only be given in love. He dared me to bite. And this time I wouldn't have just one black eye, but two, and maybe worse. 'And I'll tell everybody you are sick. Your period has you so badly cramped you can't dance – and you won't skip out on me, or make any phone calls, for I'll bind you to the bed and hide your passport.' He grinned and slapped my face lightly. 'Now, honey-chile, what are you going to do this time?'

Smiling and himself again, Julian sauntered naked to the breakfast table, flung himself down, sprawled out his long, beautifully shaped legs and asked casually, 'What's for breakfast?' He held out his arms so I could come and kiss his lips, which I did. I smiled, brushed the lock of dangling hair from his forehead, poured his coffee, and then said, 'Good morning, darling. Same old breakfast for you. Fried eggs and fried ham. I'm having a cheese omelet.'

'I'm sorry, Cathy,' he murmured. 'Why do you try to bring out the worst in me? I only use those girls to spare you.'

'If they don't mind, then I don't mind ... but don't ever force me to do what I did last night. I'm very good at hating, Julian. Just as good as you are at forcing. And at harbouring revenge I'm an expert!'

I slid on to his plate two fried eggs and two slices of ham. No toast and no butter. Both of us ate in silence. He sat across the checkered red and white tablecloth, closely shaven, clean and smelling of soap and shaving lotion. In his own dark and light exotic way he was the most beautiful man I'd ever seen.

'Cathy ... you haven't said you love me today.'

'I love you, Julian.'

An hour after breakfast I was madly searching every room to find my passport, while Julian slept on the bed, where I'd dragged him from the kitchen after he fell asleep from all the sedatives I'd dumped in his coffee.

He wasn't nearly as good at hiding as I was at finding. Under the bed, and under the blue rug, I found my passport. Quickly I threw clothes into my suitcases. When I was packed, dressed and ready to go, I leaned above him and kissed him goodbye. He was breathing deeply and regularly, and smiling slightly; perhaps the drugs were giving him pleasant dreams. Though I'd drugged him, I hesitated, wondering if I'd done the right thing. Shrugging off my indecision, I headed towards the garage. Yes, I did what I had to do. If he were awake now, he'd be burred to my side all through the day, with my passport in his pocket. I'd left a note telling him where I was going.

Paul and Carrie met me at the airport in North Carolina. I hadn't seen Paul in three years. Down the ramp I went, my eyes locked with his. His face tilted up to mine, the sun in his eyes so he had to squint. 'I'm glad you could come,' he said, 'though I'm sorry Julian couldn't make it.'

'He's sorry too,' I said, looking up into his face. He was the type of man who improved with age. The moustache I'd persuaded him to grow was still there, and when he smiled dimples showed in both his cheeks.

'Are you searching to find grey hair?' he teased when I stared too long and perhaps with too much admiration. 'If you see any let me know and I'll have my barber touch them up. I'm not ready for grey hair yet. I like your new hair style; it makes you even more beautiful. But you're much too thin. What you need is lots of Henny's home cooking. She's here, you know, in a motel's small kitchen, whipping up homemade rolls your brother so loves. It's her gift to him for becoming another doctor-son.'

'Did Chris get my telegram? He does know I'm coming?'

'Oh, indeed yes! He was fretting through every moment, afraid Julian would refuse to let you leave him, and knowing Julian wouldn't come. Honestly, Cathy, if you hadn't shown up, I don't think Chris *would* accept his degree.'

To sit beside Paul, with Henny on his far side and Carrie next to me, and watch my Christopher stride down the aisle and up the steps to accept his diploma, and then stand behind the podium and make the valedictory speech, put tears in my eyes and a swelling happiness in my heart. He did it so beautifully I cried. Paul, Henny and Carrie also had tears to shed. Even my success on stage couldn't compare to the pride I felt now. And Julian, he should be here too, making himself a part of my family and not stubbornly resisting all the time.

I thought of our mother too, who should be here to witness this. I knew she was in London, for I was still following her movements about the world. Waiting, always waiting to see her again. What would I do when I did? Would I chicken out and let her get away again? I knew one thing, she'd learn that her eldest son was now a doctor – for I'd be sure she knew – just as I kept her informed about what Julian and I were doing.

Of course I knew by now why my mother kept always on the move – she was afraid, so afraid I'd catch up with her! She'd been in Spain when Julian and I arrived. The news had been published in several papers, and not long after that I picked up a Spanish paper to see the lovely face of Mrs Bartholomew Winslow, flying to London as fast as she could.

Tearing my thoughts from her, I glanced around at the thousands of relatives crowded into the huge auditorium. When I looked back at the stage I saw Chris up there, ready to step behind the podium. I don't know how he managed to find me, but somehow he did. Our gazes met and locked, and across all the heads of those who sat between us, we met in silent communication and shared an overwhelming jubilation! We'd done it! Both of us! Reached our goals; become what we'd set out to be when we were children. It wouldn't have mattered at all about those years and months we'd lost – if Cory hadn't died, if our mother hadn't betrayed us, if Carrie had gained the height that should have been hers, and would have been if Momma had found another solution. Maybe I wasn't a prima ballerina yet – but I would be one day, and Chris would be the finest doctor alive.

Watching Chris, I believed we shared the same thoughts. I saw him swinging a bat when he was ten to smash a ball over the fence, and then he'd run like mad to touch all bases in the quickest possible time, when he could have walked and made his home run. But that wasn't his way, to make it look too easy. I saw him racing on his bike yards ahead of me, then slowing down deliberately so I could catch up and we'd both reach home at the same time. I saw him in the locked room, in his bed three feet from mine, smiling encouragingly. I saw him again in the attic shadows, almost hidden in the immense space, looking so lost and bewildered as he turned away from the mother he loved . . . to me. Vicariously we'd shared so many romances while lying on a dirty old mattress in the attic while the rain pelted down and separated us from all humanity. Was that what did it? Was that why he couldn't see any girl but me? How sad for him, for me.

The university planned a huge luncheon celebration, and at our table babbled away, but Chris and I could only stare at each other, each of us trying to find the right words to say.

'Dr Paul has moved into a new office building, Cathy,' gushed Carrie breathlessly. 'I'd hate him being so far away, but I am going to be his secretary! I am going to have a brand new electric typewriter coloured red! Dr Paul thought a custom-painted typewriter of purple might look a little garish, but I didn't think it would, so I settled for second best. And nobody is going to have a better secretary than I'll be! I'll answer his phone, make his appointments, keep his filing system, do his bookkeeping, and every day he and I will eat lunch together!' She beamed on Paul a bright smile. It seemed he'd given her the security to regain the exuberant self-confidence that she'd lost. But I was to find out later, sadly, this was Carrie's false façade, one for Paul, Chris and me to see, and when she was alone, it was far different.

Then Chris frowned and asked why Julian hadn't come. 'He wanted to come, Chris, really he did,' I lied. 'But he has obligations that keep him so busy he couldn't spare the time. He asked me to give you his congratulations. We do have very tight schedules. Actually, I can only stay two days. We're going to do a TV production of *Giselle* next month.'

Later we celebrated again in a fine hotel restaurant. This was our chance to give Chris the gifts each of us had for him. It had been our childish habit to always shake a present before it was opened, but the big box Paul gave Chris was too heavy to shake. 'Books!' said Chris rightly. Six huge, fat, medical reference volumes to represent an entire set that must have cost Paul a fortune. 'I couldn't carry more than six,' he explained. 'The remainder of the set will be waiting for you at home.' I stared at him, realizing his home was the only real home we had.

Deliberately Chris saved my gift for last, anticipating this would be the best and in that way, just as we used to, we could stretch out the enjoyment. It was too large and much too heavy to shake and besides I cautioned him it was fragile, but he laughed, for we used to always try and trick the other, 'No, it's more books – nothing else could be as heavy.' He gave me a funny, wistful smile that made him seem a boy again.

'I give you one guess, my Christopher Doll, and one hint. Inside that box is the one thing you said you wanted more than anything else – and our father said he would give it to you the day you got your black doctor's bag.' Why had I used that kind of soft voice, to make Paul turn his eyes and narrow them, and see the blood that rose to stain my brother's cheeks? *Were we never to forget, and change? Were we forever going to feel too much?* Chris fiddled with the ribbons, careful not to tear the fancy paper. When he stripped off the paper, tears of remembrance welled in his eyes. His hands trembled as he carefully lifted from the cushioned box a French mahogany case with a gleaming brass lock, key and carrying handle. He gave me a tortured look even as his lips quivered, seeming incredulous that after all these years I'd remembered.

'Oh, damn it, Cathy,' he said all choked up with emotion, 'I never really hoped to own one of these. You shouldn't have spent so much . . . it must have cost a fortune . . . and you shouldn't have!'

'But I wanted to, and it's not an original, Chris, only a replica of a John Cuff Side Pillar Microscope. But the man in the shop said it was an exact duplicate of the original and a collector's item nevertheless. And it works too.' He shook his head as he handled the solid brass and ivory accessory instruments, and the optical lens, the tweezers, and the leather-bound book titled *Antique Microscopes, 1675–1840.*

I said faintly, 'In case you decide to play around in your spare time, you can do your own research on germs and viruses.'

'Some toy you give,' he said, gritty-voiced, and now the two tears in the corners of his eyes began to slide down his cheeks. 'You remembered the day Daddy said he would give me this when I became a doctor.'

'How could I forget? That little catalogue was the one thing you took of yours that wasn't clothes, when we went to Foxworth Hall. And every time he swatted a fly, or killed a spider, Paul, Chris would long to have a John Cuff microscope. And once he said he wanted to be the Mouseman of the Attic, and discover for himself why mice die so young.'

'Do mice die young?' asked Paul seriously. 'How did you know they were young? Did you capture baby ones, and mark them in some way?'

Chris and I met eyes. Yeah, we'd lived in another world back when we were young and imprisoned, so that we could look at the mice who came to steal and nibble on our food, especially the one named Mickey.

Now I had to go back to New York and face Julian's wrath. But first I had to have a little time alone with my brother. Paul took Henny and Carrie to a movie while Chris and I strolled the campus of his university. 'And you see that window up there on the second floor, the fifth from the end there – that was my room I shared with Hank. When we dated, we dated together.'

'Oh,' I sighed. 'Did you date a lot?'

'Only on the weekends. The study schedule was too heavy for socializing during the week. None of it was easy, Cathy.'

'You're not telling me what I want to hear. Who did you date? Was there, or is there, someone special?'

He caught my hand and drew me closer to his side. 'Well, should I begin to list them one by one, and by name? If I did it would take several hours. If there had been someone special, all I would do is name one – and I can't do that. I liked them all ... but I didn't like any well enough to love, if that's what you want to know.'

Yes, that was exactly what I wanted to know. 'I'm sure you didn't live a celibate life, even though you didn't fall in love ...?'

'That's none of your business,' he said lightly.

'I think it is. It would give me peace to know you had a girl you loved.'

'I do have a girl I love,' he answered. 'I've known her all my life. When I go to sleep at night, I dream of her, dancing overhead, calling my name, kissing my cheek, screaming when she has nightmares, and I wake up to take the tar from her hair. There are times when I wake up to ache all over, as she aches all over, and I dream I kiss the marks the whip made ... and I dream of a certain night when she and I went out on the cold slate roof and stared up at the sky, and she said the moon was the eye of God looking down and condemning us for what we were. So there, Cathy, is the girl who haunts me and rules me, and fills me with frustrations, and darkens all the hours I spend with other girls who just can't live up to the standards she set. And I hope to God you're satisfied.'

I turned to move as in a dream, and in that dream I put my arms about him and stared up into his face, his beautiful face that haunted me too. 'Don't love me, Chris. Forget about me. Do as I do, take whomever knocks first on your door, and let her in.'

He smiled ironically and put me quickly from him. 'I did exactly what you did, Catherine Doll, the first who knocked on my door *was* let in – and now I can't drive her out. But that's my problem – not yours.'

'I don't deserve to be there. I'm not an angel, not a saint ... you should know that.'

'Angel, saint, Devil's spawn, good or evil, you've got me pinned to the wall and labelled as yours until the day I die. And if you die first, then it won't be long before I follow.'

Both Chris and Paul, to say nothing of Carrie, persuaded me to go back to Clairmont and spend a few days with my family. When I was there, surrounded by all the cosy comforts, the charm of the house and the gardens had their chance to beguile me again. I told myself this was the way it would have been if I'd married Paul. No problems. A sweet, easy life. Then, when I let myself wonder how Julian was faring, I thought of all the mean and spiteful ways he had of annoying me by opening my mail from Paul or Chris, as if he were looking for incriminating evidence. No doubt when he flew back from Spain, he'd deliberately let my house plants die as a way to punish me.

There must be something weird about me, I was thinking as I stood on the balcony overlooking Paul's magnificent gardens. I wasn't that beautiful, or that unforgettable, or that indispensable, to any man. I stayed there and let Chris come up behind me and put his arm about my shoulders. I leaned my head against him and sighed, staring up at the moon. The same old moon that had known our shame before, still there to witness more. I didn't do anything; I swear I didn't, just let his arm stay about me. Maybe I moved a little to contour myself against him when he had me in a tight embrace. 'Cathy, Cathy,' he groaned, pressing his lips down into my hair, 'sometimes life just doesn't have any meaning without you. I'd throw away my MD and set out for the South Pacific if you'd go with me ...'

'And leave Carrie?'

'We could take her with us.' I thought he was playing a game of wishing, like we had when children. 'I'd buy a sailboat and take out tourists, and if they cut themselves I'd have all the training to bandage their cuts.' He kissed me then with the fervour of a man gone wild from denial. I didn't want to respond, yet I did, making him gasp as he tried to coax me into his room.

'Stop!' I cried. 'I don't want you except as a brother! Leave me alone! Go find someone else!'

Dazed and hurt-looking, he backed off. 'What kind of woman are you anyway, Cathy? You returned my kisses – you responded in every way you could – and now you draw away and pull the virtuous act!'

'Hate me then!'

'Cathy, I could never hate you.' He smiled at me bitterly. 'There are times when I want to hate you, times when I think you are just the same as our mother, but I don't ever stop loving once I start!' He entered his room and slammed the door, leaving me speechless, staring after him.

No! I wasn't like Momma, I wasn't! I'd responded only because I was still seeking my lost identity. Julian stole my reflection and made it his. Julian wanted to steal my strength and call it his own; he wanted me to make all the decisions, so he couldn't be blamed when a mistake was made. I was still trying to prove my worth, so in the end I could disprove the grandmother's condemnation. *See, Grandmother, I am not bad or evil. Or else everyone wouldn't love me so much.* I was still that selfish, ravenous, demanding attic mouse who had to have it proven time and time again that I was worthy enough to live in the sunlight.

I was thinking about this one day when I was on the back veranda, and Carrie was planting pansies she'd grown from seed, and beside her were little pots with tiny petunia settings. Chris came out from the house and tossed me the evening newspaper. 'There's an article in there that might be of some interest to you,' he said in an off-hand way. 'I thought about not showing it to you, but then I decided I should.'

The husband and wife ballet team of Julian Marquet and Catherine Dahl, our own local celebrities, seems to have parted company. For the first time Julian Marquet will partner a ballerina other than his wife in a major television production of *Giselle*. It has been rumoured about that Miss Dahl is ill, and also rumoured that the ballet team are about to split.

There was more to read, including the fact that Yolanda Lange was to replace me! This was our big chance – another of many, to make stars of ourselves, and he was putting Yolanda in my part! Damn him! Why didn't he grow up? Every chance we had he blew it. He couldn't lift Yolanda easily, not with his bad back.

Chris threw me a strange look before he asked, 'What are you going to do about it?' I yelled back, 'Nothing!' For a second or two he didn't say anything.

'Cathy, he didn't want you to come to my graduation, did he? And that's why he's put Yolanda in your role. I warned you not to let him be your manager. Madame Zolta would have treated you more fairly.'

I got up to pace the porch. Our original contract with Madame Z had expired two years ago, and all we owed her now was twelve performances a year. The rest of the time Julian and I were freelance, and could dance with whatever company we chose.

Let Julian have Yolanda. Let him make a fool of himself – I hoped to God he dropped her! Let him have all his playmates for sex games . . . I didn't care. Then I was running in the house and up to my bedroom where I flung myself face down and bawled.

Everything was made worse by the fact that I had made a secret trip to the gynaecologist the day before. Two missed periods didn't really mean anything for a woman like me, who was so irregular. I might not be pregnant; it might be just another false alarm . . . and if it wasn't, I prayed I'd have the strength to go through with an abortion! I didn't need a baby in my life. I knew once I had a child, he or she would become the centre of my world, and *luv* would again spoil a ballerina who could have been the best.

Ballet music was in my head when I drove Chris's car to visit Madame Marisha one hot spring day when all the world seemed sleepy and lazy. I sat in the shadows near the far wall of a huge auditorium and watched the large class of boys and girls dance. It was scary to think of how soon those girls would grow up to replace the stars of the present. Then I too would become another Madame Marisha and the years would flow by like seconds, until I was Madame Zolta, and all my beauty would be preserved only in old, faded photographs.

'Catherine!' called Madame M joyfully when she spied me. She came striding swiftly, gracefully, my way. 'Why do you sit in shadows?' she asked. 'How nice to see your lovely face again. And don't think I don't know why you look so sad! You're one big fool to leave Julian! He's a big baby; you know he can't be left alone or he does things to hurt himself, and when he hurts himself, he hurts you too! Why did you let him get control of management? Why did you let him burn up your money as fast as it hits your pockets? I tell you this, in your place, I would never, never have let him put another in my role of *Giselle*!'

God, what a blabbermouth he was!

'Don't worry about me, Madame,' I said coolly. 'If my husband doesn't want me for his partner any more, I'm sure there will be others who will.'

She scowled, advanced. She put those bony hands on me and shook me as if to wake me up. Up close, I could see she'd aged terribly since Georges had died. Her ebony hair was almost white now, and streaked with charcoal. She snarled then, baring teeth whiter than they used to be and far more perfect. 'Are you going to let my son make a fool of you? You let him put another dancer in your place? I gave you credit for having more backbone! Now you hightail it back to New York and push that Yolanda out of his life! Marriage is sacred, and wedding vows are meant to be kept!'

Then she softened and said, 'Come now, Catherine,' and led me into her small cluttered office. 'Now you tell me about this foolishness going on between you and your husband!'

'It is really none of your business!'

She swung another straight chair to where she could straddle it. Leaning forward upon her arms, she stabbed me with her hard penetrating glare. 'Anything, and everything concerning my son is my business!' she snapped. 'Now you just sit there and keep quiet, and let me tell you what you don't know about your husband.' Her voice turned a little kinder. 'I was older than Georges when we were married, and even so I dared putting off having a child until I believed the best of my career was behind

239

me, and then I became pregnant. Georges never wanted a child to hold him down, and back, and so, from the beginning Julian had two strikes against him.

'I tell myself we didn't force the dance upon our son, but we did keep him with us, so the ballet became part of his world, the most important part.' She sighed heavily and wiped a bony hand over her troubled brow. 'You know,' she went on with a wistful expression, 'only after my husband was dead and buried did I realize that he never spoke to our son unless it was an order not to do something, or an order to improve his dancing technique. I never realized that Georges could have been jealous of his own son, seeing that he was a better dancer and would achieve more fame. It wasn't easy for me to become only a ballet mistress, and for Georges to be only an instructor. Many a night we lay on our bed and held to each other, craving the applause, the adulation ... It was a hunger that would not be satisfied until we heard the applause for our son.'

Again she paused, and birdlike craned her neck to peer at me and see if I was paying full attention. Oh, yes, she had my attention. She was telling me so much I needed to know.

'Julian tried to hurt Georges and Georges got hurt because Julian made light of his father's reputation. One day he called him only a second-class performer. Georges didn't speak to his own son for a whole month! They never got back together after that. Farther and farther they drifted apart ... until one fine Christmas Day when another prodigy drifted into our lives, and offered herself. *You*! Julian had flown back to visit us, only because I had pleaded with him to try and make it up with his father ... and Julian saw you.'

She paused, flicked her stony eyes over me and went on breathlessly, 'You came, you admired him, you loved him when you were dancing with him, and when you weren't, you were indifferent. The harder you were to win, the more determined he was to have you. I thought you clever, playing a skilful woman's game when you were only a child! And now you, you ... you go and leave him when he was in a foreign country, when you must have learned that he cannot bear to be alone!'

She jumped up like a black, scrawny alleycat and stood above me. 'Without Julian to give you inspiration and enhance your talent with his own, where would you be? Without him would you be in New York, dancing with what is fast becoming one of the leading ballet companies? No! You'd be here, raising babies for that doctor. God knows why you said yes to Julian, and how you can keep from loving him. For he tells me you don't, and never have! So you drug him. You leave him. You take off to see your brother become a doctor, when you know damn well your place is at your husband's side, making him happy and taking care of his wants!

'Yes! Yes!' she shrilled, 'he called me long distance and told me everything! Now he thinks he hates you! Now he wants to cut you off. And when he does, he won't have a heart left to keep him alive! For he gave you his heart years and years ago!'

Slowly I rose to my feet; my legs felt weak and trembly. I brushed a hand over my aching forehead, and held back tired tears. All of a sudden it hit me hard, I did love Julian! Now I saw how very much we were alike, him with his hate for his father who had denied him as a son. And me with my hatred for my mother, making me do crazy things, like sending off hateful letters and Christmas cards to sadden her life and never, never let her find peace. Julian in competition with his father, never knowing he'd won, and was better ... and me in competition with my mother – but I had yet to prove myself better. 'Madame, I am going to tell you something Julian might not know, and I didn't really know until today; I do love your son. Perhaps I always loved him, and just couldn't accept it.'

She shook her head, then fired her words like bullets. 'If you love him, why did you leave him? Answer me that! You left him because you found out he has a liking for young girls? Fool! All men have yearnings for young girls – but still they go on loving their wives! If you let his desire for young flesh drive you away, you are crazy! Slap his face – tell him to leave those girls alone or you will divorce him! Say all of that, and he will be what you want. But when you say nothing, and act like you don't care, you tell him plainly you don't love him, or want him, or need him!'

'I'm not his mother, or a priest, or God,' I said wearily, sick of all the passion she used. Backing towards the door, I tried to leave. 'I don't know if I can keep Julian from young girls, but I'm willing to go back and try. I promise to do better. I'll be more understanding, and I'll let him know I love him so much, I can't abide the thought of him making love to anyone but me.'

She came to take me in her arms. She soothed, 'Poor baby, if I have been hard on you, it was for your own good. You have to keep my son from destroying himself. He has a death wish, always I've known it. He thinks he's not good enough to live on because his father could never convince him he was, and that was my fault too, as well as Georges's. But you go back and tell Julian Georges did love him. To me he said it many times. Tell him too that his father was proud of him. Tell him, Catherine. Go back and convince him of how much you need and love him Tell him how sorry you are to have left him alone. Go quickly before he does something terrible to himself!'

It was time to say goodbye to Carrie, Paul and Henny again. Only this time I didn't have to bid adieu to Chris. He put his foot down. 'No! I'm coming with you! I'm not letting you go back to a crazy man. When you've made your peace with him, and I know everything is all right – only then will I leave.'

Carrie cried, as she always did, and Paul stood back and let only his eyes speak and say yes, I could find a place in his heart again.

I looked down as the plane began to lift, and saw Paul holding Carrie's small hand, as she tilted her face to stare up at us and waved, and waved until we could see her no more. I squirmed into a comfortable position and put my head on Chris's shoulder, and told him to wake me when we reached New York. 'A fine travelling companion you make,' he grumbled, but soon his cheek was on my hair as he dozed off too. 'Chris,' I said sleepily, 'remember that book about Raymond and Lily who were always seeking the magical place where purple grass grew that would fulfil all their wishes? Wouldn't it be wonderful to look down and see purple grass?'

'Yeah,' he said as sleepily as I. 'I keep looking for it too.'

The plane set down at La Guardia around three. A hot, sultry day. The sun played coy, darting in and out of gathering storm clouds. We were both tired. 'At this hour Julian will be in the theatre rehearsing. They'll use the rehearsals as a promotion film. There have to be a lot of rehearsals; we've never danced in this theatre before and it's important to get the feel of the space you have to move in.'

Chris was lugging along my two heavy suitcases, while I carried his much lighter bag. I laughed and smiled his way, glad he was with me, though Julian would be furious. 'Now you stay in the background ... and don't let him even see you if everything goes all right. Really, Chris, I'm sure he'll be glad to see me. He's not dangerous.'

'Sure,' he said glumly.

We sauntered on into the darkened theatre. The stage up ahead was very brightly lit. The TV cameras were in position, ready to shoot the warm-ups. The director, producer and a few others were lined up in the front-row seats.

The heat of the day was chased by the chill of the huge space. Chris opened up one of my bags and spread a sweater about my shoulders after we both sat down near the aisle, midway back in the centre section. Automatically I lifted both my legs to stretch them on top of the seat just ahead. Though I shivered, the *corps de ballet* were sweating from the hot klieg lights. The eye was down and a few flats were up. I looked for Julian but didn't see him.

Just to think of Julian was to bring him out of the wings, on to the stage in a series of whirling *jetés*. Oh, he looked terrific in that snug, white leotard with bright green leg warmers.

'Wow!' whispered Chris in my ear. 'Sometimes I forget how sensational he is on stage. No wonder every ballet critic thinks he will be the star of this decade when he learns some discipline. Let it be soon ... and I mean you too, Cathy.' I smiled, for I too needed discipline. 'Yes,' I said, 'I too, of course.'

No sooner had Julian finished his solo performance than Yolanda Lange pirouetted out from the wings, wearing red. She was more beautiful than ever! She danced extraordinarily well for a girl so tall. That was, she danced well until Julian came to partner her, and then everything went wrong. He reached for her waist and got her buttocks, then he had to quickly shift his hold, so she slipped and nearly fell and again he adjusted to save her. A male dancer who let a ballerina fall would soon never have a partner to lift. They tried again the same jump, lift, and fall back, and this time it went almost as awkwardly, making Yolanda seem ungainly, and Julian unskilled.

Even I, sitting halfway down the row of seats, could hear her loud curse. 'Damn you!' she screeched. 'You make me look gauche – if you let me fall, *I'll see you never dance again!*'

'Cut!' called the director, getting to his feet and looking impatiently from one to the other.

The *corps de ballet* milled about, grumbling, throwing angry looks at the pair centre stage that was wasting so much time. Obviously, from the sweaty, hot looks of all of them, this had been going on for some time, and badly. 'Marquet!' called the director, well known for having little patience for those who required two, or even more takes. 'What the hell is wrong with your timing? I thought you said you knew this ballet. I can't think of one thing you've done right in the past three days.'

'Me?' Julian railed back. 'It's not me . . . she jumps too soon!'

'Okay,' the director said sarcastically, 'it's always *her* fault and never yours.' He tried to control his impatience, knowing Julian would walk out in a second if criticized too much. 'When is your wife going to be well enough to dance again?'

Yolanda screamed out, 'Hey, wait a minute! I came all the way from Los Angeles and now you're sounding as if you're going to replace me with Catherine! I won't have it! I'm written into that contract now! I'll sue!'

'Miss Lange,' said the director smoothly, 'you are the cover only – but while you are, let's attempt it again. Marquet, listen for your cue – Lange, make ready – and pray to God this time it will be fit to show an audience who might expect better from professionals.'

I smiled to hear she was only the cover; I had thought I was really written out.

I perversely enjoyed watching Julian make a fool out of himself and Yolanda as well. Yet, when the dancers on stage groaned, I groaned along with them, feeling their exhaustion, and despite myself I began to feel pity for Julian who was diligently trying to balance Yolanda. Any second the director could call 'take ten' and that's when I would make my move.

Up ahead, first row, Madame Zolta suddenly turned her wizened giraffe neck to crane my way, and those sharp little beady eyes saw me sitting tensely, watching like an eagle. 'Hey, you, Catherine,' she called with great enthusiasm. *Come*, she gestured, *sit by my side.*

'Excuse me a minute, Chris,' I whispered. 'I've got to go up there and save Julian before he ruins both our careers. I'll be all right. There's not much he can do with an audience – is there?'

Once I was seated beside Madame Zolta, she hissed, 'Sooo, you not so sick after all! Thank God for small favours. Your husband up there is ruining my reputation along with his and yours. I should have known better than to always let him partner you, so now he can dance with no one as well.'

'Madame,' I asked, 'who arranged for Yolanda to be my stand-in?'

'Your husband, my love,' she whispered cruelly. 'You let him get control – you were a fool to do that. He is impossible! He is a tempest, a devil, so unreasonable! Soon he will go mad, if he doesn't see your face – or we will go mad. Now run fast and put on dance clothes and save me from extinction!'

It was only a matter of seconds before I had on a practice outfit and, as soon as I had my hair bound up and securely fastened in place, I strapped on my *pointes*. At the dressing-room barre I warmed up quickly, doing my *pliés*, and the *rond de jambes* to pump blood into each limb. Soon enough I was ready. Not a day passed I didn't do my exercises for several hours.

In the darkened wings I hesitated. I was prepared, I thought, for almost anything when Julian saw me – what would he do? While I watched him on stage, suddenly from behind I was brutally shoved aside! 'You've been replaced,' hissed Yolanda. 'Get out – and stay out! You had your chance and loused it up – now Julian is *mine*! You hear that – he's *mine*! I have slept in your bed, and used your makeup and worn your jewellery – I have taken your place in everything.'

I wanted to ignore her and not believe anything she said.

When the cue came for Giselle to go on, Yolanda tried to hold me – that's when I turned savagely upon her and pushed her so hard she fell. She blanched with pain, while I went on *pointe* and glided on to the stage, making my perfect little string of pearls ... Each tiny step could have been measured and proven to be of an exact distance. I was the shy young village girl, sweetly, sincerely falling in love with Loys. Others on stage gasped to see me. Relief lit up Julian's dark eyes – for an instant. 'Hi,' he said coolly as I neared him, and fluttered my dark lashes to enchant him more. 'Why'd you come back? Your doctors kick you out? Sick of you already?'

'You are a nasty, inconsiderate brute, Julian, to replace me with Yolanda! You know I despise her!'

His back was to the onlookers as he sneered wickedly, all the while keeping time, 'Yeah, I know you hate her; that's why I wanted her.' He curled his beautiful red lips so they looked ugly. 'Listen to this, dancing doll. Nobody runs out on me, especially my wife, and comes back and thinks she can still fit in my life. My love, my dearest heart, I don't want you now, I don't need you now, and you can go and play bitch to any man you want! Get the hell out of my life!'

'You don't mean that,' I said, as we both performed perfectly, and no one called cut. How could they when we did everything so exquisitely right?

'You don't love me,' he said bitterly. 'You've never loved me. No matter what I did, or what I said, and now I don't give a damn! I gave you the best I had to give, and it wasn't enough. So, dear Cath-er-ine – *I give you this!*' And with those sudden words, he broke the routine, jumped high into the air, to come down forcefully and directly on to my feet. All his weight, brought down like a battering ram to crush my toes!

I uttered some small cry of pain, then Julian was whirling back to chuck me under the chin. 'Now, see who will dance Giselle with me. Certainly it won't be you, will it?'

'Take ten!' bellowed the director, too late to save me.

Julian gripped my shoulders and shook me like a rag doll. I stared at him rattle-eyed, expecting anything. Then suddenly he whirled away leaving me centre stage, alone, on two damaged feet that hurt so badly I could have screamed. Instead, I sank to the floor and sat there staring at my rapidly swelling feet.

From out of the darkened auditorium Chris came running to my assistance. 'Damn him to hell for doing this!' he cried, falling on his knees to take off my *pointe* shoes and examine my feet. Tenderly he tried to move my toes, but I cried out from the awful pain. Then he picked me up easily and held me tight against him. 'You'll be all right, Cathy. I'll see that your toes heal properly. I fear a few are broken on each foot. You'll need an orthopaedist.'

'Take Catherine to our orthopaedist,' ordered Madame Zolta who teetered forward and stared at my darkening, enlarging feet. She peered more closely at Chris, having seen him only a few times before. 'You're Catherine's brother who caused all this trouble?' she asked. 'Take her quick to the doctor. We have insurance. But that fool husband, this is it. I *fire* him!'

THE THIRTEENTH DANCER

Both of my feet were X-rayed, disclosing three broken toes on my left foot, and one broken small toe on my right. Thank God both my big toes were spared, or else I might never dance again! An hour later Chris was carrying me out of the doctor's office with a plaster cast that reached to my knee, drying on one foot, while the small toe was only taped and left to heal without such protection. Each of the toes in the cast was nestled securely in its own little padded compartment so I couldn't move a one, and left exposed for everyone to admire the lovely shades of black, blue and purple. In my thoughts the sour lemon-drops of the doctor's last words failed to melt and sweeten the future. 'You may, or you may not dance again, it all depends.' On what it depended, he didn't say.

So I asked Chris. 'Sure,' he said confidently, 'of course you'll dance again. Sometimes a doctor likes to be overly pessimistic so you can think how great he was when everything works out fine – due to his special skill.' Clumsily he tried to support me while he used my key to open the door of the apartment Julian and I shared. Then he carefully lifted me up again, carried me inside and kicked the door closed behind him. He tried to make me as comfortable as possible on one of the soft couches. I had my eyes squeezed tightly together, trying to suppress the pain I felt at every move

Chris tenderly supported both legs so he could stuff pillows under and keep them elevated to reduce the swelling. Another fat pillow was carefully eased under my back and head . . . and he never said one word . . . not one word.

Because he was so silent, I opened my eyes and studied his face that loomed above me. He tried to look professional, detached, but he failed. He showed shock each time his eyes moved from one object to another. Fearfully I looked around. My eyes bulged. My mouth opened. This room! The mess! Oh,

God, it was awful!

Our apartment was a wreck! Every painting Julian and I had so carefully selected was torn down from the walls, smashed on the floor. Even the two watercolours Chris had painted especially for me, portraits with me in costume. All the expensive bric-à-brac lay broken on the hearth. Lamps were on the floor, the shades slashed to ribbons and the wire frames bent. Needlepoint pillows I'd made during the long tedious flights from here to there while on tour were ripped, destroyed! Houseplants had been dumped from their pots and left with roots exposed to die. Two cloisonné vases that Paul had given as a wedding gift, gone too. Everything fine and costly, and very cherished, things he and I had planned to keep all our lives and leave to our children – all beyond restoration.

'Vandals,' said Chris softly. 'Just vandals.' He smiled and kissed my forehead and squeezed my hand as tears came to my eyes. 'Stay calm,' he said, then he went to check the other three rooms, while I sank back on the pillows and sniffed back my sobs. Oh, how he must hate me to do this! Shortly Chris was back with his expression very composed, in that same eye-of-the-hurricane way I'd seen a few times on his face. 'Cathy,' he began, settling cautiously down on the edge of the sofa and reaching for my hand, 'I don't know what to think. All your clothes and shoes have been ruined. Your jewellery is scattered all over the bedroom floor, the chains ripped apart, the rings stepped on, bracelets hammered out of shape. It looks as if somebody set out deliberately to ruin all of your things and left Julian's in perfect condition.' He gave me a baffled, troubled look, and maybe the tears I tried to hold back jumped from my eyes to his. With glistening blue eyes he extended his palm to show me the setting of a once exquisite diamond engagement ring, given to me by Paul. The platinum band was now a crooked oval. The prongs had released their clasp on the clear and perfect two-carat diamond.

Sedatives had been shot into my arm so I couldn't feel the pain of my broken toes. I felt fuzzy and disoriented, and rather detached. Someone inside me was screaming, screaming – hatred was near again – the wind was blowing, and when I closed my eyes, I saw the blue-misted mountains all around me, shutting out the sun – like upstairs, like in the attic.

'Julian,' I said weakly, 'he must have done this. He must have come back and vented his rage on all my belongings. See the things left whole – they are things he chose for himself.'

'Damn him to hell!' cried Chris. 'How many times has he vented his rage on you? How many black eyes – I've seen one – but how many others?'

'Please don't,' I said sleepily, hazily. 'He never hit me that he didn't cry afterwards, and he'd say he was sorry.' Yes, so sorry, my sweetheart, my only love ... *I don't know what makes me act as I do when I love you so much!*

'Cathy,' began Chris tentatively, tucking the platinum band in his pocket, 'are you all right? You look close to fainting. I'll go in and straighten up the bed, so you can rest in that. Soon you'll fall asleep and forget all of this, and when you wake up, I'm taking you away. Don't cry for the clothes and things he gave you, for I'll give you better and more. As for this ring Paul gave you, I'll search around the bedroom until I find the diamond.'

He looked, but he didn't find the diamond, and when I drifted into sleep, he must have carried me to the bed he'd made up with clean sheets. I was under a sheet and a thin blanket when I opened my eyes, and he was sitting on the edge of the bed, watching my face. I glanced towards the windows and saw it was getting dark. Any moment Julian would come home, and find Chris with me – and there'd be hell to pay!

'Chris ... did you undress me and put on this gown?' I asked dully, seeing the sleeve of a blue gown that was one of my favourites.

'Yes. I thought you'd be more comfortable than wearing that pantsuit with the leg split up the seam. And I'm a doctor, remember? I'm used to seeing all there is – and I took care not to look.'

The darkness of late twilight was in the room, turning all the shadows soft and purplish. Fuzzily I saw him as he used to be, when the attic atmosphere was like this, purplish, dim, scary, and we were alone and facing some unknown horror ahead. Always he gave me comfort when nothing else could. Always he was there when I needed him to do and say the right thing.

'Remember the day Momma received the letter from the grandmother saying we could stay in her home? We thought wonderful things were ahead of us then; we later thought all joy lay in the past. Never, never in the present.'

'Yes,' he said softly, 'I remember. We believed we'd be rich as King Midas, and everything we touched would turn to gold. Only we'd have more self-control, enough to keep those we loved still made of flesh and blood. We were young and silly then, and so trusting.'

'Silly? I don't think we were silly, only normal. You've achieved your goal of being a doctor. But I'm still not a prima ballerina.' I said this last bitterly.

'Cathy, don't belittle yourself. You will be a prima ballerina yet!' he said fervently. 'You would have been a long time ago, if Julian could control his fits of temper that make every company manager afraid to sign the pair of you on. You get stuck in a minor company just because you won't leave him.'

I sighed, wishing he hadn't said that. It was true enough Julian's fiery temper tantrums had scared off more than one offer that would have placed us in a more prestigious company. 'You've got to leave, Chris. I don't want him to come home and find you here. He doesn't want you near me. And I can't leave him. In his own way he loves me and needs me. Without me to keep him steady he would be ten times more violent, and I do love him after all. If he struck out sometimes, he was just trying to make me see that. Now I do see.'

'*See?*' he cried. 'You're not seeing! You're letting pity for him rob you of good common sense! Look around you, Cathy! Only a crazy man could have done this. I'm not leaving you alone to face a madman! I'm staying to protect you. Tell me what you could do if he decides to make you pay again for leaving him alone in Spain? Could you get up and run? No! I'm not leaving you here, unprotected, when he might come home drunk, or on drugs –'

'He doesn't use drugs!' I defended, protective of the good that was in Julian, and for some reason, wanting to forget all that wasn't.

'He jumped on your toes, when you need those toes to dance

on – so don't tell me you will have a sane man to deal with. When you were putting on your clothes, I overheard someone say that since Julian started running around with Yolanda he's been an entirely different man. Everyone else suspects he's on drugs – that's why I said it,' and here he paused, 'and besides, I know for a fact that Yolanda takes anything she can get.'

I was sleepy, in pain and worried about Julian who should be home by now, and there was the baby in me whose fate I had to decide. 'Chris, stay then. But when he comes home, let me do the talking – just fade into the background – promise?'

He nodded, while I began to drift off again, feeling as if nothing was real but the bed underneath me and the sleep I needed. Lazily, without thought, I tried to turn on my side, and my legs slipped from the heaped pillows, making me cry out. 'Cathy ... don't move,' said Chris, quickly adjusting my legs back on the pillows. 'Let me lie beside you, and hold you until he comes. I promise not to sleep, and the minute he comes through the door, I'll jump up and fade away.' He smiled to charm me into cheer again, so I too nodded and welcomed the warm, strong arms he put around me as again I sought the sweet relief of sleep.

As in a dream I felt soft lips move on my cheek, in my hair, then lightly over my eyelids, and finally my lips. 'I love you so much, oh, God, how much I love you,' I heard him say, and I thought for a disoriented moment it was Julian who'd come home to say he was sorry for hurting and humiliating me ... for this was his way, to give me pain, and then apologize, and make love with passionate abandon. So I turned a bit on my side and responded to his kisses, and put my arms around him, and twined my fingers into his strong dark hair. That's when I knew. The hair I felt wasn't strong and crisp, but silky and fine, like my own. 'Chris!' I cried out, 'stop!'

'Don't cry stop,' he murmured, caressing and stroking me, 'all my life I've had nothing but frustrations. I try to love others, but it's always you ... you, whom I can never have! Cathy ... leave Julian! Come away with me! We'll go to some distant place, where no one knows us, and together we can live as man and wife. We won't have any children ... I'll see to that. We can adopt babies. You know we make good parents ... you know we love each other and always will! Nothing can change that! You can run from me and marry twelve other men, but your heart is in your eyes when you look at me – it's me you want – as I want you!'

He was carried away with his own persuasions and wouldn't listen to my weak words. 'Cathy, just to hold you, to have you again! This time I'll know how to give you the pleasure I couldn't before – please, if you ever loved me – leave Julian before he destroys us both!'

I shook my head, trying to focus on what he was saying and what he was doing. His blond hair was beneath my chin, nuzzling at my breasts, and he didn't see my denial, but he did hear my voice. 'Christopher – I'm going to have Julian's baby. Julian and I are having a baby.'

Chris sat up on the side of the bed and bowed his head into his hands. Then he sobbed, 'Always you manage to defeat me, Cathy! First Paul, then Julian ... and now a baby.' Then suddenly he faced me. 'Come away and let me be the father to that child! Julian isn't fit! If you never let me touch you, let me live near enough so I can see you every day and hear your voice. Sometimes I want it back like it used to be ... just you and I, and our twins.'

Silence that we both knew well came and took us, and shut us away in our own secret world where sin lived and unholy thoughts dwelled, and we'd pay, pay, pay, if ever ... but no, there wouldn't be any if ever ...

'Chris, I'm going to have the baby with Julian,' I said with a firm resolution that surprised me. 'I want Julian's child – for I do love him, Chris – and I've failed him in so many ways. Failed him because you and Paul got in my eyes, and I didn't appreciate what I could have had in him. I should have been a better wife, and then he wouldn't have needed those girls. I'll always love you – but it's a love that can't go anywhere, so I give it up. You give it up! Say goodbye to yesterday and a Catherine Doll who doesn't exist anymore.'

'You forgive him for breaking your toes?' he asked, astonished.

'He kept begging me to say I loved him, and I never would. I kept a deceptive parasol over my head, to keep dark doubts in my mind, and I refused to see anything that was noble and fine about him but his dancing. I didn't realize that to love me, even when I denied him, was noble and fine in itself. So, let me go, Chris – even if I never dance again, I'll have his child ... and he will go on to fame without me.'

He slammed the door and left me, and I soon fell asleep to dream of Bart Winslow, my mother's second husband. We were waltzing in the grand ballroom of Foxworth Hall, and upstairs, near the balcony balustrade, two children were hidden inside the massive chest with the wire screen backing. The Christmas tree over in the corner towered up to heaven, and hundreds of people danced with us, but they were made of transparent cellophane, not of the healthy flesh, blood and muscle that was the beauty of Bart and I. Bart suddenly stopped dancing, and picked me up to carry me up the broad stairs, and down on the sumptuous swan bed he laid me. My beautiful gown of green velvet and softer green chiffon melted beneath the touch of his burning hands – and then that powerful male shaft that entered me and wound about me started shrieking, screaming, and each loud cry sounded exactly like a telephone ringing.

I bolted awake ... why did a telephone ringing in the dead of night always have such a threatening sound? I sleepily reached for the receiver. 'Hello?'

'Mrs Julian Marquet?'

I came awake a bit more, and rubbed at my eyes. 'Yes, this is she.'

She named a hospital on the other side of town. 'Mrs Marquet, would you please come as quickly as possible? If you can, have someone else drive you. Your husband was in an auto accident, and is even now in surgery. Bring with you his insurance papers, identification, and any medical history you have ... Mrs Marquet ... are you there?'

No. I wasn't there. I was back in Gladstone, Pennsylvania, and I was twelve years old. Two state troopers were in the driveway, with a white car parked ... and swiftly they were striding to interrupt a birthday party to tell us all that Daddy was dead. Killed in an accident on Greenfield Highway.

'Chris! Chris!' I screamed, terrified he might have gone.

'I'm here. I'm coming. I knew you'd need me.'

In that dim and lonely hour that comes before dawn, Chris and I arrived at the hospital. In one of those sterile waiting rooms we sat down to wait and find out if Julian would survive the accident and the surgery. Finally, around noon, after hours in the recovery room, they brought him down.

They had him laid out on what they called a 'fracture bed' – a torturous looking device that strung up his right leg which wore a cast from his toes to his hip. His left arm was broken, and in a cast, and strung up in a peculiar way too. His pale face was lacerated and bruised. His lips, usually so full and red, were as pale as his skin. But all of that was nothing compared to his head! I shivered to look! His head had been shaved and small holes drilled for metal calipers to be hooked in to pull his head up and backwards! A leather collar lined with fleece was fastened about his neck. *A broken neck!* Plus a leg fracture, and a compound fracture of his forearm – to say nothing of the internal injuries that had kept him on the operating table three hours!

I cried out, 'Will he live?'

'He is on the critical list, Mrs Marquet,' they answered so calmly. 'If he has other close relatives, we suggest you contact them.'

Chris made the call to Madame Marisha, for I was deathly afraid he'd pass away any moment, and I might miss the only chance to tell him I loved him. And if that happened, I'd be cursed and haunted all through the rest of my life.

Days passed. Julian flitted in and out of consciousness. He stared at me with eyes lacklustre, unfocused. He spoke but his voice came so thick, heavy and unintelligible I couldn't understand. I forgave him for all the little sins, and the big ones too, as you are apt to when death is around the corner. I rented a room in the hospital next to his where I could catch naps, but I never had a full night's rest. I had to be there when he came to, where he could see and know me, so I could plead with him to fight, to live, and, most of all, say all the words I'd so stingily kept from his ears. 'Julian,' I whispered, my voice hoarse from saying it so often, 'please don't die!'

Our dancing friends and musicians flocked to the hospital to offer what consolation they could. His room filled with flowers from hundreds of fans. Madame Marisha flew up from South Carolina and stalked into the room wearing a dreary black dress. She gazed down on the unconscious face of her only child without any expression of grief. 'Better he die now,' she said flatly, 'than to wake up and find himself a cripple for life.'

'How dare you say that?' I flared, ready to strike her. 'He's alive – and he's not doomed. His spinal cord wasn't injured! He'll walk again, and dance again too!'

Then came the pity and disbelief to shimmer her jet eyes – and then she was in tears. She who'd boasted she never cried, never showed grief, wept in my arms. 'Say it again, that he'll dance – oh, don't lie, he's got to dance again!'

Five horrible days came and went before Julian could focus his eyes enough to really see. Unable to turn his head, he rolled his eyes my way. 'Hi.'

'Hello, dreamer. I thought you were never going to wake up,' I said.

He smiled, a thin ironic smile. 'No such luck, Cathy love.' His eyes flicked downwards to his strung-up leg. 'I'd rather be dead than like this.'

I got up and went to his fracture bed that was made with two wide strips of rough canvas slipped over strong rods, with a mattress beneath this that could be lowered enough to allow a bedpan to be placed in position. It was a hard, unyielding bed to lie on, yet I stretched beside him very carefully, and curled my fingers into his tangle of uncombed hair – what he had left. My free hand stroked his chest. 'Jule, you're not paralysed. Your spinal cord was not severed, crushed, or even bruised. It's just in shock, so to speak.'

He had an uninjured arm that could have reached to hold me, but it stayed straight at his side. 'You're lying,' he said bitterly. 'I can't feel one damn thing from my waist down. Not your hand on my chest either. Now get the hell out of here! You don't love me! You wait until you think I'm ready to kick off, and then you come with your sweet words! I don't want or need your pity – *so get the hell out, and stay out!*'

I left his bed and reached for my bag. Crying, even as he cried and stared at the ceiling. 'Damn you for wrecking our apartment!' I stormed when I could talk. 'Damn you for breaking my toes!' I rampaged, angry now, and wanting to slap his face that was already bruised and swollen. 'Damn you for breaking all our beautiful things! You knew how painstakingly we chose all those lamps, the accessories that cost a fortune. You know we wanted to leave them as heirlooms for our children. Now we've got nothing left to leave anyone!'

He grinned, satisfied. 'Yeah, nothing left for nobody.' He yawned, as if dismissing me, but I was unwilling to be dismissed. 'Got no kids, thank God. Never gonna have any. You can get a divorce. Marry some son of a bitch and make his life miserable too.'

'Julian,' I said with such heavy sadness. 'Have I made your life miserable?'

He blinked, as if not wanting to answer that, but I asked him again, and again, until I forced him to say, 'Not altogether miserable – we had a few moments.'

'Only a few?'

'Well ... maybe more than a few. But you don't have to stay on and take care of an invalid. Get the hell out while you can. I'm no good, you know that. I've been unfaithful to you time and again.'

'If you are again, I'll cut your heart out!'

'Go 'way, Cathy. I'm tired.' He sounded sleepy from the many sedatives they fed into him and shot into him. 'Kids are not good for people like us anyway.'

'People like us ... ?'

'Yeah, people like us.'

'How are we different?'

He mockingly, sleepily laughed, bitterly too. 'We're not real. We don't belong to the human race.'

'What are we then?'

'Dancing dolls, that's all. Dancing fools, afraid to be real people and live in the real world. That's why we prefer fantasy. Didn't you know?'

'No, I didn't know. I always thought we were real.'

'It wasn't me who ruined your things, it was Yolanda. I watched, though.'

I felt sick, scared he was telling the truth. Was I only a dancing doll? Couldn't I make my way in the real world, outside the theatre? Wasn't I, after all, any better at coping than Momma?

'Julian ... I do love you, honest I do. I used to think I loved someone else, because it seemed so unnatural to go from one love to another. When I was a little girl, I used to believe love came only once in a lifetime, and that was the best kind. I thought once you loved one person, you never could love another. But I was wrong.'

'Get out and leave me alone. I don't want to hear what you've got to say, not now. Now I don't give a damn.'

Tears coursed down my face and dropped on him. He closed his eyes and refused to see, or listen. I leaned to kiss his lips, and they stayed tight, hard, unresponding. Next he spat, '*Stop! You sicken me!*'

'I love you, Julian,' I sobbed, 'and I'm sorry if I realized it too late, and said it too late – but don't let it *be* too late. I'm expecting your baby, the fourteenth in a long line of dancers ... and that baby is a lot to live for, even if you don't love *me* any more. Don't close your eyes and pretend not to hear, because you are going to be a father, whether or not you want to be.'

He rolled his dark, shining eyes my way, and I saw why they shone, for they were full of tears. Tears of self-pity, or tears of frustration, I didn't know. But he spoke more kindly, and there was a tone of love in his voice. 'I advise you to get rid of it, Cathy. Fourteen is no luckier a number than thirteen.'

In the room next door, Chris held me in his arms all through the night.

I woke up early in the morning. Yolanda had been thrown from the car in that accident, and today she would be buried. Cautiously I eased from the fold of Chris's arms, and I arranged his nodding head more comfortably before I stole away to take a peek into Julian's room. He had a night nurse on duty, and she was sound asleep beside his bed. I stood in the doorway and watched him in the dim, greenish light from the lamp covered by a green towel. He was asleep, deeply asleep. The intravenous tube that led to his arm ran under the sheet and into his vein. For some reason I fixed my eyes upon that bottle with the pale yellow liquid that seemed more water than anything else, so quickly it was being depleted. I ran back to shake Chris awake. 'Chris,' I said, as he tried to pull himself together, 'isn't that IV supposed to just trickle into his arm? It's running out very quickly – too quickly, I think.'

Hardly were the words out of my mouth when Chris was up and running towards Julian's room. He snapped on the ceiling light as he entered, then wakened the sleeping nurse. 'Damn you for falling asleep! You were in here to watch him!' By the time he had that said, he'd pulled back the covers and there was Julian's casted arm with the opening for the needle – and the needle was still inserted, and taped in position – but the tube had been cut! 'Oh, God,' sighed Chris, 'an air bubble must have reached his heart.'

I stared at the shiny scissors held so loosely in Julian's slack right hand. 'He cut the tube himself,' I whispered, 'he cut the tube himself, and now he's dead, dead, dead ...'

'Where did he get the scissors?' snapped Chris, while the nurse began to tremble. They were her small embroidery scissors she used to cut her crochet thread. 'They must have fallen out of my pocket,' she said weakly. 'I swear I don't remember losing them – or maybe he took them when I was leaning over ...'

'It's all right,' I said dully. 'If he hadn't done it this way, it would have been another. I should have known and warned you. There was no life for him if he could never dance again. No life at all.'

Julian was buried next to his father. On the headstone, I made sure Madame Marisha agreed to the name I added: *Julian Marquet Rosencoff, beloved husband of Catherine, and thirteenth in a long line of Russian male ballet stars.* Maybe it was ostentatious and gave away my own failure to love him enough while he lived, but I had to let him have it the way he wanted – or as I thought he wanted.

Chris, Paul, Carrie and I paused at the foot of Georges's grave too, and I bowed my head to show respect to Julian's father. Respect I should have given him too. Graveyards with their marble saints, angels, all so sweetly smiling, so pious or sober – how I hated them! They patronized we who lived; we who were made of fragile tissue and blood, who could grieve and cry while they would stand there for centuries, smiling piously down on all. And I was right back where I'd started.

'Catherine,' said Paul when we were all seated in the long black limousine, 'your room is still as it was, all yours. Come home and live with Carrie and me until your baby is born. Chris will be there too, doing his internship at Clairmont Hospital.'

I stared over at Chris who was seated on the jumpseat, knowing he'd won a much better position in a very important hospital – and he was interning in a small, unimportant one. 'Duke is so far away, Cathy,' he said with his eyes avoiding mine. 'It was bad enough travelling when I was in college and medical school ... so if you don't mind, let me be somewhere near so I can be here the day my nephew or niece arrives in the world.'

Madame Marisha jolted so her head almost struck the ceiling of the car. 'You carry Julian's child?' she cried. 'Why didn't you tell me before? How wonderful!' She glowed, so the sadness dropped from her like a gloomy cloak. 'Now Julian's not dead at all – for he will father a son, who will be exactly like him!'

'It may be a girl, Madame,' Paul said softly, while he reached for my hand. 'I know you long for a boy like your son, but I long for a little girl like Cathy and Carrie ... but if it's a boy, I won't object.'

'Object?' cried Madame. 'God in his infinite wisdom and mercy will send to Catherine the exact duplicate of Julian! And he will dance, and he will reach the fame that was waiting just around the corner for the son of my Georges!'

Midnight found me all alone on the back veranda, rocking back and forth in Paul's favourite chair. My head was full of thoughts for the future. Thoughts of the past conflicted and nearly drowned me. The floorboards squeaked faintly; they were old and had known grief like mine before; they sympathized. The stars and moon were out; even a few fireflies came to bob about in the garden darkness.

The door behind me opened and closed quietly. I didn't look to see who it was, for I knew. I was good at sensing people, even in the dark. He sat in the chair next to mine, and rocked his chair in the same rhythm as I rocked.

'Cathy,' he said softly. 'I hate to see you sitting there with that lost and drained expression. Don't think all the good things in your life have passed you by and nothing is left. You're still very young, very beautiful, and after your baby is born, you can quickly whip yourself back into shape, and dance until you feel you're ready to retire and teach.'

I didn't turn my head. Dance again? How could I dance when Julian lay in the ground? All I had was the baby. I would make the baby the centre of my life. I would teach my child to dance, and he or she would reach the fame that should have been Julian's and mine. Everything that Momma failed to give us I would bestow on *my* child. Never would my child be neglected. When my child reached for me, I would be there. When my child cried out for Momma, he wouldn't have to make do with only an older sister. No . . . I'd be like Momma was when she had Daddy. That was what hurt the most, that she could change from someone loving and kind into what she was, a monster. Never, never would I treat my child as she'd treated hers!

'Good night, Paul,' I said as I stood to go. 'Don't stay out here too long. You have to get up early, and you looked tired at dinner.'

'Catherine . . . ?'

'Not now. Later. I need time.'

Slowly I ascended the back stairs, thinking of the baby in my womb, how I had to be careful and not eat junk food; I had to drink plenty of milk, take vitamins, and think happy thoughts . . . not vengeful ones. Every day from now on I would play ballet music. Inside me my baby would hear, and even before he or she was born a small living soul would be indoctrinated to the dance. I smiled, thinking of all the pretty tutus I could buy for my little girl. I smiled even more to think of a boy like his father with a wild tumble of dark curls. Julian Janus Marquet would be his name. Janus for looking both ways, ahead and behind.

I passed Chris who was ready to come down the stairs. He touched me. I shivered, knowing what he wanted. He didn't have to say the words. I knew them backwards and forwards, inside and out, upside down, or right side up; I knew them . . . as I knew him.

Though I tried diligently to think only of the innocent child growing within me, still my thoughts would steal to my mother, filling me with hate, filling me with unwanted plans for revenge. For somehow she had caused Julian's death too. If we'd never been locked away in the first place and needed to escape and run, then I would never have loved Chris, or Paul, and perhaps Julian and I would have met inevitably in New York. Then I could have loved him as he needed and wanted to be loved.

INTERLUDE FOR THREE

As my baby grew within me, I began to find the identity I had lost, for the ballet kept the real me always in an embryo state, enclosed by my desire to dance and succeed. I was now standing firmly on the ground with the fantasy of glamorous life pushed to the background. Not that I didn't still crave the stage and the applause now and then. Oh, I had my sorrowful moments – but I had one sure way to shut them out. I turned my thoughts on my mother, on what she'd done to us. Another death on your record, Momma!

Dear Mrs Winslow,
    Are you still running away from me? Don't you know yet you can never run fast enough or far enough? Someday I will catch up, and we will meet again. Perhaps this time you will suffer as you made me suffer, and, hopefully, thrice the amount.
    My husband has just died as the result of a car accident, just as your husband died many years ago. I am expecting his baby, but I won't do anything as desperate as you did. I will find a way to support him or her, even if I have triplets!

I mailed that letter off, addressed to her home in Greenglenna, but the newspapers later informed me she was in Japan. Japan! Wow, she did get about.
    I was turning into a woman I'd never seen before. Mirrors showed I wasn't slim and supple any more. That terrified me. I saw my breasts become rounder, fuller, as my middle swelled outward. I hated to move less than gracefully, but my hands loved to caress the swell of my baby's small rump.
    One day I realized I was luckier than most widows, I had two men needing me. Men who let me know in subtle ways they were ready to take Julian's place. And I had Carrie, Carrie who

considered me a model by which she could mould her own life. Dear, sweet little Carrie who was now sixteen, and had never had a date, or a boy-friend, or been to a prom. Not that she couldn't have, if she'd forget her smallness. Chris persuaded his friends to date a younger sister who was dying on the vine for want of romance. She complained to me: 'Chris doesn't have to make dates for *you*! That college student, he doesn't want me. He just comes to worm in closer to you.' I laughed at how ridiculous that was. Nobody would want me in the condition I was, pregnant, a widow, and too old for a college boy.

Carrie heard this, but sulked near the window. 'Since you came back, Dr Paul doesn't take me out to the movies and to dinner like he used to. I used to pretend he wasn't my guardian, but my sweetheart, and that made me feel good inside, because all the ladies look at him, Cathy. He is handsome, even if he is old.'

I sighed, for to me Paul would never be old. He was wonderfully young looking for his age of forty-eight. I took Carrie in my arms and consoled her, saying love was waiting for her just around the corner. 'He'll be young too, Carrie, near your own age. And once he sees you, and really knows what you are, he won't have to be coerced, he'll be more than willing to love you.' Quietly she got up and entered her own room, not convinced by anything I'd said.

Madame Marisha came often to check on my condition, and filled me with authoritative advice. 'Now you keep up your practising; play the ballet music to fill Julian's baby with love for beauty before he is born; inside you he'll know the dance is waiting for him.' She glanced down at my feet that had finally healed. 'How do those toes feel now?'

'Fine,' I answered dully, though they ached when it rained.

Henny was there to wait on me hand and foot when Carrie wasn't around. She was growing old amazingly fast. I worried about her. She diligently tried to keep to the rigid diet both her 'doctor-sons' insisted on, but she ate what she wanted to, never counting calories or cholesterol.

The long days of grief sped by more quickly because I had

Julian's baby, part of him to keep with me. Soon Christmas was upon us, and I was so large I didn't feel I should show myself. Chris insisted, along with Paul, that it would be good therapy to go shopping.

I bought an antique gold locket to send to Madame Zolta, and inside I put two small photos of Julian and I, in our Romeo and Juliet costumes.

Shortly after Christmas her thank-you note arrived.

Dear Catherine,

Yours is the best gift of all. I grieve for your beautiful dancing husband. I grieve for you most of all if you decide not to dance again just because you are to become mother! Long ago you would have been a prima ballerina if your husband had shown less arrogance and more respect for those in authority. Keep in shape, do exercises, bring your baby with you and we will all live together in my place until you find new *danseur* to love. Life offers many chances, not just one. Come back.

Her note put a wistful smile on my face. 'What is it that makes you smile like that?' asked Paul, laying aside the medical journal that must have held only a part of his interest. Awkwardly I leaned forward to hand the note to him. He read it, then held out his arms, inviting me to come and cuddle on his lap and in his arms. Eagerly I accepted his invitation, I was hungry for affection. Life seemed to me nothing without a man.

'You could go on with your career,' he said softly. 'Though I pray to God you won't go back to New York and leave me again.'

'Once upon a time,' I began, 'there was a beautiful set of blond parents who gave life to four children who should never have been. And they adored them beyond reason. Then one day the father was killed, and the mother changed, and forgot all about the love, affection and attention those four children so desperately needed. So, now that another beautiful husband is dead, I will not have my child feel neglected, or fatherless, or unwanted and unnecessary. When my child cries, I'll be there. I'll be there always to make my child feel secure, and very loved, and I'll read to him, and sing to him, and he'll never feel left out, or betrayed – as Chris felt betrayed by the one he loved most.'

'He? You sound as if you know.' His iridescent eyes looked sad. 'And are you going to be both mother and father to this child? Are you going to close the gates to any man who might want to share your life? Catherine, I hope you're not going to be one of those women who lets herself go sour because life doesn't always fulfil her wishes.'

I leaned my head backwards to stare into his eyes. 'You don't still love me, do you?'

'Don't I?'

'That's no answer.'

'I didn't think I needed to answer. I thought you could tell. I thought too, from the way you look at me, that you would turn to me again. I love you, Catherine . . . Since the day you first came up my veranda steps, I've loved you. I love the way you talk, the way you smile, the way you walk – that is, before you became pregnant and started leaning backwards and holding on to your back – does it hurt that much?'

'Oh,' I said in disgust, 'why did you have to stop saying all those sweet words to ask if my back hurts? Of course it bothers me. I'm not used to carrying an extra nineteen pounds in front – go on with what you were saying before you remembered you're a doctor.'

He slowly lowered his lips to brush mine, just lightly, before passion came and he pressed them hard with his own. My arms found their way around his neck and ardently I returned kiss for kiss.

The front door opened and then banged shut. I pulled quickly away from Paul and tried to stand up before Chris came into the room – but I wasn't quick enough. He strode in, his overcoat covering his white intern's suit. He carried a bag with a quart of pistachio ice cream that I had expressed a desire for at dinner. 'I thought you were on duty tonight,' I said too quickly to hide my distress and surprise. He thrust the ice cream into my hands and looked at me coldly.

'I *am* on duty. But it's a dull night, so I thought I could take a few minutes off to drive and get you the dessert you seemed to want so much.' He flicked his glance to Paul. 'I'm sorry I arrived at the wrong time. Go on with what you were doing.' He spun on his heel and left the room, then slammed the front door a second time.

'Cathy,' said Paul who got up to take the ice cream from me, 'We have to do something about Chris. What he wants can never be. I've tried to talk to him about it, but he won't listen. He closes his ears and walks away. You must make him understand that he's ruining his life by refusing to let any other girl into his heart.' He went on into the kitchen, coming back in a few minutes with two sherbet dishes of the green ice cream I didn't want now.

He was right. Something did have to be done about Chris – but what? I couldn't hurt him; I couldn't hurt Paul. I was like a battlefield wanting both sides to win.

'Catherine,' said Paul softly, as if he'd been watching my reaction, 'you don't owe me if you don't love me. Cut Chris off, make it clear that he has to let go and find someone else. Anyone else but you ...'

'I find it so difficult to tell him that,' I said in a low voice, ashamed to admit I didn't want Chris to find anyone else. I wanted him with me always – just the nearness of him, the confidence he gave me – nothing else. I was trying to balance my time between Chris and Paul, to give each of them enough, but not too much. I watched the jealousy between them grow, and felt it was none of my fault – only Momma's! As everything wrong in my life was her fault.

It was a cold February night when I felt my first contraction. I gasped from the sharp pain – I had known it would hurt, but not so much! I glanced at the clock – two in the morning of St Valentine's Day. Oh, how marvellous, my baby would be born on what would have been our sixth wedding anniversary! 'Julian,' I cried out, as if he could hear me, 'you are about to become a father!'

I got up and dressed as speedily as I could before I crossed the hall to rap on Paul's door. He mumbled something by way of a question. 'Paul,' I called, 'I think I just had my first contraction.'

'Thank God!' he cried from the other side, instantly wide awake. 'Are you all set to go?'

'Of course. I've been ready for a month.'

'I'll call your doctor, then alert Chris – you sit down and take it easy!'

'Would it be all right if I came in?'

He swung open the door, wearing only his trousers. His chest was bare. 'You're the calmest mother-to-be I've ever seen,' he said as he helped me sit. He raced next to swipe at his face with an electric razor, then he was running to put on a shirt and tie. 'Had any more contractions?' It was on the tip of my tongue to say no, when another seized me. I doubled over. 'Fifteen minutes since the last,' I gasped. He looked pale as he pulled on his jacket, then came to help me up. 'Okay, I'll put you in the car first, then go for your suitcase. Keep calm, don't worry, this baby will have three doctors doing their very best ...'

'To get in each other's way,' I concluded.

'To see you have the best medical attention possible,' he corrected, then he bellowed towards the kitchen. 'Henny, I'm taking Catherine to the hospital! Tell Carrie when she wakes up.'

It seemed forever before the hospital loomed up ahead. Under a protective canopy at the emergency entrance, a solitary doctor paced restlessly back and forth. Chris, who said 'Thank God you're here! I was picturing all sorts of calamities,' even as he assisted me out, while someone else rushed up with a wheelchair, and without any of the preliminaries other patients had to endure, I was snug in bed in no time at all – and gasping from another contraction.

Three hours later, my son was born. Chris and Paul were there, both of them with tears in their eyes, but it was Chris who picked up my son, still with the cord attached, messy and bloody. He put him upon my belly and held him there while another doctor did what he had to. 'Cathy ... can you see him?'

'He's beautiful,' I breathed in awe, seeing all the dark, curling hair, the perfect little red body. With a fierce anger so like his father's he waved his tiny fists and flailed his thin legs, screaming at all the indignities inflicted upon him – and all the light that

268

came so suddenly to shine in his eyes, and put him centre stage, so to speak.

'His name is Julian Janus Marquet, but I'm going to call him Jory.'

Both Chris and Paul heard my thin whisper. I was so tired, so sleepy.

'Why would you call him Jory?' asked Paul, but it wasn't I who had the strength to answer. It was Chris who understood my reasoning.

'If he had been blond, she would have named him Cory – but the J will stand for Julian, and the rest for Cory.'

Our eyes met and I smiled. How wonderful to be understood, and never have to explain.

PART FOUR

MY SWEET SMALL PRINCE

If ever a child was born into a palace of adoring worshippers, it was my Jory with his blue-black curls, his pale creamy skin, and his dark, dark blue eyes. He was Julian all over, and to him I could give the lavish affection I'd been unable to give his father.

From the very first Jory seemed to know I was his mother. He seemed to know my voice, my touch, even the sound of my footsteps. Yet he had almost as great a love for Carrie who ran home every night straight from Paul's office to gather him in her arms and play with him for hours.

'We should find our own place,' said Chris, who wanted to establish himself firmly as Jory's father. In Paul's home, this wasn't possible.

I didn't know what to say to that. I loved Paul's big house, and being with him and Henny. I wanted Jory to have the garden paths where I could push him in his carriage and he'd be surrounded by beauty. And in no way could Chris and I give him as much. Chris didn't know about my sky-high debts.

Upstairs Paul had made a nursery, completely refurbished with crib, playpen, bassinet and dozens of soft plushy stuffed animals a baby could enjoy without harming himself. There were times when both Paul and Chris would rush home with the same toy. They'd look at each other, and both would force a smile to hide the embarrassment. Then I had to rush forward and exclaim, 'Two men with the same idea.' And one would have to be taken back ..., but never, never did I let either one know whose gift it was that I returned.

Carrie graduated from school the June she was seventeen. She didn't want college; she was very much contented to be Paul's private secretary. Her small fingers could fly over the typewriter keyboard; she took dictation with remarkable speed and accuracy – but still she kept wishing for someone to love her, despite her small size.

To see her unhappy made me furious with my mother – again! I began to dwell on what I would do when I had my chance. Now I was free, no husband to hold me back – make her pay, as Carrie was paying!

Each day she saw Paul and Chris battling for my attention, each desiring me, each beginning to look at the other with enmity. I had to settle something that should have been settled a long time ago. If only Julian hadn't put himself in the way, I would now be Paul's wife, and Jory would be Paul's son, and yet, and yet . . . I loved Jory for who he was, and on second thought I was glad I'd had Julian for a while. I was no longer a sweet, innocent virgin – two men had taught me well. I would have the knowledge to hold my own when it came time to steal my mother's husband away from her. I'd be like she'd been with Daddy. I'd cast Bart Winslow shy glances, meaningful long, long looks. I'd reach to caress his cheek . . . And my biggest asset of all was I looked like her, but I was years younger! How could he resist? I'd put on a few pounds to make myself curvier – like her.

Christmas came and Jory, less than a year old, sat amidst his presents, wide-eyed and bewildered, not knowing what to do, or which toy to pick up first. Snap, snap, snap went the click of three cameras. But Paul had the movie camera, not Chris, Carrie or I.

'Lullabye and good night,' sang Carrie softly to my son, rocking him to sleep on Christmas night, '. . . may heaven's sweet charms hold you safe in its arms.'

I couldn't help but cry to see her there, like a child herself, but so longing to have a child of her own. Chris came up behind me and put his arms around my waist as I leaned back against him. 'I should run for a camera,' he whispered, 'they look so sweet together, but I don't want to break the spell. Carrie is so much like you, Cathy, except in size.'

One little word, 'except'. One little word that kept Carrie from ever feeling really happy.

Footsteps sounded on the stairs. Quickly I jerked from Chris's arms and went in to tuck my small son into his crib. I sensed Paul in the doorway now that Chris had gone on to his room. 'Cathy,' whispered Carrie so Jory wouldn't awaken, 'do you think I'll ever have a baby?'

'Yes, of course you will.'

'*I* don't think I will,' she said, and then ambled away, leaving me to stare after her.

Paul came into the nursery, kissed Jory good night, then turned as if to take me in his arms. 'No,' I said in a small voice, 'not while Chris is in the house.' He nodded stiffly, then said good night, and I went to lie awake until almost dawn – wondering how I could solve the dilemma I was in.

Jory seemed quite happy with his situation; he wasn't spoiled; he didn't whine and cry or make unnecessary demands, he just accepted. He could sit for minutes staring from one to the other of us, as if sizing us up, and our relationship to him. He had the patience of Chris; the quiet sweetness of Cory, and only occasionally the brashness of his father – and his mother. But nothing at all about Jory reminded me of Carrie; he smiled so much more than she. Nevertheless, when Carrie strolled through Paul's gardens with Jory in her arms, she pointed out the differences between this tree and that. Incessantly explaining. She forced Jory to imitate speech sooner than he would have otherwise.

'Now, if I were a bee, you could bet I'd go straight for the violets and pansies too, even though they don't stand as tall.' She lifted her eyes to meet mine and said in a strange, tight small voice, 'You are like a rose, Cathy. All the bees come to you, and they don't even see me down so low. Please don't get married again before I have my chance. Please don't be around if ever some man looks my way ... Don't you smile at him, please.'

Oh, how fast the years go when you have a baby to fill all the hours. All of us took snapshots like crazy: Jory's first smile; his first tooth; his first crawl from me to Chris, and then over to Paul, and to Carrie.

Paul began his courtship that was to last two years; the same two years Chris interned in the Clairmont Hospital. They couldn't hurt each other when each loved and respected the other. They couldn't even speak of the barrier between them, except through me.

'It's this town,' said Chris. 'I think Carrie would fare better in another city. All of us together.'

It was twilight in the gardens, our favourite time there. Paul was off making his rounds in three hospitals, and Carrie was entertaining Jory before she put him to bed. Henny rattled pots and pans to let us know she was still up – and still busy.

Chris had completed his two years of internship, and had started on his residency which would take another three years. When he told me he was considering another hospital, far more famous, to further his training, I felt a deep shock. He was leaving me!

'I'm sorry, Cathy, the Mayo Clinic has accepted me, and that's an honour. I'll only be there nine months, and then back here to complete my training. Why don't you and Jory come with me?' His eyes were very bright and lambent. 'Carrie can stay to keep Paul company.'

'Chris! You know I can't do that!'

'You are going to stay on here after I'm gone?' he asked bitterly.

'If Julian's insurance company would pay off, I could afford a house of my own, and start my own dance school. But they keep insisting his death was suicide. I know that policy has a two-year suicide clause, and we paid on it since the day we married – so it was not in effect when he died. Yet, they won't pay.'

'What you need is a good attorney.'

My heart jumped. 'Yes. Yes, I do. Chris, go on to the Mayo Clinic without me. I'll make out fine, and I swear not to marry anyone until you are back and give your approval. Worry about finding someone yourself. After all, I'm not the only woman who resembles our mother.'

He flared. 'Why the hell do you put it like that? It's *you*, not *her*! It's everything about you that's not like her that makes me need and want you so!'

'Chris, I want a man I can sleep with, who will hold me when

I feel afraid, and kiss me, and make me believe I am not evil or unworthy.' My voice broke as tears came. 'I wanted to show Momma what I could do, and be the best ballerina, but now that Julian's gone all I want to do is cry when I hear ballet music. I miss him so, Chris.' I put my head on his chest and sobbed. 'I could have been nicer to him – then he wouldn't have struck out in anger. He needed me and I failed him. You don't need me. You're stronger than he was. Paul doesn't really need me either, or he would insist on marrying me right away ...'

'We could live together, and, and ...' And here he faltered as his face turned red.

I finished for him, 'No! Can't you see it just wouldn't work?'

'No, I guess it wouldn't work for you,' he said stiffly. 'But I'm a fool; I've always been a fool, wanting the impossible. I'm even fool enough to want us locked up again, the way we were – with me the only male available to you!'

'You don't mean that!'

He seized me in his arms. 'Don't I? God help me but I do mean it! You belonged to me then, and in its own peculiar way our life together made me better than I would have been ... and you made me want you, Cathy. You could have made me hate you, instead you made me love you.'

I shook my head, denying this; I'd only done what came naturally from watching my mother with men. I stared at him, trembling as he released me. I stumbled as I turned to run towards the house. Before me Paul loomed up! Startled I faltered guiltily and stared at him as he turned abruptly and strode in the opposite direction. Oh! He'd been watching and listening! I pivoted about, then raced back to where Chris had his head resting against the trunk of the oldest oak. 'See what you've done!' I cried out. '*Forget me, Chris!* I'm not the one and only woman alive!'

He appeared blind as he turned his head and he said, 'You are for me the only woman alive.'

October came, the time for Chris's departure. To see him pack, to know he was going, to say goodbye as if I didn't care when he came back made me deathly ill while I smiled.

I cried in the rose arbour. It would be easier now. I wouldn't have to keep putting Paul off so Chris wouldn't be hurt. No longer would I have to weigh each smile and balance it off against what I'd given the other. Now I had a clear, straight path to Paul – but something got in my eyes. The vision of my mother as she stepped off the plane with her husband on the step behind her. She was coming back to Greenglenna! I clipped out the newsphoto and the caption and put that in my scrapbook. Perhaps if she'd stayed away, I would have married Paul then and there. As it was, I did something entirely unplanned.

Madame Marisha was getting older and needed an assistant, so I went to convince her I should be the one to keep her school running – if ever, well, you could never tell ...

'I don't intend to die,' she snapped. Then begrudgingly she nodded, her ebony eyes suspicious. 'Yes, I suppose *you* would think of me as old, though I never do. But don't you try and take over, and try to run *me*. I am still the boss here, and will be until I am in my grave!'

By the time November rolled around I realized working with Madame was impossible. She had fixed ideas about everything, while I had a few ideas of my own. But I needed money, I needed a place of my own. I wasn't ready to marry Paul, and if I stayed there, that's just what would happen. I had spent enough years plotting and planning. It was time to make my move. The first pawn to play would be Mr Attorney at Law. It wouldn't work if I stayed with Paul, and though he objected, saying it was an unnecessary expense, I explained I had to have a chance to be my own person, and in my own home to find out what I really wanted. He gave me a puzzled look, then a more shrewd one. 'All right, Catherine, do what you must. You will anyway.'

'It's only because Chris insisted that I not marry again until Carrie has her chance, and Chris objects to my staying here with you ... when he isn't here ...' My ending was lame, and oh, such a lie!

'I understand,' he said with a wry smile. 'Since the day Julian died, it has been very clear that I am in competition with your brother for your affection. I've tried to talk to him about it, but *he* won't let me. I try to talk to you about it, and *you* won't let me. So go live in your own home, and be your own person, and find your own self, and when you feel grown up enough to act adult, come back to me.'

OPENING GAMBIT

As soon as I was installed in a small, rented cottage, halfway between Clairmont and Greenglenna, I sat down to draft a blackmail letter to my mother. I was deeply in debt, with one child, but I had Carrie too. The enormous bills Julian had run up in New York stores were still unpaid; there was also his hospital bill, his funeral bill, plus my own hospital bills made when Jory was born. Credit cards just didn't solve everything. Not for one moment was I going to accept more from Paul. He'd done enough. I needed to prove I was better than Momma, more able, smarter ... and what did I do but write her a letter, as she'd written to *her* mother after Daddy died. Why not ask for just one paltry million? Why not? She owed us! It was ours too! With that money I could pay off all the debts I owed, pay back Paul and do something to make Carrie happier. And if I felt some shame to do the same thing she'd done – in a way – I rationalized it away by thinking it was her own fault! She'd asked for it! Jory was not going to live his life in need, when she had so much!

Finally, after many futile attempts, I came up with what I believed the perfect letter of extortion:

Dear Mrs Winslow:

Once upon a Gladstone, Pennsylvania time, there lived a man and wife who had four children everyone referred to as the Dresden dolls. Now one of those dolls lies in a lonely grave and another of those dolls fails to grow to the height that should have been hers if she'd have been given sunlight and fresh air, and the love that a mother owed her when she needed it most.

Now the ballerina doll has a small son of her own, and not much money. I know, Mrs Winslow, you don't have much compassion for children who might cast a shadow over your sunny days, so I will come directly to the point. The ballerina doll *demands* payment of one million dollars – if you are to keep any of *your* millions – or billions. You may send that amount to the post office box I name, and be assured, Mrs Winslow, that if you fail to do so, the ears of Mr Bartholomew Winslow, Attorney at Law, will be filled with horror tales I'm sure you'd rather he not hear.

Cordially yours, the ballerina doll.

Each day I waited for a cheque to come in the mail. Each day I was disappointed. I wrote another letter, then another, and another. Each day for seven days I mailed off a letter to her, with a fierce anger growing in my heart. What was one measly million to her who had so many? I wasn't asking for too much. Part of that money belonged to us anyway.

Then, after fruitless months of waiting while Christmas and the New Year came and went, I decided I'd waited long enough. She was going to ignore me. I looked up a number in the Greenglenna telephone book, and in no time at all I had an appointment to see Bartholomew Winslow, Attorney at Law.

It was February and Jory was three. He was to spend the afternoon with Henny and Carrie as I, dressed in my very best with my hair becomingly styled, sauntered into the posh office to gaze upon my mother's husband. At last I was looking at him up close – and this time he had his eyes open. Slowly he rose to his feet, wearing a bemused expression – as if he'd seen me before and couldn't quite remember where. I thought back to the night I had stolen to Momma's grand suite of rooms in Foxworth Hall and found Bart Winslow asleep in the chair. He'd had a big dark moustache then, and I had dared to kiss him while he dozed, believing as I did that he was fully asleep . . . and he hadn't been! He'd seen me and thought me part of his dream. Because of one stolen kiss that Chris was to hear about later, the repercussions had led Chris and me down a path we'd determined never to follow. Now we were paying the price – and it was *her* fault that Chris was now living apart from me, trying to deny what she'd started. I could not accept Paul as my husband until I had made her pay – and not just in money.

He smiled at me then, my mother's ruggedly handsome

husband, and I saw for the first time the dazzling charisma of him. A light of recognition came into his dark brown eyes. 'As I live and breathe, if it isn't Miss Catherine Dahl, the lovely ballerina who takes my breath away even before she dances. I'm enchanted you have need of a lawyer and you chose me, though I cannot possibly imagine why you are here.'

'You've seen me dance?' I asked, stunned to hear he had. If he had seen me, then Momma must have too! Oh, and I never knew! Never knew! I glowed, I dimmed, saddened, became confused. Somewhere deep within me, despite all the hate on top, I still felt some of the love I'd had for her when I was young and trusting.

'My wife is a ballet buff,' he went on. 'Actually, I didn't care much for it when she first started dragging me to every one of your performances. But soon I learned to enjoy it, especially when you and your husband were featured in the lead roles. In fact, my wife seemed to have no interest in ballet at all unless you and your husband *were* featured. I used to fear she had a crush on your husband – he looks a little like me.' He took my hand and lifted it to his lips, flashing his eyes upward and smiling with the easy charm of a man who knew what he was, a ladies' man used to putting notches on his belt. 'You are even more beautiful off stage than on. But what are you doing in this part of the country?'

'I live here.'

He pulled out a chair for me, sat me down so close he could watch my legs when I crossed them. He perched on the edge of his desk to offer me a cigarette, which I refused. He lit one for himself, then asked, 'You're on vacation? Visiting your husband's mother?'

I realized he didn't know about Julian. 'Mr Winslow, my husband died from injuries sustained in an auto accident more than three years ago – didn't you hear about it?'

He appeared shocked and a bit embarrassed. 'No, I didn't hear. I'm very sorry. Please accept my belated condolences.' He sighed and ground out his half-smoked cigarette. 'The two of you were sensational on stage – it's a terrible pity. I've seen my wife cry, she was so impressed.'

Yeah! I'll bet she was impressed. I shrugged off more questions and came directly to the object of my visit by handing him Julian's insurance policy. 'He took out this policy shortly after we were married and now they won't pay because they think he cut the intravenous tube that was feeding him. But, as you can see, after two years the suicide clause is no longer in effect.'

He sat down to read it carefully, and then looked up at me again. 'I'll see what I can do. Are you in immediate need of this money?'

'Who isn't in need of money, Mr Winslow, unless they are millionaires?' I smiled and tilted my head in the manner of my mother. 'I have hundreds of bills and I have a small son to support.'

He asked the age of my son; I told him. He appeared puzzled and confounded in more ways than one as I looked at him with sleepy, half-closed eyes, my head tilted backwards and slightly to one side, in a mannerism that was my mother's way of looking at a man. I was only fifteen when I'd kissed him. He was far more handsome now. His mature face was long and lean, his bones too prominent, but in a very virile, masculine way he was strikingly good looking. Something about him suggested an exaggerated sensuality. And no wonder my mother hadn't sent a cheque. Probably all my blackmail letters were still following her from place to place.

Bart Winslow asked a dozen or more questions, then he said he'd see what he could do. 'I'm a pretty good lawyer once my wife allows me to stay home and get my hand into practice.'

'Your wife is very rich, isn't she?'

This appeared to annoy him. 'I suppose you could say she is,' he answered stiffly, letting me know he didn't like discussing the subject.

I stood to leave. 'I'll bet your rich wife leads you around like a pet poodle on a jewelled leash, Mr Winslow. That's the way rich women are. They don't know the least thing about working for a living, and I wonder if you do.'

'Well, by God,' he said, jumping off the desk and standing with feet wide apart, 'why did you come if you feel that way? Go to another attorney, Miss Dahl. I don't want a client who insults me and has no regard for my abilities.'

'No, Mr Winslow, I want you. I want you to prove you know your business as you claim to. Maybe, in a way, you can then prove something to yourself as well – that you aren't, after all, just a rich woman's plaything.'

'You have the face of an angel, Miss Dahl, but a bitch's tongue! I'll see your husband's insurance firm pays off. I'll petition them to appear in court, and threaten to sue. Ten to one they'll settle within ten days.'

'Good,' I said. 'Let me know, for as soon as I have the money, I'm moving.'

'Where?' he asked, striding forward to take hold of my arm.

I laughed, looking up into his face and using the ways a woman had to make a man interested. 'I'll let you know where I go, in case you want to keep in touch.'

In ten days, true to his word, Bartholomew Winslow came by the dance school to hand me the cheque for one hundred thousand dollars. 'Your fee?' I asked, waving off the girls and boys who came running to surround me. I was wearing a tight practice outfit, and he was all eyes.

'Dinner at eight, next Tuesday night. Wear blue to match your eyes, and we'll discuss the fee then,' he said, then turned to leave, not even waiting for my answer.

When he was gone, I turned around and looked at the children doing their warm-up positions, and somewhere above I hovered, looking down, and feeling scorn for the pitiful thing I was that innocence should admire me so much. I felt sad for them, for me.

'Who was that man who came to give you cheque?' Madame Marisha asked me when class was over.

'An attorney I hired to force Julian's insurance company to pay off – and they did.'

'Ah,' she said, falling into her old swivel desk chair, 'now you have money and can pay off bills – I suppose you will quit working for me and go off somewhere, yah?'

'I'm not sure just what I plan to do yet. But you must admit,

282

Madame, you and I don't get along very well, do we?'

'You have too many ideas I don't like. You think you know more than me! You think now that you work here few months, you can go away and start new school of your own!' She smiled evilly to see my start of surprise, revealing the truth she only guessed at.

'Madame, I am taking Jory away.'

'Why? You think you can teach him as well as I can?'

'I don't know for certain, but I think I can. My son may not choose to be a dancer,' I continued, ignoring her hard stony eyes. 'If he does decide one day, I think I will make an able teacher – as good as any.'

'*If he choose to dance!*' Words like cannonshot. 'What other choice does Julian's son have *but to dance*? It is in his bones, in his brain – and most of all in his blood and in his heart! *He dances – or he dies!*'

I got up to leave. It was in my heart to be kind to her, to let her share in Jory's life . . . but the meanness in her hard eyes changed my mind. She would take my son and make of him what she'd made of Julian, someone who could never find fulfilment because life offered to him but one choice.

'I didn't expect to say this today, Madame, but you force me. You made Julian believe if he couldn't dance, then life held nothing. He would have recovered from that broken neck and his internal injuries, except you said he would never dance again – and he overheard you. He wasn't sleeping. So, he chose to die! The very fact that he could move the arm that wasn't strapped down, enough to steal the scissors from that nurse's pocket, proved he was already recovering but all he could see was a bleak desert where the ballet didn't exist! Well, Madame . . . you *are not doing that to my son!* My son will have the chance to choose for himself what kind of life he wants – and I hope to God it *is not* the ballet!'

'You fool!' she spat at me, jumping up to pace back and forth in front of her old, beat-up desk, 'there is nothing better than adulation from your fans, the sound of thundering applause, the feel of roses in your arms! And soon enough you will find that out for yourself! You think to take my husband's grandson away, and hide him from the stage? *Jory will dance, and before I die I will live to see him on stage – doing what he must – or he too will die!*

'Yes, go on ... marry that big doctor you've had a yen for since you came starry-eyed and fresh faced as a kid to me – and ruin his life too!'

'Ruin his life too?' I repeated dully.

She spun about. '*You got something eating at you, Catherine! Something gnawing at your guts. Something so bitter it simmers in your eyes and grits your teeth together! I know your kind. You ruin everyone who touches your life and God help the next man who loves you as much as my son did!*'

Unexpectedly, some enigmatic, invisible cloak dropped down to wrap me in my mother's cool, detached poise. Never before had I felt so untouchable. 'Thank you for enlightening me, Madame. Goodbye and good luck. You won't be seeing me again, or Jory.' I turned and left. Left for good.

Tuesday night Bart Winslow showed up at my cottage door. He was dressed in his best, and I was wearing blue; he smiled, pleased I'd obeyed. He took me to a Chinese restaurant where we ate with chopsticks, and everything was black or red.

'You are the most beautiful woman I have ever seen, with the exception of my wife,' he said while I read my fortune cookie slip. '*Beware of impulsive actions.*'

'Most men don't mention their wives when they take another woman out –'

He interrupted: 'I am not an ordinary man. I'm just letting you know, you are not the most beautiful woman I know.'

I smiled at him sweetly, closely watching his eyes. I saw I irritated him, charmed him, but most of all intrigued him, and when we danced, I also learned I excited him. 'What is beauty without brains?' I asked, my lips brushing his ear as I stood on tiptoes. 'What is beauty that is growing old, and overweight, and no challenge at all?'

'You are the damnedest female I've ever known!' His dark eyes flashed. 'How dare you imply my wife is stupid, old and fat? She looks very young for her age!'

'So do you,' I said with a small mocking laugh. His face reddened. 'But don't worry, Mr Attorney . . . I'm not competing with her – I don't want a pet poodle.'

'Lady,' he said coldly, 'you won't have one, not in me. I'm leaving soon to set up my offices in Virginia. My wife's mother isn't well and needs some attendants. As soon as you've settled your account with me, you can say goodbye to a man who obviously brings out the worst in you.'

'You haven't mentioned your fee.'

'I haven't decided yet.'

Now I knew where I was going – back to Virginia to live somewhere near Foxworth Hall.

Now I could begin the real revenge.

'But Cathy,' wailed Carrie tearfully, very upset because we were leaving Paul and Henny. 'I don't want to leave! I love Dr Paul and Henny! You go anywhere you want to, but leave me here! Can't you see Dr Paul doesn't want us to go? Don't you care when you hurt him? You're always hurting him! I don't want to!'

'I care very much about Dr Paul, Carrie, and I don't want to hurt him. However, there are certain things I must do, and I must do now. And Carrie, you belong with me and Jory. Paul needs his chance to find a wife without so many dependants. Don't you see, we are an encumbrance to him?'

She backed off and glared at me. 'Cathy, he wants you for his wife!'

'He hasn't said so in a long, long time.'

'That's because you got your mind set on going and doing something else. He told me he wants you to have what you want. He loves you too much. If I were him, I'd make you stay, and wouldn't care what you wanted!' She sobbed then, and ran from me to slam her bedroom door.

I went to Paul and told him where I was going and why. His happy expression turned sad, and then his eyes went vague. 'Yes, I suspected all along you would feel it necessary to go back there and confront your mother face to face. I've seen you making your plans and I hoped you'd ask me to go with you.'

'It's something I have to do myself,' I said, holding both his hands now. 'Understand, please understand I still love you and always will.'

'I understand,' he said simply. 'I wish you luck, my Catherine. I wish you happiness. I wish all your days are bright and sunny and you get what you want – whether or not I am included in your plans. When you need me, *if* you ever need me, I'll be here, waiting to do what I can. Every minute I'll be loving you and missing you . . . Just remember, when you want me I'll be there.'

I didn't deserve him. He was much too fine for the likes of me.

I didn't want Chris or Carrie to know what part of Virginia I was headed for. Chris wrote to me once or twice a week and I responded letter for letter – but not one word did I tell him . . . he'd find out when he saw the change of address.

The month was May, and the day after Carrie's twentieth birthday party, celebrated without Chris there, Carrie, Jory and I set off in my car, backing out of Paul's driveway where we had come to say goodbye. Paul waved and when I looked in the rear-view mirror I saw him reach in his breast pocket for his handkerchief. He touched the tears in the corners of his eyes even as he kept on waving.

Henny stared after us. I thought I saw written in her expressive brown eyes. *Fool, fool, fool to go away and leave good man!*

Nothing proved more what a fool I was than the sunny day I set out for the mountains of Virginia with my small sister and son in the front seat next to me. But I had to do it – compelled by my own nature to seek the revenge in the place of our incarceration.

THE SIREN CALL OF THE MOUNTAINS

At the last moment I decided I couldn't risk seeing Bart Winslow even long enough to pay his fee, so I dropped a cheque for two hundred dollars in a mailbox and considered that enough – whether or not it was.

With Carrie beside me and Jory on her lap I headed straight for the Blue Ridge Mountains. Carrie was very excited now that we were on our way, her big blue eyes wide as she commented on everything we passed. 'Oh, I love to travel!' she said happily. When Jory grew sleepy, she carefully made a bed for him on the back seat and sat with him to be sure he didn't roll off and fall to the floor. 'He's so beautiful, Cathy. I am going to have at least six children, or maybe even more. I want half to look just like Jory, and half like you and Chris, and two or three like Paul.'

'I love you, Carrie, and I pity you too. You're planning on a dozen children, not just six.'

'Don't worry,' she said settling back to take a nap herself. 'Nobody is going to want me, so I won't ever have any children but yours to love.'

'That's not true. I've got the feeling, once we are in our new home, Miss Carrie Dollanganger Sheffield is going to have a love of her own. I'll even bet you five dollars – is it a bet?' She smiled, but she refused to take on the bet.

As I drove on northwest and the night began to descend Carrie grew very quiet. She stared out the windows and then back at me, and her large blue eyes held a look of fear. 'Cathy, are we going back *there*?'

'No, not exactly.' That's all I'd say until we'd found a hotel and settled in for the night.

The first thing in the morning a real estate woman I'd contacted in advance came to drive us in her car to look over the properties for sale. She was a large, mannish woman and all business. 'What you need is something compact, utilitarian and not too expensive. In this neighbourhood all the houses run into big money. But there are a few small houses that the rich people used to use for guest homes, or they housed their servants in some. There's one that's very pretty with a nice flower garden.'

She showed us that five-room cottage first and immediately I was won over. I think Carrie was too, but I'd warned her to show no signs of approval. I picked at small details to lead the agent astray. 'The chimney looks like it won't work.'

'It's a fine chimney, a good draught.'

'The furnace – does it use oil or gas?'

'Natural gas was installed five years ago and the bath has been remodelled, the kitchen too. A couple used to live here who worked for the Foxworths on the hill, but they sold out and went down to Florida. But you can tell they loved this house.'

Of course they had. Only a house that had been very beloved would have all the nice little details that made it exceptional. I bought it and signed all the papers without a lawyer, though I'd read up on the subject and insisted on having the deed checked.

'We'll have a wall oven put in with a glass door,' I said to Carrie who loved to cook – thank God, for I'd hardly have the time. 'And we'll repaint the whole interior of the house ourselves and save the money.'

Already I was finding out that one hundred thousand, after paying all the accounts I had to settle and putting the down payment on the cottage, was not going to last long. But I hadn't gone into this venture blindfolded. While Carrie stayed with Jory in a motel, I visited the ballet instructor who was selling her school and retiring. She was blonde and very small, and nearing seventy. She seemed pleased to see me as we shook hands and settled on the amount she wanted. 'I've seen you and your husband dance and really, Miss Dahl, though I'm delighted you want my school, it's a shame you are retiring at such an early age. I couldn't have given up performing at twenty-seven, never!'

She wasn't me. She didn't have my past or my kind of childhood. When she saw my determination to go through with the deal, she gave me the list of her students. 'Most of these children belong to the wealthy people who live around here, and I don't think any of them seriously intend to become professional dancers. They come to please their parents who like to see them looking pretty in little tutus during the recitals. I have failed to turn out one gifted performer.'

All three bedrooms in our cottage were very small, but the living room was L-shaped and of reasonable proportions, with a fireplace sided by bookcases. The short part of the L could be used as a dining room. Carrie and I set to with paint brushes and in one week we had painted every room a soft green. With the white woodwork it looked delicious. The space opened up and everything seemed larger. Carrie, of course, would have to have red and purple accessories for her room.

In three weeks we had both settled into a new routine, with me teaching the ballet school located over the local pharmacy and Carrie doing the housework and most of the cooking while she looked after Jory. As often as possible I took Jory with me to class, not only to relieve Carrie of the responsibility, but also to have him near me. I was remembering Madame Marisha's talk of letting him look and listen and get the feel of the dance.

I sat one Saturday morning in early June staring out the windows at the blue-misted mountains that never changed. The Foxworth mansion was still the same. I could have turned back the clock to 1957 and on this night taken Jory and Carrie by the hand and followed those meandering trails from the train depot. It would have been the same as when Momma led her four children up to their prison of hope and despair, then left them to be tortured, whipped and starved. I went over and over everything that had happened: the wooden key we'd made to escape our prison room, the money we'd stolen from our mother's grand bedroom, that night when we found a large book of sexual pleasures in the nightstand drawer. Maybe if we'd never seen that book ... maybe then things would have turned out differently.

'What are you thinking of?' asked Carrie. 'Are you thinking we should go back to visit Dr Paul and Henny – I hope that's what you're thinking.'

'Really, Carrie, you know I can't do that. It's recital time and the little girls and boys in my class will be rehearsing every day. It's the recitals the parents pay to see. Without them they have nothing to boast of to their friends. But maybe we could ask Paul and Henny to visit us.'

Carrie pouted and then for some reason brightened. 'You know, Cathy, the day the man came to put in the new oven he was young and good looking, and when he saw me with Jory he asked if that was my son. That made me giggle, and he smiled too. His name was Theodore Alexander Rockingham, but he asked me to call him Alex.' Here she paused and looked at me fearfully, with hope trembling her all over. 'Cathy, he asked me for a date.'

'Did you accept?'

'No.'

'Why not?'

'I don't know him well enough. He said he's going to college and works part-time doing electrical work to help pay his tuition. He says he's going to be an electrical engineer or maybe a minister ... He hasn't decided yet which one.' She gave me a small smile of both pride and embarrassment. 'Cathy, he didn't seem to notice how little I am.'

The way she said that made me smile too. 'Carrie – you're blushing! You tell me one moment you don't know this fella very well, and then you come up with all sorts of pertinent facts. Let's invite him to dinner. Then I can find out if he's good enough for my sister.'

'But, but ...' she stammered, her small face flushed red. 'Alex asked me to go home with him to Maryland for a weekend. He told his parents about me ... but Cathy, I'm not ready to meet his parents!' Her blue eyes were full of panic. That's when I realized that Carrie must have seen this young man many, many times while I was teaching my ballet classes.

'Look, darling, invite Alex here to dinner and let him fly home alone. I think I should know him better before you go off with him alone.'

She gave me the strangest long look, then lowered her eyes to the floor. 'Will you be here if he comes to dinner?'

'Why, of course I will.' Only then did it dawn on me. Oh, God! I drew her into my arms. 'Look, sweetheart, I'll ask Paul to come up this weekend, so when Alex sees I go for older men he won't even glance my way. Besides, you saw him first and he saw *you* first. He won't want an older woman with a child.'

Happily she threw her thin arms about my neck. 'Cathy, I love you! And Alex can fix toasters, steam irons. Alex can fix anything!'

One week later Alex and Paul were at our dinner table. Alex was a nice-looking young man of twenty-three who complimented my cooking. I was quick to point out that Carrie had prepared most of the meal. 'No,' she denied modestly, 'Cathy did most of it. I only stuffed the chicken, made the dressing, mashed the potatoes, made the hot rolls and the lemon meringue pie – Cathy did the rest.' Suddenly I felt I'd done nothing but set the table. Paul winked to show he understood.

When Alex took Carrie to the movies and Jory was snug in bed with his favourite stuffed toy, Paul and I settled down before the fire like an old married couple.

'Have you seen your mother yet?' he asked.

'They're here, my mother and her husband,' I said quietly. 'Staying in Foxworth Hall. The local newspaper is full of their comings and goings. It seems my dear, stone-eyed grandmother has suffered a slight stroke, so the Bartholomew Winslows will now make their home with her – that is, until she is dead.'

Paul didn't say anything for the longest time. We sat before the fire and watched the red coals burn down to grey ashes. 'I like what you've done with this house,' he said finally. 'It's very cosy.'

He got up then and came to sit close by my side on the sofa. Tenderly he drew me into his arms. He just held me, with our eyes locked. 'Where do I fit in?' he whispered. 'Or don't I fit anywhere now?'

My arms tightened about him. I'd never stopped loving him, even when Julian was my husband. It seemed there wasn't any one man who could give me everything.

'I want to make love with you, Catherine, before Carrie comes back.'

Quickly we shed our clothes. Our passion for each other had not lessened in all the years since we'd first met in this most intimate way. It didn't seem wrong. Not when he could murmur, 'Oh, Catherine, if there is one thing I wish for, it is to have you as mine all my life through, and when I die, let it be after such as this, with you in my arms, your arms about me, and you will be looking at me as you are now.'

'How beautiful and poetic,' I said. 'But you won't be fifty-two until September. I know you'll live to be eighty or ninety. And when you are, I pray passion will still rule both of us as it does now.'

He shook his head. 'I don't want to live to eighty unless you're with me and still love me. When you don't love me, let my time on earth be over.' I didn't know what to say. But my arms spoke for me, drawing him closer so I could kiss him again and again. Then the phone was ringing. Lazily I reached for it – then bolted straight up in the bed.

'Hello, my lady Cath-er-ine!' It was Chris. 'Henny had a friend over when I called Paul, and her friend gave me your phone number. Cathy, what the hell are you doing in Virginia? I know Paul is with you – and I hope to God he can persuade you not to do whatever it is you've got on your mind!'

'Paul is much more understanding than you are. And you are the one who should know best why I'm here!'

He made some noise of disgust. 'I do understand, that's the worst of it. But you'll be hurt, I know that. And there's Momma. I don't want you to hurt her more than she already hurts, and you know she does. But more than anything I don't want you to be hurt again, and you will be. You're always running from me, Cathy, and you can't ever run far enough or fast enough, because I'll be right at your heels, loving you. Whenever anything good happens to me I sense you by my side, clinging to my hand, loving me as I love you, but refusing to recognize it because you think it's sin. If it is a sin, then hell would be heaven with you.'

I felt a terrible sense of panic, as I hastily said goodbye and hung up, then turned to cuddle close to Paul, hoping he wouldn't know why I trembled.

In the dead of night, with Paul deeply asleep in the tiny third bedroom, I woke suddenly. I thought I heard the mountains calling out, *Devil's spawn*! The wind through the hills whistled and shrieked and added its voice to call me unholy, wicked, evil and everything else the grandmother had named us.

I got up and padded over to the windows to stare at the shadowy, dark peaks in the distance. The same mountain peaks I'd gazed on so often from the attic windows. And yes, just like Cory, I could hear the wind blowing and howling like a wolf searching for me, wanting to blow me away too, just as it had blown Cory and made him into only dry dust.

Quickly I ran to Carrie's room and crouched by her bed, wanting to protect her. For it seemed to me, in my nightmarish state, it was more likely the wind would take her before it got me.

CARRIE'S BITTERSWEET ROMANCE

Carrie was twenty now, I was twenty-seven, and this November Chris would be thirty. That seemed an impossible age for him to be. But when I looked at my Jory it hit me hard how quickly time moves as you get older.

Time that had once moved so slowly speeded up, for our Carrie was in love with Alex! It sparkled from her blue eyes and danced her tiny feet around the room as she dusted, ran the vacuum, washed the dishes or planned menus for the next day. 'Isn't he handsome, Cathy?' she asked and I agreed, though honestly he was just an average, nice-looking boy with light brown hair that ruffled up easily and gave him a shaggy-dog appearance that was somehow appealing, for he was so neat in other ways. His eyes were turquoise and his expression that of someone who has never once had an ugly, unkind thought.

Carrie thrilled to hear the phone ring. She bubbled with excitement for so often the call was for her. She wrote Alex long, passionate love poems, then gave them to me to read and stored them away without mailing them off to the one who should read them.

I was happy for her and for myself too, for my ballet school was progressing nicely and any day Chris would be coming home! 'Carrie, can you believe it? Chris's extended course is almost up!' She laughed and came running to me, as she had when she was a little girl, and in my outstretched arms she flung herself. 'I know!' she cried. 'Soon we will be a whole family again! Like we used to be. Cathy, if I have a little boy with blond hair and blue eyes, guess who I'll name him after.' I didn't have to guess, I knew. Her firstborn, blond, blue-eyed son would be called Cory.

Carrie in love was pure enchantment to watch. She stopped talking of her small size and even began to feel she wasn't inadequate. For the first time in her young life she began to use makeup. Her hair was naturally wavy, like mine, but she had it cut shoulder length and there it curled upwards in a wild tumble.

'Look, Cathy!' she cried when she came home from the beauty parlour with her new, smarter hair style. 'Now my head doesn't look so big, does it? And have you noticed how much taller I've grown?'

I laughed. She was wearing shoes with three-inch heels and two inches of platform! But she was right. The shorter hair did make her head look smaller.

Her youth, her loveliness, her joy all touched me so much my heart ached in the awful apprehension that something might happen to spoil it for her.

'Oh, Cathy,' said Carrie, 'I would want to die if Alex didn't love me! I want to make him the best possible wife. I'll keep his house so clean dust motes won't dance in the sunlight. Every night he'll eat the gourmet meals I prepare – never frozen TV junk. I'll make my own clothes and his and our children's. I'll save him loads of money in lots of ways. He doesn't say much; he just sits and looks at me in that special, soft way. So, I take what I can from that and not what words he says – for he hardly says any.'

I laughed and hugged her close. Oh, I did so long for her to be happy. 'Men don't talk as freely about love as women do, Carrie. Some like to tease you, and that's a pretty good indication you've got their interest, and it can grow into something larger. And the way you find out how much they care is by looking into the eyes – eyes never learn how to lie.'

It was easy to see that Alex was enchanted with Carrie. He was still working part-time as an electrician for a local appliance store while he took summer courses at the university, but he spent every spare minute with Carrie. I suspected he either had asked or was about to ask her to marry him.

I woke suddenly a week later to see Carrie sitting before the bedroom windows and staring off towards the shadowy mountains. Carrie who never had insomnia as I often did. Carrie who could sleep through thunderstorms, a tornado, telephone shrills a foot from her ear and a fire across the street. So naturally I was alarmed to see her there. I got up and went to her.

'Darling, are you all right? Why aren't you asleep?'

'I wanted to be with you,' she whispered, her eyes still riveted on the distant mountains, dark and mysterious in the night. They were all around us, boxing us in like they used to do. 'Alex asked me to marry him tonight.' She told me this in a flat, dull tone and I cried out, 'How wonderful! I'm so happy for you, Carrie, and for him!'

'He told me something, Cathy. He's decided he wants to be a minister.' Pain and sorrow were in her voice, and I didn't understand at all.

'Don't you want to be a minister's wife?' I asked, while I was so frightened underneath. She seemed so remote.

'Ministers expect people to be perfect,' she said in that deadly, scary tone, 'especially their wives. I remember all the things the grandmother used to say about us. About us being Devil's issue and evil and sinful. I didn't used to understand what she meant, but I remember the words. And she was always saying we were wicked, unholy children who should never have been born. *Should* we have been born, Cathy?'

I choked, overwhelmingly frightened, and swallowed over the lump that rose in my throat. 'Carrie, if God hadn't wanted us to be born He wouldn't have given us life in the first place.'

'But ... Cathy, Alex wants a perfect woman – and I'm not perfect.'

'Nobody is, Carrie. Absolutely nobody. Only the dead are perfect.'

'Alex is perfect. He has never done even one bad thing.'

'How would you know? Would he tell you if he had?'

Her lovely young face was darkly shadowed. Falteringly she explained. 'It seems Alex and I have known each other for a long, long time, and until recently he didn't tell me much about himself. I've talked my head off to him, but I've never told him about our past, except how we became wards of Dr Paul's after our parents died in an auto accident. And that's a lie, Cathy. We aren't orphans. We still have a mother who is alive.'

'Lies are not deadly sins, Carrie. Everyone tells little lies now and then.'

'Alex doesn't. Alex has always felt drawn towards God and

religion. He wants a wife and children. He told me he's never had sex with anyone because he's been looking all his adult life for just the right girl to marry – somebody perfect, like me. Somebody godly, like him. And *Cathy*,' she wailed pitifully, '*I'm not perfect! I'm bad!* Like the grandmother was always telling us, I'm evil and unholy too! I have ugly thoughts! I hated those mean little girls who put me on the roof and said I was like an owl! I wished them all to die! And Cathy, did you know Sissy Towers drowned when she was twelve? I never wrote and told you, but I felt it was my fault for hating her so much! I hated Julian too for taking you away from Paul, and he died too! You see how it is; how can I tell Alex all of that and then tell him our mother married her half-uncle too? He'd hate me, Cathy. He wouldn't want me then, I know he wouldn't. He'd think I would give birth to deformed children, like me – and I love him so much!'

I knelt by the side of her chair and held her close as a mother would. I didn't know what to say, and how to say it. I longed for Chris and his support, and for Paul who always knew how to say everything just right. And remembering this I took his words, said to me, and I repeated them to Carrie, even as I felt a terrible wrath against the grandmother who'd implanted all these crazy notions in the head of a five-year-old child. 'Darling, darling, I don't know how to say everything right, but I'm going to try. I want you to understand that what is black to one person is white to another. And nothing in this world is so perfect that it is pure white, or so bad it is pure black. Everything concerning human beings comes in shades of grey, Carrie. None of us is perfect, without flaws. I've had the same doubts about myself as you have.'

Her teary eyes widened to hear this, as if she considered me, of all people, perfect. 'It was our doctor Paul who set me straight, Carrie. He told me long ago, if a sin was committed when our parents married and conceived children, it was *their* sin and not ours. He said God didn't intend to make *us* pay the price for what our parents did. And they weren't that closely related, Carrie. Do you know in ancient Egypt the pharaoh would only allow his sons and daughters to marry a brother or sister? So you see, society makes the rules; and never forget, our parents had four children and not one of us is a freak – so God didn't punish them, or us.'

She glued her huge blue eyes to my face, desperately wanting to believe. And never, never should I have mentioned freak.

'Cathy, maybe God did punish me. I don't grow; that is punishment.'

I laughed shakily and drew her closer. 'Look around you, Carrie. Many other people are smaller than you. You aren't a midget or a dwarf, you know that. Even if you were, which you aren't, still you would have to accept it and make the best of it, just as many do who consider themselves too tall, or too fat, or too thin, or too something. You have a beautiful face, sensational hair, a lovely complexion, an adorable figure with everything where it should be. You have a beautiful singing voice, and you've got a brilliant mind; look at how fast you can type and how well you take shorthand and keep Paul's books, and you can cook twice as well as I can. You are also a much better housekeeper than I am, and look at the dresses you sew. They look better than anything I see in a store. When you add all that up, Carrie, how can you think you aren't good enough for Alex or any other man!'

'But, Cathy,' she wailed, stubbornly unappeased by what I'd said, 'you don't know him like I do. We went by an X-rated movie theatre and he said anybody who did any of those things was evil and perverted! And you and Dr Paul told me sex and making babies was a natural, loving part of living – and I'm bad, Cathy. Once I did something very wicked.'

I stared at her, taken by surprise. With whom? It was as if she read my mind, for she shook her head while tears streamed down her cheeks. 'No ... I've never had ... had ... intercourse, not with anybody. But I did other things that were wicked, Alex would think so, and I should have known it was evil.'

'What did you do, darling, that was so terrible?'

She gulped and bowed her head in shame. 'It was Julian. One day when I was visiting and you weren't home he wanted to do ... do something with me. He said it would be fun and wasn't real sex, the kind that made babies – so I did what he wanted, and he kissed me and said next to you he loved me best. I didn't know it was wicked just to do what I did.'

I swallowed over the huge, aching lump in my throat, smoothed her silken hair from her fevered forehead and wiped away her tears. 'Don't cry and feel ashamed, darling. There are all kinds of love and ways to express love. You love Dr Paul and Jory and Chris in three different ways, and me in another – and if Julian convinced you to do something you feel was wicked, that was *his* sin, not yours. And mine too, for I should have told you what he might want. He promised me never to touch you or do anything sexual with you, and I believed him. But if you did it, don't be ashamed any longer – and *Alex doesn't have to know.* Nobody will tell him.'

Very slowly her head lifted, and the moon that suddenly came into view from behind dark clouds shone in her eyes full of self-torture. 'But *I'll* know.' She began to sob, wild, hysterical sobs. 'That's not the worst thing, Cathy,' she screamed, 'I liked doing what I did! I liked him wanting me to do it – I tried not to let my face show I was feeling any pleasure for God might have been watching. So you see why Alex won't understand? He'd hate me, he would, I know he would! And even if he never knows, I'll still hate myself for doing it and liking it!'

'Please stop crying. What you did isn't that bad, really. Forget our grandmother who kept talking about our evil blood. She's a bigoted, narrow-minded hypocrite who can't tell right from wrong. She did all kinds of horrible things in the name of righteousness and nothing at all in the name of love. You're not bad, Carrie. You wanted Julian to love you, and if what you did gave him pleasure and you pleasure, then that's normal too. People are made to feel sensual pleasure, made to enjoy sex. Julian was wrong and he shouldn't have asked you, but that was *his sin*, not yours.'

'I remember lots of things you don't think I do,' she whispered. 'I remember the funny way Cory and I used to talk to each other, so you and Chris couldn't understand. We knew we were the Devil's issue. We heard the grandmother. We talked about it. We knew we were locked up because we weren't good enough to be out in the world with people better than us.'

'Stop!' I cried. 'Don't remember! Forget! We did get out, didn't we? We were four children not responsible for the actions of our parents. That hateful old woman tried to steal our confidence and our pride in ourselves – don't let her succeed! Look at Chris, aren't you proud of him? Weren't you proud of *me* when I was on stage dancing? And one day, after you and Alex are married, he will change his mind about what is perverted and what isn't – for I did. Alex will grow up and stop being overly righteous. He doesn't know yet the pleasures love can give.'

Carrie pulled from my arms and went to stare out of the windows at the dark and distant mountains, and at the quarter moon that sailed as an uptilted Viking ship through the black seas of night. 'Alex won't change,' she said dully. 'He's going to be a minister. Religious people think everything is bad, just like grandmother. When he told me he was going to give up the idea of being an electrical engineer, I knew it was all over between us.'

'Everybody changes! Look at the world about us, Carrie. Look at the magazines and the movies that decent people go to and enjoy, and the stage plays with everyone naked, and the kind of books being published. I don't know if it's for the better, but I do know people aren't static. We all change from day to day. Maybe twenty years from now our children will look back to our time and be shocked, and maybe they will look back and smile and call us innocents. Nobody knows how the world will change – so if the world can change, so can one man named Alex.'

'Alex won't change. He hates today's lack of morals, hates the kinds of books being published, the movies that are dirty and the magazines with couples doing wicked things. I don't think he even approves of the kind of dancing you used to do with Julian.'

I wanted to yell out, *To hell with Alex and his prudery*! Yet I couldn't slander the only man Carrie had found to love. 'Carrie, sweetheart, go to bed. Go to sleep and remember in the morning that the world is full of all sorts of men who would be delighted to love someone as pretty, sweet and domestically oriented as you are. Think of what Chris tells us always, "things always happen for the best." And if it doesn't work out for you and Alex, then it will work out for you and someone else.'

She threw me a quick glance of deepest despair. 'How was it for the best when God made Cory die?'

Dear Lord, how to answer a question like that?

'Was it for the best when Daddy was killed on the highway?'

'You don't remember that day.'

'Yes I do. I've got a good memory.'

'Carrie, absolutely no one is perfect, not me, not you, not Chris, not Alex. Not anybody.'

'I know,' she said, crawling into her bed like a good little girl obeying her mother. 'People do bad things and God sees them and punishes them later on. Sometimes he uses a grandmother with her whip, like she beat you and Chris. I'm not dumb, Cathy. I know you and Chris look at each other in the way Alex and I look at each other. I think you and Dr Paul were lovers too – and maybe that's why Julian died, to punish you. But you're the kind of woman men like and I'm not. I don't dance; I don't know how to make everybody love me. Only my family loves me, and Alex. And when I tell Alex he won't love me or want me.'

'You won't tell him!' I ordered sternly.

She lay with her eyes fixed on the ceiling until finally she drifted off to sleep. Then I was the one left to lie awake, hurting inside, still astonished by the effect one old woman had on the lives of so many. I hated Momma for taking us to Foxworth Hall. She'd known what her mother was like and still she took us there. She'd known her mother and father better than anyone and still she married a second time and left us alone, so she had the fun and we had the torture. And it was we who were still suffering while she had the fun!

Fun that would soon be over, for I was here and Bart was here, and sooner or later we would meet. Though how he had managed to avoid me so far I wasn't to learn until later.

I comforted myself with the thoughts of how Momma would be suffering soon too, like we had suffered. Pain for pain, she'd learn how we had felt when *she* was left alone and unloved. She wouldn't be able to cope . . . not again. One more blow would be her undoing. Somehow I knew that – perhaps because I was so much like her.

'Are you sure you're all right?' I asked Carrie a few days later. 'You haven't been eating well. Where has your appetite gone?'

She said quietly, her face expressionless, 'I'm just fine. I just don't feel like eating much. Don't take Jory with you today to your dance studio. Let me keep him all day. I miss him when he goes away with you.'

I felt uneasy about leaving her all day with Jory who could be a handful, and Carrie didn't look like she was feeling well. 'Carrie, be honest with me, please. If you feel unwell, let me take you to a doctor.'

'It's my time of the month,' she said with her eyes downcast, 'I just feel crampy in my middle three or four days before it starts.'

Only the blues of the month – and when you were her age you did feel more cramps than at mine. I kissed my small son goodbye while he set up a terrible wail, wanting to go with me and watch the dancers.

'Wanna hear the music, Mommy,' objected Jory who knew very well what he wanted and what he didn't. 'Wanna watch the dancers!'

'We'll go for a walk in the park. I'll push you in the swing and we'll play in the sandbox,' said Carrie hastily, picking up my son and holding him close. 'Stay with me, Jory. I love you so much and I never see enough of you ... Don't you love your aunt Carrie?'

He smiled and threw his arms about her neck, for yes, Jory loved everyone.

It was a terribly long day. Several times I called to check on Carrie to see if she was all right. 'I'm fine, Cathy. Jory and I had a wonderful time in the park. I'm going to lie down now and take a nap – so don't call and wake me up again.'

Four o'clock came, and my last class of the day, when my six- and seven-year-olds moved on out into the centre of the studio.

While the music played I counted, '*Un, deux, pliés, un, deux, pliés,* and now, *un, deux, tendu,* close up, *un, deux, tendu,* close up.' And on and on I instructed, when suddenly I felt that prickly rise of my neck hackles to inform me that someone was staring at me intently. I whirled about to see a man standing far to the rear of the studio. Bart Winslow – my mother's husband!

The minute he saw I recognized him he came striding towards me. 'You do look sensational in purple tights, Miss Dahl. May I have a moment of your time?'

'I'm busy!' I snapped, annoyed that he could ask when I had twelve little dancers I couldn't take my eyes off. 'My day will be over at five. If you care to you can sit over there and wait.'

'Miss Dahl, I've had one devil of a time finding you, and you've been right here under my nose all the time.'

'Mr Winslow,' I said coolly, 'if I didn't mail you an adequate fee you could have written a letter and it would have been forwarded to me.'

He knitted his dark, thick brows together. 'I'm not here about the fee – though you didn't pay me the price I had in mind.' Smiling and assured, he slipped a hand inside his jacket and pulled from the breast pocket a letter. I gasped to see my own handwriting and all the postmarks and cancellation marks on that letter that had followed my mother all about Europe! 'I see you recognize this letter,' he said with his keen brown eyes watching my every flicker of expression.

'Look, Mr Winslow,' I said, very much in a state of flurry, 'my sister isn't feeling well today and she's taking care of my son who is hardly more than a baby. And you can see I've got my hands full here. Can we talk about this some other time?'

'At your convenience, Miss Dahl, any time.' He bowed and then handed me a small business card. 'Make it as soon as possible. I've many questions to ask you – and don't try skipping out. This time I'm keeping close tabs on you. You don't think one dinner date was enough, do you?'

It upset me so much to see him with that letter that the moment he was gone I dismissed my class and went into my office. There I sat down to pore over my green ledger, totalling the figures and seeing I was still in the red. Forty students I'd been assured when I bought out this school, but I hadn't been told most of them went away during the summers and didn't return until fall. All the spoiled little rich kids in the winter and the middle-class children in the summer who could only come once or twice a week. No matter how I stretched the money I earned it didn't cover all my costs of redecorating and installing new mirrors behind the long barre.

I glanced then at my watch, saw it was almost six o'clock, then changed into my street clothes and ran the two blocks to my small house. Carrie should have been in the kitchen preparing dinner while Jory played in the fenced-in yard. But I didn't see Jory, nor was Carrie in the kitchen!

'Carrie,' I called, 'I'm home – where are you and Jory hiding?'

'In here,' she responded in a thin whisper.

All the way I ran to find her still in bed. Weakly she explained Jory was staying with the next-door neighbour. 'Cathy … I don't really feel very good. I've thrown up four or five times; I can't remember how many … and I'm so crampy. I feel funny, real funny …'

I put my hand to her head and found it strangely cold, though the day was very warm. 'I'm going to call a doctor.' No sooner were the words out of my mouth than I had to laugh bitterly at myself. There wasn't a doctor in this town who made house calls. I ran back to Carrie and stuck a thermometer in her mouth, then gasped to read the figures.

'Carrie, I'm going to get Jory and then I'm driving you to the nearest hospital. You have a temperature of one hundred and three point six!'

Listlessly she nodded, then drifted off to sleep. I rushed next door to check on my son who was happily playing with a little girl a month older than he was. 'Look, Mrs Marquet,' said Mrs Townsend, a sweet, motherly woman in her early forties who was taking care of her granddaughter, 'if Carrie is sick, let me keep Jory until you come home. I do hope Carrie isn't seriously ill. She's such a dear little thing. But I've noticed she's been looking pale and miserable for a day or so.'

I'd noticed the same thing and had tied it all to her romance with Alex that was going awry.

How wrong I was!

The very next day I called Paul. 'Catherine, what's wrong?' he said when he heard the panic in my voice.

I spilled it all out, how Carrie was sick and in the hospital where they had already made several tests, and still they didn't know what was wrong with her. 'Paul, she looks dreadful! And she's losing weight fast, unbelievably fast! She's vomiting, can't keep any food down and has diarrhoea too. She keeps calling for you and Chris too.'

'I'll have another doctor fill in for me here and fly right up there,' he said without hesitation. 'But wait before you try and get in touch with Chris. The symptoms you name are so common to a number of minor ailments.'

I took him at his word and didn't try and contact Chris who was enjoying a two-week tour of the West Coast before he came home and continued his residency. In three hours Paul was with me in the hospital room staring down at Carrie. She smiled weakly to see him there and held out her thin arms. 'Hello,' she whispered thinly, 'I'll bet you didn't think you'd see me in an old hospital bed, did you?'

Immediately he took her in his arms and began to ask questions. What were her first signs that something was wrong?

'About a week ago, I started feeling very tired. I didn't tell Cathy 'cause she worries so much about me anyway. Then I had headaches and I felt sleepy all the time, and I got big bruises and didn't know how I got them. Then I combed my hair and lots and lots of it came out, and then I just started throwing up ... and other things that other doctors have already asked me and I told them.' Her thin, whispering voice drifted off. 'I wish I could see Chris,' she mumbled before her eyes closed and she was asleep.

Paul had already seen Carrie's chart and talked to her doctors. Now he turned to me with that blank expression that put dread in my heart ... it was so fraught with meaning. 'Maybe you ought to send for Chris.'

'Paul! Do you mean ... ?'

'No, I don't mean that. But if she wants him, he should be here with her.'

I was in the hall, waiting for the doctors to do certain tests on Carrie. They had chased me from the room. As I paced back and forth before the closed door to her room, I sensed him before I saw him. I whirled about, catching my breath to see Chris striding down the long corridor, bypassing nurses carrying bedpans and trays of medicines who gaped to see him in all his splendid glory.

Time rolled backward and I saw Daddy, Daddy as I best remembered him, dressed in white tennis clothes. I couldn't speak when Chris took me in his arms and bowed his tanned face down into my hair. I heard the thud of his heart beating strong and regular. I sobbed, so near a deluge of tears, 'It didn't take you long to get here.' His face was in my hair and his voice was husky. 'Cathy,' he asked, raising his head and looking me directly in the eyes, 'what is wrong with Carrie?'

His question stunned me – for he should know! 'Can't you guess? It's that damned arsenic; I know it is! What else could it be? She was fine until a week ago, then all of a sudden she's sick.' I broke then and sobbed, 'She wants to see you.' But before I led him to Carrie's small room, I put in his hand a note I'd found in the diary she'd started the day she met Alex. 'Chris, Carrie knew for a long time something was going wrong, but she kept it to herself. Read this and tell me what you think.' While he read, my eyes stayed glued to his face.

Dear Cathy and Chris,

Sometimes I think you two are my real parents, but then I remember my real momma and daddy, and she seems like a dream that never was, and I can't picture Daddy unless I have his photograph in my hand – though I can picture Cory just like he was.

I've been hiding something. So if I don't write this you are going to blame yourselves. For a long time I've felt I was going to die soon, and I don't care any more, like I used to. I can't be a minister's wife. I wouldn't have lived this long if you two, and Jory, and Dr Paul and Henny hadn't loved me so much. Without all of you to hold me here, I would have gone on to Cory a long time ago. Everybody has somebody special to love, except me. Everybody has something special to do, except me. I've always known I'd never get married. I knew I was fooling myself about having children, for I think I'm too small. I'd never be anybody special, like you, Cathy, who can dance and have babies and everything else. I can't be a doctor like Chris, so I'd just be nothing much, just somebody to get in the way and worry everybody because I'm unhappy.

So, right now, before you read on further, promise in your heart you won't let the doctors do anything to make me live on. Just let me die, and don't cry. Don't feel sad and miss me after I'm buried. Nothing has been right, or felt right since Cory went away and left me. What I regret most is I won't be around to watch Jory dance on stage like Julian used to. Now I have to confess the truth, I loved Julian, the same as I love Alex. Julian never thought I was too little, and he was the only one who made me feel a normal woman, for a short time. Though it was sinful, even when you say it was not, I know it was, Cathy.

Last week I started thinking about the grandmother and what she used to say to us all the time about being the Devil's spawn. The more I thought about it, the more I knew she was right – *I* shouldn't have been born! I am evil! When Cory died because of the arsenic on the sugared doughnuts the grandmother gave us, I should have died too! You didn't think I knew, did you? You thought all the time I was sitting on the floor, in the corner, I couldn't hear and didn't take notice, but I was seeing and hearing, but I didn't believe, back then. Now I believe.

Thank you, Cathy, for being like my mother and the best sister alive. And thank you, Chris, for being my substitute father and my second best brother, and thank you, Dr Paul, for loving me even though I didn't grow. Thank all of you for never being ashamed to be seen with me, and tell Henny I love her. I think maybe God won't want me either, until I grow taller, and then I think about Alex, who thinks God loves everybody, even when they aren't so tall.

She'd signed that letter in a huge scrawl to make up for her small size. 'Oh, dear God!' cried Chris. 'Cathy, what does this mean?'

Only then could I open my purse and take from it something I'd found hidden away in the dark, far end of the closet in Carrie's room. His blue eyes grew wide and the colour seemed to fade as he read the name on the rat poison bottle, then saw the package of sugared doughnuts with only one left. One left. It had been bitten into just once. Tears began to course down his cheeks, then he was really sobbing on my shoulder. 'Oh, God ... she put that arsenic on the doughnuts, didn't she, so she could die in the same way Cory did?'

I broke free from his clutching arms and backed a few feet away, feeling I was drained of all blood. 'Chris! Read that letter over again! Didn't you notice what she wrote, how she didn't believe, and "Now I believe." Why wouldn't she believe back then, and believe now? Something happened! Something happened to make her believe that our mother could poison us!'

He shook his head in a bewildered fashion, the tears still eking from his eyes. 'But if she knew all along, how could anything more happen to convince her, when overhearing us talking and seeing Mickey die didn't?'

'How can I tell you?' I cried out desperately. 'But the doughnuts have been liberally coated with arsenic! Paul had them tested. Carrie ate those, knowing they would kill her. Can't you see this is another murder our mother committed?'

'She isn't dead yet!' Chris cried. 'We'll save her! We won't let her die. We'll talk to her, tell her she has to hold on!'

I ran to hold him, fearing it was too late and desperately hoping it wasn't. Even as we clung together, made parents again by our common suffering, Paul came from Carrie's room. The solemn expression on his drawn face told me everything.

'Chris,' said Paul calmly, 'how wonderful to see you again. I'm sorry the circumstances are so sad.'

'There's hope, isn't there?' cried Chris.

'There's always hope. We are doing what we can. You look so

tan and vibrant. Hurry in to see your sister and pass along some of that vitality to her. Catherine and I have said all we can think of to try to make her fight back and gain her will to live. But she has given up. Alex is in there on his knees by her bed, praying for her to live, but Carrie has her head turned towards the windows. I don't think she realizes what is said or what is done. She's gone off somewhere out of our reach.'

Paul and I trailed along behind Chris who ran to Carrie. She lay thin as a rail beneath a pile of heavy covers, when it was still summer. It just didn't seem possible she could age so quickly! All the firm, ripe, rosy roundness of youth had fled, leaving her small face gaunt and hollow. Her eyes were deep pits to make her cheekbones very prominent. She even seemed to have lost some of her height. Chris cried out to see her so. He leaned to gather her in his arms, called her name repeatedly, stroked her long hair. To his horror hundreds of the golden strands clung to his fingers when he drew them away. 'Good God in heaven – what's being done for her?'

When he brushed the hair from his fingers I hurried forward to pluck them from his hands, and in a plastic box I carefully laid them out. The electric static of the box kept them in place. An idiot notion, but I couldn't bear to see her beautiful hair swept up and thrown away. Her hair glinted on the pillows, on the bedspread, on the white lace of her bedjacket. As in a trance of nightmares unending I gathered up the long hairs and arranged them neatly while Alex prayed on and on. Even as he was introduced to Chris he paused only long enough to nod.

'Paul, answer me! What is being done to help Carrie?'

'Everything we know how to do,' answered Paul, his voice low and soft, the way people speak when death is near. 'A team of good doctors are working around the clock to save her. But her red blood cells are being destroyed faster than we can replace them with transfusions.'

Three days and nights all of us lingered beside Carrie's bedside while my neighbour took care of Jory. Each of us who loved her prayed that she'd live. I called Henny and told her to go to church and have all her family and church members pray for Carrie too. She tapped over the line her signal for 'Yes, Yes!'

Flowers arrived daily to fill her room. I didn't look to see who sent them. I sat beside Chris or Paul, or between both, and held their hands and silently prayed. I looked with distaste upon Alex, whom I believed responsible for much of what was wrong with Carrie. Finally I could keep my question to myself no longer; I got up and stalked Alex and backed him into a corner. 'Alex, why would Carrie want to die during the happiest days of her life? What did she tell you and what did you say?'

He turned his bewildered, unshaven, grief-stricken face to mine. 'What did I say?' he asked, his eyes red-rimmed from lack of sleep. I repeated my question with an even harder edge to my voice. He shook his head as if to clear it, looking hurt and sleepy as he ran long fingers through the tumble of his uncombed brown curls. 'Cathy, God knows I've done everything I can to convince her I love her! But she won't listen to me. She turns her face aside and says nothing. I asked her to marry me and she said yes. She threw her arms about my neck and said yes over and over again. Then she said, "Oh, Alex, I'm not nearly good enough for you." And I laughed and said she was perfect, just exactly what I wanted. Where did I go wrong, Cathy? What did I do to make her turn against me so now she won't even look my way?'

Alex had the kind of sweet, pious face you expect to see carved only on marble saints. Yet, as he stood there, so humbled, so racked by grief and torn by love turned against him, I reached out and soothed him as best I could, for he did love Carrie. In his own way he loved her. 'Alex, I'm sorry if I sounded harsh; forgive me for that. But did Carrie confess anything to you?'

Again his eyes clouded. 'I called and asked to see her a week ago and her voice sounded strange, as if something terrible had happened and she couldn't speak about it. I drove as fast as I could to be with her, but she wouldn't let me in. Cathy, I love her! She's told me she's too small and her head is too large, but in my eyes her proportions are just right. To me she was a dainty doll who didn't know she was beautiful. And if God lets her die I will never in this life find my credence again!' That's when he buried his face in his hands and began to cry.

It was the fourth night after Chris arrived. I dozed beside

Carrie. The others were trying to catch a catnap before they too were ill and Alex was napping in the hall on a cot when I heard Carrie call my name. I ran to her bed and knelt beside it, then reached for her small hand under the covers. It was only a bony hand now, with skin so translucent her veins and arteries could be seen.

'Darling, I've been waiting for you to wake up,' I whispered in a hoarse voice. 'Alex is in the hall and Chris and Paul are napping in the doctors' quarters – shall I call them in?'

'No,' she whispered. 'I want to talk only to you. I'm going to die, Cathy.' She said it so calmly, as if it didn't matter, as if she accepted it and was glad. 'No!' I objected strongly. 'You are *not* going to die! I'm not going to let you die! I love you as my own child. Many people love and need you, Carrie! Alex loves you so much and he wants to marry you, and he won't be a minister now, Carrie; I've told him it makes you uncomfortable. He doesn't really care what his career is, as long as you stay alive and love him. He doesn't care if you are small or if you have children. Let me call him in so he can tell you all . . .'

'Nooo,' she whispered thinly. 'I've got something secret to tell you.' Her voice was so faint it seemed to come from over hundreds of soft, rounded, little hills far, far away. 'I saw a lady on the street.' Her voice was so low I had to lean to hear. 'She looked so much like Momma I had to run up. I caught hold of her hand. She snatched hers away and turned cold hard eyes on me. "I don't know you" she said. Cathy, that was our mother! She looks like she used to almost, only a little older. She even had on the pearl necklace with the diamond butterfly clasp that I remember. And, Cathy, when your own mother doesn't want you – doesn't that mean nobody can want you? She looked at me and she knew who I was; I saw it in her eyes, and still she didn't want me because she knows I'm bad. That's why she said what she did – that she didn't have any children. She doesn't want you or Chris either, Cathy, and all mothers love and want their children unless they're evil, unholy children . . . like us.'

'Oh, Carrie! Don't let her do this to you! It's the love of money that made her deny you . . . not that you are bad or wicked or unholy. You haven't done anything evil! It's money that matters to her, Carrie, not us. But we don't need her. Not when you have Alex and Chris, Paul and me ... and Jory too, and Henny ... Don't break our hearts, Carrie, hang on long enough to let the doctors help you. Don't give up. Jory wants his aunt back; every day he asks where you are. What am I going to tell him – that you didn't care enough to live?'

'Jory don't need me,' she said in the manner she'd spoken when she was a child. 'Jory's got lots of people besides me to love and care for him ... but Cory, he's waiting for me, Cathy. I can see him right now. Look over there behind your shoulder; he's standing next to Daddy and they want me more than anyone here.'

'Carrie, don't!'

'It's nice where I'm going, Cathy, flowers everywhere, and beautiful birds, and I can feel myself growing taller ... Look, I'm almost as tall as Momma, like I always wanted to be. And when I get there nobody's ever going to say again I got eyes big and scary as an owl's. Nobody will ever call me "dwarf" again, and tell me to use a stretching machine ... 'cause I'm just as tall as I want to be.'

Her weak and trembling voice faded away. Her eyes rolled heavenward and stayed open without blinking. Her lips stayed parted, as if she had something else to tell me. *Dear God, she was dead!*

Momma had started all of this. Momma who got out of everything scot-free! Scar-free! And rich, rich, rich! All she had to do was shed a few tears of self-pity after she went home. That's when I screamed! I know I screamed. I wailed and wanted to rip the hair from my head and tear the skin from my face – for I looked too much like that woman who had to pay, pay, pay ... and then pay some more!

On a hot August day we buried Carrie in the Sheffield family plot, a few miles outside the city limits of Clairmont. No rain this time. No snow on the ground. Now death had claimed every season but winter and left only that cold, blustery weather for me to rejoice in. We covered Carrie over with the crimson flowers she so loved, and purple ones too. The sun above was a rich saffron colour, almost orange before it turned to vermilion as it sank to the horizon and turned the heavens rosy-red.

My thoughts were like the dry leaves blowing in the strong wind of hate as I sat on and on and on, though the marble bench beaneath me was hard and uncomfortable. I made those dry leaves, after I gathered them together and twisted them, into a cruel witch's stick, a thing to stir up a neglected brew of revenge!

Out of the four Dresden dolls only two were left. And *one* would do nothing. He had taken an oath to do what he could to preserve life and keep alive even those who didn't deserve to live.

I was loath to leave Carrie alone in the night, the first one she'd spend in the ground. I had to spend this one night with her and comfort her in some unknown way. I threw a glance at where Julia and Scotty lay asleep too, near Paul's parents, and an older brother who had died even before Amanda was born. I wondered what we, the Foxworths, were doing in the Sheffield family plot? What meaning was there to any of this?

If Alex hadn't come into Carrie's life when he did and given her love, would she have been better off? If Carrie hadn't spied Momma on the street and raced to catch up with her, happy enough to take hold of her hand and call her Momma, would that have made a difference? It must have made *all* the difference! It must have! Straight from her mother's denial she had gone to purchase rat poison because she didn't feel fit to live, not when even her mother could deny her. And the poison on her doughnuts hadn't been just a trace, but heavily laced – pure arsenic!

Someone spoke my name softly. Someone reached with tenderness to lift me up by my elbows. With his arm about my waist, supporting me, he led me from the cemetery where I would have stayed until dawn to see the sun come up. 'No, darling,' said Chris. 'Carrie doesn't need you now. But others do. Cathy, you must forget the past and your plans for revenge. I see the look on your face and read your mind. I'll share with you my secret for finding peace. I've tried to give it to you before but you refuse to listen. *Now this time listen and believe!* Do as I do and force yourself to forget everything that gives you pain, and remember only what gives you joy. It is the whole secret to happy living, Cathy. Forgetting and forgiving.'

Bitter, bleak eyes I turned upon him and scornfully I said, 'You are indeed very good at forgiving, Christopher – but at forgetting, now that is another matter.'

He flushed as red as the dying sun. 'Cathy, please! Isn't forgiving the better half? I only remember the sweeter part.'

'No! No!' But I clung to him as one who approaches Hell holds tight to salvation.

Though I'm not sure, I thought I saw a woman dressed in black, with her head and face covered by a black veil, duck behind a tree as we approached the road and the parked car. Hiding so we wouldn't see her. But I caught a glimpse, enough to reveal the rope of lustrous pearls she wore. Pearls that were there for a thin white hand to lift and nervously, out of long habit, twist and untwist into a knot.

Only one woman I knew did that – and she was the perfect one to wear black, and should run to hide! *Forever hide!*

Colour all her days black! Every last one!

I'd see to it that all her remaining days on earth were black. Blacker than the tar put on my hair. Blacker than anything in that locked room and in the darkest shadows in the attic that had been given to us when we were fearful and young and needing so much to be loved enough. Blacker than the deepest pit in hell.

I'd waited long enough to deliver what I must. Long enough. And even with Chris here to try and stop me – even he wouldn't be enough to prevent what I had to do!

PART FIVE

THE TIME FOR VENGEANCE

The untimely death of Carrie left a gaping hole in the lives of all of us who loved her. Now the little porcelain dolls were mine to cherish and keep. Chris went away to be a resident at the University of Virginia just so he wouldn't be too far from me.

'Stay, Catherine,' pleaded Paul when I told him I was going back to my place in the mountains to pick up my life as dance instructor. 'Don't go and leave me alone again! Jory needs a father; I need a wife; he needs a man to emulate. I'm sick to death of having you to love only once in a while.'

'Later,' I said with hard determination, backing off from his arms. 'I'll come to you one day and we will be married, but I have some unfinished business to attend to first.'

Soon I was back into my routine of work, not far from where the Foxworths lived in their mansion. I settled down to scheming. Jory was a problem now that I didn't have Carrie. He grew tired at the dance school and wanted to play with children his own age. I enrolled him in a special preschool and hired a maid to help out with the housework and stay with Jory when I wasn't there. At night I went on the prowl, looking, of course, for one particular man. So far he had eluded me, but sooner or later fate would see that we met – God help you then, Momma!

The local newspaper gave Bartholomew Winslow a big write-up when he opened his second law office in Hillendale while his junior partner ran his first office in Greenglenna. Two offices, I thought. What money couldn't buy! I didn't plan on being so bold as to approach him directly; ours would be an accidental confrontation. Leaving Jory in the care of Emma Lindstrom, as he played in our fenced-in yard with two other children, I drove my car to the woods that weren't so far from Foxworth Hall.

Bart Winslow was a celebrity of sorts, with all the details of his life explored, so I knew from the news story that it was his habit to jog a few miles each day before breakfast. Indeed, he would need a strong heart for what was coming up in his near future. For days on end I jogged myself, using dirt paths that twisted and turned, cluttered by dead, dry and crackling leaves. It was September and Carrie had been dead a month. Sad thoughts while I sniffed the pungent aroma of woodfires burning and heard the noise of wood being chopped. Sounds and smells Carrie should be enjoying – they'll pay, Carrie! I'll make them pay, and somehow I forgot, Bart Winslow didn't have anything to do with it. Not him, only *her*! How quickly time passed and I was getting nowhere! Where was he? When we met, and some day we had to, he'd say something that was a cliché, or I would, and that would be the beginning – or the ending I had in mind since the first time I laid eyes on Bartholomew Winslow dancing with my mother on Christmas night.

As contrary as life would be, I didn't meet him jogging. One Saturday noon I sat in a café and suddenly Bart Winslow sauntered in the door! He glanced around, spied me seated by the windows and came towards me in his three-piece lawyer's suit that must have cost a fortune. With attaché case in hand, he actually swaggered! His smile was wide, his lean, tanned face slightly sinister – or maybe it was me scaring myself.

'We-ll,' he drawled, 'as I live and breathe, if it isn't Catherine Dahl, the very woman I've been hoping to run into for months.' He set down his attaché case, sat across from me without my invitation, then leaned on his elbows to peer into my eyes with intense interest. 'Where the hell have you hidden yourself?' he asked, using his foot to draw his case nearer and guard it.

'I haven't hidden myself,' I said, feeling nervous and hoping it wouldn't show.

He laughed as his dark eyes scanned over my tight sweater and skirt and what he could see of my foot that nervously swung. Then his face grew solemn. 'I read in the newspaper about your sister's death. I am very sorry. It always hurts to read of someone so young dying. If it's not too personal, may I ask what killed her? A disease? An accident?'

My eyes opened wide. What killed her? Oh, I could write a book about that!

'Why don't you ask your wife what killed my sister?' I said stiffly.

He appeared startled, then shot out, 'How can she know when she doesn't know you or your sister? Yet, I saw her with the clipping cut from the obituary page, and she was crying when I snatched it from her hand. I demanded an explanation; she got up and ran upstairs. She still refuses to answer my questions. Just who the hell are you, anyway?'

I bit again into my ham, tomato and lettuce sandwich and chewed irritatingly slowly just to watch his vexation. 'Why not ask *her*?' I said again.

'I do hate people who answer questions with questions,' he snapped, then motioned to a red-haired waitress who hovered nearby and gave her his order to have the same as I. 'Now,' he said, scooting his chair forward. 'Some time ago I came to your dance studio and showed you those blackmail letters you keep writing to my wife.' He reached into his pocket and pulled out three I'd written years ago. From the dog-eared look of them, and the many stamps and cancellations, they had followed her about the world to end up again in my hands, with him almost shouting again, 'Who the hell are you?'

I smiled to charm him. My mother's smile. I tilted my head as she did hers and fluttered one hand up to play with my simulated pearls. 'Do you really have to ask – can't you guess?'

'Don't play coy with me! Who are you really? What is your relationship to my wife? I know you look like her, same hair, same eyes, and even some of your mannerisms are the same. You must be some kind of relative ... ?'

'Yes. You could say that.'

'Then why haven't I met you before? A niece, cousin?' He had a strong animal magnetism that almost frightened me from playing the kind of game I had in mind. This was no adolescent boy who would be timidly impressed with a former ballerina. His dark appeal was strong, almost overwhelming me. Oh, what a wild lover he'd make. I could drown in his eyes and, making love with him, I'd be forever lost to any other man. He was too confidently masculine, too assured. He could smile and be at ease while I fidgeted and longed to escape before he led me down the trail I thought I'd wanted up until this very moment.

'Come,' he said, reaching to forcefully restrain my departure when I rose to go, 'stop looking frightened and play the game you've had in mind for some time.' He picked up the letters and held them before my eyes. I looked away, unhappy with myself. 'Don't turn away your eyes. Five or six of your letters came while my wife and I were in Europe, and she'd see them and pale. She'd swallow nervously – as you are swallowing nervously now. Her hand would lift to play with her necklace, just as you are playing with your beads now. Twice I saw her write on the envelope, "Address unknown." Then one day I collected the mail and I found these three letters you'd written to her. I opened them. I read them.' He paused, leaned forward so his lips were only inches from mine. His voice came hard and cold and fully in control of any savagery he might feel. 'What right have you to try and blackmail my wife?'

I'm sure the colour left my cheeks. I know I felt sick and weak and wanted to flee this place and him. I imagined I heard Chris's voice saying, *Let the past rest in peace. Let it go, Cathy. God in his own way will eventually work the vengeance you want. In his own way, at his own speed He will take the responsibility from your shoulders.*

Here was my chance to spill it forth – *all of it*! Let him know just what kind of woman he'd married! Why couldn't my lips part and my tongue speak the truth? 'Why don't you ask your wife who I am? Why come to me when she has *all* the answers?'

He leaned back against the gaudy, bright orange, plastic-covered chair and took out a silver cigarette case with his monogram in diamonds. That just had to be a gift to him from my mother – it looked like her. He offered that case to me. I shook my head. He tapped the loose tobacco from one end and then lit the other with a silver lighter with diamonds too. All the while his dark, narrowed eyes held mine and, like a fly caught in a web of its own making, I waited to be pounced upon.

'Each letter you write says you need desperately a million

dollars,' he said in a flat monotone, then blew smoke directly into my face. I coughed and fanned the air. All around the walls bore signs reading NO SMOKING. 'Why do you need a million?'

I watched the smoke; it circled and came directly to me, wreathed about my head and neck. 'Look,' I said, struggling to regain my control, 'you know my husband died. I was expecting his child and I was inundated with bills I couldn't pay, and even after the insurance paid off, with some assistance from you, still I'm going under. My dance school is in the red. I have a child to support, and I need things for him, to save for his college education, and your wife has *so* many millions. I thought she could part with just one.'

His smile was faint, cynical. He blew smoke rings to made me dodge and cough again. 'Why would an intelligent woman like you presume to think my wife would be so generous as to turn over one dine to a relative she doesn't even claim?'

'Ask her why!'

'I have asked her. I took your letters and pushed them in her face and demanded to know what it was all about. A dozen times I've asked just who you are and how you are connected to her. Each time she says she doesn't know you, except as a ballerina she's seen dance. This time I want straight answers from you.' To assure that I didn't turn my face and hide my eyes, he reached forward to grip my chin firmly so I couldn't turn my head. *'Who the hell are you?* How are you connected to my wife? Why should you think she would pay you blackmail money? Why should your letters send her running upstairs to take out a picture album she keeps locked in her desk drawer or in a safe? An album she quickly hides and locks away whenever I come into the room.'

'She took the album – the blue album with a gold eagle on the leather cover?' I whispered, shocked that she would do that.

'Everywhere we go the blue album goes with her in one of her locked trunks.' His dark eyes narrowed dangerously. 'You described that blue and gold album exactly, though it's old and worn shabby now. While my wife looks in a picture album, my mother-in-law reads her Bible to rags. Sometimes I catch my wife crying over the photographs that blue album holds, which I presume are pictures of her first husband.'

I sighed heavily and closed my eyes. *I didn't want to know she cried!*

'Answer me, Cathy. *Who are you?*' I felt he would grip my chin and hold me there throughout eternity if I didn't speak up and say something, and for some stupid reason I lied. 'Henrietta Beech was your wife's half-sister. You see, Malcolm Foxworth had an extramarital affair, and three children were the result. I am one. Your wife is my half-aunt.'

'Ahhh,' he sighed, releasing my chin and leaning back in his chair, as if satisfied I was telling the truth. 'Malcolm had an affair with Henrietta Beech who gave him three illegitimate children. What extraordinary information.' He laughed mockingly. 'I never thought the old devil had it in him, especially after that heart attack soon after my wife married the first time. Gives a man inspiration to know that.' He sobered then to give me a long and searching look. 'Where is your mother now? I'd like to see and talk to her.'

'Dead,' I said, hiding my hands under the table and keeping my fingers crossed like a superstitious, silly child. 'She's been dead a long, long time.'

'Okay. I get the picture. Three young, illegitimate Foxworth children hoping to cash in on their bloodline by blackmailing my wife – right?'

'Wrong! It was only me. Not my brother or my sister. I only want what is due us! At the time I wrote those letters I was in a desperate situation, and even now I'm not much better off. The hundred thousand the insurance paid didn't go very far. My husband had run up huge bills and we were behind in our rent and car payments; plus I owed hospital bills for him, the money for his funeral, and then the costs of having my baby. I could go on all night telling you my dance school's problems and how I was tricked into believing it was a profitable, going concern.'

'And it's not?'

'Not when it consists of so many little rich girls who take off and go on vacations two or three times a year and aren't really serious about dancing anyway. All they want to do is look pretty and feel graceful. If I had one really good student it would be worth all my efforts. But I don't have one, not one.'

He drummed his strong fingertips on the tablecloth, looking deeply reflective. Next he had a cigarette lit again, not as if he truly enjoyed smoking, but more as if he had to have something to keep his restless fingers busy. He inhaled deeply, then looked me straight in the eyes. 'I'm going to speak very frankly to you, Catherine Dahl. First, I don't know if you are lying or telling the truth, but you do look like a member of the Foxworth clan. Second, I don't like you trying to blackmail my wife. Third, I don't like to see her unhappy, so much so that she cries. Fourth, I happen to be very much in love with her, though there are times, I admit, I'd like to choke the past from her throat. She never speaks of it; she is full of secrets my ears will never hear. And one great big secret I've never heard before is that Malcolm Neal Foxworth, the good, pious, saintly gentleman, had a love affair after he had heart trouble. Now before his heart trouble, I happen to know he had at least one, possibly, but no more.'

Oh! He knew more than I. I had shot an arrow into the sky, not knowing it would hit a bulls-eye!

Bart Winslow glanced about the café. Families were coming in to dine early, and I suppose he feared someone might recognize him and report back to his wife, my mother.

'C'mon, Cathy, let's get out of here,' he urged, getting to his feet and reaching to pull me on mine. 'You can invite me to have a drink in your home, then we can sit and talk and you can tell me everything in more detail.'

Twilight came like a quickly dropped shade to the mountains – suddenly it was evening – and we'd been hours in that café. We were on the sidewalk when he held my cardigan sweater for my arms to fill the sleeves, though the air was so brisk I needed a jacket or coat.

'Your home, where is it?'

I told him and he looked disconcerted. 'We'd better not go there ... too many people might see me go inside.' (He didn't know then, of course, I had chosen that cottage mainly because it backed up to a wooded area, and there was plenty of privacy for a man to come and go on the sly.) 'My face is in the newspapers so often,' he continued, 'I'm sure your neighbours would see me.

Could you call your babysitter and have her stay on a while longer?'

I did just that, speaking first to Emma Lindstrom, and then to Jory, telling him to be a good boy until Mommy was home again.

Bart's car was sleek and black, a Mercedes. It purred along like one of Julian's sleek luxury cars, so heavy it didn't rattle or clank, and firmly it gripped the curved mountain roads. 'Where are you taking me, Mr Winslow?'

'To a place where we can talk and no one will see us or hear us.' He looked my way and grinned. 'You've been studying my profile. How do I rate?'

A hot rush of blood heated my face. Knowing I was blushing made me blush again, so then I felt damp. My life was full of handsome men, but this man was far different from any I had known. A rakish, bandit type of man who was filling me with alarm signals – go slow with this one! My intuitiveness warned as I studied his face and took note. Everything, his expensive, beautifully fitted suit, shouted that he should be as determined as I was in getting what he wanted, when he wanted.

'Well,' I drawled to make a mockery of this, 'your looks tell me to run fast and lock the door behind me!'

Wickedly he grinned again, seemingly satisfied. 'So, you find me exciting and a bit dangerous. Nice. To be handsome but boring would be worse than being ugly and charming, wouldn't it?'

'I wouldn't know. If a man is charming and intelligent enough, I often forget how he actually looks and think he's handsome regardless.'

'Then you must be easily pleased.'

I shifted my eyes and sat up primly. 'Truthfully, Mr Winslow –'

'Bart.'

'Truthfully, Bart, I am very difficult to please. I'm inclined to put men up on a pedestal and think of them as perfect. As soon as I find out they have feet of clay, I fall out of love, become indifferent.'

'Not many women know themselves so well,' he mused. 'Most go around never knowing what they are beneath their façade. At least I know where I stand – a sex symbol not on a pedestal.'

322

I'd never put *him* on a pedestal. I knew him for what he was, a womanizer, a skirt-chaser, wind and fire, enough to drive a jealous wife crazy! Certainly my mother had never bought that sex manual to instruct him how to or when to and where to! He'd know everything. Abruptly he pulled his car to a stop, then turned to meet my gaze. Even in the darkness the whites of his dark eyes shone. Too virile, too vibrant for a man who should be showing signs of ageing. He was eight years younger than my mother. That made him forty years old, a man's most attractive time, his most vulnerable time, his time to think youth would soon be over. He'd have to make his new conquests now, before the sweet and fleeting bird of youth had flown away and taken with it all the young and pretty girls that could have been his. And he must be tired of the wife he knew so well, though he professed to love her. Why then were his eyes gleaming, challenging me? *Oh, Momma, wherever you are, you should be down on your knees praying! For I'm not going to show you mercy, no more than you showed us!*

Yet as I sat there summing him up I realized he was no self-sacrificing, quiet man like Paul. This one wouldn't need seducing. He'd do that himself, staccato time. He'd stalk like a black panther until he had what he wanted, and then he'd walk out and leave me and it would be all over. He was not going to give up his chance to inherit millions and the pleasures millions gave for some chance mistress who came his way. Red lights were flashing behind my eyes ... go easy ... do it right, for there's danger if you do it wrong.

As I measured him, he was measuring me in just about the same way. Did I remind him too much of his wife so there would be no real difference? Or was my likeness to her an advantage? After all, didn't men always fall over and over again for the same type?

'Beautiful night,' he said. 'This is my favourite season. Fall is so passionate, even more than spring. Come walk with me, Cathy. This place puts me in a strange, melancholy mood, as if I've got to run fast to catch up with the best thing in my life, which up until now has always eluded me.'

'You sound poetic,' I said as we left his car and he caught hold of my hand. We began to stroll, with him deftly guiding me – would you believe it – alongside a railroad track in the country! It seemed so familiar. Yet it couldn't be, could it? Not the same railroad track that had taken us as children to Foxworth Hall fifteen years ago when I was twelve!

'Bart, I don't know about you, but I've got the weirdest feeling that I have walked this path with you before, on some other night before this.'

'Déjà vu,' he said. 'I have that same feeling. As if once you and I were deeply in love, and we walked through those woods over there. We sat on that green bench beside these train tracks. I was compelled to bring you here, even when I didn't know where it was I was driving to.'

He turned to smile with a great deal of winsome charm. 'I think you and I have much in common, Catherine Dahl. I have the need of the mysterious, the need to be confounded, and the need to have someone to worship. So I fell in love with an heiress to millions, but those millions she wanted to inherit got in my way. They put me off and scared me. I knew everyone would think I was marrying her just for her money. I think she thought it too, until I convinced her otherwise. I fell for her hard, before I knew who she was. In fact I used to think she was like you.'

'How could you think that?' I asked, all tight inside from hearing his revelations.

'Because she was like you, Cathy, for a while. But then she inherited millions, and in great orgies of shopping she'd buy everything her heart desired. Soon there was nothing to wish for at all – but a baby. And she couldn't have a baby. You can't imagine all the time we spent in front of shops that sold infant clothes, toys and furniture. I married her knowing we couldn't have children and I thought I didn't care. Soon I began to care too much. Those infant shops held a fascination for me too.'

The faint path we followed led straight to the green bench stretched between two of the four rickety old green posts that supported a rusty tin roof. There we sat in the cold mountain air, with the moon bright, the stars flickering on and off; bugs were humming, just as my blood was singing.

'This used to be a mail pick-up and drop-off station, Cathy.'

He lit another cigarette. 'They don't run the trains by here anymore. The wealthy people who live nearby finally won their petition against the railroad company and put an end to trains that so inconsiderately blew their whistles at night and disturbed their rest. I was very fond of hearing the train whistles at night. But I was only twenty-seven, a bridegroom living in Foxworth Hall. I'd lie on my bed near my wife, with a swan overhead – can you believe that? She would sleep with her head on my shoulder or we'd hold hands all through the night. She took pills so she'd sleep soundly. Too soundly, for she never heard the beautiful music coming from overhead. It puzzled me so – and she said, when I told her, it was my imagination. Then one day it stopped, and I guessed she was right, it was only my imagination. When the music ended I missed it. I longed to hear it again. The music had given that old dry house some enchantment. I used to fall asleep and dream of a lovely young girl who danced overhead. I thought I was dreaming of my wife when she was young. She told me that often, as a way of punishment, her parents would send her into the attic schoolroom and force her to stay there all day, even in the summers when the temperature up there must have been over a hundred degrees. And they sent her up there in the winters too – she said it was frigidly cold and her fingers would turn blue. She said she spent her time crouched on the floor near the window, crying because she was missing out on some fun thing her parents considered wicked.'

'Did you ever go and take a look in the attic?'

'No. I wanted to, but the double doors at the top of the stairs were always locked. And besides, all attics are alike; see one and you've seen them all.' He flashed me a wicked smile. 'And now that I've revealed so much about myself – tell me about you. Where were you born? Where did you go to school? What made you take up dancing – and why haven't you ever attended one of those balls the Foxworths throw on Christmas night?'

I sweated, though I was cold. 'Why should I tell you everything about myself. Just because you sat there and revealed a little about yourself? You didn't tell me anything of real importance. Where were you born? What made you decide to become an attorney? How did you meet your wife? Was it in the summer, the winter, what year? Did you know she'd been married before, or did she tell you only after you were married?'

'Nosy little thing, aren't you? What difference does it make where *I* was born. I haven't led an exciting life like you have. I was born in the nothing little town called Greenglenna, South Carolina. The Civil War ended the prosperous days of my ancestors, and we went steadily downhill, as did all the friends of the family. But it's an old story, told so many times. Then I married a Foxworth lady and prosperity reigned again in the South. My wife took my ancestral home and practically had it reconstructed, and refurbished, and spent more than if she had bought a new place. And what was I doing during all of this? I've done very little with my education; I've become a social butterfly. I've had a few court cases and I helped you with your difficulties. And, by the way, you never paid the fee I had in mind.'

'I mailed you a cheque for two hundred dollars!' I objected hotly. 'If that wasn't enough, please don't tell me now; I don't have another two hundred to give away.'

'Have I mentioned money? Money means little to me now that I have so much of it at my disposal. In your special case I had another kind of fee in mind.'

'Oh, come off it, Bart Winslow! You've brought me way out into the country. Now do you want to make love on the grass? Is it your lifelong ambition to make love to a former ballerina? And what's so attractive about you, a lap dog for a pampered, spoiled, rich woman who can buy anything she wants – including a much younger husband! Why, it's a wonder she didn't put a ring through your nose to lead you around and make you sit up and beg!'

He seized me then hard and ruthlessly, then pressed his lips down on mine with a savagery that hurt! I fought him off with my fists, battering his arms as I tried to twist my head from beneath his, but whichever way my head went, right or left, up or down, he kept his kiss, demanding my lips to separate and yield to his tongue! Then, realizing I couldn't escape the arms of steel he banded about me to mould my form to his, against my will, my arms stole up around his neck. My unruly fingers betrayed me and twined into his thick, dark hair, and that kiss lasted, and lasted, and lasted until both of us were hot and panting – and then he thrust me from him so cruelly I almost fell from the bench.

'Well, Little Miss Muffet – what kind of lap dog do you call me now? Or are you Little Red Riding Hood who has just met the Wolf?'

'Take me home!'

'I'll take you home – but not until I've enjoyed a little more of what you just gave.' He lunged again to seize me, but I was up and running, running for his car, running to seize my purse so that when he got there I held my manicuring scissors ready to stab with.

He grinned, reached out and wrested them from me. 'They would deliver a nasty scratch,' he mocked. 'But I don't like scratches except on my back. When I let you out you can have your little two-inch scissors back again.'

In front of my cottage he handed me the scissors. 'Now, do your worst. Cut out my eyes; stab me in the heart – you might as well. Your kiss has begun it, but I still demand my total payment.'

TIGER BY THE TAIL

Early on a Sunday morning a few days later I was warming up at the barre in my bedroom. My small son was earnestly trying to do as I did. It was sweet to watch him in the mirror I'd moved from the dresser over to the barre.

'Am I dancing?' asked Jory.

'Yes, Jory. *You are dancing!*'

'Am I good?'

'Yes, Jory. *You are wonderful!*'

He laughed and hugged my legs and looked up into my face with that ecstatic rapture only the very young can express – all the wonder of being alive was in his eyes, all the wonder of learning something new every day. 'I love you, Mommy!' It was something we said to each other a dozen or more times each day. 'Mary's got a daddy. Why don't I have a daddy?'

That really hurt. 'You did have a daddy, Jory, but he went away to heaven. And maybe some day Mommy will find you a new daddy.'

He smiled because he was pleased. Daddies were big in his world, for all the children in the nursery school had one ... all but Jory.

Just then I heard the front door bang. A familiar voice called my name. Chris! He strode through the small house as I hurried towards him in my blue tights, leotards and *pointe* shoes. Our eyes met and locked. Without a word he held out his arms and I ran unhesitatingly into them, and though he sought my lips to kiss he found only my cheek. Jory was pulling on his grey flannel trousers, eager to be swept up in strong, manly arms. 'How's my Jory?' asked Chris after he kissed both round, rosy cheeks. My son's eyes were huge as they stared at him. 'Uncle Chris, are you my daddy?'

'No,' he said gruffly, putting Jory again on his small feet, 'but I sure wish I had a son like you.' This made me shift around uncomfortably so he couldn't see my eyes, and then I asked what he was doing here when he should be attending his patients.

'Got the weekend off, so I thought I'd spend it with you; that is, if you'll let me.' I nodded weakly, thinking of someone else who was likely to come this weekend. 'I was as good as a resident can be and was rewarded and given a weekend without duty.' He gave me one of his most winning smiles. 'Have you heard from Paul?' I asked. 'He doesn't come as often as he used to, and he doesn't write much either.'

'He's away on another medical convention. I thought he always kept in touch with you.'

He put just a little stress on the 'you'. 'Chris, I'm worried about Paul. It isn't like him not to answer every letter I write.'

He laughed and fell into a chair, then lifted Jory up on his lap. 'Maybe, dear sister, you have finally met a man who can get over loving you.'

Now I didn't know what to say or what to do with my legs and hands. I sat and stared down at the floor, feeling Chris's long, steady gaze trying to read my intentions. No sooner did I think that than he was asking, 'Cathy, what are you doing here in the mountains? What are you planning? Is it your scheme to take Bart Winslow from our mother?'

My head jerked up. I met his narrowed blue eyes and felt the heat that sprang up from my heart. 'Don't question me like I'm some ten-year-old without a brain. I do what I have to – just as you do.'

'Sure, you do. I didn't have to ask, I know. It doesn't take a crystal ball to read you. I know what makes you tick and how your thoughts range – but leave Bart Winslow alone! He'll never leave her for you! She's got the millions and all you have is youth. There are thousands of younger women he can choose from – why should he choose you?'

I didn't say anything, just met his scowling look with my own confident smile, making him flush, then turn aside his face. I felt mean, cruel and ashamed. 'Chris, let's not argue. Let's be friends and allies. You and I are all that's left out of four.'

His blue eyes grew soft as they studied me. 'I was only trying, as I am always trying.' He looked around, then back to me. 'I

329

share a room with another resident at the hospital. It would be nice if I could live here with you and Jory. It would be like it used to be, just us.'

What he said made me stiffen. 'It would be a long drive for you every morning, and you couldn't be on immediate call.'

He sighed. 'I know – but how about the weekends? Every other weekend I have off-duty time – would that bug you too much?'

'Yes, it would bug me too much. I have a life of my own, Christopher.'

I watched him bite down on his lower lip before he forced a smile. 'Okay, have it your way ... do what you must, and I hope to God you won't be sorry.'

'Will you please drop the subject?' I smiled and went to him and hugged him close. 'Be good. Take me as I am, obstinate as Carrie. Now, what would you like for lunch?'

'I haven't had breakfast yet.'

'Then we'll eat brunch – and that can do for two meals.' From then on the day went swiftly. On Sunday morning he came to the table ready for the cheese omelet he favoured. Jory, thank God, would eat anything. Despite myself I thought of Chris as a father to Jory. It seemed so right to have him at the table, like it used to be ... him and I playing at being parents. Doing the best we could, all we could, and we had been only children ourselves.

We ambled through the woods after breakfast, using all the trails I followed when I jogged. Jory rode on Chris's shoulder. We looked at the world that was just outside Foxworth Hall, all the places we hadn't been able to see when we were on the roof or locked away. Together we stood and stared at that huge mansion. 'Is Momma in there?' he asked in a tight, thick voice.

'No. I've heard she's down in Texas in one of those beauty spas for very wealthy women, trying to lose fifteen extra pounds.'

Alerted, he swivelled his head. 'Who told you that?'

'Who do you think?'

He shook his head violently, then lifted Jory down and set him on his feet. 'Damn you for playing with him, Cathy! I've seen

330

him. He's dangerous – leave him alone. Go back to Paul and marry him if you must have a man in your life. Let our mother live out her life in peace. You don't believe for one moment, do you, that she doesn't suffer? Do you think she can be happy knowing what she did? All the money in the world can't give her back what she's lost – and that is *us*! Let that be enough revenge.'

'It isn't enough. I want to confront her in front of Bart with the truth. And you can stay one hundred years and get down on your knees and plead until your tongue falls out – I will still go ahead and do what I must!'

The time Chris stayed with me he slept in the room that had been Carrie's. We did very little talking, though his eyes followed my every movement. He looked drained, lost ... and, most of all, hurt. I wanted to tell him that when I'd finished what I had to do I'd go back to Paul and live a safe life with him, and Jory would have the father he needed, but I said nothing.

Mountain nights were cold, even in September when the days were warm still. In that attic we'd nearly melted from the sweltering heat, and I guess this was on both our minds as we sat before the guttering log fire on the night before Chris had to leave. My son had been in bed for hours when I rose, yawned, stretched wide my arms, then glanced at the clock on the mantel which read eleven. 'It's time for bed, Chris. Especially for you who have to get up so early tomorrow.'

He followed me towards Jory's room without speaking and together we looked down on Jory, sleeping on his side, his dark curls damp and his face flushed. In his arms he cuddled a stuffed, plushy pony, much like the real one he said he had to have when he was four.

'When he's sleeping he looks more like you than Julian,' whispered Chris.

Paul had said the same thing.

'Good night, Christopher Doll,' I said as we paused by the door of Carrie's room, 'sleep tight, don't let the bedbugs bite.'

What I said made his face contort in pain. He turned from me, opened the door to Carrie's room, then swung back to face me. 'That's the way we used to say good night when we slept in the same room,' he said, then he turned and closed the door behind him.

Chris was gone by the time I got up at seven o'clock. I cried a little. Jory stared at me with widened, surprised eyes. 'Mommy ... ?' he asked fearfully.

'It's all right. Mommy just misses your uncle Chris. And Mommy is not going to work today.' No, why should I? Only three students were due and I could teach them tomorrow when the class would be full.

My plans were moving too slowly. To speed them up I asked Emma to come and stay with Jory while I jogged through the woods. 'I won't be gone longer than an hour. Let him play outside until lunchtime, and by then I'll be back.'

Dressed in a bright blue jogging outfit trimmed with white, I set off down the dirt trails. This time I used a right fork I'd never tried before and into a denser pine forest I ran. The trail was faint and jaggedly crooked, so I had to keep a keen eye on the ground for tree roots that might trip me up. The mountain trees that grew between the pines were a brilliant blaze of fall colours, like fire against the emerald green of the pines, firs and spruces. And it was, as I'd told myself long ago, the year's last passionate love affair before it grew old and died from the frosty bite of winter.

Someone was jogging behind me. I didn't turn to look. The crispy crackle of the dead leaves pleased my ears, so I ran faster, faster, letting the wind take my loose hair just as I let the beauty of the day take my grief, remorse, shame and guilt and make them transparent shadows that didn't hold up beneath the sun.

'Cathy, hold up!' called a man's strong voice. 'You run too fast!'

It was Bart Winslow, of course. As it had to be sooner or later. Fate couldn't always outwit me, and my mother couldn't always win. I threw a glance over my shoulder, smiling to see him panting as he ran in his stylish jogging costume of maple-sugar tan, trimmed with bands of orange and yellow knit at the cuffs, neck and waistband. Two vertical lines of yellow and orange ran down the sides of the loose pants. Just what a local runner should wear when on the prowl.

'Hello, Mr Winslow,' I called back as I speeded up. 'A man who can't catch a woman is no man at all!'

He took the challenge and put more speed into his long legs and I really had to put out to keep ahead! I flew, my long hair bannering behind. Squirrels on the ground scrounging around for nuts had to scamper to get out of my way. I laughed with the power I felt, then threw out my arms and pirouetted, feeling I was on stage playing out the best role of my life. Then from nowhere a knobby tree root caught beneath the toe of my dirty sneaker and down I fell, flat on my face. Luckily, the dead leaves cushioned me.

In a flash I was up and running again, but my fall had given Bart the chance to draw nearer. Panting, gasping, clearly indicating he didn't have nearly the stamina I had, despite the advantage of his longer legs, he cried out again, 'Stop running, Cathy! Have mercy! This is killing me! There are other ways I can prove my manhood!'

I had no mercy! It was catch me if you can, or else I'd never be taken. I shouted this back to him and ran on, rejoicing in my powerful dancer's legs, my supple, long muscles and all that ballet training had done to make me feel a blue streak of light.

No sooner did this self-conceit flash through my mind than my stupid knee suddenly gave way and down I went again, on my face in the dead leaves. And this time I was hurt, really hurt. Had I broken a bone? Sprained an ankle, torn a ligament – again?

In a few moments Bart was beside me, down on his knees, rolling me over so he could see my face before he asked with a great deal of concern, 'Are you hurt? You look so pale – what's paining?'

I wanted to say of course I was all right, for dancers knew how to fall, except when they didn't know they were going to fall – and why was my knee aching so badly? I stared down at it, feeling betrayed by a knee that was always the one to foul me up and hurt me in more than one way. 'It was my stupid knee. If I bump my elbow on the shower door, my right knee hurts. When I have a headache, my knee hurts along with it to keep it company. Once I had a tooth filled, and the dentist was careless enough to let the drill slip and cut my gum, and my right knee shot right out and kicked him in the stomach.'

'You're kidding.'

'I'm serious – don't you have anything peculiar about your physical makeup?'

'Nothing I'm going to speak of.' He smiled and the devil made his dark eyes sparkle, then he assisted me to my feet and felt my knee as if he knew what he was doing. 'Seems a good, functional knee to me.'

'How would you know?'

'My knees are functionally good, so I know one when I feel one – but if I could see the knee I could tell more.'

'Go home and look at your wife's functional knee.'

'Why are you being so hateful to me?' He narrowed his eyes. 'Here I was, delighted to see you again, and you act so antagonistic.'

'Pain always makes me antagonistic – are you any different?'

'I'm sweet and humble when I'm suffering, which isn't often. You get more attention that way – and remember you threw down the challenge, not me.'

'You didn't have to accept it. You could have gone along your merry way and let me go along mine.'

'Now we're arguing,' he said, disappointed. 'You want to fight when I want to be friendly. Be nice to me. Say you're glad to see me. Tell me how much better looking I've grown since you saw me last, and how exciting you find me. Even if I don't run like the wind I have my own bag of tricks.'

'I'll bet you do.'

'My wife is still in that beauty spa and I've been all by my lonesome for long, long months, bored to death by living with an old lady who can't talk and can't walk, but manages to scowl every time she sees me. One evening I was just sitting before the fire, wishing someone around here would commit murder so I'd have an interesting case for a change. It's damn frustrating to be an attorney and be surrounded by nothing but happy, normal people with no suppressed emotions to erupt suddenly.'

'Congratulations, Bart! Before you stands someone full of

334

aggressive resentment and mean, hateful spite seeking revenge that will erupt – you can count on that!'

He thought I was joking, playing a cat and mouse, man and woman game, and willingly he rose to that challenge too, not at all suspicious of my real purpose. He looked me over good, stripping off my sapphire jogging suit with the sensual eyes of a man starving for what I could give. 'Why did you come to live up here near me?'

I laughed. 'Arrogant, aren't you? I came to take over a dance school.'

'Sure you did ... There's New York and your home town, wherever that is, and you come here – to enjoy the winter sports as well?' His eyes insinuated the kind of indoor sport he had in mind, if I didn't.

'Yes, I do like all kinds of sports, inside and outside,' I said innocently.

Confidently he chuckled, assuming as all conceited men do that already he'd scored a point in the only intimate game a man really wanted to play with women.

'That old lady who can't talk, does she get around at all?' I asked.

'A little. She's my wife's mother. She speaks but her words come out jumbled and unintelligible to anyone but my wife.'

'You leave her there all alone – is that safe?'

'She's not alone. There's a private duty nurse there with her all the time, and a staff of servants.' He frowned as if he didn't like my questions, but I persisted. 'Why stay there at all then, why not go and have fun while the cat's away?'

'You do have a shrewish way about you. Though I've never cared much for my mother-in-law, as she is now I feel sorry for her. And human nature being what it is, I don't trust servants to take proper care of her without a family member in the house to keep check on what's done to keep her comfortable. She's helpless and can't rise from a chair without assistance, or get out of bed unless she's lifted out. So, until my wife is home again, I'm in charge to see that Mrs Malcolm Foxworth is not abused or neglected or stolen from.'

An overwhelming curiosity came over me then. I wanted to

know her first name, for I'd never heard it. 'Do you call her Mrs Foxworth?'

He hadn't understood my interest in an old lady, and tried to turn the conversation elsewhere, but I persisted. 'Olivia, that's what I call her!' he said shortly. 'When I was first married, I tried not to speak to her at all, to try to forget she existed. Now I use her first name; I think it pleases her, but I can't be sure. Her face is of stone, fixed in one expression – icy.'

I could picture her, unmoving but for her flintstone eyes of grey. He'd told me enough. Now I could make my plans – just as soon as I found out one more small thing. 'Your wife, when is she due back?'

'Why should you know?'

'I too get lonely, Bart. I have only my small son after Emma, his babysitter, goes home. So . . . I thought maybe some evening you might like to have dinner with us . . .'

'I'll come tonight,' he said immediately, his dark eyes aglow.

'Our schedule revolves around my son. We eat at five-thirty in the summer, but now that the days are shorter five is dinner time.'

'Great. Feed him at five and put him to bed. I'll be there at seven-thirty for cocktails. After dinner we can get to know each other better.' He met my considering look with grave intensity, as a proper attorney should. Then, because of that look we held too long, simultaneously we both broke into laughter.

'And incidentally, Mr Winslow, if you cut through the woods back of your place, you can reach mine and no one will see you unless, of course, you make a big show of yourself.'

He put his palm up and nodded, as if we were both conspiring. 'Discretion is the password, Miss Dahl.'

THE SPIDER AND THE FLY

Exactly at seven-thirty the door chimes sounded, punched by an impatient finger, forcing me to hurry lest he waken Jory who hadn't liked being put to bed at such an early hour.

If I had taken pains to look my best, so had Bart. He strode in as if he already owned the place and me. He left behind a drift of shaving lotion with a piney forest scent, and every hair on his head was carefully in place, making me wonder if he had a thinning spot – which I'd find out for myself sooner or later. I took his coat and hung it in the hall closet, then sashayed over to the bar where I busied myself as he sat down before the log fire I had burning (nothing had been overlooked; I even had soft music playing). By this time I knew enough about men and the ways of pleasing them best. There wasn't a man alive who wasn't charmed by a lovely woman bustling about, eager to wait on him, pamper and wine and dine him. 'Name your weakness, Bart.'

'Scotch.'

'On the rocks?'

'Neat.'

He watched all my movements, which were deliberately graceful and deft. Then, turning my back I mixed a fruity drink for myself, lacing it lightly with vodka. And with my two little stemmed goblets on a silver tray, I seductively ambled his way, leaning to give him an enticing view of my bra-less bosom. I sat across from him and swung one leg over the other to allow the long slit of my rose-coloured dress to open and expose one leg from silver sandal midway to the hip. He couldn't take his eyes off it. 'Sorry about the glasses,' I said smoothly, well pleased with his expression; 'I don't have room in this cottage to unpack everything I own. Most of my crystal is in storage and I have here only wine glasses and water goblets.'

'Scotch is scotch no matter how it's served. And what in the world is that thing you're sipping?' By this time he'd shifted his gaze to the low V of my gown.

'Well, you take orange juice freshly squeezed, a dab of lemon juice too, a dash of vodka, bit of coconut oil, and drop in a cherry to dive after. I call it a Maiden's Delight.'

After a few minutes of conversation, we drifted to the dining table, not so far from the fireplace, to eat by candlelight. Every so often he'd drop his fork, or spoon, or I would, and both of us would go for it, then laugh to see who was fastest. I was, every time. He was much too distracted to spot a missing fork or spoon when a neckline opened up so obligingly.

'This is delicious chicken,' he said after demolishing five hours of hard labour in about ten minutes. 'Usually I don't like chicken – where'd you learn to prepare this dish?'

I told him the truth. 'A Russian dancer taught me, she was on tour over here, and we liked each other. She and her husband stayed with Julian and me, and we'd cook together whenever we weren't dancing or shopping or touring. It took four chickens to feed four people. Now you know the nasty truth about dancers; when it comes to eating we are not in the least dainty. That is, after a performance. Before we go on we have to eat very lightly.'

He smiled and leaned across the small drop-leaf table. Candlelight was in his eyes, sparkling them devilishly. 'Cathy, tell me honestly why you came to live in this hick town and why you've got your heart set on me for a lover.'

'You flatter yourself,' I said in my most aloof manner, thinking I was very successful in appearing cool on the outside while inside I was a web of conflicting emotions. It was almost as if I had stage fright and was in the wings waiting to go on. And this was the most important performance of my life.

Then almost magically I felt I *was* on stage. I didn't have to think of how to act or what to say to charm him and make him forever mine. The script had been written a long time ago when I was fifteen and locked away upstairs. *Yes, Momma, it's first act time.* Expertly written by someone who knew him well from all the answers to her many questions. How could I fail?

After dinner I challenged Bart to a game of chess, and he accepted. I hurried to bring out the chessboard as soon as the table was cleared and the dishes were stacked in the sink. We began to set up the two armies of medieval warriors. 'Exactly what I came for,' he said, darting me a hard look, 'to play chess! I showered, shaved and put on my best suit – so I could play chess!' Then he smiled, devastatingly winsome. 'If I win – what reward?'

'A second game.'

'When I win the second game – what reward?'

'If you win two games, then comes the playoff. And don't sit there and grin at me so smugly. I was taught this game by a master.' Chris, of course.

'*After* I win the playoff – what reward?' he insisted.

'You can go home and fall asleep very satisfied with yourself.'

Very deliberately he picked up the chessboard with its handcarved ivory chessmen and put it on top of the refrigerator. He caught my hand and drew me into the living room. 'Put on the music, ballerina,' he said softly, 'and let's dance. No fancy footwork, just something easy and romantic.'

Popular music I could listen to only on the car radio to cheer up a long, lonely drive, but when it came to spending my money on records I bought classical or ballet. However, today I'd made a special purchase of 'The Night was Made for Love'. And, as we danced in the dimness of the living room with only the fire for light, I was reminded of the dry and dusty attic and Chris.

'Why are you crying, Cathy?' he asked softly, then turned my head so his cheek was smeared by my tears. 'I don't know,' I sobbed. And I didn't ...

'Of course you know,' he said, rubbing his smooth cheek against mine as we danced on and on. 'You are an intriguing combination, part child, part seductress, part angel.'

I laughed shortly and bitterly. 'That's what all men like to think about women. Little girls they have to take care of – when I know for a fact it is the male who is more boy than man.'

'Then say hello to the first grown-up man in your life.'

'You're not the first arrogant, opinionated man in my life!'

'But I'll be the last. The most important one – the one you will never forget.' Oh! Why did he have to say that? Chris was right. I was over my head with this one.

'Cathy, did you really think you could blackmail my wife?'

'No, but I gave it a try. I'm a fool. I expect too much, then I'm angry because nothing ever works out the way I want. When I was young and full of hopes and aspirations, I didn't know I would get hurt so often. I think I'll get tough and won't ache again, then my fragile shell shatters, and again, symbolically, my blood is spilled with the tears I shed. I pull myself back together again, go on, convince myself there is a reason for everything, and at some point in my life it will be disclosed. And when I have what I want, I hope to God it stays long enough to let me know I have it, and it won't hurt when it goes, for I don't expect it to stay, not now. I'm like a doughnut, always being punched out in the middle, and constantly I go around searching for the missing piece, and on and on it goes, never ending, only beginning ...'

'You're not being honest with yourself,' Bart said softly. 'You know better than anyone where that missing piece is, or I wouldn't be here.'

His voice was so low and seductive I put my head on his shoulder as we went on dancing. 'You're wrong, Bart, I don't know why you're here. I don't know how to fill my days. When I'm teaching class and when I'm with my son, then I'm alive – but when he's in bed and I'm alone, I don't know what to do with myself. I know Jory needs a father, and when I think of his father I realize I've always managed to do the wrong thing. I've read my reviews that rave about the potential I had ... but in my personal life I've made only mistakes, so what I accomplished professionally doesn't matter at all.' I stopped moving my feet and sniffled, then tried to hide my face – but he tilted it upwards, then dried my tears and held his handkerchief so I could blow my nose.

Then came the silence. The long, long silence. Our eyes met and clung and my heart started a faster thumping. 'Your problems are all so simple, Cathy,' he began, 'all you need is someone like me, who needs someone like you. If Jory needs a father, then I need a son. See how simply all complicated matters are solved?'

Too simply, I thought, when he had a wife and I was discerning and cynical enough to know he couldn't possibly care for me enough. 'You have a wife you love,' I said bitterly. I shoved him away. I didn't want to get him too easily, but only after long and difficult struggles against my mother, and she wasn't here to know.

'Men are liars too,' he said flatly, with some of the zest gone from his eyes. 'I have a wife and occasionally we sleep together, but the fire has gone out. I don't know her. I don't think anyone knows her. She's a bundle of secrets, wound up tight, and she won't let me inside. It's gone on so long I don't care to be let in now. She can keep her secrets and her tears, and eat her way out of her anxieties and whatever it is that makes her wake up in the night and go and look in that damned blue album! Now she's overweight and she's written she's just had plastic surgery – a face lift – and I won't know her when she comes back. As if I ever really knew her!'

I panicked inside – he had to care! How could I break up a marriage that was already coming apart? I needed to feel I'd accomplished this against overwhelming odds! 'Go home!' I said, pushing at him. 'Get out of my house! I don't know you well enough to even listen to your problems – and I don't believe you. I don't trust you!'

He laughed, mocking me, aroused by my puny efforts to push him away. His libido was fired ... It flamed in his eyes as he grabbed my upper arms and drew me hard against him. 'Now *you* come off it! Look at the way you're dressed. You had me come here for a reason. So here I am, ready to be seduced. You seduced me the first time I saw you – and for the life of me it seems I've known you much longer than I actually have. Nobody plays games with me, then calls it a draw. You win or I win, but if we go to bed together we might wake up in the morning and find out we've both won.'

Red lights flashed, *Stop! Resist! Fight!* I did none of those things. I beat on his chest with ineffectual small fists as he laughed and picked me up and threw me over his shoulder. With one hand he gripped both of my legs to keep them from kicking, and with the other he turned out the lamps. In the dark, with me still beating on his back, he carried me into my bedroom and threw me down on the coverlet. I scrambled to get up, but he came at me fast! There wasn't a chance to use the knee I had ready. He sensed my dancer's ability could defeat him so he lunged, caught me about the waist so we both tumbled to the floor! I opened my mouth to scream. He clamped his hand upon my open lips, then pinioned my arms with his iron strength and sat on the legs that tried to kick myself free.

'Cathy, my lovely seductress, you went to such a lot of trouble. You seduced me long ago, ballerina. Until the week before Christmas you are mine, and then my wife will be home – and I won't need you.'

His hand eased away from my lips and I thought I would scream, but instead I bit out, 'At least *I* didn't have to buy you with my father's millions!' That did it. He crushed his lips down brutally hard on mine before I realized what was happening. This wasn't the way I wanted it! I wanted to tempt him, set him on fire, make him chase me, and give in only after a long and arduous pursuit that my mother could watch and suffer through, knowing she could do nothing or I'd talk. And yet he was taking me heartlessly, more ruthless than Julian at his worst! Savagely he bore down on me. He squirmed and writhed to grind in, even as his hands ripped and tore off my clinging rose dress. All I had on then was pantyhose, and soon he had those pulled down so my silver slippers came off and stayed inside of them.

With his lips still crushed brutally hard on mine, he carried my resisting hand to his zipper and squeezed until my knuckles cracked. It was either tug it down or have my fingers broken! How he managed to wiggle out of his clothes, even as he held me naked beneath him, I'll never know. When he was naked, but for his socks, I kept on wiggling, writhing, squirming, butting and trying to scratch or bite while he kissed, fondled and explored. I had my chance to scream several times – but I too was breathing fast and hard, and jerking upwards to force him off. But he took this as a welcoming arch of invitation. He entered, and had his too-quick satisfaction, then pulled out before I had any!

'Get out of here,' I screamed. 'I'm calling the police! I'll have you thrown in jail, charged with assault and rape!'

He laughed scornfully, chucked me under the chin playfully, then stood up to pull on his clothes. 'Oh,' he said, mocking me

342

with an imitation of my own voice, 'I am so frightened.' Then his voice was deeply earnest. 'You aren't happy, are you? It didn't work out the way you planned it, but don't you worry, tomorrow night I'll be back, and maybe then you can please me enough, so I'll feel like taking the time to please you.'

'I've got a gun!' (I didn't.) 'And if you dare set foot in this house again you're a dead man! Not that you are a man. You are more brute than human!'

'My wife often says the same thing,' he said casually, zipping up his trousers shamelessly, without the decency to even turn his back. 'But she likes it just the same, just as you did. Beef Wellington, you can have that tomorrow night, plus a tossed salad and a chocolate mousse for dessert. If you make me fat, we can burn off the calories in the most pleasant way possible – and I don't mean jogging.' He grinned, saluted me, put one foot behind the other to turn smartly, military fashion, then paused at the doorway as I sat up and clutched the remnants of my gown to my breasts. 'Same time tomorrow night, and I'll stay the night – that is, if you treat me right.'

He left, and slammed the front door behind him. *Damn him to hell!* I began to cry, not from pity for myself. It was frustration so huge I could have torn him limb from limb! *Beef Wellington!* I'd lace it with arsenic!

A small timid sound came from outside my door. 'Mommy . . . I'm scared. Are you cryin', Mommy?'

Hastily I pulled on a robe and called him in, then held him close in my arms. 'Darling, darling, Mommy is all right. You had a bad dream. Mommy isn't crying . . . see?' I brushed away the tears – for I'd get even.

Three dozen red roses arrived while Jory and I were eating breakfast – the long-stemmed variety from the florist. A small white card read:

> I'm sending you a big bouquet of roses,
> One for every night you'll have my heart.

No name. And what the devil was I supposed to do with three

dozen roses in a matchbox house? I couldn't send them to a children's ward; the hospital was miles and miles away. Jory decided what to do with them. 'Oh, Mommy, how pretty! Uncle Paul's roses!'

For Jory I kept the roses instead of throwing them out, and in many vases I scattered them throughout the house. He was delighted, and when I took him with me to dancing school he told all my students roses were all over his home – even in the bathroom.

After lunch I drove Jory to the nursery school he so loved. It was a Montessori school that was inspiring him to want to learn by appealing to his senses. Already he could print his name, and he was only three! He was like Chris, I told myself, brilliant, handsome, talented – oh, my Jory had everything – but a father. From his bright brown eyes shone the quick intelligence of someone who would have a lifetime curiosity about everything. 'Jory, I love you.'

'I know that, Mommy.' He waved goodbye as I drove off.

I was there to meet him when he came from his school, his small face flushed and troubled. 'Mommy,' he said as soon as he was beside me in the car, 'Johnny Stoneman, he said his mommy slapped him when he touched her – there.' And he shyly pointed at my breast. 'You don't slap me when I touch you there.'

'But you don't touch me there, not since you were a little baby and Mommy nursed you for a short while.'

'Did you slap me then?' He looked so worried.

'No, of course not. I would never slap you for touching there – so if you want to try me, go ahead and touch.' His small hand reached out tentatively while he watched my face to see if I'd be shocked. Oh, how fast the young learned all the taboos! And when he'd touched, he smiled, very relieved. 'Oh, it's just a soft place.' He'd made a pleasant discovery, and around my neck he threw his arms. 'I love you too, Mommy. 'Cause you love me even when I'm bad.'

'I'll always love you, Jory. And if you're bad sometimes, I'll try and understand.' Yes, I was not going to be like my grandmother – nor my mother. I was going to be the perfect mother, and some day he'd have a father too. How was it that

344

little children, such young ones, would already be talking of sin and being slapped for only touching? Was it because it was too high here, too near God's eyes? So that everyone lived under His spell, living afraid, acting righteous, while they committed every sin in the book? *Honour thy father and thy mother. Do unto others as thou wouldst have done unto you. An eye for an eye.*

Yes ... *an eye for an eye* – that's why I was here.

I stopped to buy stamps before I reached my cottage, and left Jory dozing on the front seat. *He* was in the post office, which was no larger than my living room, buying stamps too. Charmingly he smiled at me, as if nothing untoward had happened between us the night before. He even had the nerve to follow me to my car so he could ask how I liked the roses. 'Not your kind of roses,' I snapped, then got primly into my car and slammed the door in his face. I left him staring after me without a smile – in fact, he looked rather miserable.

At five-thirty a special-delivery man brought a small package to our front door. It was certified so I had to sign for it. Inside a larger box was another box, and inside of that was a velvet jewellery case which I quickly opened while Jory watched, all eyes. On black velvet lay a single rose comprised of many diamonds. Also a card with a note that read, 'Perhaps this kind of rose is more to your liking.' I put the thing away as a trifle bought with *her* money, so it wasn't really from him – no more than the real roses.

He had the nerve to come that night at seven-thirty just as he'd said he would. Nevertheless, I readily let him in, then led him silently to the dining table with no to-do about cocktails or other niceties. The table was set even more elaborately than the night before. I'd hauled out some boxes and done some unpacking, and on the table were my best lace mats and covered silver serving dishes. Neither of us had as yet spoken. All his forgive-me roses I'd gathered together and they were in the box near his plate. On his empty plate was the jeweller's velvet container with the diamond rose brooch inside. I sat to watch his expression as he put the jewellery box aside casually, and just as casually moved the flower box out of his way. He then took from his breast pocket a folded note that he handed to me. He'd written in a bold hand:

I love you for reasons that have no beginning and no ending. I loved you even before I knew you, so that my love is without reason or design. Tell me to go and I will. But know first, if you turn me away, I will remember all my life that love that should have been ours, and when I'm stretched out cold, I will but love you better after death.

I glanced upwards to meet his eyes squarely for the first time since he'd entered. 'Your poetry, it somehow has a familiar ring, with a bit of strangeness.'

'I composed it only a few minutes ago – how could it sound familiar?' He reached for the domed silver lid, ostensibly hiding the Beef Wellington underneath. 'I warned you I was an attorney, not a poet – so that accounts for the strangeness. Poetry was not my best subject in school.'

'Obviously.' I was very interested in his expression. 'Elizabeth Barrett Browning is sweet, but not your type.'

'I did my best,' he said with a wicked grin, meeting my eyes and challenging me before his gaze lowered to stare at the huge platter that held one hot dog and a small dab of cold canned beans. The disbelief in his eyes, his utter offended shock gave me so much satisfaction I almost liked him.

'You are now gazing upon Jory's favourite menu,' I said, gloating. 'It is exactly what he and I ate tonight for dinner, and since it was good enough for us, I thought it was good enough for you, so I saved some. Since I've already eaten, *all* of that is yours alone, and you may help yourself.'

Scowling, he flashed me a burning, hard look, then savagely bit down into the hot dog which I'm sure had grown cold as the beans. But he gobbled down everything and drank his glass of milk, and for dessert I handed him a box of animal crackers. First he stared at the box in another expression of dumbfounded amazement, then ripped it open, seized up a lion and snapped off the head in one bite.

Only when he'd eaten every animal cracker and then picked

346

up each crumb did he take the trouble to look at me with so much disapproval I should have shrunk to ant size. 'I take it you are one of those despicable liberated women who refuses to do anything to please a man!'

'Wrong. I am liberated only with *some* men. Others I can worship, adore and wait on like a slave.'

'You made me do what I did!' he objected strongly. 'Do you think I planned it that way? I wanted us to find our relationship on an equal basis. Why did you wear that kind of dress?'

'It's the kind all chauvinist men prefer!'

'I am not a chauvinist – and I hate that kind of dress!'

'You like what I've got on better?' I sat up straighter go give him a better view of the old nappy sweater I had on. With it I wore faded blue jeans, with dirty sneakers on my feet, and my hair was skinned back and fastened in a granny's knot. Deliberately I'd pulled long strands free so they hung loose about my face, slovenly fringes to make me look more appalling. And no makeup prettied my face. He was dressed to kill.

'At least you look honest and ready to let me do the pursuing. If there is one thing I despise, it's women who come on strong, like you did last night. I expected better from you than that kind of sleazy dress that showed everything to take the thrill from discovering for myself.' He knitted his brows and mumbled, 'From a damned harlot's red dress to blue jeans. In the course of one day, she changes into a teenybopper.'

'It was rose-coloured, *not red*! And besides, Bart, strong men like you always adore weak and passive stupid women, because basically you're meek yourself and afraid of an aggressive woman!'

'I am not weak or meek or anything but a man who likes to feel a man, not to be used for your own purposes. And as for passive women I despise them as much as I do aggressive ones. I just don't like the feeling of being the victim of a huntress leading me into a trap. What the hell are you trying to do to me? Why dislike me so much? I sent you roses, diamonds, imitation poetry, and you can't even comb your hair and take the shine from your nose.'

'You are looking at the natural me, and now that you've seen, you can leave.' I got up and walked to the front door and swung it open. 'We are wrong for each other. Go back to your wife. She can have you, for *I* don't want you.'

He came quickly, as if to obey, then seized me in his arms and kicked the door closed. 'I love you, God knows why I do, but it seems I've always loved you.'

I stared up in his face, disbelieving him, even as he took the pins from my hair and let it spill down. Out of long habit I tossed it about so it fluffed out and arranged itself, and smiling a little he tilted my face to his. 'May I kiss your *natural* lips? They are very beautiful lips.' Without waiting for permission he brushed his lips gently over mine. Oh – the shivery sensation of such a feathery kiss! Why didn't all men know that was the right way to start? What woman wanted to be eaten alive, choked by a thrusting tongue? Not me, I wanted to be played like a violin, strummed pianissimo, in largo timing, fingered into legato, and let it grow into crescendo. Deliciously I wanted to head towards the ecstatic heights that could only happen for me when the right words were spoken and the right kind of kisses given before his hands came into play. If he'd done for me only a little last night, this night he used all the skills he had. This time he took me to the stars where we both exploded, still holding tight to each other, and doomed to do it again, and then again.

He was hairy all over. Julian had been hairless but for one thatch that grew in a thin line up to his navel. And Julian had never kissed my feet that smelled of roses from a long perfumed bath before I put on old work clothes. Toe by toe he mouthed before he started working upwards. I felt the grandmother watching, blazing her hard, grey eyes to put us both in hell. I turned off my mind, shut her out, and gave in to my senses and to this man who was now treating me like a lover.

But he didn't love me, I knew that. Bart was using me as a substitute for his wife, and when she came back I'd never see him again. I knew it, knew it, but still I took and I gave until we fell asleep in each other's arms.

When I slept, I dreamed. Julian was in the silver music box my father had given me when I was six. Round and round he spun, his face ever turning towards me, accusing me with his jet eyes, and then he grew a moustache and was Paul, who only looked sad. I ran fast to set him free from death in a music box turned into a coffin – and then it was Chris inside, his eyes closed, his hands folded one over the other on his chest ... dead, dead. Chris!

I awoke to find Bart gone and my pillow wet with tears. *Momma, why did you start this, why?*

Holding tight to my son's small hand I led him out into the cold morning air on my way to work. Faint and far away I heard someone calling my name, and with it came the scent of old-fashioned roses. Why don't you come, Paul, and save me from myself – why only call in your thoughts?

Part one was done. Part two would begin when my mother knew I had Bart's child – and then there was the grandmother who had to pay as well. And when I looked I saw that the mountains curved upwards into a satisfied smirk. At last I had responded to their call. Their vengeful, tormenting wail.

THE GRANDMOTHER REVISITED

Foxworth Hall was at the end of a cul-de-sac, the largest and most impressive of many fine, large homes and the only one that sat high, high on the hillside, looking down on all the others like a castle. For days I went to stare at it, making my plans.

Bart and I didn't have to sneak around furtively to meet. The houses where he lived were far apart and no one could see us when he came to me through the back door that opened out into a yard with a fence. Behind that was a country lane, shrubbed and made private by many trees. Sometimes we met in a distant town and our lovemaking in a motel room was wild, sweet, tender, erotic and altogether satisfying, and yet I froze when he told me at lunch. 'She called this morning, Cathy. She'll be home before Christmas.'

'That's nice,' I said and went right on eating my salad and anticipating the Beef Wellington that would show up soon. He frowned and his fork loaded with salad hesitated on the way to his mouth. 'It means we won't be able to see as much of each other. Aren't you sorry?'

'We'll find ways.'

'If you aren't the damnedest woman!'

'Don't get so worked up over nothing. All women are monsters to men, and maybe to ourselves. We are our own worst enemies. You don't have to divorce her and give up your chance to inherit her fortune. Though she could outlive you and have the chance to buy another younger husband.'

'Sometimes you are just as bitchy as she is! She *did not buy me*! I loved her! She loved me! I was crazy about her, as crazy for her as I am for you now. But she changed. When I met her she was sweet, charming, everything I wanted in a woman and wife, but she changed.' He stabbed the salad fork towards his mouth and chewed viciously. 'She's always been a mystery – like you.'

'Bart, my love,' I said, 'very soon all mystery walls will crumble.'

He went on, as if I hadn't interrupted, 'That father of hers, he too was a mystery; you'd look at him and see a fine old gentleman, but underneath was a heart of steel. I thought I was his only attorney, but he had six others, each of us assigned to different tasks. Mine was to make out his wills. He changed them dozens of times, putting this family member in, and writing another out, and adding codicils like a madman, though he was sane enough right up until the very end. The last codicil was the worst.'

Of course, no children for him, ever. 'Then you really were a practising lawyer?' He smiled bitterly, then answered, 'Of course I was. And now I am again. A man needs something meaningful to do. How many times can anyone tour Europe before boredom sets in? You see the same old faces, doing the same old things, laughing at the same jokes.'

'Why don't you divorce her and do something meaningful with your life?'

'She loves me.' That's the way he said it. Short. Sweet. He stayed because she loved him, forcing me to say, 'You told me when we first met that you loved her, and then you say you don't – which is it?' He thought about it for a long time.

'Honestly, ballerina, I'm ambivalent and resentful. I love her, I hate her. I thought she was what you seem to be now. So please, smother that bitchy side that reminds me of her and don't try and do to me what she did. You are putting a wall between us because you know something I don't. I don't fall in love easily, and I wish I didn't love you.'

He seemed suddenly a small boy, wistful, as if his pet dog might betray him and life would never be good again. I was touched and dared to say, 'Bart, I swear there will come a day when you know all my secrets and all of hers – but until that time comes say you love me, even if you don't mean it, for I can't enjoy being with you if I don't feel you love me just a little.'

'A little? It seems I've loved you all my life. Even when I kissed you the first time it seemed I'd kissed you before – why is that?'

'Karma.' I smiled at his baffled expression.

There was something I had to do before my mother came home. One day when I had no classes and Jory was in his special school I slipped over to Foxworth Hall, using all the hidden ways. At the back door I used the old wooden key that Chris had fashioned so long ago. It was Thursday. All the servants would be in town. Since Bart had told me in detail his routine, that also told me a lot of the grandmother's daily life. I knew at this time the nurse would be napping, as my grandmother had her rest time in the afternoon too. She'd be in the same little room beyond the library, the same room that had confined our grandfather during his last days, while upstairs we four children waited for him to pass on to his rewards, and death would set us free.

I strolled through all those rich, grand rooms and hungrily stared at all the fine furnishings and saw again the dual winding staircases in the front foyer large enough to be used as a ballroom. Where the curving staircases met was a balcony on the second floor, and from that rose another flight of stairs, straight up to the attic. I saw the massive chest which Chris and I had hidden inside to watch a Christmas party going on below. So long ago, and yet my clock of time turned swiftly backward. I was twelve again and scared, afraid this mammoth house would swallow me down if I moved or spoke above a whisper. I was awed again by the three giant crystal chandeliers suspended from a ceiling some forty feet above the floor. And because it was a dance floor of mosaic tiles, I automatically had to dance just a little to see how it felt.

I ambled on, taking my time, admiring the paintings, the marble busts, the huge lamps, the fabulous wall hangings that only the super-rich, who could be so stingy in small ways, could buy. Imagine my grandmother buying bolts of grey taffeta just to save a few dollars, when they bought the best to furnish their rooms and they had millions!

The library was easy to find. Lessons learned at an early age and under miserable conditions could never be forgotten. Oh, such a library! Clairmont didn't have a library with so many fine books! Bart's photograph was on the ponderous desk that had been my grandfather's. Many things were there to indicate that Bart often used this room for his study, and to keep his mother-in-law company. His brown house-slippers were beneath a comfortable-looking chair near the immense stone fireplace with a mantel twenty feet long. French doors opened on to a terrace facing a formal garden with a fountain to spray water into a bird bath formed by a rock garden of steps, with the water trickling down into a pool. A nice, sunny place for an invalid to sit, protected from the wind.

At last I'd seen enough to satisfy my curiosity, harboured for years, and I sought out the heavy door at the far end of the library. Beyond that closed door was the witch-grandmother. Visions of her flashed through my mind. I saw her again as she'd been the first night we came, towering above us, her thick body strong, powerful, her cruel, hard eyes that swept over us all and showed no sympathy, no compassion for fatherless children who had lost so much, and she couldn't even smile to welcome us or touch the pretty round cheeks of the twins who had been so appealing at age five.

The second night flashed, when the grandmother ordered our mother to show us her naked back striped with red and bleeding welts. Even before we'd seen that horror she'd picked Carrie up by the hair and Cory had hurled himself against her, trying to inflict some pain with his small white shoe that kicked her leg and his small sharp teeth that bit – and with one powerful slap she'd sent him reeling. All because he had to defend his beloved twin who had screamed and screamed. Again I saw myself before the mirror in the bedroom without a stitch on, and her punishment had been so harsh, so heartless, trying to take from me what I admire the most, my hair. A whole day Chris had spent trying to take the tar from my hair and save it from the shears. Then no food or milk for two whole weeks! *Yes!* She deserved to see me again! Just as I'd vowed the day she whipped me that there would come a day in the future when she would be the helpless one and I would be the one to wield the whip and keep the food from her lips!

Ah, the sweet irony of it – that she would gloat to see her

husband dead, and now she was in his bed and even more helpless – and alone! I took off my heavy winter coat, sat down to tug off my boots, and then I put on the white satin *pointes*. My leotards were white and sheer enough to let the pink of my skin show through. I unbound my hair so it fell in a luxuriant, golden cascade of rippling waves down my back. Now she would see and envy the hair the tar hadn't ruined after all:

Get ready, Grandmother! Here I come!

Very quietly I stole to her door. Then carefully I eased it open. She was on the high, high hospital bed, her eyes half-closed. The sun through the windows fell upon her pink and shining scalp, clearly revealing how nearly bald she was. And oh, how old she looked! So gaunt, so much smaller. Where was the giantess I used to know? Why wasn't she wearing a grey taffeta dress to whisper threats? Why did she have to look so pitiful?

I hardened my heart, closed out mercy, for she'd never had any for us. Apparently she was on the verge of sleep, but as the door opened slowly, slowly her eyes widened. Then her eyes bulged. She recognized me. Her thin, shrivelled lips quivered. She was afraid! Glory hallelujah! My time had come! Still, I paused in the open doorway, appalled. I had come for revenge and time had robbed me! Why wasn't she the monster I recalled? I wanted her that way, not what she was now, an old, sick woman with her hair so scant most of her scalp showed, and the hair left was pulled to the top of her head and fastened up there by a pink satin ribbon bow. The bow gave her a ghoulish-girlish look, and even bunched together as they were, the thin wisps were no wider than my small finger – just a tuft like a worn-out, bleached brush for watercolour painting.

Once she'd stood six feet tall and weighed over two hundred pounds and her huge breasts had been mountains of concrete. Now those breasts hung like old socks to reach her puffy abdomen. Her arms were withered old dry sticks, her hands corded, her fingers gnarled. Yet, as I stared and she stared in complete silence as a small clock ticked relentlessly on, her old despicable personality flared hot to let me know her outrage. She tried to speak to order me out. *Devil's issue*, she'd scream if she could, *get out of my house! Devil's spawn, out, out, out!* But she couldn't say it, any of it.

While I could greet her pleasantly, 'Good afternoon, *dear* Grandmother. How very nice to see you again. Remember me? I'm Cathy, one of the grandchildren you helped hide away, and each day you brought us food in a picnic basket – every day by six-thirty you were there, with your gallon Thermos of milk, and your quart Thermos of lukewarm soup – and canned soup at that. Why couldn't you have brought us hot soup at least once? Did you deliberately heat that soup to only warm?' I stepped inside and closed the door behind me. And only then did she see the willow switch I'd hidden behind my back.

Casually I tapped the switch on my palm. 'Grandmother,' I said softly, 'remember the day you whipped our mother? How you forced her to strip in front of her father, and then you whipped her, and she was an adult – a shameless, wicked, evil deed, don't you agree?'

Her terrified grey eyes fixed on the switch. A terrible struggle was going on in her brain – and I was *glad*, so *glad* Bart had told me she wasn't senile. Pale, watery, grey eyes, red-rimmed and crinkled all about with deep crow's feet, like cuts that never bled. Thin, crooked lips now shrunken to only a tiny buttonhole and puckered about by a radiating sunburst of deep lines, etching beneath her long hooked nose a spiderweb design of crosshatch lines. And, believe it or not, to the high and severe neckline of that yellow cotton jacket was fastened *the* diamond brooch! Never had I seen her without the brooch pinned to the neckline of her grey taffeta dresses with the white crocheted collars.

'Grandmother,' I chanted, 'remember the twins? The dear little five-year-olds you enticed into this house, and not once while they were here did you ever speak their names – or any of our names. Cory's dead, and you know that – but did my mother tell you about Carrie? Carrie is dead too. She didn't grow very tall because she was robbed of sunlight and fresh air in the years when she needed it most. Robbed too of love and security and given trauma instead of happiness. Chris and I went on to the roof to sit and sun ourselves, but the twins were afraid of the high roof. Did you know we went out there and we'd stay for hours and hours . . . no, you didn't know, did you?'

She moved a bit, as if trying to shrink into the thin mattress. I gloated to see her fear, rejoiced that she could move a little. Her eyes now were as mine used to be, windowpanes to reveal all her terrified emotions – and she couldn't cry out for help! At my mercy. 'Remember the second night, dearest, loving Grandmother? You lifted Carrie up by her hair, and you must have known that hurt, yet you did it. Then you sent Cory spinning with one blow, and that hurt too, and he was only trying to protect his sister. Poor Carrie, how she grieved for Cory. She never got over his death, never stopped missing him. She met a nice boy named Alex. They fell in love and were going to be married when she found out he was going to be a minister. That shook Carrie up. You see, *you* made us all deeply fearful of religious people. The day Alex said he was going to be a minister Carrie went into a despairing depression. She had learned the lesson you taught very well. You taught us that no one can ever be perfect enough to please God. Something dormant came to life the day Carrie was weakened by shock, depression and the lack of the spirit to go on.

'Now listen to what she did – because of you! Because you impressed on her young brain that she was born evil and she'd be wicked no matter how much she sought to be good! She believed you! Cory was dead. She knew he had died from the arsenic put on sugared doughnuts . . . So when she felt she could no longer put up with life and all the people who expected perfection, she bought rat poison! She bought a package of twelve doughnuts and coated them with that rat poison full of arsenic! She ate all but one – and that had a bite mark. Now . . . shrink into your mattress and try and run from the guilt that is yours! You and my mother killed her as much as you killed Cory! I despise you, old woman!'

I didn't tell her I hated my mother more. The grandmother had never loved us, so anything *she* did was to be expected. But our mother who had borne us, who had cared for us, who had loved us well when Daddy lived – that was another story – an unbearable horror story! And her time would come!

'Yes, Grandmother, Carrie is dead now too, because she

wanted to die in the same way Cory had and be with him in heaven.'

Her eyes squinched and a small shudder rippled the covers. I gloated.

I brought from behind my back the box containing a long length of Carrie's hair that had taken me hours to arrange and brush into one long, shimmering switch of molten gold. At one end it was tied with a red satin bow, and at the other, a bow of purple satin. '*Look old woman*, this is Carrie's hair, some of it. I have another box full of loose, tangled strands, for I can't bear to part with a piece of it. I saved it to keep not only for Chris and myself, but to show you and our mother ... for the two of you killed Carrie as surely as you killed Cory!'

Oh, I was near mad with hate. Revenge blazed my eyes, my temper, and shook my hands. I could see Carrie as she lay near death, turning old, withered, bony until she was only a little skeleton covered by loose, pale skin, so translucent all her veins showed – and the remains had to be sealed quickly in a box of pretty metal to shut away the stench of decay.

I stepped nearer the bed and dangled the bright hair with its gay ribbons before her wide and frightened eyes. 'Isn't this beautiful hair, old woman? Was yours ever so beautiful, so bountiful? *No!* I know it wasn't! Nothing about you could ever have been pretty, nothing! Not even when you were young! That's why you were so jealous of your husband's step-mother.' I laughed to see her flinch. 'Yes, dear Grandmother, I know a lot more about you now than I did. Your son-in-law has told me all the family secrets my mother told him. Your husband Malcolm was in love with his father's younger wife, ten times more beautiful and sweeter than you ever were! So when Alicia had a son, you suspected that child was your own husband's, and that's why you hated our father, and why you sent for him, deceiving him into believing he'd found a good home. And you educated him and gave him the best of everything so he'd have a taste of the good, rich life and be more hurt and disappointed later on, when you threw him out and left him nothing in your wills. But my father fooled you instead, didn't he? He stole your only daughter, whom you hated too, because her father loved her

357

more than he loved you. And half-uncle married half-niece. Yet how wrong you were about Malcolm and Alicia, for my father's mother despised Malcolm! She fought him off time and again – and the baby she had was not your husband's son! Though he would have been, if Malcolm had had his way!'

Blankly she stared at me, as if the past was of no importance to her now. Only the present mattered, and the switch in my hand. 'I'm going to tell you something now, old woman, that you need to know. There was never a better man born than my father, or a more honourable woman than his mother. But don't lie there and think I've inherited any of Alicia's or my father's godly traits – for I am like *you*! Heartless! I never forget, never forgive! *I hate for you killing Cory and Carrie! I hate you for making of me what I am!*' I screamed this, out of control, forgetful of the nurse napping down the hall. I wanted to feed her arsenic by the handful and sit to watch her die and rot before my eyes, like Carrie had. I pirouetted around the room to release my frustrations, lashing my legs, showing off my fine young body, and then I drew up short and snapped in her face, 'All those years you locked us up, you never said our names, never looked at Chris because he was our father all over again – and your husband too, when he was young, and before you made him evil too. You blame everything wrong with human beings on their evil souls, and ignore the truth. *Money* is the god who rules in this house! It's *money* that's always made the worst things happen! You were married for your money and you knew it! And greed brought us here, and greed locked us up and stole three years and four months from our lives, and put us at your mercy and you didn't have any, not even for your grandchildren, the only grandchildren you'd ever have, and we never touched you, did we? Though we tried in the beginning, remember?' I jumped up on the bed and lashed at her with the length of Carrie's golden hair. A soft whip that didn't hurt, though she cringed from the touch. Then I tossed Carrie's precious hair to her bedside table and snapped the switch before her eyes. I danced and whirled on her bed, over her frozen body, displaying my fine agility as my long hair flared in a golden circle.

'Remember how you punished our mother before we grew to

hate her too? I owe you for that,' I said, legs apart and straddling her covered body. 'From your neck down to your heels, I owe you that, plus the whip lashes you gave Chris and me, I owe you that too. And all the other things, each one of them is etched in my memory. Didn't I tell you there would come a day when I held the switch in my hand, and there would be food in the kitchen you'd never eat? Well ... *that day is here, Grand-mother.*'

The sunken grey eyes in her gaunt face sparkled hate, malicious and strong. Daring me to strike her – daring me!

'What shall I do first,' I said as if to myself, 'shall it be the switch, or the hot tar in your hair? Where did you get the tar, old woman? I always wondered where you got it. Did you plan it way in advance and wait for an excuse to use it? I'm going to confess something now you don't know. Chris never cut off all my hair, only the front part to fool you into thinking I was baldheaded. Beneath that towel I wrapped on my head was all the long hair he saved. Yes, old woman, love saved my hair from being cut off. He loved me enough to work for hours and hours to save what hair he could – more love than you've ever known, and from a brother.'

Deep in her throat she made a strangling sound, and how I wished she could speak!

'Grandmother darling,' I taunted, hands on my hips as I leaned to look down on her, 'why don't you tell me where to get the tar? I haven't been able to find any. No road construction going on anywhere near – so I guess I'll have to use hot wax. *You* could have used melted wax, for it would have done the job just as well. Didn't you think of melting a few of your candles?' I smiled, menacingly, I hoped. 'Oh, dear Grandmother, what fun you and I are going to have! And nobody will know, for *you can't talk* and *you can't write*, all you can do is lie there and suffer.'

I didn't like myself or what I was saying or what I was feeling. My conscience hovered near the ceiling, looking down with shame at this released fury in white tights that was me. Aghast, I was up there feeling pity for this old woman who'd suffered through two strokes – but on the bed was another kind of me. A vicious, mean, vindictive Foxworth, with blue eyes as cold as hers used to be as I stared her down, and then suddenly, cruelly I bent; I yanked down the sheet and blanket that covered her and she was exposed. Her garment was like a hospital jacket that was slit and tied down the back, for there was no front opening. Just a plain yellow cotton thing with that incongruous diamond brooch at the throat. No doubt they would attach that brooch to her funeral garments.

Naked. She had to be stripped, as Momma was, as Chris had been, as I had been too. She had to suffer through the humiliation of being without clothes while contemptuous eyes made her shrivel even smaller. Relentlessly I seized hold of the hem of her stingy, cheap cotton garment and without compunction I yanked it upward to her armpits. In rumpled unironed folds it half-hid her face, and carefully I pulled back the cloth that could hide from me any expression she might manage to reveal. Then I stared down at her body, expressing scorn and revulsion as she had expressed it with her hard eyes and knife-slashed lips when I was a child of fourteen and she had caught me looking at myself in the mirror, admiring the beauty of a figure I'd never seen before nude.

The body in its youth is a beautiful thing . . . a joy to behold, the sweet young curves, the smooth unblemished skin, firm and taut flesh, but oh, to grow old! Her flabby loose breasts sagged to her waist, and the blue veins stood up like thin ropes covered by a translucent sheath. The pasty whiteness of her skin was dimpled, furrowed, creased by stretch marks from childbirth, and a long scar from navel to her almost hairless mound of Venus showed she'd either had a hysterectomy or a Caesarean section. It was an old scar, pale and shinier than the doughy, white, wrinkled skin around it. Her thin, long legs were gnarled old branches of a tired tree. I sighed – would *I* some day look like this?

Without pity or an attempt to be gentle I rolled her over and yanked her back into the centre of the bed. And all the while I was babbling on of how Chris and I had joked she either nailed on her clothes or glued them on and never, of course, did she take off her underclothes unless she was in a closet with the light out.

Her back showed fewer ravages than her front, though her buttocks were flat, flabby and too white.

'I'm going to whip you now, Grandmother,' I said tonelessly, my heart gone out of this now. 'I promised a long time ago I was going to do this if ever I had the chance and so I will do it!' And closing my eyes and, asking God to forgive me for what I was about to do, I lifted my arm high and then brought down that willow switch as hard as I could, and flat on her bare buttocks!

She shuddered. Some noise came from her throat. Then she seemed to sink into unconsciousness. She relaxed so much she released her bladder. I began to cry. Terrible sobs from *me* as I ran to the adjoining bath to find a washcloth and soap, and back I hurried with toilet tissue to clean her. Then I washed her and put salve on the awful welt I'd made.

I turned her over on the bed, straightened out her gown so she was covered modestly, neatly, and only then did I check to see if she was alive or dead. Her grey eyes were open and staring at me without expression as tears streaked *my* face. Next, slowly, as I sobbed on, her eyes began to gleam in unspoken triumph! Mutely she called me *coward! I knew you couldn't be anything but a soft weakling! No spine, no starch! Kill me. Go on, kill me! I dare you, do it, do it, go on!*

Down from the bed I jumped, and I ran fast into the library and on into the parlour I'd seen. In a frenzy of anger I grabbed up the first candelabra I saw and dashed back to her – but I didn't have matches! Back again to the library where I rummaged through the desk Bart used. He smoked; he'd have matches or a cigarette lighter. I found a book of matches from a local disco.

The candles were ivory coloured, dignified, like this house. Terror was in her iron eyes now. She wanted that bit of tufted hair tied with a pink ribbon. I lit a candle and watched it flame, then I held it angled over her head so the melting wax dribbled down drop by drop on to her hair and her scalp. Maybe six or seven drops fell before I could stand no more. She was right. I was a coward, I couldn't do to her what she'd done to us. I was a Foxworth twice over, and yet God had changed the mould so I didn't fit.

I blew out the ivory candle, replaced it in the candelabra, then left.

No sooner was I in the ballroom than I remembered I'd forgotton the precious length of Carrie's hair. I raced back to get it. I found the grandmother lying as I'd left her, only her head was turned and two huge glistening tears were in her eyes that stared at the switch of Carrie's beautiful hair. Ahh! Now I had my pound of flesh!

Bart spent more time at my small home than at his huge one. He plied me with gifts, as he did my son. He ate his breakfast, lunch and dinner with us on the days he didn't spend in his office, which I privately believed was more a façade for appearing useful than a functioning law office. My dancing school suffered from his attention, but it didn't matter. I was now a kept woman. Paid to be his mistress.

Jory was delighted with the little leather boots Bart gave him. 'Are you my daddy?' asked my son who would be four in February. 'No, but I sure wish I was and I could be.'

As soon as Jory was out in the yard, tromping around and staring down at his feet that fascinated him now that they sported cowboy boots, Bart turned to me and flung himself wearily down in a chair. 'You'd never guess what happened over at our place. Some sadistic idiot put wax in my mother-in-law's hair. And there's a long welt on her buttocks that won't heal. The nurse can't explain it. I've questioned Olivia, and asked if it was anyone she knew, one of the servants, and she blinked her eyes twice, meaning no. Once is for yes. I'm mad as hell about it! It must have been one of the servants, yet I can't understand why one would be so cruel as to torment a helpless old woman who can't move to defend herself. She refuses to identify anyone I name. I promised Corrine I'd take good care of her, and now her bottom is such a raw mess she has to lie on her stomach two to four hours each day, and she is turned during the night.'

'Oh,' I breathed, feeling a bit sick. 'How awful – why won't it heal?'

'Her circulation is bad. It would have to be, wouldn't it, since she can't move about normally?' He smiled then, brilliantly, like the sun coming out after a storm. 'Don't concern yourself, darling. It's my problem, not yours – and, of course, hers.' He held out his arms and I went quickly into them to snuggle in his lap, and we kissed fervently before he carried me into my bedroom. He laid me down and began to undress. 'I could wring the neck of the fiend who did that to her!'

We lay entwined after our lovemaking, listening to the wind blending with Jory's shrill laughter, racing after the toy poodle Bart had given him. A few snow flurries were beginning to fall. I knew I had to get up soon so Jory wouldn't run in and catch us, just to tell us it was snowing. He couldn't remember other snows, and barely would the ground be sugar-coated than he'd want to make a snowman. Sighing first, I kissed Bart, then reluctantly pulled from his embrace. I turned my back to pull on bikini panties as he propped up on an elbow and watched. 'You've got a lovely behind,' he said. I said thanks. 'What about my front?' He said it wasn't bad. I threw a shoe at him.

'Cathy, why don't you say you love me?'

I whirled about, startled. 'Have you ever said it to me and meant it?' I snapped on a tiny bra.

'How do you know I don't mean it?' he asked with anger.

'Let me tell you how I know. When you love, you want that person with you all of the time. When you avoid the subject of divorce, that alone is an indication of how much you care for me and just where I belong in your life.'

'Cathy, you've been hurt, haven't you? I don't want to hurt you more. You play games with me. I've always known that. What does it matter if it is only sex and not love? And tell me how to know where one ends and the other begins?'

His teasing words were a knife in my heart, for somehow, without meaning to let it happen, I'd fallen madly, idiotically in love with him.

According to Bart's enthusiastic report, his long-gone wife came home from her rejuvenation trip looking smashingly young and beautiful. 'She's lost twenty pounds. I swear, that face lift has done wonders! She looks sensational, and damn it, so unbelievably like you!'

It was easy to see how impressed he was with his new, younger-looking wife, and if he was only trying to take the wind from my too confident sails, I didn't let it show. Then he was telling me I was just as necessary to him as before in a tone that said I was not. 'Cathy, while she was in Texas she changed. She's like she used to be, the sweet, loving woman I married.'

Men! How gullible they were! Of course my mother was sweeter and nicer to him now – now that she knew he had a mistress who was very accessible, and that the other woman was her own daughter. She'd have to know, for it was whispered all about now – everyone knew.

'So, why are you here with me when your wife is back and so like me? Why don't you put your clothes on and say goodbye and never come back? Say it was sweet while it lasted, but it's all over now, and I'll say thank you for a wonderful time before I kiss you farewell.'

'Well–ll,' he drawled, pulling me hard against his naked body. 'I didn't say she was *that* sensational looking. And then again, there is something special about you. I can't name it. I can't understand it. But I don't know if I can live without you now.' He said it seriously, truth in his dark eyes.

I'd won, won!

Quite by accident my mother and I met in the post office one day. She saw me and shivered. Her lovely head lifted higher as she turned it slightly away, pretending she didn't know me. She would deny me as she'd denied Carrie, even though it was so obvious that we were mother and daughter and not strangers. I wasn't Carrie. So I treated her as she treated me, indifferently, as if she were nobody special and never would be again. Yet, as I waited impatiently for my roll of stamps, I saw my mother dart her eyes to follow the restless prowl of my young son who had to stare at everything and everyone. He was handsome, graceful, a charming boy who drew the eyes of everyone who had to stop and admire him and pat his head. Jory moved with innate style, unstudied and relaxed, at ease wherever he was, because he thought the whole world was his, and he was loved by everyone.

He turned to catch my mother's long stare and he smiled. 'Hello,' he greeted. 'You're pretty – like my mommy.'

Oh, the things children say! What innocent knowledge they had, to see so readily what others instinctively refused to acknowledge. He stepped closer to reach out and tentatively touch her fur coat. 'My mommy's got a fur coat. My mommy is a dancer. Do you dance?'

She sighed, I held my breath. *See, Momma, there is the grandson your arms will never hold. You'll never hear him say your name ... never!*

'No,' she whispered, 'I'm not a dancer.' Tears filmed her eyes.

'My mommy can teach you how.'

'I'm too old to learn,' she whispered, backing off.

'No, you're not,' said Jory, reaching for her hand as if he'd show her the way, but she pulled back, glanced at me, reddened, then fumbled in her purse for a handkerchief. 'Do you have a little boy I can play with?' questioned my son, concerned to see her tears, as if having a son would make up for not knowing how to dance.

'No,' she said in a quivering weak whisper, 'I don't have any children.'

That's when I moved in to say in a cold, harsh voice, 'Some women don't deserve to have children.' I paid for my roll of stamps and dropped them in my purse. 'Some women like you, Mrs Winslow, would rather have money than the bother of children who might get in the way of good times. Time itself will sooner or later let you know if you made the right decision.'

She turned her back and shivered again as if all her furs couldn't keep her warm enough. Then she strode from the post office and headed towards a chauffeur-driven, black limousine. Like a queen she rode off, head held high, leaving Jory to ask, 'Mommy, why don't you like that pretty lady? I like her a lot. She's like you, only not so pretty.' I didn't comment, though it was on the tip of my tongue to say something so ugly he would never forget it.

In the twilight of that evening I sat near the windows, staring towards Foxworth Hall and wondering what Bart and my mother were doing. My hands were on my abdomen which was still flat, but soon it would be swelling with the child that might be started. One missed period didn't prove anything – except I wanted Bart's baby, and little things made me feel sure there was a baby. I let depression come and take me. He wouldn't leave her and her money to marry me and I'd have another fatherless child. What a fool to start all of this – but I'd always been a fool.

And then I saw a man slipping through the woods, coming to me, and I laughed, made confident again. He loved me! He did ... and as soon as I knew for certain, I would tell him he was to be a father.

Then the wind came in with Bart and blew the vase of roses from the table. I stood and stared down at the crystal pieces and the petals scattered about. Why was the wind always trying to tell me something? Something I didn't want to hear!

STACKING THE DECK

'Cathy, you told me there was no need for precautions!'

'There was no need. I want your baby.'

'*You want my baby?* What the hell do you think I can do, marry you?'

'No. I did my own assuming. I presumed you'd have your fun with me and when it was over you'd go back to your wife and find yourself another playmate. And I'd have just what I set out to get – your baby. Now I can leave. So kiss me off, Bart, as just another of your little extramarital dalliances.'

He looked furious. We were in my living room, while a fierce blizzard raged outside. Snow heaped in mounds window-high, and I was before the fireplace, knitting a baby bunting before I began a bootee. I was getting ready to slip a stitch then knit two together when Bart seized my knitting from my hands and hurled it away. 'It's unravelling!' I cried in dismay.

'What the hell are you trying to do to me, Cathy? You know I can't marry you! I never lied and said I would. You're playing a game with me.' He choked and covered his face with his hands, then took them down and pleaded. 'I love you. God help me but I do. I want you near me always, and I want my child too. What kind of game are you playing now?'

'Just a woman's game. The only game she can play and be sure of winning.'

'Look,' he said, trying to regain his control of the situation, 'explain what you mean, don't double talk. Nothing has to change because my wife is back. You'll always have a place in my life –'

'In your life? Don't you mean more correctly, on the fringes of your life?'

For the first time I heard humility in his voice. 'Cathy, be reasonable. I love you, and I love my wife too. Sometimes I can't separate you from her. She came back different, as I told you, and now she is like she was when we first met. Maybe a more youthful figure and face has given her back some confidence she lost, and because of it she can be sweeter. Whatever the cause, I'm grateful. Even when I disliked her, I loved her. When she was hateful, I'd try and strike back by going to other women, but still I loved her. The one big issue we fight over is her unwillingness to have a child, even an adopted one. Of course she's too old to have one now. Please, Cathy, *stay! Don't leave! Don't take my child away so I will never know what happens to him, or to her ... or to you.*'

I laid it out flat. 'All right, I will stay on one condition. If you divorce her and marry me, only then will you have the child you always wanted. Otherwise, I'm taking myself, and that means your child too, far away. Maybe I'll write to let you know if you have a son or a daughter, and maybe I won't. Either way, once I leave, you are out of my life for good.' I thought, *look at him, acting as if that codicil weren't in the will forbidding his wife to have children*. Protecting her! Just like Chris, when all along he had to know. He'd drawn up the will. He had to know.

Before the fireplace he stood with his arm up on the mantel, then he rested his forehead on that and stared down at the fire. His free hand was behind his back and clenched into a fist. His confused thoughts were so deep they reached out and touched me with pity. He turned then to face me, staring deep into my eyes. 'My God,' he said, shocked by his discovery. 'You planned this all along, didn't you? You came here to accomplish what you have, but why? Why should you choose me to hurt? What have I ever done to you, Cathy, but love you? True, it started with sex, and sex only was what I wanted it to stay. But it has grown into something much more than that. I like being with you, just sitting and talking, or walking in the woods. I feel comfortable with you. I like the way you wait on me, and touch my cheek when you pass, and rumple my hair and kiss my neck, and the sweet, shy way you wake up and smile when you see me beside you. I like the clever games you play, keeping me always guessing, and always amused. I feel I have ten women in one, so now I feel I can't live without you. But I can't abandon my wife and marry you. She needs me!'

368

'You should have been an actor, Bart. Your words move me to tears.'

'Damn you for taking this so lightly!' he bellowed. 'You've got me on a rack and you're twisting the screws! Don't make me hate you and ruin the best months of my life!'

With that he stormed out of my cottage, and I was left alone, ruefully regretting that always I talked too much, for I would stay as long as he needed me.

Emma, Jory and I thought it a wonderful idea to make an excursion to Richmond and do some Christmas shopping. Jory had never seen Santa Claus that he could remember, and most fearfully he approached the red-suited, white-bearded man who held out his arms to encourage him. Tentatively he perched on Santa's knee, and stared disbelievingly into twinkling blue eyes while I snapped pictures from every angle, even crawling to get what I wanted.

Next we visited a dress shop I'd heard about where I handed to them a sketch I'd drawn from memory. I selected the exact shade of dark green velvet, and then the lighter green chiffon for the skirt. 'And make the straps of the velvet bodice shoestrings of rhinestones – and remember, the floating panels must reach the hem.'

While Jory and Emma watched a Walt Disney movie, I had my hair cut and styled differently. Not just trimmed, as was my habit, but really cut shorter than I'd ever worn it. It was a style that flattered me, as it should, for it had flattered my mother when she wore her hair this way, fifteen years ago.

'Oh, Mommy!' cried Jory, distress in his voice. 'You've lost your hair!' He began to cry. 'Put your long hair back on – you don't look like my mommy now!'

No, that was the purpose. I didn't want to look like me this Christmas – not this special Christmas when I had to duplicate exactly what my mother had been when first I saw her dancing with Bart. Now, at long last, my chance – in a gown the same as hers, with her hair style, her younger face, I would confront my mother in her own home, on *my* terms. Woman to woman – and let the best one win! She'd be forty-eight, with a recent face lift –

still I knew she was very beautiful. But she couldn't compete with her daughter who was twenty-one years younger! I laughed when I looked in the mirror after slipping on the new green gown. Oh, yes, I'd made myself into what she was – the kind of woman men just couldn't resist. I had her power, her beauty – and ten times more brains – how could she win?

Three days before Christmas I called Chris and asked if he'd like to go with me to Richmond. I'd forgotten a few necessary items the little local shops didn't have. 'Cathy,' he said sternly, his voice cold and hostile, 'when you give up Bart Winslow you will see me again, but until you do, I don't care to be near you!'

'All right!' I flared. 'Stay where you are! You can miss out on your revenge, but I am not going to miss out on mine! Goodbye, Christopher Doll, and I hope all the bedbugs bite!' I hung up!

I didn't teach ballet class as often as I used to, but at recital times I was always there. My little dancers delighted in dressing up, and showing off before their parents, grandparents and friends. They looked adorable in their costumes for *The Nutcracker*. Even Jory had two minor roles to play, a snowflake and a sugarplum.

In my opinion there was no more magical way to spend at least one Christmas Eve than as a family attending a performance of *The Nutcracker*. And it was a thousand times more wonderful when one of those gifted, small, graceful children was your own small son, fifty-two days short of being four years old. The sweet babyness of him dancing on stage with so much passion drew applause time and again from the audience who stood up to cheer his solo performance that I'd choreographed especially for him.

And best of all, I'd made Bart swear he'd force my mother to attend that recital – and they were there; I checked by peeking through the curtains: front row centre, Mr and Mrs Bartholomew Winslow. He looked happy; she looked grim. So I did have some control over Bart. It showed up in a huge bouquet of roses for the dance instructor, and a huge box for the solo performing snowflake.

'What can it be?' asked Jory, his face flushed, his happiness rebounding from the sky. 'Can I open it now?'

'Sure, soon as we're home, and tomorrow morning Santa will leave a hundred gifts for you.'

'Why?'

'Because he loves you.'

'Why?' asked Jory.

'Because he couldn't help but love you – that's why.'

'Oh.'

Before five in the morning Jory was up, playing with the electric train Bart had sent him. All over the living-room floor were the splendid wrappings from hundreds of gifts from Paul, Henny, Chris, Bart, and Santa Claus. Emma gave him a box of homemade cookies that he polished off between ripping open the packages. 'Gee, Mommy,' he cried, 'I thought it would be lonely without my uncles, but I'm not lonely. I'm having fun.'

He wasn't lonely, but I was. I wanted Bart with me, not over there with her. I waited for him to make up some excuse to drive to the drugstore and slip over to see me and Jory. But all I saw of Bart on Christmas morning was the two-inch-wide diamond bracelet he enclosed in a box with two dozen red roses. His card read, 'I love you, Ballerina'.

If ever there was a woman who dressed more carefully than I did that night it must have been Marie Antoinette. Emma complained it was taking me forever. I painted my face as if a camera was going to shoot me close up for a magazine cover. Emma styled my hair as my mother had worn hers long ago. 'Wave it back softly from the face, Emma, then catch it high at the crown with a cluster of curls, and make sure a few hang long enough to brush my shoulders.'

When she finished, I gasped to see I was almost an exact duplicate of what my mother had been when I was twelve! My high cheekbones were emphasized just as hers had been with this hair style. As in a dream I never truly expected to happen I stepped into the green gown with the velvet bodice and chiffon skirt. This was the type of gown that never went out of fashion. I spun around before the mirror, getting the feel of being my mother with her power to control men, while Emma stood back and flattered me with compliments.

Even my perfume was the same. Musky with an Oriental garden scent. My slippers were straps of silver with four-inch heels. My silver evening bag matched. All I needed now was the emerald and diamond jewellery she had worn. Soon I'd have that too. Surely fate wouldn't let her be wearing green tonight. At some point in my life fate had to be on my side. I figured it was due tonight.

Tonight I'd deliver the surprises and the slaps. She would feel the pain of losing! What a pity Chris wouldn't come and enjoy the ending of a long, long play, started the day our father was killed on the highway.

I threw myself one more admiring glance, picked up the fur stole Bart had given me, gathered up my faltering courage, took a last peek at Jory who was curled up on his side and looking angelic. I leaned over to kiss tenderly his round, rosy cheek. 'I love you, Jory,' I whispered.

He partially awakened from a hazy dream and stared up at me as if I were part of that dream. 'Oh, Mommy, you look so pretty!' His dark brown eyes shone with childish wonder as he asked quite seriously, 'Are you going to a party to get me a new daddy?'

I smiled and again kissed him and said yes, in a way I was. 'Thank you, darling, for thinking I look pretty. Now go back to sleep and dream of happy things, and tomorrow we'll build a snowman.'

'Bring a daddy to help.'

On the table by the front door was a note from Paul. 'Henny is very ill. It's a pity you can't give up your plans to visit her before it is too late. I wish you good luck, Catherine.' With a sigh I put that note aside and picked up the note Henny had enclosed with Paul's, written on festive red paper, with the letters made crooked because of painful arthritic knuckles.

Dear Fairy-Child,
    Henny is old; Henny is tired; Henny is glad own son is by her side, but unhappy because other children far away.

I tell you now, before I go on to better place, the simple secret of living happy. All you need do is say goodbye to yesterday's loves, and hello to the new. Look around and see who needs you most and you won't go wrong. Forget who needed you yesterday.

You write and say you have new baby inside you made by husband of your mother. Rejoice in child, even if mother's husband will stay married to her. Forgive your mother, even if once she did evil. Nobody all bad, and a lot of the good in her children must have come from her. When you can forgive and forget the past, peace and love will come again to you, and this time it will stay.

And if you never in this world see Henny again, remember that Henny loved you well, as her own daughter, just as I loved your angel-sister whom I expect to meet again soon.

Soon to be in heaven,
Henny

I put the note down with a heavy feeling of sadness in my chest, then shrugged my shoulders. What had to be done would be done. A long time ago I'd set my feet on this path, and I'd follow it, come what may.

How strange the wind wasn't blowing when I stepped out the door and turned to wave to Emma who was spending the night with Jory. With boots covering my silver slippers, I headed for my car. How hushed it was, like nature was holding back in suspense as it focused on me.

Soft as eiderdown snow began to drift down. I glanced up at the grey, leaden sky, so much like the grandmother's eyes. Resolved again, I turned the key in the ignition and headed towards Foxworth Hall, though I wasn't an invited guest. I'd stormed at Bart for that. 'Why didn't you insist and force her to invite me?'

'Really, Cathy, isn't that a bit too much to ask? Can I insult my wife by asking my mistress to her party? I may be a fool, Cathy, but I am not that cruel.'

That first Christmas of imprisonment when I was twelve I'd lain with my head on Chris's boyish chest, wistfully wishing to be grown up, with curves as shapely as my mother's, with a face as beautiful as hers, wearing clothes as stunning as hers. And most of all I'd wished to be in control of my life.

Some Christmas wishes did come true.

REVELATIONS

Just a little after ten o'clock I used the wooden key Chris had carved so many years ago to slip unseen through a back door into Foxworth Hall. Already many guests were there and more were still arriving. The orchestra was playing a Christmas carol and faintly it drifted up to me. Music so sweetly haunting I was taken back to my childhood. Only this time I was alone in alien territory with no one to back me up as I stole quietly up the back stairs, keeping to the shadows, ready to hide quickly if necessary. I wended my solitary way to the grand central rotunda to stand near the cabinet where Chris and I had hidden to look down on another Christmas party. I gazed downwards to spy upon Bart Winslow standing beside his wife, who was wearing bright red lamé. His strong voice was hearty as he greeted his arriving guests warmly, shaking hands, kissing cheeks, acting the genial host in true fashion. My mother seemed somehow secondary to him, hardly needed at all in this huge mansion that was soon to be hers.

Smiling bitterly to myself, I stole on to my mother's grand suite of rooms. It took me back in time! Oh, golly-lolly! I used my little-girl exclamation of delight, of surprise, of dismay or frustration, though I had better and more accurate words at my disposal now. Tonight I had no frustrations, only a lilting sense of justification. Whatever happened, she had brought it upon herself. Look, I thought, there was the splendid swan bed, still there, with the little swan bed across the foot. I glanced around, seeing it was all the same, but for the brocade fabric on the walls – that was different. Now it was a soft plum colour, and not strawberry pink. There was a brass valet to hold a man's suit ready, and unwrinkled, until he put it on. That was new. I hurried on into my mother's dressing room. On my knees, I pulled out a special bottom drawer to feel around for the tiny button that had to be pushed in a certain combination of numbers to trigger the complicated lock. And would you believe it – she still used her birthday numbers of month, day and year! My! She was a trusting soul.

In no time at all I had the huge velvet tray on the floor before me, so I could help myself to the emeralds and diamonds she had worn to that Christmas party when first Chris and I beheld Bartholomew Winslow. How we'd loved her then, and how we'd resented *him*. We had been still in the shadow of our grief for our father, and hand't wanted Momma to marry again – not ever again.

As in a dream I donned the emerald and diamond jewellery that went so well with my green velvet and chiffon gown. I glanced in the mirror to see if I looked as she had way back then. I was a few years younger, but yes, I did look like her. Not exactly, but almost – and enough to convince – for were two leaves from the same tree ever duplicates? I replaced the jewellery tray, put back the drawer, leaving everything as it had been. Except now I wore several hundred thousand dollars worth of gems I didn't own. One more look at my watch. Ten-thirty. Too soon. At twelve I wanted to make my grand entrance, like Cinderella in reverse.

With utmost caution, I crept stealthily along the long halls to the northern wing, and found that end room with the door locked. The wooden key still fitted. But my heart didn't seem to fit my chest. It beat too fast, too fierce, too loud and my pulse raced too excitedly. I had to keep calm, self-possessed, do everything right and not be intimidated by this awesome house that had done its best to destroy us.

When I stepped into that room with the two double beds, I stepped back into childhood. The gold-coloured, quilted satin spreads were still on the beds, precisely made without a wrinkle. The ten-inch TV was still in the corner. The doll's house with its porcelain people and antique made-to-scale furniture waited for Carrie's hands to bring it to life again. The old rocker that Chris had brought down from the attic, still there. *Why, it was as if in here time stood still and we'd never left!*

Even Hell was still on the walls gruesomely represented by three reproductions of masterpieces. Oh, God! I hadn't known this room would make me feel so – so shredded inside. I couldn't afford to cry. That would make my mascara run. Yet I wanted to cry. All about me flitted the ghosts of Cory and Carrie, just five years old, laughing, crying, wanting outside, the sunlight, and all they could do was push tiny trucks to make-believe San Francisco or Los Angeles. There used to be train tracks that ran all over the room and under the furniture. Oh, where did the train tracks go – the coal cars, the engines? I pulled a tissue from my tiny evening bag and held it to the corner of one eye and then the other. I leaned to peer into the doll's house. The porcelain maids were still cooking in the kitchen; the butler still stood near the front door to welcome the guests arriving in a coach pulled by two horses – and lo, when I looked in the nursery, the cradle was there! The missing cradle! For weeks we'd hunted to find it, fearful all the time the grandmother would notice it missing and punish Carrie – and there it was, just where it should be! But the baby wasn't in it, nor were the parents in the front parlour. Mr and Mrs Parkins and baby Clara were now mine and never would they reside in this doll's house again.

Had the grandmother herself stolen the cradle, so she could then see it missing, and ask Carrie where it was, and when it couldn't be produced, she'd have good reason to punish Carrie? And Cory as well, for he would automatically, without fear for himself, run to protect his twin sister. It was like her to do something mean and cruel like that. But if she had, why had she stayed her hand, and not played out her role to the end? I laughed bitterly to myself. She had played out her role to the end – not just a whipping, but something better, something worse. Poison. Arsenic on four sugared doughnuts.

I jumped then. It seemed I heard a child laugh. My imagination, of course. And then, when I should have known better, I headed for the closet and the high and narrow door at the very back end and the steep and narrow dark stairs. A million times I'd ascended these stairs. A million times in the dark, without a candle, or a flashlight. Up into the dark, eerie, gigantic attic, and only when I was there did I feel around for the place where Chris and I had hidden our candles and matches.

Still there. Time did stand still in this place. We'd had several candle holders, all of pewter with small handles to grasp. Holders we'd found in an old trunk along with boxes and boxes of short, stubby, clumsily made candles. We'd always presumed them to be homemade candles, for they had smelled so rank and old when they burned.

My breath caught! Oh! It was the same! The paper flowers still dangled down, mobiles to sway in the draughts, and the giant flowers were still on the walls. Only all the colours had faded to indistinct grey – ghost flowers. The sparkling gem centres we'd glued on had loosened, and now only a few daisies had sequins, or gleaming stones, for centres. Carrie's purple worm was there only now he too was a nothing colour. Cory's epileptic snail didn't appear a bright, lopsided beach ball now, it was more a tepid, half-rotten squashy orange. The BEWARE signs Chris and I had painted in red were still on the walls, and the swings still dangled down from the attic rafters. Over near the record player was the barre Chris had fashioned, then nailed to the wall so I could practise my ballet positions. Even my outgrown costumes hung limply from nails, dozens of them with matching leotards and worn out *pointe* shoes, all faded and dusty, rotten smelling.

As in an unhappy dream I was committed to, I drifted aimlessly towards the distant schoolroom, with the candlelight flickering. Ghosts were unsettled, memories and spectres followed me as things began to wake up, yawn and whisper. No, I told myself, it was only the floating panels of my long chiffon wings ... that was all. The spotted rocking-horse loomed up, scary and threatening, and my hand rose to my throat as I held back a scream. The rusty red wagon seemed to move by unseen hands pushing it, so my eyes took flight to the blackboard where I'd printed my enigmatic farewell message to those who came in the future. How was I to know it would be me?

We lived in the attic,
Christopher, Cory, Carrie and me –
Now there are only three.

Behind the small desk that had been Cory's I scrunched

378

down, and tried to fit my legs under. I wanted to put myself into a deep reverie that would call up Cory's spirit that would tell me where he lay.

As I sat there waiting, the wind outside began to blow, picking up strength so it howled and hurled the snow slantwise. Another blizzard was on, full force. With the storm came the draughts to blow out my candle! The darkness shrieked, and I had to run to get out! Run fast ... run, run, run before I became one of them!

The next hour had been choreographed to the smallest detail. As the big grandfather clock began to strike twelve, I positioned myself in the centre of the second-floor balcony. I did nothing spectacular to pull all eyes my way, just stood there with my flesh warmed by the flashing jewels. In her crimson dress of lamé, so high in front it reached her throat that was encircled with a lavish choker of diamonds, my mother slightly turned. I saw the backless gown made up for the severity in front, so a hint of her buttock cleavage showed. Her blonde hair was styled shorter than I'd ever seen it, and fluffed out around her face in a flattering way. From this distance she looked very young and lovely, and nowhere near her actual age. Ahh ... the last stroke of twelve sounded ...

Some sixth sense must have warned her, for she turned her head slowly to look my way. I began my descent. She froze in shock. Her eyes grew wide and dark as her hand that held a cocktail glass trembled so much a bit of the liquid sloshed out and fell to the floor. Because she stared, Bart followed the direction of her gaze. He gawked as if at an apparition. Now that both host and hostess were mesmerized, each guest had to look where no doubt they expected to see Santa Claus, and it was only me. Only me as once my mother had been years ago, wearing the same gown, and before many, I was sure, of those very same people who were here that other Christmas when I was twelve. I even recognized a few, older, but I knew them! Oh, the joy to have them here!

This was my moment of triumph! Moving as only a ballerina can, I meant to play my role to the utmost of my dramatic ability.

As the guests stared upwards, clearly caught in thrall by time moved backwards, I gloated to see my mother blanch. Then I rejoiced to see Bart's eyes widen more as they jumped from me, to her, then back to me. Slowly, in a dead silence, for the music had stopped, I descended the left side of the dual winding staircases, thinking I was Caraboose, the wicked fairy who put upon Aurora the curse of death. Then I made myself the Lilac Fairy to steal away Aurora's prince while she slept her sleep of one hundred years. (It was clever of me not to think of myself as my mother's daughter, and how soon I would destroy her. Very clever to make of this a stage production, when I was dealing with reality, and not fantasy and the blood that could be spilled.)

Gracefully I trailed my sparkling fingers along the rosewood railing, feeling my green chiffon wings fluttering and floating as step by step, and second by second, I neared the place where my mother and Bart were standing very close together. She was trembling all over, but managing to hold on to her poise. I thought I glimpsed a flicker of panic in the blue of her Dresden eyes. I kindly bestowed on her my most gracious smile while standing on the second step from the bottom. In this way I gave myself the height I needed to be taller than anyone else. All had to look up to me wearing four-inch silver heels on platform soles like Carrie's, so as to be on an even height with my mother when we met eye to eye. The better to see her dismay. Her discomfort. Her utter collapse!

'Merry Christmas!' I called to one and all in a loud clear voice. It resounded like a heralding trumpet to attract others from different rooms, and they came in by the dozen, as if drawn more by the total silence but for my voice. 'Mr Winslow,' I called invitingly, 'come dance with me, just as you danced with my mother fifteen years ago, when I was twelve and hiding above, and she wore a gown just like the one I have on now.' Bart was visibly jolted. Stunned shock made his dark eyes blacken, but he refused to move from my mother's side!

He forced me to do what I did next. As everyone stood there and waited, held in breathless suspense, expecting more explosive revelations, I gave them what they wanted.

'I'd like to introduce myself.' My voice was high-pitched so it would carry well. 'I am Catherine Leigh Foxworth, the firstborn daughter of Mrs Bartholomew Winslow, whom most of you must remember was first married to my father, Christopher Foxworth. Remember too that he was my mother's half-uncle, the younger brother of Malcolm Neal Foxworth who disinherited his only daughter, his sole remaining heir, because she had the unholy temerity to wed his half-brother! I also have an older brother, named Christopher too – he's a doctor now. Once I had a younger brother and sister, twins seven years younger than I – but Cory and Carrie are dead now – for they were –' I stopped short for some reason, then went on. 'That Christmas party fifteen years ago, Chris and I were hiding in the chest on the balcony, while the twins slept in the end room of the northern wing. Our playground was the attic, and never, never did we go downstairs. We were attic mice, unwanted and unloved once money came into the picture.' And I would have screamed it all out, every last detail, but Bart came striding over to me.

'Bravo, Cathy!' he cried. 'You play your part to perfection! Congratulations.' He put his arm about my shoulders, charmingly smiled at me, then turned to the guests who appeared not to know what to think, or whom to believe, much less how to react. 'Ladies, gentlemen,' he said, 'let me introduce to you Catherine Dahl, whom many of you must have seen on stage when she danced with her husband, Julian Marquet. And as you have just witnessed, she is also an actress of merit. Cathy here is a distant relative of my wife, and if you can see any resemblance, that explains it. In fact, Mrs Julian Marquet is one of our neighbours now, you may know that. Since her resemblance to my wife is so remarkable, we cooked up this little farce between us, and did what we could to enliven and make different this party with our little joke.'

He ruthlessly pinched my upper arm, before he caught my hand, put his arm about my waist and asked me to dance. 'Come now, Cathy, certainly you want to show of your dancing ability after that fine dramatic performance.' As the music began to play, he forcibly made me dance! I turned my head to see my mother sagging against a friend, her face so pale her makeup stood out like livid blotches. Even so, she couldn't take her eyes from me in the arms of her husband.

'You brazen little bitch!' Bart hissed at me. 'How dare you come in here and pull such a stunt? I thought I loved you. I despise you. I won't have you ruining my wife! You little idiot, whatever made you tell so many lies?'

'You are the idiot, Bart,' I said calmly, though I was panicked inside – what if he refused to believe? 'Look at me. How would I know she wore a gown like this, if I hadn't seen her with it on? How would I know you went with her to see her bedroom with the swan bed, if my brother, Chris, hadn't hidden and heard and seen everything the two of you did up on the second-floor rotunda?'

He met my eyes, and he looked so strange, so distant and strange.

'Yes, Bart darling, I am your wife's daughter, and I know if your law firm finds out your wife had four children born from the union of her first marriage, then you and she lose everything. All that money. All your investments. Everything you have bought will be taken back. Oh, the pity of that makes me want to cry.'

We danced on, his cheek inches from mine. A smile was fixed to his lips. 'That gown you're wearing, how the hell did you find out she had one exactly like that the first time I came to this house to a party?'

I laughed with fake merriment. 'Dear Bart, you are so stupid. How do you think I know? I saw her in this gown. She came to our room and showed us how pretty she looked, and I was so envious of all her curves and the way Chris looked at her with so much admiration. She wore her hair as I am wearing mine now. These jewels were taken from her safe in the dressing-room table drawer.'

'You're lying,' he said, but doubt was in his voice now.

'I know the combination,' I went on softly, 'she used her birthday numbers. She told me that when I was twelve. She *is* my mother. She *did* keep us locked in that room, waiting for her father to die, so she could inherit. And you know why she had to keep us a big, dark secret. You wrote the will, didn't you? Think back to a certain night when you fell asleep in her grand suite of rooms, and you dreamed a young girl wearing a short blue nightie stole in and kissed you. You weren't dreaming, Bart. That kiss was from me. I was fifteen then, and had snuck into your room to steal money – remember how you used to miss cash? You and she thought the servants were stealing, but it was Chris, and one time it was me ... who didn't find anything because you were there to scare me away.'

'Nooo,' he said with a sigh. '*No!* She wouldn't do that to her own children!'

'Wouldn't she? She did. That big chest up there near the balcony balustrade has a backing of wire mesh screening. Chris and I could see just fine. We saw the caterers fixing crêpes and waiters in red and black and a fountain spraying champagne, and there were two huge silver punch bowls. Chris and I could smell everything so delicious and we drooled to have a taste of what was down there. Our meals were so boring, and always cold or lukewarm. The twins hardly ate anything. Were you there the Thanksgiving Day dinner when she got up and down so much? Do you want to know why? She was preparing a tray of food to take up to us whenever the butler John was out of his pantry.'

He shook his head, his eyes dazed.

'Yes, Bart, the woman you married had four children she hid away for three years and almost five months. Our playground was in the attic. Have you ever played in an attic in the summertime? In the winter? Do you think it was pleasant? Can you imagine how we felt, waiting year after year for an old man to die so our lives could begin? Do you know the trauma we suffered knowing she cared more for the money than she did for us, her own children? And the twins, they didn't grow. They stayed so small, grew so large-eyed and haunted looking, and she'd come and never look at them! She pretended not to notice their ill health!'

'Cathy, please! If you are lying, stop! Don't make me hate her!'

'Why not hate her? She deserves it,' I went on as my mother went to lean against a wall, and looked sick enough to throw up. 'Once I lay on the swan bed, with the little swan bed across the foot. You had a book in your nightstand drawer about sex, disguised under a dustjacket that read *How to Create and Design Your Own Needlepoint* or something like that.'

'*How to Create Your Own Needlepoint Designs,*' he corrected, looking sick and as pale as my mother, though he kept on smiling, hatefully smiling.

'You are making all of this up,' he said in an odd tone that showed no sincerity. 'You hate her because you want me, and connive to deceive me and destroy her.'

I smiled and lightly brushed his cheek with my lips. 'Then let me convince you more. Our grandmother always wore grey taffeta with hand-crocheted collars, and never without a diamond brooch with seventeen stones pinned at her throat. Very early each morning, before six-thirty, she brought us food and milk in a picnic hamper. At first she fed us rather well, but gradually, as her resentment grew, our meals grew worse and worse until we were fed mostly sandwiches of peanut butter and jelly and occasionally fried chicken and potato salad. She gave us a long list of rules to live by, including one that forbade us to open the draperies to let in light. Year after year we lived in a dim room without sunlight. If only you knew how dreary life is, shut away, without light, feeling neglected, unwanted, unloved. Then there was another rule very hard to abide by. We were not supposed to even look at each other – especially one of the opposite sex.'

'Oh, God!' he exclaimed, then sighed heavily. 'That sounds like her. You say it was more than three years you were locked up there?'

'Three years and almost five months, and if that seems a long time to you, how do you think it was for small children of five, and one of twelve, and the other of fourteen? Back then, five minutes passed like five hours, and days were like months, and months were like years.'

Doubt fought clearly with his legal mind that saw all the ramifications, if my tale were true. 'Cathy, be honest, totally honest. You had two brothers and one sister – and all that time, when I was here too, you were living locked up?'

'In the beginning, we believed in her, every word she said, for we loved her, trusted her – she was our only hope, and our salvation. And we wanted her to inherit all that money from her father. We agreed to stay up there until the grandfather died, although when our mother explained how we were to live in Foxworth Hall she failed to mention we were to be hidden away. At first we thought it would only be for a day or so, but it went on and on. We filled our time by playing games – and we prayed a lot, slept a lot. We grew thin, half-sick, malnourished, and suffered through two weeks of starvation while you and our mother travelled throughout Europe on your honeymoon. And then you went to Vermont to visit your sister, where our mother bought a two-pound box of maple-sugar candy. But by then we'd already been eating doughnuts with arsenic laced in the powdered sugar.'

He gave me a hard, fierce look of terrible anger. 'Yes, she did buy a box of that kind of candy in Vermont. But Cathy! Whatever else you may say, I can never believe my wife would deliberately set out to poison her own children!' His scornful eyes raked over me, then back to my face. '*Yes, you do look like her!* You could be her daughter, I admit that! But to say Corrine would kill her own children, I can't believe that!'

I shoved him away forcefully, and whirled about. '*Listen everyone!*' I yelled out. 'I *am* the daughter of Corrine Foxworth Winslow! She *did* lock her four children in the end room of the northern wing. Our grandmother was in the scheme and gave us the attic for our playroom. We decorated it with paper flowers, to make it pretty for our little twins, all so our mother could inherit. Our mother told us we had to hide, for if we didn't our grandfather would never have her written into his will. All of you know how he despised her for marrying his half-brother. Our mother persuaded us to come and live upstairs, and be as quiet as attic mice; we went, trusting and believing she would keep her word and let us out the day her father died. *But she didn't!* She didn't! She let us suffer up there for nine months after he was dead and buried!'

I had more to spill out. But my mother shrilled out in a loud voice, '*Stop!*' She stumbled forward; her arms outstretched as if she were blind. '*You lie!*' she screamed. 'I've never seen you before! Get out of my house! Get out this instant before I call the

385

police and have you thrown out! *Now you get out, and you stay out!*

Everyone was staring at her now, not me. She, the ultra-poised and arrogant had lost control, was trembling, her face livid, wanting to scratch the eyes from my face! I don't think a soul there believed her then, not when they could see I was her very image – and I knew too many truths.

Bart left my side and went to his wife to whisper something in her ear. He put his arms consolingly around her, and kissed her cheek. She clung to him helplessly, with pale, shaky hands of desperation, beseeching his help with great teary eyes of cerulean blue – like mine, like Chris's, like the twins' blue eyes.

'Thank you again, Cathy, for a fine performance. Come into the library with me and I'll pay you your fee.' He scanned over the guests clustered around and quietly he said, 'I'm sorry, but my wife has been ill, and this little joke was ill-timed on my part. I should have known better than to plan such a show. So, if you will please forgive us, do go on with the party; enjoy yourselves; eat, drink and be merry; and stay as long as you like, Miss Catherine Dahl may have some more surprises in store for you.'

How I hated him then!

As the guests milled about and whispered and looked from me to him, he picked up my mother and carried her towards the library. She was heavier than she used to be, but in his arms she seemed a feather. Bart glanced over his shoulder at me, gestured with his head that I was to follow, which I did.

I wanted Chris here with me, as he should be. It shouldn't be left up to me to confront her with the truth. I was strangely alone, defensive, as if in the end Bart would believe her and not me, no matter what I said, no matter what proof I gave him. And I had plenty of proof. I could describe to him the flowers in the attic, the snail, the worm, the cryptic message I'd written on the blackboard, and, most of all, I could show him the wooden key.

Bart reached the library and carefully put my mother into one of the leather chairs. He snapped an order my way. 'Cathy, will you please close the door behind you.'

Only then did I see who else was in the library! My grand-mother was seated in the same wheelchair her husband had used.

Ordinarily you can't tell one wheelchair from another, but this one was custom-made and much finer. She wore a grey-blue robe over her hospital jacket, and a lap robe covered her legs. The chair was placed near the fireplace so she could benefit from the heat of a roaring log fire. Her bald head shone as she turned it my way. Her flintstone grey eyes glowed maliciously.

A nurse was in the room with her. I didn't take the time to look at her face.

'Mrs Mallory,' said Bart, 'will you please leave the room and leave Mrs Foxworth here.' It wasn't a request, but an order.

'Yes, sir,' said the nurse who quickly got up and scuttled to leave as fast as possible. 'You just ring for me when Mrs Foxworth wants to be put to bed, sir,' she said at the door and then disappeared.

Bart seemed on the verge of exploding as he stalked the room, and what wrath he felt now seemed directed not only at me, but also at his wife. 'All right,' he said as soon as the nurse was gone, 'let's have done with it, all of it. Corrine, I've always suspected you had a secret, a big secret. It occurred to me many times you didn't truly love me, but it never once crossed my mind you might have four children you hid away in the attic. *Why?* Why couldn't you have come to me and told me the truth?' He roared this, all control gone. 'How could you be so selfishly heartless, so brutally cruel as to lock away your four children and then try and kill them with arsenic?'

Sagging limply in a brown leather chair, my mother closed her eyes. She seemed bloodless as she asked in a dull voice. 'So, you are going to believe her and not me. You know I could never poison anyone, no matter what I had to gain. And you know that I don't have any children!'

I was stunned to know Bart believed me and not her, and then I guessed he didn't truly believe me, but was using a lawyer's trick, attacking and hoping to take her off guard, and maybe get to the truth. But that would never work, not with her. She'd trained herself over too many years for anyone to take her by surprise.

I strode forward to glare down at her, and in the harshest of voices I spoke. 'Why don't you tell Bart about Cory, Momma?

Go on, tell him how you and your mother came in the night and wrapped him in a green blanket and told us you were taking him to a hospital. Tell him how you came back the next day and told us he died from pneumonia. Lies! All lies! Chris sneaked downstairs and overheard the butler, John Amos Jackson, telling a maid of how the grandmother carried arsenic up to the attic to kill the little mice. *We were the little mice who ate those sugared doughnuts, Mother!* And we proved those doughnuts were poisoned. Remember Cory's little pet mouse that you used to ignore? He was fed only a bit of sugared doughnut and he died! Now sit there and cry, and deny who I am, and who Chris is, and who Cory and Carrie used to be!'

'I have never seen you before in my life,' she said strongly, bolting upright and staring me straight in the eyes, 'except when I went to the ballet in New York.'

Bart narrowed his eyes, weighing her, then me. Then he looked at his wife again and his eyes grew even more slitlike and cunning. 'Cathy,' he said, still looking at her, 'you are making very serious allegations against my wife. You accuse her of murder, premeditated murder. If you are proven right, she will face a jury trial for murder – is that what you want?'

'I want justice, that is all. No, I don't want to see her in prison or put in an electric chair – if they still do that in this state.'

'She is lying,' whispered my mother, 'lying, lying, lying.'

I had come prepared for accusations like this and calmly I pulled from my tiny purse duplicates of four birth certificates. I handed them to Bart who took them over to a lamp and bent to study them. Cruelly and with great satisfaction I smiled at my mother. 'Dear Mother, you were very foolish to sew those birth certificates in the lining of our old suitcases. Without them I wouldn't have had any proof at all to show your husband and, no doubt, he would go on believing you – for I am an actress and accustomed to putting on a good show.

'It's a pity he doesn't know you are an even better actress. Cringe away, Momma, but I have the proof!' I laughed wildly, near tears as I saw them begin to glisten in her eyes, for once I had loved her so well, and under all the hatred and animosity I felt for her, a little light of innate love still waxed and waned, and it hurt, oh, it did hurt to make her cry. Yet she deserved it, she did, I kept telling myself she did!

'You know something else, Momma, Carrie told me how she met you on the street and you denied her, and shortly afterwards she became so ill she died – so you helped kill her too! And without the birth certificates you could have escaped all retribution, for that courthouse in Gladstone, Pennsylvania, burned down ten years ago. See how kind fate would have been to you, Mother? But you never did anything well. Why didn't you burn them? Why did you save them . . . ? That was very thoughtless of you, dearest loving Mother, to save the evidence; but then you were always careless, always thoughtless, always extravagant about everything. You thought if you killed your four children you could have others – but your father tricked you, didn't he?'

'*Cathy! Sit down and let me handle this!*' ordered Bart. 'My wife has just undergone surgery and I'll not have you threaten her health. *Now sit before I push you down!*'

I sat.

He glanced at my mother, then at *her* mother.

'Corrine, if you have ever cared for me, loved me even a little – is any of what this woman says true? *Is she your daughter?*'

Very weakly my mother answered, '. . . Yes.'

I sighed. I thought I heard the whole house sigh, and Bart along with it. I lifted my eyes to see my grandmother staring at me in the oddest way.

'Yes,' she continued flatly, her dull eyes fixed on Bart. 'I couldn't tell you, Bart. I wanted to tell you, but I was afraid you wouldn't want me if I came with four children and no money, and I loved and wanted you so much. I racked my brains trying to figure out a solution so I could keep you, my children and the money too.' She sat up and made a ramrod of her spine as her head lifted regally high. 'And I *did* figure out a solution! I *did*! It took me weeks and weeks of scheming, but I *did* figure a way!'

'Corrine,' said Bart with ice in his voice as he towered above her, 'murder is never a solution to anything! All you had to do was tell me, and I would have thought of a way to save your children and your inheritance.'

'But don't you see,' she cried out excitedly, 'I figured out a way all by myself! I wanted you; I wanted my children and the money too. I thought my father owed me that money!' She laughed hysterically, beginning to lose control again, as if hell was at her heels and she had to speak fast to escape its burn. 'Everyone thought I was stupid, a blonde with a pretty face and figure but no brains. Well, I fooled you, Mother,' she threw out at that old woman in the chair. And at a portrait on the wall she screamed, 'And I fooled you too, Malcolm Foxworth!' Then at me she flared her eyes, 'And you too, Catherine. You thought you had it so tough up there, locked away, missing out on schooldays and friends, but you don't realize how good you had it compared to what my father did to me! You, you and your accusations, always at me, when could I let you out? When down below my father was ordering me to do this, do that, for if you don't you won't inherit one penny and I'll tell your lover about your four children too!'

I gasped. Then jumped to my feet. 'He knew about us? The grandfather knew?'

Again she laughed, hard, diamond-brittle laughter. 'Yes, he knew, but I didn't tell him! The day Chris and I ran away from this horrible house he hired detectives to follow and keep tabs on us. Then, when my husband was killed in that accident, I was persuaded by my lawyer to seek their help. How my father rejoiced! Don't you see, Cathy,' she said so fast her words piled one on the other, 'he *wanted* me and my children in his house and under his thumb! He had it planned along with my mother, to deceive me and let me think he didn't know you were hidden upstairs. But he knew all the time! It was his plan to keep you locked up for the rest of your lives!'

I gasped and stared at her. I doubted her too; how could I trust anything she said now after she'd done so much? 'The grandmother, she went along with his plan?' I asked, feeling a numbing sensation creeping up from my toes.

'Her!' said Momma, tossing her mother a hard look of contempt. 'She'd do anything he said, for she hated me; she's always hated me; he loved me too much when I was a girl, and cared nothing at all about his sons whom she favoured more.

And after we were here, snared in his trap, he gloated to have his half-brother's children captured as animals in a cage, to keep locked up until they were dead. So, while you were up there, playing your games and decorating the attic, he kept at me, day in, day out. "They should never have been born, should they?" he'd slyly say, and cunningly suggest you would all be better off dead than kept prisoners until you grew old, or sickened and died.

'I didn't truly believe he meant this at first. I thought it was only another of his ways to torture me. Each day he'd say you were wicked, flawed, evil children who should be destroyed. I'd cry, plead, go down on my knees and beg, and he'd laugh. One evening he raged at me. "You fool," he said. "Were you idiot enough to think I could ever forgive you for sleeping with your half-uncle – the ultimate sin against God? Bearing his children?" And on and on he'd rave, screaming sometimes. Then he'd lash out with his walking cane, striking whatever he could reach. My mother would sit nearby and smirk with pleasure. Yet, he didn't let me know he knew you were up there for several weeks . . . and by that time, I was trapped.'

She pleaded with me to believe, to have mercy. 'Can't you see how it was? I didn't know which way to turn! I didn't have any money, and I kept thinking his terrible temper tantrums would kill him, so I provoked him so he would die – but he kept on living, and berating me and my children. And every time I went into your room, you'd be pleading to be let out. *Especially you, Cathy – especially you.*'

'And what else did he do to make you keep us prisoners?' I asked sarcastically, 'except scream and rail and hit you with his cane? It couldn't have been very hard, for he was very frail, and we never saw any marks on you after the first whipping. You were free to come and go as you wanted. You could have worked out some plan to slip us outside unknown to him. You wanted his money, and you didn't care what you had to do to get it! You wanted that money more than you wanted your four children!'

Before my very eyes her delicate and lovely restored face took on the aged look of her mother. She seemed to shrivel and grow haggard with the countless years she had yet to live with her regrets. Her gaze took wild flight, seeking some safe refuge in which to hide forever, not only from me, but from the fury she saw in her husband's eyes.

'Cathy,' pleaded my mother, 'I know you hate me, but –'

'Yes, Mother, I do hate you.'

'You wouldn't if you understood –'

I laughed, hard and bitterly. 'Dearest Mother, there is not one thing you could tell me to make me understand.'

'Corrine,' said Bart, his tone sterile, as if his heart had been removed. 'Your daughter is right. You can sit there and cry, and talk about your father forcing you to poison your children – but how can I believe when I can't remember him even giving you a hard glance? He looked at you with love and pride. You did come and go as you chose. Your father lavished money on you, so you could buy new clothes and everything else you wanted. Now you come up with some ridiculous tale of how you were tortured by him, and forced by him to kill your hidden children. God, you sicken me!'

Her eyes took on a glassy stare; her pale and elegant hands trembled as they unfolded and fluttered up from her lap to her throat, and there they fingered over and over again the diamond choker that must be keeping her gown from falling off. 'Bart, please, I'm not lying . . . I admit I've lied to you in the past, and deceived you about my children – but I'm not lying now. Why can't you believe me?'

Bart stood with his feet spread apart, as a sailor would to brace himself on a rocky sea. His hands were behind his back and clenched into fists. 'What kind of man do you think I am – or was?' he asked bitterly. 'You could have told me anything then, and I would have understood. I loved you, Corrine. I would have done anything legally possible to thwart your father and help you gain his fortune, and at the same time keep your children alive, free to live normal lives. I'm not a monster, Corrine, and I didn't marry you for your money. I would have married you if you were penniless!'

'You couldn't outwit my father!' she cried, jumping up and beginning to pace the floor.

In that shiny crimson dress my mother appeared a bright lick of flame, a colour that made her eyes dark purple as they darted from one to the other of us. Then, finally, when I couldn't stand to watch her as she was, broken, wild, with all her queenly poise gone, her eyes came to rest on her mother – that old woman who slumped in the wheelchair, as if without bones. Her gnarled fingers worked weakly at the afghan, but her grey zealot's eyes burned with a strong, mean fire. I watched as the eyes of mother and daughter clashed. Those grey eyes that never changed, never softened with old age or fear of the hell that must be lying in wait for her.

And, to my surprise, from this confrontation my mother rose straight and tall, the winner in this battle of wills. She began to speak in a dispassionate way, as if discussing someone else. It was like hearing a woman talk who knew she was killing herself with each razored word, and yet she didn't care, not any more – for I was the winner, after all, and to me, her most severe judge, she turned to appeal. 'All right, Cathy. I knew sooner or later I would have to face up to you. I knew it would be you who would force the truth from me. It has always been your way to look through me, and guess I wasn't always what I wanted you to believe I was. Christopher loved me, trusted me. But you never would. Yet in the beginning, at the time your father was killed, I was trying to do the best I could by you. I told you what I believed to be the truth, when I asked you to come and live here hidden away until I won back my father's favour. I didn't truly think it would take more than one day, or possibly two.'

I sat as frozen, staring at her. Her eyes pleaded mutely, *have mercy, Cathy, believe me! I speak the truth.*

She turned from me, and in great distress she appealed to Bart and spoke of their first meeting in a friend's home. 'I didn't want to love you, Bart, and involve you in the mess I was in. I wanted to tell you about my children and the threat my father posed to them, but just when I would he'd worsen and appear ready to die, so I'd put it off and keep quiet. I prayed that when eventually I did tell you, you'd understand. It was stupid of me, for a secret kept too long becomes impossible to explain. You wanted to marry me. My father kept saying no. My children pleaded every day to be let out. Even though I knew they had every right to complain, I began to resent them, the way they kept harassing me, making me feel guilty and ashamed when I was trying to do the best I could for them. And it was Cathy, always it was Cathy, no matter how many gifts I gave her, who kept at it the most.' She threw me another of her long, tormented looks, as if I'd tortured her beyond endurance.

'Cathy,' she whispered then, her watery, drowning look of anguish brightening a little, as once more she turned to me. 'I did do the best I could! I told my parents all of you did have hidden afflictions, especially Cory. They wanted to think God had punished my children, so they believed easily. And Cory was always having one cold after another, and his allergy. Can't you see what I tried to do, make all of you just a little sick, so I could rush you one by one to the hospital, then report back to my mother you died. I used a minute bit of arsenic, but not enough to kill you! All I wanted to do was make you a little bit sick, just enough to get you out!'

I was appalled by her stupidity to scheme in such a dangerous way. Then I guessed it was all a lie, just an excuse to satisfy Bart who was staring at her in the oddest way. I smiled at her then, while inside I was hurting so badly I could cry. 'Momma,' I said softly, interrupting her pleas, 'have you forgotten your father was dead before the sugared doughnuts started coming? You didn't have to trick him in his grave.'

She darted her tormented eyes to the grandmother who had a stern, forbidding look fixed on her daughter.

'Yes!' cried Momma, 'I knew that! But for that codicil I would never have needed the arsenic! But my father let our butler John in on our secret, and he was alive to see that I followed through and kept you upstairs until each one of you was dead! And if he didn't, then my mother was to see he didn't inherit the fifty thousand dollars promised to him. Then there was my mother, who wanted John to inherit everything!'

A terrible silence came while I tried to digest this. The grandfather knew all the time and had wanted to keep us prisoners for life? And as if that weren't enough punishment, he then tried to force her to kill us? Oh, he must have been even more evil than I thought! Not human at all! Then, as I watched her and took note of her anxiously waiting blue eyes, her hands busily trying to twist an invisible rope of pearls, I knew she was lying. I glanced at the grandmother and saw her frown as she tried to speak. Fierce indignation was in her eyes, as if she would deny all my mother had said. But she hated Momma. She would want me to believe the worst – oh, God, how was I to find out the truth?

I glanced at Bart who stood before the fire, his dark eyes gazing at his wife as if he'd never seen her before, and what he was seeing now appalled him.

'Momma,' I began in a flat voice, 'what did you really do with Cory's body? We have looked in all the cemeteries around here and checked their records, and not one little boy of eight years died in that last week of October, 1960.'

She swallowed first, then wrung her hands, flashing all the diamonds and other jewels. 'I didn't know what to do with him,' she whispered. 'He died before I could reach the hospital. Suddenly he stopped breathing, and when I looked in the back seat I knew he was dead.' She sobbed with the memory. 'I hated myself then. I knew I could be charged with murder, and I hadn't meant to kill him! Only make him a little sick! So I threw his body in a deep ravine and covered him over with dead leaves, sticks and stones . . .' Her huge desperate eyes pleaded with me to believe.

I too had to swallow, thinking of Cory in a deep dark ravine, left to decay there. 'No, Momma, you didn't do that.' My soft voice seemed to cut through the frozen atmosphere of the huge library. 'I visited the end room of the northern wing before I came down here.' I paused for better effect and made my next words more dramatic. 'Before I came down the stairs to confront you I first used stairs that lead directly to the attic, then the hidden little stairway in the closet of our prison. Chris and I always suspected there was another way into the attic, and correctly we reasoned there had to be a door hidden behind the giant heavy armoires we couldn't shove out of the way no matter how hard we pushed. Momma . . . I found a small room we'd never seen before. There was a very peculiar odour in that room, like something dead and rotten.'

For a moment she couldn't move. Her expression went totally blank. She stared at me with vacant eyes and then her mouth and her hands began to work, but she couldn't speak. She tried, but she couldn't speak. Bart started to say something, but she put her hands up to her ears to shut out anything anyone would say.

Suddenly the library door opened. I whirled in a fury.

My mother turned as in a nightmare to see why I kept staring. Chris pulled up short and gazed at her. She jumped then, as if terribly startled, then put up both her hands in a gesture that seemed to ward him off. Was she seeing a ghost of our father? 'Chris . . . ?' she asked. 'Chris, I didn't mean to do it, really I didn't! Don't look at me like that, Chris! I loved them! I didn't want to give them the arsenic – but my father made me! He told me they should never have been born! He tried to tell me they were so evil they deserved to die, and that was the only way I could make amends for the sin I'd committed when I married you!' Tears streamed her cheeks as she went on, though Chris kept shaking his head. 'I loved my children! *Our* children! But what could I do? I only meant to make them a little sick – just enough to save them, that's all, that's all . . . Chris, don't look at me like that! You know I wouldn't ever kill our children!'

His eyes turned icy blue as he stared at her. 'Then you did deliberately feed us arsenic?' he asked. 'I never fully believed it once we were free of this house and had time to think about it. But you did do it!'

She screamed then. In all my life I'd never heard such a scream as that one that rose and fell hysterically. Screams that sounded like the howls of the insane! On her heel she whirled about, still screaming, as she raced for a door I hadn't even known was there, and through it she ran and disappeared.

'Cathy,' said Chris, tearing his eyes from the door and scanning the library to take note of Bart and the grandmother, 'I've come to fetch you. I've had bad news. We have to go back to Clairmont immediately!'

Before I could answer Bart spoke up, 'Are you Cathy's older brother, Chris?'

'Yes, of course. I came for Cathy. She's needed some place

else.' He stretched out his hand as I drifted towards him.

'Wait a minute,' said Bart. 'I need to ask you a few questions. I've got to know the full truth. Was that woman in the red dress your mother?'

First Chris looked at me. I nodded to tell him Bart knew, and only then did Chris meet Bart's eyes with some hostility. 'Yes, she is my mother and Cathy's mother, and once the mother of twins named Cory and Carrie.'

'And she kept all four of you locked up in one room for more than three years?' asked Bart, as if he still didn't want to believe.

'Yes, three years and four months and sixteen days. And when she took Cory away one night she came back later and told us he died of pneumonia. And if you want more details, you will have to wait, for there are others we have to think about now. Come, Cathy,' he said, reaching for my hand again. 'We've got to hurry!' He looked then at the grandmother and gave her a wry smile. 'Merry Christmas, Grandmother. I had hoped never to see you again, but now that I have I see time has worked its own revenge.' He turned again to me. 'Hurry, Cathy, where is your coat! I have Jory and Mrs Lindstrom out in my car.'

'Why?' I asked. Sudden panic filled me. What was the matter?

'No!' objected Bart. 'Cathy can't leave! She's expecting my child and I want her here with me!'

Bart came to take me in his arms and tenderly he gazed with love at my face. 'You have lifted the blinkers from my eyes, Cathy. You were right. Certainly I was meant for better things than this. Perhaps I can still redeem my existence by doing something useful for a change.'

I threw the grandmother a look of triumph and avoided looking directly at Chris, and with Bart's arm about my shoulders we left the library and the grandmother and strode through all the other rooms until we reached the grand foyer.

Bedlam had broken loose! Everyone was screaming, running, searching to find a wife or a husband. Smoke! I smelled smoke.

'My God, the house is on fire!' Bart cried. He shoved me towards Chris. 'Take her outside and keep her safe! I've got to find my wife!' He looked wildly about, calling, 'Corrine,

Corrine, where are you?'

The milling throng were all headed for the same exit. From the stairs above black smoke billowed down. Women fell and people stepped over them. The merry guests of the party were hell-bent now on getting out, and woe to those who didn't have the strength to fight their way to the door. Frantically I tried to follow Bart with my eyes. I saw him pick up a telephone, no doubt to call the fire department, and then he was racing up the right side of the dual staircase and into the very heart of the fire! '*No!*' I screamed. 'Bart – don't go up there! You'll be killed! Bart – don't! Come back!'

I think he must have heard me, for he hesitated midway up and smiled back at me as I was frantically waving. He mouthed the words *I love you* – and then pointed towards the east. I didn't understand what he meant. But Chris took it that he was telling us of another way out.

Coughing and choking, Chris and I sped through another parlour, and finally I had the chance to see the grand dining room – but it was full of smoke too! 'Look,' cried Chris, pulling me on, 'there are French doors – the fools, there must be a dozen or more exits on the first floor, and everyone rushes for the front door!'

We made it outside and finally over to the car I recognized as Chris's, and there Emma held Jory in her arms as she stared at the great house that was burning. Chris reached inside and pulled out a car robe to throw over my shoulders, and then he held to me as I leaned against him and sobbed for Bart – where was he? Why didn't he come out?

I heard the wail of fire engines winding around the hills, screaming in the night that was already wild with the wind and the snow. The snow that fell above the house on fire was speckled red dots that sizzled as they met the flames. Jory put out his arms, wanting me, and I held him close as Chris put his arms about me and held us both. 'Don't worry, Cathy,' he tried to comfort, 'Bart must know all the ways to get out.'

Then I saw my mother in her red flame dress, being restrained by two men. She screamed on and on, crying out her husband's name – and then that of the grandmother. 'My mother! She's in there! She can't move!'

Bart was on the front steps when he heard her voice. He whirled about and sped back into the house. Oh, my God! He was going back to save the grandmother who didn't deserve to live! Risking his life – doing what he had to to prove, after all, he wasn't just a lap dog.

This was the fire of my childhood nightmares! This was what I'd always feared more than anything! This was the reason I'd insisted we make the rope ladder of torn-up sheets so we could escape and reach the ground – just in case.

It was more than horrible to watch that mammoth house burn when once I would have been glad to see it go. The wind blew relentlessly and whipped the flames higher, higher until they lit up the night and fired the heavens. How easily old wood burned along with the antique furnishings, the priceless heirlooms that could never be replaced. If anything survived, despite what those heroic firemen did, it would be a miracle! Someone screamed, 'People are trapped inside! Get them out!' The firemen worked with superhuman speed and agility to get them out while I cried, wild and frantic. 'Bart! I didn't want to kill you! I only wanted you to love me, that's all. Bart, don't die, please don't die!' My mother heard and she came running to where Chris was holding me tight in his arms.

'*You!*' she screamed, her distraught expression that of the insane. '*You think Bart loved you? That he would marry you? You are a fool!* You betrayed me! As you've always betrayed me, and now Bart will die because of you!'

'No, Mother,' said Chris who tightened his arms about me, and his tone was that of ice, 'it wasn't Cathy who cried out to remind your husband your mother was still inside. You did that. You must have seen he couldn't go back in that house and live. Perhaps you would rather see your husband dead than married to your daughter.'

She stared at him. Her hands worked nervously. Her cerulean blue eyes were darkly shadowed by the pools of black mascara. And as I watched and Chris watched something in her eyes broke – some minute thing that had lent clarity and intelligence to the eyes dissolved and she seemed to shrink. 'Christopher my son, my love, I'm your mother. Don't you love me any more, Christopher? Why? Don't I bring you everything you need and ask for? New encyclopedias, games and clothes? What is it you lack? Tell me, so I can go out and buy it for you, please tell me what you want. I'll do anything, bring you anything to make up for what you're losing. A thousandfold over you will be rewarded when my father dies, and he will die any day, any hour, any second, I know! I swear you won't have to be up here much longer! No, not much longer, not much longer, not much longer.' And on and on until I could have screamed. Instead I put my hands over my ears and pressed my face against Chris's broad chest.

He made some signal to one of the ambulance drivers, and warily they approached our mother who saw them, shrieked and then tried to run. I saw her stumble and fall, her heel caught in the long hem of her flaming red, glittering gown, and on the snow she fell flat, kicking, screaming and pounding her fists.

They took her away in a straitjacket, still screaming of how I had betrayed her, while Chris and I clung to one another and watched with wide eyes. We felt like children again, helpless with the fresh grief and shame we bore. I followed him about while he did what he could for those who had been burned. I only got in his way, but I couldn't let him out of my sight.

The body of Bart Winslow was found on the floor of the library with the skeletal grandmother still clutched in his arms – both suffocated by the smoke and not the flames. I stumbled over to fold down the green blanket and stared into his face to convince myself death had come again into my life. Again and again it kept coming! I kissed him, cried on his unyielding chest. I raised my head and he was looking straight at me – and through me – gone on to where I could never reach him and confess that I had loved him from the start – fifteen years ago.

'Cathy, please,' said Chris, tugging me away. I sobbed when Bart's hand slipped from my grasp. 'We have to go! There's no reason for us to stay on now that it is all over.'

All over, all over – it was all over.

My eyes followed the ambulance with Bart's body inside, and

my grandmother too. I didn't grieve for her – for she had got out of life what she put in.

I turned to Chris and cried again in his arms, for who would live long enough to let me keep the love I had to have? Who?

Hours and hours passed while Chris pleaded with me to leave this place that had brought us nothing but unhappiness and sorrow. Why hadn't I remembered that? Sadly I leaned to pick bits and pieces of craft paper that once had been orange and purple, and other pieces of our attic decorations blew on the wind, torn petals, jagged leaves, ripped from their stems.

It was dawn before the fire was brought under control. By that time the mammoth greatness that had once been Foxworth Hall was only a smouldering ruin. The eight chimneys still stood on the sturdy brick foundation, and, oddly enough, the dual winding staircases that curved up into nowhere still remained.

Chris was eager to depart, but I had to sit and watch until the last wisp of smoke was blown away and became part of the wind called nevermore. It was my salute, the final one to Bartholomew Winslow whom I'd first seen at the age of twelve. On first sight I'd given my heart to him. So much so that I had to have Paul grow a moustache so he'd look more like Bart. And I'd married Julian because his eyes were dark, dark like Bart's . . . Oh, God, how could I live with the knowledge I had killed the one man I'd loved best?

'Please, please Cathy, the grandmother is gone and I can't say I'm sorry, though I am about Bart. It must have been our mother who started the fire. From what the police say, it began in that attic room at the top of the stairs.'

His voice came to me as from a far distance, for I was locked up in a shell of my own making. I shook my head and tried to clear it. Who was I? Who was that man next to me – who was the little boy in the back seat asleep in the arms of an older woman?

'What's the matter with you, Cathy?' Chris said impatiently. 'Listen, Henny had a massive stroke tonight! In trying to help her Paul suffered a heart attack! He needs us! Are you going to sit here all day too and grieve for a man you should have left alone, and let the one man who has done the most for us die?'

The grandmother had said a few things so right. I was evil, born unholy. Everything was my fault! All my fault! If I'd never come, if I'd never come, on and on I kept saying this to myself as I cried bitter tears for the loss of Bart.

REAPING THE HARVEST

It was autumn again, that passionate month of October. The trees this year were ablaze from the touch of early frost. I was on the back veranda of Paul's big white house, shelling peas and watching Bart's small son chase after his older half-brother Jory. We'd named Bart's son after him, thinking it only right, but his last name was Sheffield, not Winslow. I was now Paul's wife.

In a few months Jory would be seven years old, and though at first he'd been a bit jealous he was now delighted to have a younger brother to share his life – someone he could boss, instruct and patronize. However young, Bart was not the kind to take orders. He was his own person, right from the beginning.

'Catherine,' called Paul's weak voice. I put the bowl of green peas quickly aside and hurried to his bedroom on the first floor. He was able to sit up in a chair for a few hours a day now, though on our wedding day, he'd been in bed. On our wedding night he'd slept in my arms, and that was all.

Paul had lost a great deal of weight; he looked gaunt. All his youth and vitality, held on to so valiantly, had disappeared almost overnight. Yet he'd never moved me more than when he smiled at me and held out his arms. 'I just called to see if you'd come. I ordered you to get out of this house for a change.'

'You're talking too much,' I cautioned. 'You know you aren't supposed to talk but a little.' This was a sore point with him, to only listen and not join in, but he tried to accept it. His next words took me by complete surprise. I could only stare at him, mouth agape and eyes wide. 'Paul, you don't mean that!'

Solemnly he nodded, his still beautiful iridescent eyes holding mine. 'Catherine, my love, it's been almost three years that you have been a slave to me, doing your best to make my last days happy. But I'm never going to get well. I could live on like this for years and years, like your grandfather did, while you grow older and older, and miss out on the best years of your life.'

'I'm not missing out on anything,' I said with a sob in my throat.

He smiled at me gently and held out his arms, and gladly I went to cuddle on his lap, though his arms about me no longer felt strong. He kissed me, and I held my breath. Oh, to be loved again ... but I wouldn't let him, I wouldn't!

'Think about it, my darling. Your children need a father, the kind of father I can't be now.'

'It's my fault!' I cried. 'If I had married you years ago, instead of Julian, I could have kept you well, and forced you not to work so hard and drive yourself night and day. Paul, if we three hadn't come into your life, you wouldn't have had to earn so much money, enough to send Chris through college and me to ballet classes ...'

He put his hand over my mouth, and told me but for us, he would have died years ago from overwork. 'Three years, Catherine,' he said again. 'And when you think about it, you will realize you are very much a prisoner, just as when you were in Foxworth Hall, waiting for your grandfather to die. I don't want you and Chris to grow to hate me ... so think about it, and talk to him about it — and then decide.'

'Paul, Chris is a doctor! You know he wouldn't agree!'

'Time is running out, Catherine, not only for me, but for you and Chris too. Soon Jory will be seven years old. He will be remembering everything more clearly. He will know Chris is his uncle, but if you leave now and forget about me, he will consider Chris his step-father, not his uncle.'

I sobbed. 'No! Chris would never agree.'

'Catherine, listen to me. It wouldn't be evil! You are now unable to have more children. Though I was terribly sorry you had such a difficult time giving birth to your last son, maybe it was a blessing in disguise. I'm impotent; I'm not a real husband, and soon you will be a widow again. And Chris has waited for so long. Can't you think about him, and forget the sin?'

And so, like Momma, we'd written our scripts too, Chris and I. And maybe ours were no better than hers, though I'd never plotted to kill anyone, nor had I meant to drive her over the

404

brink of insanity so the rest of her life she'd live in a home. And the irony of ironies, when all that she'd inherited from her father had been taken away, it had reverted to her mother. Then the grandmother's will had been read and her entire fortune, plus the remains of Foxworth Hall, now belonged to a woman who could only sit in a mental institution and stare at four walls. Oh, Momma, if only you could have looked into the future when first you considered taking your four children back to Foxworth Hall! Cursed with millions – and unable to spend a cent. Nor would one penny come to us. When our mother died, it would be distributed to different charities.

In the spring of the following year we sat near the river water where Julia had led Scotty, then held him under so he drowned in the shallow, greenish water where my own two small sons sailed small boats and waded in water that only reached their ankles.

'Chris,' I began falteringly, embarrassed, and yet happy too, 'Paul made love to me last night for the first time. We were both so happy, we cried. It was safe enough, wasn't it?'

He bowed his head to hide his expression, and the sun blazed his golden hair. 'I'm happy for the both of you. Yes, sex is safe enough now, as long as you don't work him up to a great pitch of excitement.'

'We took it easy.' After four severe heart attacks, it had to be easy sex.

'Good.'

Jory shrieked out then he'd caught a fish. Was it too small? Would he have to throw back another? 'Yes,' called Chris, 'that's just a baby. We don't eat baby fish, only the big ones.'

'Come,' I called, 'let's head for home and dinner.' They came running and laughing, my two sons, both so much alike they appeared whole brothers, and not halfs. And as yet we hadn't told them any different. Jory hadn't asked, and Bart was too young to question. But when they did, we would tell them the truth, as difficult as it was.

'We've got two daddies,' cried Jory, flinging himself into Chris's arms as I picked up Bart. 'Nobody at school but me has two daddies and they don't understand when I tell them ... but maybe I don't tell it right.'

'I'm sure you don't tell it right,' said Chris with a small smile.

In Chris's new blue car we drove home to the big white house that had given us so much. As we had the first time we came, we saw a man on the front veranda with his white shoes propped up on the balustrade. As Chris took my sons into the house I went over to Paul and smiled to see him dozing with a pleased smile upon his face. The newspaper he'd been reading had slipped from his slack hand to fan on the veranda floor. 'I'll go in and bathe the boys,' whispered Chris, 'and you can pick up the newspapers before the wind blows them on to our neighbours' lawns.'

As quietly as you can try to pick up papers and fold them neatly, somehow they will crackle and rustle, and soon Paul half-opened his eyes and smiled at me. 'Hi,' he said sleepily. 'Did you have a good day? Catch anything?'

'Two small fish bit on Jory's line, but he had to throw them back. What were you dreaming before you woke?' I asked, leaning to kiss him. 'You looked so happy – was it a sexy dream?'

Again he smiled, sort of wistfully. 'I was dreaming of Julia,' he said. 'She had Scotty with her, and they were both smiling at me. You know, she very seldom smiled at me after we married.'

'Poor Julia,' I said, kissing him again. 'She missed out on so much. I promise my smiles will make up for all she didn't give.'

'They already have.' He reached to touch my cheek and stroked my hair. 'It was my lucky day when you climbed my veranda steps on that Sunday ...'

'That damned Sunday,' I corrected. He smiled. 'Give me ten minutes more before you call me in to dinner. I'd like to get hold of that bus driver and tell him no Sundays are damned when you are on the bus.'

I went in to help Chris with the boys, and while he washed Jory, I helped Bart Scott Winslow Sheffield with his yellow pyjamas. We ate early, so we could dine with our children.

Soon the ten minutes were up and again I went to waken Paul. Three times I said his name softly and stroked his cheek gently, then blew in his ear. Still he slept on. I started to say his name again, and louder, when he made some small sound that sounded like my name. I looked, already trembling and afraid. Just the strangeness of the way he said that filled me with a terrible dread.

'Chris,' I called weakly, 'come quick and look at Paul.'

He must have been in the hall, sent by Emma to see what was taking us so long, for he stepped out of the door immediately, then ran to Paul's side. He seized his hand and felt for his pulse, and then in another second he was pulling his head back and holding his nose and breathing into his mouth. When that didn't work he struck him several times very hard on his chest. I ran into the house and called an ambulance.

But, of course, none of it did any good. Our benefactor, our saviour, my husband was dead. Chris put his arm about my shoulder and drew me to his chest. 'He's gone, Cathy, the way I would like to go, in my sleep, feeling well and happy. It's a good way for a good man to die, with no pain and no suffering – so don't look like that, it's not your fault!'

Nothing was ever my fault! Behind me lay a trail of dead men. But I wasn't responsible for the death of even one, was I? No, of course not. It was a wonder Chris had the nerve to climb in the car and sit beside me, heading his car west. Going west like the pioneers to seek a new future and find different kinds of lives. Paul had left everything he owned to me, including his family home. Though his will had stated, if I decided to sell, he wanted Amanda to have the final bid.

So at last Paul's sister had their ancestral home she had always wanted and schemed to get – but I made sure it was at a steep price.

Chris and I rented a home in California until we could have a custom-designed ranchhouse built to our specifications. My sons call my brother Daddy. They both know they have other fathers who went on to heaven before they were born. So far, they don't realize Chris is only their uncle. A long time ago Jory forgot that. Maybe children too forget when they want to, and ask no questions that would be embarrassing to answer.

At least once a year we travel East to visit friends, including

Madame Marisha and Madame Zolta. Both make a great to-do about the dancing abilities of Jory, and both try with fervent zeal to make Bart a dancer too. But so far, he doesn't have the inclination to be anything but a doctor. We visit all the graves of our beloved ones, and put flowers there. Always red and purple ones for Carrie, and roses of any colour for Paul and Henny. We have even sought out our father's grave in Gladstone, and paid our respects to him too with flowers. And Julian is never overlooked, or Georges.

Last of all, we visit Momma.

She lives in a huge place that tries unsuccessfully to look homey. Usually she screams when she sees me. Then she jumps up and tries to tear the hair from my head. When she is restrained, she turns the hatred upon herself, trying time after time to mutilate her face, and free herself forever of any resemblance to me. Just as if she no longer looked in the mirrors that would tell her we no longer look alike. Remorse has made of her something terrible to see. And once she'd been so very beautiful. Her doctors allow only Chris to visit with her an hour or so, while I wait outside with my two sons. He reports back that if she recovers, she won't be faced with a murder charge, for both Chris and I have disclaimed there ever was a fourth child named Cory. She doesn't fully trust Chris, sensing he is under my evil influence, and if she lets go her façade of being insane, she will end up with a death penalty. So year after year passes as she clings to her calculated fallacy as a way to escape both justice and the future with no one who really cares for her. Or perhaps, more truly, she seeks to torment me through Chris and the pity he insists on feeling for her. She is the one issue that keeps our relationship from being perfect.

So, the dreams of perfection, of fame, of fortune, of undying, ever-abiding love without one single flaw, like the toys and games of yesteryear, and all other youthful fantasies I have outgrown, I have put away.

Often I look at Chris, and wonder just what it is he sees in me. What is it that binds him to me in such a permanent way? I wonder too why he isn't afraid for his future and the length of it, since I am better at keeping pets alive than husbands. But he comes home jauntily, wearing a happy grin, as he strides into my welcoming arms that respond quickly to his greeting, 'Come greet me with kisses if you love me.'

His medical practice is large, but not too large, so he has time to work in our four acres of gardens with the marble statues we brought along from Paul's gardens. As much as possible we have duplicated what he had, except for the Spanish moss that clings, and clings, and then kills.

Emma Lindstrom, our cook, our housekeeper, friend, lives with us as Henny lived with Paul. She never asks questions. She has no family but us, and to us she is faithful, and our business is our own.

Pragmatic, blithe, the eternal, cockeyed optimist, Chris sings when he works in the gardens. When he shaves in the mornings he hums some ballet tune, feeling no trepidation, no regrets, as if long, long ago he had been the man who danced in the shadows of the attic and had never, never let me see his face. Did he know all along that just as he had won over me in all other games it would be him in the end?

Why hadn't I known?

Who had shut my eyes?

It must have been Momma who told me once, 'Marry a man with dark, dark eyes, Cathy. Dark eyes feel so terribly intense about everything.' What a laugh! As if blue eyes lacked some profound steadfastness; she should have known better.

I should know better too. It worries me because I went yesterday into our attic. In a little alcove to the side, I found two single-size beds, long enough for two small boys to grow into men.

Oh, my God! I thought, who did this? I would never lock away my two sons, even if Jory did remember one day that Chris was not his step-father but his uncle. I wouldn't even if he did tell Bart, our youngest. I could face the shame, the embarrassment, and the publicity that would ruin Chris professionally. Yet ... yet, today I bought a picnic hamper, the kind with the double lids that open up from the centre; the very same kind of hamper the grandmother had used to bring us food.

So, I go uneasily to bed and lie there awake, fearing the worst in myself, and struggling to keep firm hold of the best. It seems, as I turn over, and snuggle closer to the man I love, that I can hear the cold wind blowing from the blue-misted mountains so far away.

It's the past that I can never forget, that shadows all my days, and hides furtively in the corners when Chris is home. I do make an effort to be like he is, always optimistic, when I am not at all the kind who can forget the tarnish on the reverse side of the brightest coin.

But ... I am not like her! I may look like her, but inside I am honourable! I am stronger, more determined. The best in me will win out in the end. I know it will. It has to sometimes ... doesn't it?

Flowers in the Attic
Virginia Andrews

It was a game of happy families.

The four children had such perfect lives in such a happy, golden family.

It was a game of hide and seek.

Their father died suddenly. The children now lived alone, hidden in the airless attic.

It was a case of tender, loving murder.

Their mother promised they would stay only long enough to inherit the fortune. But gradually she forgot how much she adored those children.

Flowers in the Attic is the compelling story of a family's betrayal and heartbreak, love and revenge.

ISBN 0 00 615929 X

If There Be Thorns

Virginia Andrews

The perils of the past.

The young family lived as far as possible away from the haunting scenes of their past and, in the sunshine and joy of their new life, with the children and their shared love, tried to forget the anguish of their loveless inheritance.

But the hidden secrets of the past rose up to trouble them. Their parents' dark heritage began to haunt them once more. The rage and hatred they felt returned to torment and twist the next generation. It was only if they could forgive their mother and forgo their final revenge, that peace could at last return to the family.

If There Be Thorns is the third book in the Dollanganger family saga.

ISBN 0 00 616370 X